LUKE IRONTREE & THE LAST VAMPIRE WAR

Luke Irontree & The Last Vampire War
Book 0 - The Centurion Immortal
Book 1 - Dark Fangs Rising - March 22, 2022
Book 2 - Dark Fangs Raging - April 19, 2022
Book 3 - Dark Fangs Descending* - May 17, 2022
Book 4 - Blood Empire Reborn* - July 12, 2022
Book 5 - Blood Empire Avenged* - August 9, 2022
Book 6 - Blood Empire Burning* - September 6, 2022
Book 7 - Blood Empire Collapsing* - October 4, 2022
Book 8 - Ancient Sword Falling* - November 29, 2022
Book 9 - Ancient Sword Unyielding* - December 27, 2022
Book 10 - Ancient Sword Shattering* - February 7, 2023

The Luke Irontree Historical Adventures
Rise of the Centurio Immortalis - April 5, 2022
Fall of the Centurio Immortalis* - May 31, 2022
The Moonlight Centurion* - November 1, 2022
The Highway Centurion* - January 24, 2023

*Forthcoming

DARK FANGS RISING

LUKE IRONTREE & THE LAST VAMPIRE WAR

C. THOMAS LAFOLLETTE

BROKEN WORLD PUBLISHING

DARK FANGS RISING
C. Thomas Lafollette

A Broken World Publication
13820 NE Airport Way
Suite #K395495
Portland, OR 97251-1158
Dark Fangs Rising
Copyright © 2022 by C. Thomas Lafollette
ISBN 978-1-949410-40-2 (ebook);
ISBN 978-1-949410-41-9 (paperback)

Cover Design: Ravven
Edited by: Suzanne Lahna
Copy Editing & Proofreading: Amy Cissell

CONTENTS

Content Warning   vii
Pronunciation Guide & Author's Notes   xi

Chapter 1   1
Chapter 2   9
Chapter 3   17
Chapter 4   25
Lucius I   35
Chapter 5   43
Chapter 6   51
Chapter 7   59
Chapter 8   67
Lucius II   75
Chapter 9   83
Chapter 10   93
Chapter 11   101
Chapter 12   111
Chapter 13   121
Lucius III   135
Chapter 14   143
Chapter 15   155
Chapter 16   161
Chapter 17   173
Chapter 18   185
Lucius IIII   199
Chapter 19   207
Chapter 20   219
Chapter 21   223
Chapter 22   233
Chapter 23   243
Chapter 24   249
Lucius V   257
Chapter 25   269
Chapter 26   277
Chapter 27   289
Epilogue   305

Leave a Review   315
Luke Irontree Will Return In   317
Dark Fangs Raging

Newsletter   327
Glossary   329
Acknowledgments   331
About the Author   333
Also by C. Thomas Lafollette   335

CONTENT WARNING

This book contains some gore and body horror. There is also a brief, non-specific mention of child abuse and domestic violence.

To Amy
Your tireless support and all your work and advice are the reason this book exists

PRONUNCIATION GUIDE & AUTHOR'S NOTES

Pronunciation: Latin names and words are mentioned throughout the book and are intended to be read with the classical Latin pronunciation. For instance, "c" is always pronounced hard, like a "k." "U" is always a short "oo" sound. "V" typically sounds like a "w." There are plenty of resources on the internet if you wish to learn more about Classical Latin pronunciation.

- Lucius – Loo-kih-oos
- Silvanius – Sihl-wahn-ih-oos
- Ferrata – Fehr-rah-tah
- Cassius – Cahs-sih-oos

Latin Words: Latin words are used for effect and to add to the "flavor" of the story, not to reflect Latin grammar/declensions/conjugations.

Anachronisms: It's nearly impossible to write historical settings without some anachronisms, especially when you're writing scenes set nearly 2,000 years in the past. Those used are done so intentionally for the purpose of story telling and to convey sentiments that would be recognizable to people then and now. Also, there are vampires.

ONE

LUKE'S PREY stumbled in front of him; the weight of the intoxicated woman slung over the vampire's shoulder made him clumsy. With all the vamp's attention on the drunk woman, he had no idea what other dangers lurked in the night. The vampire maneuvered his impaired victim into the shadow of a massive statue of a woman kneeling, one of her metal hands reaching down while the other grasped a trident. Rain drizzled over the statue's body and down her arm, streaming off her outstretched fingers onto the street below. Luke reached over his shoulder into the folds of his hood, ensuring his sword's handle remained unobstructed by the damp cloth, then returned his hand to his side.

"Excuse me, sir. Could you spare a moment? I seem to be lost. Can you point me in the right direction?" Luke asked.

The overly polite and formal tone should mark him as an easy target. A bit of buzzed slur added just the right spice to Luke's charade. He distractedly scratched at his overgrown, scruffy beard. He hadn't cared enough to trim it since he'd returned from his trip to Belgium last spring. The vamp, clad in a stylish jacket, hefted the woman against the wall.

Luke waited for the man to turn around. What Luke didn't

expect was to see a woman disentangling herself from her victim to deal with Luke. Most vampires tended to be male. Without the support of the woman, the drunk slumped forward, momentum stopped by the wall. The vamp strode toward him. Luke wasn't sure how he'd misidentified his target, but he adjusted his plan as the short, dark-haired, white woman looked him over. Her expression went from annoyed to predatory to pleasantly helpful in the blink of an eye. If Luke was as drunk as he was feigning, he'd have missed it.

"Certainly!" She casually approached Luke, walking slowly with a small smile on her face. "What are you looking for?"

When she was close enough to see Luke's unsteady stance, the predatory gleam returned to her eyes. As oblivious as she was to her surroundings—letting Luke follow her and missing that his drunkenness wasn't genuine—she must be a young vamp.

Luke, dressed in dark colors—a black hoodie, baggy faded jeans, and black combat-style boots, ran his right hand through his long, dark, slightly damp hair and left it casually resting on the back of his neck as if scratching an itch. "Um, I'm not sure… I'm staying at a hotel near here, but I seem to be lost."

"Fortunately, you ran into me," the vampire said, her lips parting into a carnivorous grin.

"What's—what's wrong with your teeth?"

Needle-sharp fangs descended from her top teeth, her grin growing even more feral. She tilted her head slightly to the side. "Oh, these? In a moment, you'll forget you ever saw them."

Luke feigned a nervous chuckle and let his hand slide down into his hood to grip the well-worn handle of his gladius. Sheathed on his back, the gladius was twenty-five inches of viciously sharp Toledo steel alloyed with a bit of silver. The scabbard was angled toward his right shoulder and was open except for the last eight inches that covered the tip of the blade and the snap band at the top that held it in place, allowing for easy, quick draws.

His new friend walked closer, turned toward Luke's left side, and raised her arm as if to put it around Luke's shoulders so she could more easily guide Luke to his destination—her dinner plate.

Luke grabbed the vampire's arm and spun the creature around so her back was in front of him, keeping her fangs away from his more vulnerable spots. He pulled his gladius from its sheath and brought it down through the woman's leather clad right elbow.

"WHAT THE FUCK, MAN!" The creature whirled around as black blood splattered in an arc from her stump. Her eyes glowed red, all traces of humor disappearing from her face. "We could have done this the easy way, but now you're going to feel every moment."

A wound that would have downed a howling barbarian had merely pissed her off. The vampire crouched and flexed her remaining hand, nails extending into nasty looking claws. She launched a series of clumsy swipes at Luke's neck and torso he easily side stepped. With each subsequent miss, her rage grew, fueling her speed, but not her skill.

Luke snorted in amusement, eliciting a growl of fury from the one-armed vampire. She finally landed a swipe that cut into the cloth covering Luke's chest. Her claws screeched against hard steel. Her momentary look of triumph quickly morphed into confusion.

Luke'd had enough. He waited for the next awkward swipe, letting the vamp's rage and momentum carry her past Luke as he spun and brought the blade down on the vamp's left shoulder, relieving her of her other arm. Luke kicked her in the back of her legs, sending her crashing to the ground. The creature's rage turned to whimpering as she tried to push herself off the ground with her bloody, oozing stump. She only managed to slip and slide, landing on her face. Luke put a foot on the vampire's butt to keep her on the ground as he reached under the waistband at the back of his hoodie. He flipped the catch holding the rudis in place and withdrew it from its scabbard.

The rudis, a gladius made of wood, was a piece of art. Gleaming, razor-sharp steel lined the cutting edges and point while intricate designs made of silver filigree covered the wooden blade. The wood itself was a warm, deep honey gold intermixed with rich brown and dark brown hardwood with a pattern that highlighted the wood's grain. Luke flicked his right wrist, and the steel sword sliced into the vamp's leather jacket between the shoulder blade and the spine.

"My coat!" she whimpered. The blood was slowing to a trickle, her stumps already sealing.

"I already cut both sleeves off. What's one more rip?" With that, Luke plunged the rudis through the cut he'd just made and felt the blade scrape along the vampire's scapula, backbone, and ribs until it found the heart. As he knelt over her body, Luke rested his forehead on the pommel of the rudis, whispering an incantation he'd said more times than he could remember. The silver filigree began to glow with a pure, white light, slithering down the silver into the vampire's body and then back up again to disappear into Luke's forehead. The corpse went rigid, and steam rose where the silver touched it. Once he removed the rudis from the vampire's body, the corpse gradually deflated and dissolved into a viscous reddish-black goo.

"Damn it," Luke muttered, shaking his head. "A new vampire. All goo and no go. I thought her moves seemed weak."

The sound of retching reminded him he wasn't alone. He turned to see the vamp's intended victim on all fours, heaving up everything he'd consumed that night. Luke scanned around for something to clean his blades on. The vamp's clothes were out as the erstwhile young lady of the fang was currently drenching her trendy ensemble in the rapidly spreading goo that had been her body. He looked down, pursing his lips.

"Fucking vamp ruined my favorite hoodie." He set down the rudis and slid the blade of the gladius into the belly pocket. Gripping the blade through the rain damp fabric, he slid it clean, then resheathed it. He treated the rudis in the same manner and put it away. With the weaponry stowed, Luke slowly walked toward the man.

"W-what's wrong with me?"

"It appears you drank too much."

"Did she drug me? Was she going to rob me?"

"Something like that," Luke replied as he slowly approached, trying not to spook him. Luke followed the man's gaze to what remained of his would-be date slowly liquefying on the sidewalk and running into the gutter. He retched again.

"Pl-pl-please don't hurt me," he whimpered between dry heaves.

"I'm not going to hurt you." He pointed at the slick of vampire goo. "She was going to."

The glamour drunk man nodded.

Luke pointed west. "Let's walk up to Broadway. It's well lit. Do you have a phone? You can call a Lyft or a taxi."

"O-OK."

They stepped as quickly as the man's frightened but still slightly inebriated body would carry him. As they walked past the nearly vanished remnants of the unlucky vampire, the man was careful to look anywhere else. When they got to Broadway, Luke waited with him under a streetlight while his car arrived to take him home. Just as he stepped into the back seat, he paused, looked at Luke and said, "Thank you."

Luke nodded at him, then turned and walked back into the dreary night.

LUKE PARKED his old Volvo wagon in his garage and grabbed the equipment-filled tote from the rear hatch. Propping the tote against the door frame, he hit the garage door button, then unlocked the door and walked in. A hulking, orange tabby cat greeted him.

"Mrrrraaaoooo!"

"Hey, Alfred. Stay out of trouble tonight?" He usually did, not having opposable thumbs and all.

Luke set the tote down, then dropped a scoop of kibble into the cat's empty bowl. Alfred ran to the bowl, buried his giant head in it, and chomped down. Luke shucked his ripped, wet hoodie and grabbed a hand towel to dry his wavy hair. He unlaced his boots and left them on a mat by the door before heading to the fridge. Grabbing a Pfriem Pils out of the fridge, he walked back and snagged the tote.

"I'm headed down to the Batcave, Alfred, if you want to come…" The tinkling of the cat's collar bell as he sauntered over to Luke answered the invite.

Once in the office, he engaged the hidden mechanism that

opened the passage behind one of the bookcases, revealing a steel spiral staircase. At the bottom of the stairs was a square room with dark hardwood flooring. Along one wall, two Danish mid-century chairs sat, an end table of the same style between them. A huge rug covered the floor. Luke set the tote on the floor near a workstation recessed along the wall furthest from the stairs. Alfred ran over to one of the chairs, hopped onto the seat, spun a couple donuts, then sprawled out, taking up most of the seat.

Luke looked at the cat. "What's it going to be tonight, eh, Alfred? We feeling up? Down? Al Green?"

"Mrao!"

"Ah! Good choice, Alfred. 'Let's Stay Together' it is!" He walked to the wall of records and flipped through the albums in the "G" section until he found the right one. Pulling out the album, he stopped halfway, shoulders slumping as he stared at the wall, then slid it back into its spot. Luke stepped over to the "Ns." Taking the second disk most of the way out of "The Downward Spiral" album jacket, he hesitated again. "What do you think, Alfie? Nine Inch Nails? Or is 'sad guy listens to Nine Inch Nails' too cliché?"

Alfred responded to his name with a raspy purr.

"You're right. Al Green was the correct choice." He opened the top of the huge console unit and set the needle down on side one. Luke released an exhausted sigh as the smooth interplay of horns, guitars, and drums led into the silky voice of Al Green. He grabbed a glass from the bar shelf and poured the beer.

Luke stopped to listen for a moment before setting his glass down on the worktable. Sitting down, he popped the top off the tote and pulled out his swords, both wooden and steel. He meticulously cleaned both, checked for damage, and oiled them before placing them on a rack. He opened a tall cabinet next to the worktable and rolled out an armor stand on a rotating base. With both hands, he reached into the tote and carefully pulled out an ancient set of armor and placed it gently on the armor stand. Phrases engraved in Ancient Greek, Latin, and Old Persian covered every flawless band. The lettering—so thick the light didn't quite know how to reflect off the steel—wove protections into the armor that made it far stronger than it naturally was while also keeping it silent for the hunt.

It would take more than vampire claws to damage it. He gently ran the fingers of his right hand over the bands that sat just over his heart where there was a crescent moon engraved. The armor and swords were nearly as old as he was, his longest relationships, and after nineteen-hundred years, his only relationships besides the orange tabby grooming himself on the chair.

Luke let out a long sigh, his face drooping and his lips closing into a frown as he squeezed his eyes shut, placing his head in his hands. "A gladius, a rudis, a set of lorica segmentata, and an Alfred…"

"Mrao."

Alfred was sitting at his feet, staring up at him. He sat up and made room for the cat to jump into his lap. He scooped up the cat and held him close, supporting his weight while scratching his ears. "I'm tired, Alfie, so tired…"

He listened to the music as Alfred purred in his arms. He'd hoped Portland would be a good place to avoid vampires, at least in serious numbers. When he'd picked it as his new home all those years ago, it was a city, but only nominally, certainly not one important enough to become a hub of vampire activity. All he'd wanted was a place free from his past and all the blood, but it didn't matter how far he ran, he couldn't escape his past. The vampires wouldn't let him.

TWO

"WELL, BUDDY." Luke bent down to scratch Alfred between his ears. "I'm going to the Howling Moon for some dinner, so you're on your own tonight."

Luke slung his backpack over his shoulder and pulled the door open before turning and looking back at the cat. "See you later, Alfred. No wild parties while I'm gone."

Howling Moon Brewing had moved into an old brick building on North Lombard Avenue just over a year ago. Since then, it'd become Luke's regular watering hole. The beers and food were delicious. Best of all, the atmosphere was usually exactly what Luke liked. Often brewpubs were bright and sterile, but Howling Moon's owners created a space both dark and warm. The high back booths provided intimacy ideal for a date night, or if you preferred, you could sit at the bar and chat with the owner or one of the bartenders. Best of all, it was a short walk from his home, and they left him alone after he placed his drink order, except for the rare times he felt like human interactions. Then, they were good for some light bar chat.

"Hey, Pablo. How's it going tonight?"

Pablo stood about five foot six and had the brown complexion of Latin America that marked him as having indigenous and European heritage. His black hair was coiffed into a hip modern cut with the sides shaved and the top left long. He wore black jeans and a black tee featuring the brewery's logo of a wolf's head howling at a full moon. Tattoos covered his muscular arms.

Pablo walked over, standing across the bar from Luke. "A bit quiet. It's been that way a lot lately. All the crime on the news is keeping people home. Did you hear about the weird shit they found by the Portlandia statue this morning?"

"I must have missed that story," Luke replied.

"They found a full outfit oozing some black goop. And get this, someone had cut the arms off the leather jacket. Weird, man."

Luke chuckled nervously. "That does sound weird. Anything new on tap I should know about?"

"Yeah! I've got a Belgian-style wit I've been experimenting with. I think I got it dialed in."

"I'll take one of those. Wits are one of my favorites."

"Really? Not IPA? Seems that's all anyone orders these days." Pablo grabbed a glass and poured a hazy blond beer with a thick, frothy head. "Let me know what you think."

Luke pulled out his usual chair at the bar, hung his backpack on the hook underneath, and grabbed his beer. "Nice aroma. Good balance between citrus, coriander, and grainy notes." He took a sip.

"Excellent nose," Pablo said.

"I like the flavor. Let me finish this glass, and I'll give you a full report."

"Good man. You can't really judge a beer from one sip. I'll be back." Pablo wandered off to check on other customers.

Luke worked his way through his first beer, then another. Pablo checked back in periodically to see how he was doing. Luke's dinner and a third beer showed up about the same time three guys walked in. Their popped-collar polos under jackets and their jeans with bedazzled rear pockets marked them as young bros who could be mistaken for University of Portland students if not for Luke's ability to tell the living from the unliving. He'd have to keep an eye on them.

He distractedly ate his dinner and mixed in a couple glasses of water while he sipped his beer. The bros chatted up a trio of women and then joined them in their booth. Fortunately, the mirrored back bar afforded Luke a decent view of their booth.

Luke had only wanted a quiet night down at the local pub, but life and vampires in Portland had another plan for him. He was mildly annoyed by the turn of events. He ignored the flavor of the food, shoveling it down while trying to inconspicuously stare at the undead jackasses flirting, buying beer, and glamouring their targets.

The crowd had largely thinned out as the evening progressed on what was a work night for the Monday-Friday crowd. After the last people in the pub who weren't the vampires, their soon-to-be-victims, Luke, or Pablo left, the vampires gave it a few minutes before they ushered the three women toward the door, opting to take their meals to go. Luke made eye contact with Pablo, set some cash on the bar, grabbed his backpack, and followed the group out the door. After exiting, he heard the door shut and open again behind him. Pablo must be following him.

THE THREE BROS and the women they'd glamoured walked toward the alley behind the bar. Pablo placed his hand on Luke's shoulder to stop him from walking further into the alley and stepped in front of Luke, putting his body between the bros and his regular customer.

"Step away from the ladies, gentlemen. Doesn't seem like they're interested in what you're offering," Pablo said, trying to distract what he probably thought were sexed up bros.

Luke unzipped his backpack, grasped the hilts of the gladius and rudis, and slowly drew them from the custom sheaths in his back-pack. "Pablo, back up a bit, please. I appreciate your effort, but you don't want to tangle with this lot."

Pablo kept his eyes on the trio. "I'm OK, Luke. I can handle myself, and no one comes into my pub and assaults people in my alley."

"I'm not saying you can't handle yourself. I'm just saying you should trust me about these guys. They might be a bit more than you're expecting..."

The three bros reluctantly set aside their prey and turned toward the interlopers. The one in the lead said, "If you two don't want a rough evening, I suggest you keep walking."

"I think you're messing with more than you can handle here. Leave the innocents alone and get the fuck out of here. Otherwise, things might get a touch...splattery," Luke said.

The three vampires chuckled, casually dismissing the implied threat as non-existent.

"I guess our dinner just got tastier." The lead vampire focused, making eye contact with Luke and Pablo, and tried to glamour them.

"Look, 'bros.' Just get the fuck out of here before you regret your choices," Pablo threatened.

"*You* get the fuck out of here before we rip you a new asshole and then shove your fucking brown head up it," the lead vamp said.

"Of course, they have to be racists too. I guess they're not going to move along. I'm not sure you need the hardware, Luke." Pablo rolled his shoulders, loosening up his muscles.

"For these three, yeah, I think I'll keep them out." Luke twirled the gladius once.

Despite the distraction provided by Pablo and Luke, the three women didn't move from their positions propped against the alley wall.

"Hey, girls! Run!" Pablo shouted.

Pablo's shout failed to rouse them. The angry smiles of the three vamps got progressively meaner as their fangs descended, their razor-sharp claws joining them for the party.

Luke stepped in front of Pablo, keeping his eyes on their opponents. "OK, Pablo. Stay behind me. Try to avoid their claws and fangs, and don't let them get you pinned down. They're faster than your normal run of the mill beered up bros and a lot stronger."

Luke stalked forward, keeping himself between Pablo and the creeping vampires. The vamps opened space between the three of them, hoping to outflank Luke and attack from multiple sides. Luke

spared a thought for his armor, neatly placed on its rack in his basement. He usually didn't need it for trips to the pub.

He feinted left and low with his rudis, then whirled and lopped
off the head of the vampire on his right with a backhanded swing.
He kept his rudis between himself and the other two vampbros.
Taking a moment, he peeked over his shoulder to check on Pablo.
The bartender had peeled his shirt off and was sprouting prodigious
volumes of body hair and a lupine snout. "*Shit, what have I gotten
myself into?*" Luke thought to himself.

He carefully stepped over the decapitated vamp, trying to
maneuver himself around so the girls would be behind him and he'd
have the vampires between him and what was quickly becoming a
very large werewolf in bipedal form, the hybrid shape that only the
most powerful shifters could achieve. He hoped Pablo would keep
his cool and not go berserk on him or the victims they were trying to
save. He'd hate to have to hurt Pablo; he brewed good beer.

The two remaining vampires suddenly realized that neither of the
men were going to be the pushovers they'd initially assumed. The
lead vampire eyed the sword-wielding hunter and the hulking werewolf, then settled his gaze on Luke.

"You're the one who's been killing our brethren. You're 'The
Hunter.' You'll pay for this." His casual dude-bro dialect dropped
away and was replaced by an antiquated, upper crust English accent.
He looked at his partner. "Break free and report what's happened
here. Bring reinforcements if you can."

Things were about to get interesting. If this vamp was as old as
his accent indicated, he'd be much more powerful than the newly
whelped bloodsuckers Luke'd been dispatching with ease lately. It'd
been several months since he'd encountered an older, more powerful
fanger. Luke's eyes narrowed, and he backed off a bit, switching to a
defensive stance. He needed to protect those he could while keeping
the vamps from scampering off. Pablo had finished his transformation and was stalking toward the vampires while ensuring he cut off
their escape route.

The British vampire pulled a long double-edge dagger from
under the back of his shirt. As he slid into a fighter's stance, it

became clear he knew how to handle himself and his blade. His young companion, however, was a lot less cocksure than he'd been before Luke had shortened their pal by a head and Pablo'd turned into a massive werewolf. The younger vampire's eyes darted around nervously, looking for an escape route.

Luke narrowed his eyes, planning his next move. "Pablo, keep the little guy from getting away."

Pablo grunted and growled, answering Luke's instructions as he slashed his gladius toward the Brit's head. He met Luke's sword with his dagger as the two blades slid together and down toward their hilt guards. The fanger took a swipe at Luke's midsection with his claws. Luke slapped the vamp's hand away with the flat of his rudis; when the silver inlay touched the vampire's skin, he yanked his hand back and yelped as the metal and anti-vampiric enchantments burned his hand. He disengaged his blade from Luke's and leapt back, maintaining eye contact with Luke. Blisters rose where the silver had burned him. He lost a bit more of his confidence, but his eyes narrowed into shrewdness and speculation. Shifting his feet, he put some distance between himself and Luke.

The vampire crouched and then launched himself at Luke with a feral grin on his face, but instead of striking at Luke, he leapt high into the air over Luke's head. The vamp dropped into a crouch, landing on his hands, and rolled onto his back and spring up again. Luke sliced his gladius low, cutting deep into the back of the fanger's legs, and severed his hamstrings.

The vamp dropped like he'd been shot in the head. "You bloody bastard!"

Even downed, he was still dangerous. Out of the corner of his eye, Luke caught Pablo and the last vampire squaring off. Pablo had no problem keeping the other vamp occupied; of course, not much can trouble a werewolf in their bipedal form. Luke's vampire was trying to scuttle backwards and away from Luke and toward the dropped dagger. Luke kicked it away, keeping an eye on the vampire in case it decided to lunge.

The sound of snapping bones and tearing flesh from the direction of Pablo caused Luke to cringe involuntarily. He ducked as something flew past his head and into his field of vision and smashed into the face of the British vampire. Pablo had thrown the other vampire's head.

"It appears this night didn't go the way you wanted it to." Luke surged forward and lopped off the distracted vampire's head. He flopped backward, his black sludge-like blood leaking into the alley. "Pablo, you better shift back and get these women out of here. The glamour they're under is about to wear off."

"I'm on it," Pablo said from behind Luke.

Luke wiped his gladius on the vamp's shirt and resheathed it in his custom backpack. He knelt over the headless body and set the point of his rudis over the heart, plunged it in, lowered his forehead to the pommel, and whispered the incantation that set the rudis glowing. Instead of dissolving into goo like the vamp from last night, the old Brit transformed to dust and blew away. Luke snagged the wallet out of the vampire's pocket so he could check it later for any useful information. He repeated the process, finalizing the transformation from corpses to less solid matter on the other two bodies. When he was done, Pablo was standing at the entrance to the alley, leaning against the wall with his arms crossed.

"Let's step inside for a beer and a chat."

Luke nodded slightly and followed him in.

THREE

AS LUKE STEPPED through the entrance, Pablo turned off the "open" sign and locked the door behind them.

"The girls called an Uber and got out of here. I don't think they're any wiser. They'll probably just chalk it up to a bad interaction with booze and some douchebags," Pablo said.

"Yeah. They were glamoured pretty hard. That'll fuzz out their memories fairly aggressively."

Pablo walked behind the bar. "Can I get you a beer?"

"I'll take a pilsner, please."

"Ah, a refreshing choice after a bit of a scuffle," Pablo said sardonically.

Luke took off his backpack and slid into a chair at the bar. Pablo had his back to him as he poured Luke's beer and one for himself. The awkward silence was nearly palpable.

"So, werewolf, eh?" Luke asked.

"Yup. I know what I am. I know what they were, although this was my first encounter with one. But I don't know who or what you are."

Luke set his rudis on the bar.

"He called you 'The Hunter.' Are you some sort of vampire

slayer? I'd make a joke about watching too many episodes of Buffy and getting delusions of grandeur, but that's some weird ass hardware you're packing," Pablo said, glancing at the rudis. "I can practically feel the power pulsing off it." He continued eyeing it warily, like it was a snake about to strike.

"That's a long story. One I usually don't tell virtual strangers." Although the two men were friendly in a regular patron/bar owner way, they weren't friends. It had been a while since Luke had been close enough to anyone to tell them pieces of his extended past. He wasn't sure about breaking his silence this time either, but they'd fought together—immortal vampire slayer and werewolf. It had only been a few months since he'd last seen a Child of Tutyr. They were masters of blending into normal society and living undetected by humans. He knew there was a pack in Portland, there had to be in a city this large, but he'd never encountered any werewolves in the over sixty years he'd lived there.

Pablo looked down at his beer. "Well, you know my secret. I usually don't wolf out around strangers, but got a little over excited when the vampire fangs popped out. I'm assuming you can keep your lips shut about that."

Luke held his hands up to placate Pablo. "Have no fear. Your secret is safe with me. You're not the first werewolf I've encountered."

"You've run into other shifters?" Pablo's eyebrows shot up in surprise.

Luke nodded. "A few here and there over the years."

"It's obvious the vampires know who or what you are, but shifter lore doesn't speak of a 'hunter' or 'slayer,' at least none I've heard. I'm assuming you keep your activities limited to bloodsuckers?" Pablo took a sip of beer.

"I'm not surprised you've never heard of me. I'm guessing you were born in and lived your entire life in the Americas. My reputation, what little of it may still make the rounds, is mostly confined to Europe. You have nothing to fear from me. Bother me not and I shall not bother you."

Pablo relaxed slightly.

"Vampires though. Vampires have feared me for a long, long time." Luke chuckled. "I'm the bump in the night that terrifies the bump in the night."

"Are you human?" Pablo asked.

"I was born one. I imagine I still am, although I've not submitted myself for scientific testing." Sitting in silence, Luke took a few drinks of the pilsner, sizing up Pablo while the bartender leaned against the bar and drank from his beer.

"I guess I understand the name of the brewery a bit better."

"Ha! Yeah, it's not subtle if you're in the know. Although, most patrons are decidedly not in the know. Speaking of which, I'll have to report this to the pack leadership. Portland has been mostly vampire free, and I have no idea what to make of you. Vampires know you as their enemy. You claim to have been fighting them for a long time. Just how long are we talking? Your hardware looks like more than just an affectation. That's no ren faire souvenir," Pablo said, eyeing the rudis.

Luke gestured toward it, indicating Pablo could pick it up. "Mind the silver."

Pablo gingerly grabbed the rudis by the handle and eyed the blade. "Is the cutting edge made of silver?"

"No, silver is too soft to keep a good edge. It's a steel and silver alloy, enough silver to give it a bit of extra anti-vampire oomph."

"What kind of wood is this?" Pablo asked. "I'm not sure I've seen it before."

"It's Persian ironwood. In essence, it's a fancy stake. A rudis was granted to gladiators when they earned their freedom. This was awarded to me and symbolizes freedom from the undead."

"Like in that Russell Crowe movie?" Pablo set the rudis back on the bar.

"Yeah. Something like that. 'Shadows and dust...'"

"What?" asked Pablo, confused.

"That's what Proximo said..."

Pablo still looked confused.

Luke waved Pablo off. "Never mind. I've probably seen that movie too many times."

"Oh, OK. Can I, uh, can I see the other sword?" Pablo asked hesitantly.

"Sure." Luke chuckled lightly as he pulled the gladius out of his backpack. He flipped it around and handed it to Pablo, handle first. "Be careful; it's got some silver, and it's extremely sharp. You could shave with it if you didn't mind accidentally slicing your nose off."

Pablo stared at the blade. "What are these engravings? A sun and a crescent moon and star? Is this an Islamic symbol?"

"No. It predates the founding of Islam by a few centuries. The sun represents Sol Invictus and his cleansing flames. The moon and star represent Luna, goddess of the moon. Their symbols make it a potent anti-vampire weapon. Put it through a vampire's heart, and it'll give them a true death and start their decay."

"It's light!" Pablo exclaimed.

"Less than two pounds. Even that gets to feeling heavy after a full day of using it in earnest."

"They're...authentic?"

Luke nodded at him.

"Are...are you..." Pablo paused, searching for the right word. "'Authentic?'"

Luke raised his eyebrow in response. "'Authentic?' That feels like a loaded question. I am who I am. I use Roman era gear to slay vampires. That's my day job, I guess, or night job, to be more accurate."

He could tell the answer wasn't even coming close to satisfying Pablo. He'd lost that bit of trepidation and was getting a touch annoyed with just a soupçon of determination.

Pablo stared at Luke for a bit until his eyebrows lifted toward his hairline. "Earlier when I mentioned the weird shit at the Portlandia statue, that was you. Wasn't it?"

Luke nodded. "Yup. Sorry if I wasn't more forthcoming, but you know how it is."

"And the other similar messes the news is talking about? You?"

"Pretty much," Luke replied.

"Who are you?"

"I'm Luke. I live in the neighborhood and drink beer at your pub."

"There's something off about you..." Pablo narrowed his eyes as he stared at Luke. "You fight different. Your speech is different. Now that you're not playing the casual customer, it's almost like you're cataloging my details, seeing if you could take me."

Luke shrugged. "I am who I am."

"Yeah, yeah, yeah. You are who you are. I get it. Stop deflecting. You don't act like other...like other modern men. There's something slightly different somehow. I don't know. It's hard to put my finger on it. Just that I've never met another human like you. What are you, dude?"

"Old. Very, very old, and some days I feel my age more than others. I've seen the fall of empires and witnessed the rise of Christianity and Islam. I've served emperors and kings. I've slain vampires beyond count. I was born Lucius, son of Ambeltrix Gaius Silvanius, in a village outside what is today called Brussels in the 839th year after the founding of Rome, the year 86 of the Common Era. I enlisted in Rome's legions when I was seventeen and fought under the Emperor Trajan in his second Dacian War where I ended up killing my first vampire."

Pablo's mouth hung open, and it looked like his brain had stopped working correctly. Luke wasn't sure why he'd told Pablo. He'd always enjoyed chatting with Pablo when he came to drink, but something clicked in Luke's head. He knew when to follow his intuition about people, and Pablo was good people. That, and he figured a secret was worth a secret. Pablo had revealed his secret to Luke when he'd stepped in to defend three innocent people and help Luke slay some vampires.

"You're... You're a two-thousand-year-old Roman legionnaire from Belgium who slays vampires? That's a bit far-fetched, don't you think?" He looked like he was trying to comprehend what he'd just been told, but wasn't quite connecting all the dots.

"You said it yourself. I don't act like other humans, or more correctly, like modern humans. I mean, I try to do my best to blend in." Luke pursed his lips, frustrated with how the evening had gone.

"The swords are authentic. I typically have my armor too, but tend to not wear it to the pub. You can either accept what I've told you, or that I'm just a weirdo with a penchant for using antique weapons to kill vampires. Well, I guess both are still true no matter how you slice it."

Pablo chuckled at Luke's pun, ran a hand through his hair, and let out a long sigh. He turned away, grabbed a couple more glasses and filled them with beer, setting one in front of Luke. He leaned against the back bar, appearing to think about what Luke had told him, occasionally taking a drink from his glass.

Luke let the silence hang in the air while enjoying the freshly poured pint of pilsner.

"Shit, man. I don't know what to think. You're just a dude who comes into my pub to drink beer. You're a regular, so I know your name. Until tonight, that was the extent of our relationship. Now we've killed vampires. I mean, shit, I killed a vampire. Holy fuck. Now you tell me you're an immortal vampire slayer. My packleader is going to think I've been hitting too much of my own sauce." Pablo shook his head.

"I'll make myself available to meet with your packleader. Now that both our cats are out of the bag and we're sharing the same territory, we should probably be properly introduced as a courtesy between supernaturals. Here." Luke grabbed a notepad out of his backpack and jotted down his number. "If your packleader wants to meet me, and you haven't seen me down here drinking beer, give me a call." Luke packed up his backpack and slung it over his shoulder. "I should get home and feed my cat."

"I'll let you out. And don't worry about the mess out back. I'll burn the clothes and wash the alley out. I wouldn't want anyone sniffing around looking for their fanged friends." Pablo pushed off the wall and walked around the bar.

Luke nodded and walked out the door, keenly aware that something new had just disrupted his normal routine. Werewolves in the neighborhood could immensely complicate his life, and more complications were just what he needed.

ALFRED WAS SUITABLY ANNOYED with his later than normal dinner but still managed to be magnanimous with his affections, despite the grave insult to his feline stomach and honor.

"Well, buddy. Looks like things are going to get a little more interesting. Apparently, we live in a neighborhood with werewolves." Luke scratched Alfred's head between his ears before grabbing his backpack and heading down to clean his swords.

He set the bag down near his worktable, grabbed The Rolling Stones' "Let it Bleed" LP off the shelf, and set down the needle. He reached down and turned the volume up as the atmospheric intro to "Gimme Shelter" floated out of the speakers. Turning around, he walked to the giant map pinned to the wall. He grabbed some pins from the tray and used them to mark the site of last night's and tonight's vampire sightings. Tonight's attack was the first in North Portland.

Most of the rest were more concentrated around downtown Portland. Downtown was expected. The high concentration of bars, hotels, and entertainment venues meant a steady stream of tourists or the bridge-and-tunnel kids coming in from the suburbs looking for booze to fuel their hookups. With the concentration of people and intoxicants, downtown Portland made for an irresistible hunting ground for creatures that haunted the night and overwhelmed weak-minded prey with a magical glamour. He flipped the record and returned to pondering the map, the Stones playing in the background, when he felt a persistent rubbing over his lower legs. He absentmindedly reached down, picked up Alfred, flipped him on his back, and rubbed his chest as the cat settled into a deep, raspy purr.

"There's at least one nest in town, maybe more. This isn't good," he muttered to himself. There had been random vampires wandering through Portland over the years he'd lived there, a few here, a few there, but nothing like the current spate. He'd killed at least a dozen since he'd returned from Belgium a few months ago, mostly weak and stupid newly turned vampires, which was also troubling. Newly turned vampires rarely strayed far from their creator's territory.

Either an older vampire was getting highly ambitious and turning a lot of new vamps, or there were several powerful vampires now operating in Portland. The last track from side two shook him out of his reverie.

"You're right, Mick. I can't always get what I want. I wanted a nice, quiet city where vamps were less likely to gather, yet here we are. Although, I doubt a pack of werewolves is actually what I needed. This shit is going to get messy if we have multiple elder vampires establishing a beachhead." Luke was silent for a while before he sighed and shook his head, resigned to the evidence.

FOUR

LUKE KNOCKED on the door of the well-maintained Portland bungalow, host gifts in his left hand. A few moments later, the door opened.

"Hey, Luke! Welcome to my home. Come in!" Pablo said.

"Hello. I brought flowers and a bottle of wine."

"Thank you!" Pablo took the flowers and wine. "You can hang your coat and backpack on the rack there. Everyone's in the kitchen. Would you like a drink? We have beer, wine, cocktails, water, soda; take your pick."

"Beer, please."

Pablo set the bouquet and Syrah down on the counter and walked over to a three-faucet kegerator in the corner. "Pils, porter, or IPA?"

"I'll take the porter."

Pablo drew a pint of dark beer, brought it over to Luke, then grabbed a vase out of the cabinet and scissors from a drawer. He clipped the stems, filled the vase with water, and dropped the flowers in before setting them in the center of the kitchen table.

"Everyone, this is Luke. Luke, this is everyone!" He pointed to a short, slim white woman in jeans and a black Ramones T-shirt sitting at the table. "This is Holly. She's our packleader."

Holly wore her short, brunette hair in a spiky cut. Her arms were covered in full sleeve tattoos, while a few lines of ink peeking above the neckline of her tee hinted at more ink below. She gave a small nod of acknowledgment, which Luke returned with a smile. Next, Pablo gestured toward a shorter, curvy Japanese woman in a floral print dress. Her hair was black with bangs and the rest pulled back into a ponytail. Her hands were stuffed inside the pockets of her dress.

"Hey, it's got pockets," Luke said.

She gave him a giant grin and pushed her hands forward, demonstrating her pockets. "Yup!"

"The lady with the pockets is Samantha, Holly's partner."

Sam rolled her eyes at Pablo. "Sam, if you please!"

"Hi, Sam," Luke said and smiled at her.

"And the handsome fellow in the apron and oven mitts is my husband, Tony." Tony was a tall, trim white man. Underneath the apron, he wore a plaid shirt tucked into skinny-legged red pants cuffed above a stylish pair of black ankle boots. Tony's blond hair, like the rest of his appearance, was immaculately groomed. He capped off his look with a pair of black plastic-framed glasses.

He briefly turned his head and waved over his shoulder with an oven-mitted hand and said, "Helloooooo." He went back to pulling out whatever he was roasting in the oven. "Why don't you guys get out of my kitchen and let me finish dinner."

"Anybody need a top off on their drinks before we leave Tony to it?" Pablo asked.

He took Luke's pint and filled it up, then grabbed a pint of IPA for Holly when she raised her hand. Sam helped herself to an open bottle of red wine on the counter. Pablo filled a pint with pilsner for himself before everyone filed out of the kitchen and into the dining room. Holly and Sam took chairs along one of the long sides of the dining room table. Luke took one across from them while Pablo sat down in between them at the head of the table.

"You have a lovely home, Pablo. Thanks for inviting me for dinner."

"Cheers!" Pablo held up his pint. The others joined in, clinked glasses, and echoed his toast. "I thought this might be the most casual way to introduce you to Holly. Drinks and food always seem like the best way to break the ice."

Luke nodded in agreement.

"That and maybe some cards or a board game? Tony will be awhile still, might as well keep occupied. Do you know 'Hand & Foot'?"

"I'm not sure. What's involved?" Luke asked.

Pablo explained the rules of the card game.

"That doesn't sound too difficult to pick up."

"You and Holly will be partners leaving Sam and me as the other team." Pablo stood and walked out of the room.

"What can I tell you about myself?" Luke directed the question at Holly.

"Well, this isn't an interrogation; at least, nothing so formal. Pablo thought, and I agreed, it would probably be best to get to know the new supernatural in the neighborhood. How long have you lived in Portland?" Holly asked.

"Oh, off and on since the late fifties. I was getting tired of living in England and remembered a friend describing Portland. I booked a trip to visit and check it out. I'd never been to the United States before, so I figured a place with mountains and an ocean might make for a pleasant change of scenery. While I was here, a house burned down along with the one next to it. Both were on large lots, so I bought both and had my house built on them." He reached for his glass of beer to wet his whistle. "I've lived in other cities for a year or two, but Portland has been my home for a while now."

Holly looked a bit shocked by the date he gave. "How have you escaped our notice all this time? The pack has always tried to keep track of such things."

"Until recently, the vampire activity in Portland has been fairly negligible. I really don't exhibit any weird characteristics. It's not a failure on your part, just me keeping a low profile, like I've done for a long time. It's what I do. I keep to myself. I kill vampires." While they were discussing his status as a Portlander, Pablo had returned and dealt the cards.

"What happened to your friend?" asked Sam. "Oh, I'm sorry! That's insensitive of me. You don't have to answer that."

"It's fine. Like most people I know, it's one of three options: war, old age, or vampire. In his case, the last option killed him during the first option."

"I'm sorry, Luke." She looked earnest.

"That's OK, Sam. I've buried a lot of friends over the years." He picked two cards from the deck, organized them, then discarded.

"Where are you from originally?" Holly asked.

Luke knew she knew the answer, or at least he was pretty sure Pablo had given her the full rundown of what Luke had told him, but some people wanted to confirm for themselves; and as the leader of a shifter pack, she could probably detect lies.

"I was born in a small village near what's today called Brussels in Belgium. My parents were Gallic Celts from the Nervii tribe. I spent my youth in a village with my mother, her sister, and my cousins."

"Where was your father?" Holly asked.

Sam gently laid her hand on Holly's forearm. "Hol, you're getting a bit interrogate-y." They briefly made eye contact and when Holly faced Luke again, her face had relaxed some.

"Sam is right. My apologies, Luke. You're a guest here and have caused no problems for the pack that I know of. Plus, Pablo likes you, and that's a good place to start. I get nervous when there are new threats to my pack and our home. Vampires are something we've never dealt with. I mean, I've heard of them and know they're more than just scary stories, but multiple attacks in weeks, including at a pack business, are making some of us anxious."

"No need to apologize. I understand your concern. Some weird guy just shows up, claiming to be a nineteen-hundred-year-old Roman legionnaire. As long as you're not working with or aiding vampires in any way, you have nothing to fear from me."

"So, you're really sticking with that story?" She raised her eyebrows skeptically.

"There are probably simpler stories I could have made up, but then again, I've always found my safety to be better served by not lying to werewolves."

Holly smirked at his comment. "And you've been killing vampires the whole time?"

"Yeah, for most of it. I killed my first vampire when I was twenty in the hills just outside Sarmizegethusa in 106 CE."

"Sarmizgauh-whatsit?" Samantha asked.

"Sarmizegethusa; it was the capital of the Dacian Kingdom, basically what's called 'Romania' today. I'd just experienced two campaigning seasons on the front lines under Imperator Traianus. Sorry, you'd know him as the Emperor Trajan. I served in the legions for many years, but the XXX Ulpia Victrix will always hold a special place as my first legion. That's where I earned my honorific. You can go out now if you can, Holly," Luke said, diverting back to the card game momentarily.

"Your 'honorific?'" asked Pablo.

"Cognomen ex virtute. Basically, a named earned from virtue or deed. I was born Lucius, son of Gaius—"

"Gaius?" Pablo interrupted. "That sounds like a Roman name, didn't you say your father was Belgian? Gallic? Nervi...whatever?"

"It is Roman. My father adopted it when he signed up for his service," Luke replied.

"Wait, if your dad wasn't a citizen, how did you join the legions? I mean, if you were a Belgian Celt..." asked Sam.

"You know Roman history?" Luke asked.

Holly snorted. "No, she loves watching Spartacus and reading trashy sandal and sword novels."

"They're not trashy!" Sam replied indignantly. "See, I learned valuable history. Right, Luke?"

"Yeah, I can't speak to the veracity of the rest of your literary choices, but that fact is true. Only free citizens could join the legions. My father was granted citizenship after serving in an auxiliary cohort for a full term of service. It allowed me the privilege of citizenship and gave me the right to join the legions. He chose Gaius as his name in honor of Gaius Julius Caesar, who'd conquered the

Nervii and other Belgian tribes a century before he was born. My full name is Lucius Silvanius Ferrata. My father was taller than his fellow Gallic and Germanic tribesman, which made him significantly taller than Italian Romans. They called him the 'Tree,' so when he finished his time, he chose the Latin surname Silvanius, which means woods or trees, as his new name. So when I joined the legions, I signed up as Lucius Silvanius. The 'Ferrata,' I earned."

"How?" asked Sam, excitement gleaming in her eyes at the real-life sword and sandal story unfolding before her.

"Honorifics are earned names, bestowed for great deeds. Scipio Africanus, for instance, wasn't his name. He was born Publius Cornelius Scipio but earned his honorific, Africanus, from his exploits fighting Hannibal and the Carthaginians. Pompeius earned his Magnus leading legions. Germanicus earned his fighting the Germans. Ferrata means 'ironclad' or 'iron will,' but that's a long story for another time."

"How long did your pops have to serve to get his citizenship?" asked Pablo.

"You had to make it to the end of twenty-five years of service."

Pablo choked on the beer he was sipping and coughed heavily. "Holy shit! Twenty-five years? Fuck, man, that's a long time."

"Yeah, I didn't meet him until I was ten. I was conceived when he'd earned a furlough and returned home for a few months. He met my mom, they hit it off, and I was born eight months after he returned to his cohort in Britannia." Luke played his last card, earning the victory for Holly and him.

"Well, crap. You caught both Sam and me with our feet. And your pop made it through all twenty-five years? And your mom didn't leave him during all that time?"

"Nope. They adored each other. Apparently, it was a very intense few months before he returned to Britannia. My mom had the support of her sister and her family as well as the money that Father sent home. You have to understand, it was pretty common. I wasn't the only kid with a father off with the legions. It was good steady pay, even at the reduced rate paid to auxiliary cohorts. If you were smart with your money and your units earned plunder booty, you could come out of the military with a sizable amount of money. My father used it to set himself up with a very profitable business selling local products to the neighborhood legionary forts."

"I'll go refresh everyone's drinks, since it's not my turn to deal," Pablo said.

Holly's face had lost its skeptical edge but was a study in quiet neutrality. Sam, on the other hand, looked absolutely delighted with the tale unfolding in front of her.

"Wow! What's it like to live for that long?"

He didn't want to crush Sam's enthusiasm for his story, but the practicalities of extreme longevity, especially in the service of a harsh task and task master, weren't all peaches and unicorns.

"Long. Oft times, boring. Tedious. And frequently, lonely. Isolating." His gaze got far away. "Everyone expects to outlive their parents; but then I watched my cousins die, then their children, and then their children. After a while, I just stopped watching."

Pablo set a fresh beer down beside Luke, then gave his shoulder a reassuring squeeze before resuming his seat.

"I've been surrounded by conflict all of my life, sometimes under a flag, but always hunting the undead," Luke said.

Tony lightly coughed from the kitchen door as he brought out a tray of hors d'oeuvres. "Would you all mind lightening up a bit? It's dark and rainy enough outside without dragging that inside. You're putting a damper on my dinner party."

"I'm sorry, Tony," Luke said, looking over his shoulder. "I'll put it away." He turned around to the rest of the table. "I don't get out much. It's been a while since I've had much in the way of normal conversation with anyone except my cat, and he's kind of shit at the give and take. Anywho..."

After that, the questioning ended and settled into a mix of friendly chitchat and card playing until Tony called out to clean up the mess and set the table, dinner was ready. Luke felt a bit embarrassed about being so open, accidentally revealing too much of his mental state to the virtual strangers. They seemed like decent people, though he'd have to be more careful so he didn't weird them out with his mental messiness.

TONY'S COOKING WAS AMAZING, as was the company as everyone got to know each other in the casual environment. While they ate, the weather got more serious than the typical fall drizzle. The rain pounded on the windows, and branches scratched at the walls and roof. They'd just cleared the table and sat down for dessert when they heard explosive cracks and a loud crash, then the lights blinked out.

"I guess that throws a twist in the evening," Tony said.

Everyone broke out their cell phones, turned on their flashlight apps, and walked to the windows. One of the neighbor's trees had snapped in the heavy wind. Fortunately for them and the neighbor, it fell diagonally across and out onto the road. Its only victim was the power lines above the street.

"That explains the lights," Holly said.

"It's dry in here, and we have space. It's probably best if everyone stays the night. I'll get some candles. Tony, could you start a fire in the den? Everyone else, sit and enjoy your dessert." Pablo suggested.

Luke, Holly, and Sam shuffled back to the table and left their phone flashlights on as Tony and Pablo began the quest for fire. Pablo returned with a couple candlesticks.

"Well, gang, things just got a bit more romantic in here." He chuckled and sat down to work on his dessert. "Do you need any help with the fire, honey?" he called to Tony.

"No, I've got it. I'll be out in a moment." Tony emerged a few seconds later. "The fire is going nicely. When we're done with dessert, let's retire to the den for a nightcap."

After they all finished, Pablo grabbed the candle sticks and led everyone into their den. "Help yourself to whatever," Pablo said, gesturing toward the collection of liquor bottles along one side of a bar.

Luke walked to the bar and perused the selection of liquors and settled on a peaty scotch. He took his glass and surveyed the collection of books. Pablo and Tony's library contained what people would consider normal books for "normal" people: fiction, non-fiction, cookbooks, gardening books, etc. However, that was only a small portion of their library. Shelf after shelf was filled with books covering specialty topics like werewolves, vampires, the occult, and other paranormal topics. Some fell into the "pop" category, while some were truly spectacular pieces of lore.

"This is an impressive collection." Luke turned back to the bookshelf, needing a minute to himself, even if it was just on the other side of the room. It'd been years since he'd participated in this much interpersonal activity. Oddly, he was enjoying it, even if it felt a bit draining.

"You're welcome to borrow anything, provided you keep it safe and bring it back in a reasonable amount of time," Tony said.

Luke finished ogling the shelves and took the empty wingback armchair next to the fire. He stared at the dancing flames. All the talk about his past sent his mind drifting to the village of his boyhood as he enjoyed the murmur of conversation around him.

Sam broke his reverie. "Penny for your thoughts, Luke?"

"I was thinking about bluebells."

"The flowers?" Sam asked.

He stared into the fire. "Outside of Brussels, there's a forest called the Hallerbos. It's more of a small nature preserve these days. When I was a boy, it was a fair bit larger, wilder too. The village I grew up in was just south of the woods. It made for a great place to sneak off to when I was being less than mindful of my chores. Every spring, about mid-May, the bluebells bloomed. Coincidently, it was about then I'd find myself in the woods more frequently than other times of the year…"

LUCIUS I

LUCIUS HAD NEVER MET his father. For all of his young
life, his father had been stationed in Britannia since he'd joined the I
Cohort Tungrorum after it formed in 71 CE. His father had briefly
returned home to their small village on a furlough the winter after
he'd earned his promotion to Centurion because of his actions during
the Battle of Mons Graupius in Caledonia. He'd met Lucius's mother
and after a brief courtship, one thing led to a Lucius thing.

As his mother told him about his father and where he was, it
always felt like they were on opposite ends of the world. He knew, in
his childish mind, that Britannia was the end of the Roman Empire,
but he had no real concept of geography or the size of the world.
Today, a person can fly from Brussels to Edinburgh in an hour and a
half. Then, it felt like it must have taken his father years to get there
and back. To Lucius, his whole world was a two-hour walk from
their tiny village. Beyond that, there be dragons.

It was late spring or early summer; he wasn't sure which. Time is
a fickle and fleeting concept to a man approaching two-thousand-
years of age. It was even more variable to a ten-year-old boy in an
era where time consisted of day or night, winter or summer. Late
spring in the forests of Gaul was a damn fine time to evade chores.

His favorite place in all the world to run off to was the woods north of his village, today known as the Hallerbos. Then, it was a massive forest. If he caught the timing right, the bluebells would be in full bloom, carpeting the forest as far as his sharp, young eyes could see.

His mother would find him in some meadow lying flat on his back, surrounded by bluebells and staring up through a gap in the trees, watching shapes in the clouds. She'd lie down beside him and share some bread and cheese she'd brought with her, knowing her son invariably would have forgotten to bring anything for lunch. She'd scold him for abandoning his chores and forcing her to skip out on whatever she was working on to find him. Although, with his father's military salary, they didn't want for much and what tasks his mother took for extra money were neither onerous nor burdensome. They were not rich by any measure of their meager village's ideals, but they had a small, warm home and wanted for little, save for the presence of his father.

She'd fallen in love with him—a dashing soldier returned home with the spoils of war, flush with his new promotion and a widely celebrated victory to the greatness of the empire. Although she'd never had anyone in her family join Rome's war machine, plenty of people in the region had. Tales of far-off adventures and the occasional son returned from abroad with either a limp or a limb missing, or, if he was lucky, a furlough pass from his prefect.

Lucius heard a crash of metal and gear outside their small home as his mother prepared their evening meal. Being an inquisitive lad, he dashed out the door and quite literally ran into a giant of a man who might have made Antigoon think twice. A haystack after a windstorm looked more organized than his red beard, which had lightning slashes of gray riddled throughout. He looked down at the boy at his feet.

"Pardon, boy. Is this the home of Verlia?"

Lucius looked up at him with his jaw open like some sort of yokel. Lucius thought he'd hit his head, although he didn't remember striking the ground or the door. Then again, if you've hit your head hard enough to hallucinate a giant, would you really remember hitting it?

"Are you daft, boy? Does Verlia live here?" the man asked, raising his voice and probably thinking the boy was soft in the head.

"G-Gaius?" Lucius's mother stood just inside the door with the shadow of evening hiding her nearly out of sight.

"Verlia?" The giant took a hesitant step forward as Lucius's mother launched herself into the giant's arms.

"It's been so long…" she said with joyful tears streaming down her eyes. She released him slowly and stepped back. Both appeared embarrassed by their emotional outburst. "Lucius, this is your father, Gaius. Gaius, this is your son." Lucius's mom stepped back, making space between him and his father.

"Well, lad. You just gonna lay there like a stick?" The boy awkwardly stood up, only to be grasped under his arms and hoisted in the air above the man his mother said was his father. Lucius went from shocked and on the ground to shocked and flying above what felt like the entire village. He couldn't help but laugh as his father smiled up at him.

"Come inside. Set your stuff in the corner. Dinner should be ready soon," Lucius's mother said, then looked at her son. "Lucius, after dinner you can go stay with your aunt and cousins."

IT WAS weird having his father in the house. It had just been his mother and him for his entire life. They visited her sister and her family regularly since they lived so close. His cousins and he would roam through the woods near their homes. He'd occasionally help his uncle with the animals, but he'd never had male guidance in his household.

It took him a while to overcome his initial shyness, but as soon as he did, he peppered his father with question after question.

"What's Britannia like?"

"Much like here. It's cold and wet a lot but with more hills and mountains," Gaius answered in the deep, slow rumble that was his voice.

"Did you kill a lot of Britannians?"

"They're not called 'Britannians.'" He laughed. "There are many tribes in Brittania, many Celts like us. I fought against the Silures, Orodvices, Novantae, Votadini, Damnonii, and all the tribes of the Caledonii."

"Did you fight them all the time?"

"No." He chuckled again. "Britannia has been mostly quiet the last many years. I spent most of the last half of my time in the army marching and building. Most legions and auxiliary cohorts spend more time building roads and forts and deterring fights than actually fighting."

"Why'd you join the army?"

"I never felt much like farming and all the tilling of the earth that it involved. The joke was on me, though. I spent more time with a shovel moving dirt in the last twenty-five years than I would have in a lifetime as a farmer."

Lucius's eyes drifted toward the armor stand Gaius had set up in the corner of the room. The gleaming silver strips of overlapping steel had been polished to a high shine. The golden-colored brass hinges, lace loops, and adornments sparkled in the dim, fire-lit room. "Can...can I try on your armor?"

"It's pretty big and really heavy..."

"Please?" Lucius asked.

Gaius could see the hungry eagerness in his son's eyes. "OK."

He stood up and plucked it off the crossbar, bringing it over to where Lucius stood. He opened the front. "This style of armor is made of segmented plates. Most auxiliary use lorica hamata, ring mail, but I had a lucky night with the dice and used my winnings to have this made."

Lucius poked his arms through as Gaius settled the immense weight on his son's young shoulders. Lucius's knees nearly buckled. As it was, they wobbled like a newly born colt's. He was practically swimming inside the huge piece of armor. It felt like his shoulders would be crushed under the weight of all that steel. He couldn't even put his arms down at his sides. His father's barrel chest was much wider than Lucius's skinny torso. His arms were propped up on the bottom edge of the armholes.

"I think we'll skip the helmet. That might be more weight than you can bear. My armor is a bit bigger than a standard Roman's lorica, because I'm a fair bit bigger than most Romans. I can carry more weight, so I had it made a bit thicker, figuring I could stand a better chance of keeping my guts on the inside where they belong. Thought it was a good way to stay alive and come back home to your momma in one piece." He always had a twinkle in his eye when he spoke about Lucius's mother Verlia.

LUCIUS SPENT the next six years at his father's side, learning everything his father could teach him. Lucius's mind was pliant and quick; rarely was a second explanation needed for a complex concept. Lucius learned Latin, both spoken and written. Gaius taught him figures and how to use and track money. Lucius made an apt pupil as Gaius spun his war loot into a thriving business.

His father was the sort who could win over nearly anyone with his open nature. He quickly established himself with the local artisans and farmers as the trusted broker to sell their goods to the Legions. He let his hair grow shaggy in the style of the local men, and when dealing with his Gallic brethren, he'd go by his birth name of Ambeltrix. When dealing with the legions, he'd dress in his standard issue garb and went by his chosen name of Gaius, flashing his rank as a Centurion to earn admission and trust. In all the days Lucius assisted his father, he never saw him deal poorly with either party, Gaul or Roman. He taught Lucius that his honor and integrity were worth far more than a few extra coins. It paid off for him. Gaius quickly became the first person people chose to deal with.

Periodically, a friend would muster out of the legions and show up looking for a job. Gaius's expanding enterprises always needed a trusted body. It was a grand time for Lucius. He became the older men's mascot. From them, he learned various fighting styles, and much to his mother's dismay, the more exotic uses of a soldier's language. Lucius's mother was less than impressed with this, scolding Lucius when she caught him practicing some of the more colorful phrases he'd recently learned and later blistering his father's ears with her displeasure. Gaius took his boy aside and taught him how to select the appropriate times and places to use such language, and how neither of those were around his mother.

Gaius's success brought with it a larger, fancier home in the style of the Romans, with servants to assist his wife. Lucius took it all in stride, spending most of his time with his father, learning everything he'd need to know to be a man. While he sometimes missed the idleness and freedom of his younger years, he was having too much fun with his father and his father's friends. By and large, Gaius was a jovial and happy man, quicker to give a hearty laugh than a harsh glance.

There were exceptions. The first time was the spring of Lucius's eleventh year. Something had startled him awake. He walked around their small home until he heard a noise outside. He carefully opened the door and peeked outside. A large figure sat on the ground, back propped against the wall of the house. Periodically, the figure would bring a wine skin to its mouth and take a deep drink. Lucius stared silently, unsure of what to do. Finally, the winds shifted the clouds, letting the moonlight illuminate the figure on the ground. Lucius immediately recognized the red beard of his father. The soft moonlight igniting the white streaks in his beard to nearly incandescent silver. Lucius saw the wet streaks on his father's cheeks.

"What's the matter, Papa?"

Gaius sniffed, ran his sleeve under his nose and rubbed the heel of his hand over his cheek. As he turned his head to see who'd spoken, Lucius saw the pain in his father's eyes. "Nothing, boy. Nothing you'd understand. Go back to bed." Gaius stared back out into the distance, ignoring the presence of his son.

Lucius took one last look, then went back to his sleeping mat. After a while, Lucius could recognize the approach to the few times a year his father's mood would slip into melancholy. Gaius would never talk about it with Lucius or his mother. When the days would approach, they knew to give Gaius his distance and to forgive him his shortness of temper. Verlia explained to Lucius that it was the result of the battles Gaius had fought in. She'd heard similar stories from other legionary wives, some of those stories far worse than Gaius's occasional moodiness. Lucius wanted to go to his father, but didn't know what to say or do, or even if it was welcome. This previously unseen side of his father forced Lucius to adjust his image of the jovial giant he'd come to know, revealing a new depth in the man.

That was the rhythm of Lucius's adolescence—working, learning, training, and building a relationship with the complex man that was his father.

FIVE

ANOTHER NIGHT, another patrol. It had been a couple nights since his evening with Pablo, Tony, Holly, and Sam. The evening spent over food, drink, and conversation had been a pleasant respite, but not enough to counter all the nights he'd spent patrolling the city. Portland was practically drowning in fanged vermin. He hadn't encountered this many vampires in this short of a time in ages, and the last time it happened, something big had been going down. What had started as a trickle of vampire murders over the last half of the summer had turned into a deluge during the early fall. If he was going to stop Portland from becoming a total vampire wasteland, he'd have to get to the root of the problem. Unfortunately, he was no closer than when he'd started noticing increased bloodsucker activity. Even though the fall had been rainier than normal, the rain couldn't quite wash away the blood of the vampires' victims.

The late night advanced toward closing time for many of the bars. Technically, 2:30 a.m. was the state mandated closing time, but most bars operated on "bar time," running about fifteen minutes faster than real time, which allowed them a cushion to get people paid up and out on the streets. Luke had wandered off the more beaten track and away from the clubs, which hadn't started spilling out their drunk and libidinous patrons into the night. Even with the violence and death, twenty-somethings still felt the need to be young, maybe even more so because of it.

"Drink, bang, and be merry; for tomorrow we may be vampire chow…" Luke mused.

As Luke walked over the Morrison Bridge into shallow southeast Portland, he stopped along the rail of the bridge just over the Montage building and leaned up against the railing, absentmindedly watching people enter and exit the Montage below. Le Bistro Montage was a Portland landmark in the middle of the warehouses of industrial inner southeast Portland and one of the few places open after hours for food. It was a long way from their 4:00 a.m. closing time but getting close to midnight, so there was no shortage of tipsy people spilling into the evening as they headed home or on to their next debaucherous adventure. His mind drifted as the rhythm of the night swept over him: the sounds of cars on I-5, the occasional vehicle passing behind him, the laughter of people enjoying their night, and the occasional gust of wind. The light drizzle had stopped for a bit, allowing a few patches of starry sky to peek through the gray murk of autumn.

A slight tingle of awareness jolted him from his abstraction; vampires were nearby. He looked down at the street below and watched as a tipsy looking, tall, Black woman stumbled her way out of the Montage on the arm of a tall, pale man with shaggy, mousy blond hair. The occasional giggle escaped her mouth. The man directed her west and under the Morrison Bridge further into the darker recesses of industrial southeast. Luke knew with only the slightest of glances that it was the blond man who had set off his internal vamp alarm. His mind snapped into focus as he ran east to get to a point where he could jump over the bridge's railing and land without hurting himself or alerting the vampire.

Once Luke reached a point he judged shallow enough, he vaulted over the railing and landed like a cat—silent and nimble. There were advantages to being an immortal vampire hunter, including a lethal combination of superhuman abilities and centuries of experience. He melted behind the shadow of a car parked along the road and assessed the situation.

Their laughter echoed off the buildings and the underside of the concrete roadway above. She stumbled slightly but was held up by his army surplus jacket clad arm.

"Oh! You're cute and strong!" she crooned to him. He chuckled in reply as he steered her around a huge pile of broken pallets and up a handful of stairs onto a loading dock behind a building on the left. Luke quietly jogged across the street and slid behind the pallets, pressing his back against the wall next to them.

"This looks like a good spot," said the vamp.

"Hmm, you are anxious!" the woman replied.

Luke crept around the corner.

"Hey, bloodsucker!" Luke shouted, "Let the juice box go."

They both turned toward Luke, and he got his first clear look at the pair. The vamp was tall, probably a touch over six feet, and skinny, somewhere in the heroin chic range. He was very white, almost translucently so, and wore skintight skinny black jeans and a black tee under his olive drab army surplus jacket. Standing as tall as the vamp, the woman appeared to be broad in the shoulders and hips but it was hard to tell in the heavy three-quarter length, dark red leather trench coat she wore over a black shirt and dark jeans that gave way to thick-heeled boots. She wore her hair in a short, natural style.

"Look. I ain't looking for a white knight here. Move along. You're involving yourself where you're not wanted." She sounded sober and free from any glamour the vampire might have deployed.

The fanger was the only one who wasn't aware that things weren't going as planned. Luke, a bit behind himself, quickly adjusted his thinking about the woman and what her role in the situation might be. She was a mystery Luke would have to solve later.

"I'm sorry to interrupt your date, but he's not what he seems," Luke said.

"They never are, honey. They never are."

"You heard the lady, get the fuck out of here." The mask of boredom slipped from the vampire's face, replaced by annoyance.

"OK! I give up!" Luke said as he raised his arms as if surrendering before letting his right hand drift behind his neck to the hilt of his gladius. He began to slide the sword out of its scabbard, but the sound of banging around inside the giant industrial dumpster next to the loading dock drew his attention. Three vamps sprang out of the dumpster, while another three dropped off the dock's overhang. "Lady, now's the time to run. I can hold them off for a bit, but it'll be a lot harder if I have to keep an eye on you too."

In response, she grabbed her date by the lapels and slammed him up against the wall, plunging a stake she'd produced from an inside coat pocket directly into his chest. He slumped to the ground and started gooing up his cool threads. Luke's mouth hung open in awe at the speed with which she'd dispatched him. He nearly didn't get his gladius cleared before the first wave of vampires was on him. He sidestepped and tripped the first vampire rushing toward him, sending him sprawling to the ground.

"Yo, hero. Get killing or get running," the woman shouted as she spun a sidekick into the midsection of a vamp stupid enough to get within range. He was hurled back as a whoosh of air exited his lungs, landing on his butt and crumpling around his mid-section.

"Already on it," Luke replied, engaging the vamp stalking toward him, swinging a length of chain ominously.

He shifted his gladius to his left hand and adjusted himself to a left-handed fighting stance. It was times like this that made him wish he always carried a scutum, but while he could cover his lorica segmentata in a baggy jacket or hoodie, it was a lot harder to look inconspicuous toting a standard Roman legionary shield. Fortunately, he'd decided to strap on his manica, the segmented arm guard he'd first used two thousand years ago during the Dacian campaigns. It wasn't something he always wore, but maybe he'd have to mix it in more frequently if this was the way things were going in Portland.

The female vampire swung the chain overhead and down at Luke's head. He raised his right arm and grunted at the painful impact of the chain bouncing off his concealed armor. He responded with a lightning quick stab toward her stomach. Instead of taking the blade, she launched herself sideways and landed awkwardly on the ground five feet below the loading dock. One of her compatriots used the opportunity to follow up the dive with a two-by-four swung at Luke's head. He grimaced as he blocked its descent on his armored arm and nudged it up and over his head, then followed it with a slash to the vamp's midsection. His gladius bit deep as he pulled his cut through and out the vamp's stomach. The vampire dropped his lumber as Luke kicked him aside. He wasn't out of the fight totally, but Luke had bought a few seconds to survey the scene.

His not-so-helpless rescue victim had put down a second vampire and was swinging the discarded two-by-four in a wide arc to hold one of the vampires off. A third was eyeing the action. He heard the vamp he'd gutted moaning and slipping on his innards trying to get up. Luke tossed his gladius over to his right hand, caught it in midair, and cut down in a backhand motion, lopping off the better part of the vamp's head before he could fully rise. Luke took the opportunity to pull out his rudis while he checked on the vamp on the ground. She appeared to be unconscious, or at least she was just lying motionless on the ground. The loud crack of wood drew his attention back to the other fight.

The woman's two-by-four had snapped off about a foot above her grip, leaving her with a jagged point but not much reach. Reassessing her situation, she drew it back and launched it at her fanged adversary like a frisbee, causing it to tumble end-over-end until it thunked into his chest just above his heart. It didn't sink in deep enough to finish the job, but she was already on top of that problem and immediately spun another sidekick at him, driving the busted-off board deep into his chest with the bottom of her boot.

Luke used the distraction to charge the vamp that was standing back a bit, catching him completely flat-footed with the speed of his attack. Luke stabbed his gladius up into the soft spot under the vamp's chin and into his skull. The upward thrust shoved his head back and his arms out, leaving the vamp's chest unprotected. As fast as a striking snake, Luke plunged his rudis into the vamp's chest and through his heart. He gave the wooden sword a hard twist, fully destroying the vamp's heart before pulling out the sword and turning back to see how the woman was doing.

She used the distraction of Luke's charge to scoop up the chain. The rattle of chain on concrete pulled the attention of the remaining bloodsucker back to the situation at hand. It was too late, though, as the woman flung one end of the chain around his neck, grabbed it, and moved behind him back-to-back. She pulled the chains tight over her shoulder and bent over, pulling the vamp off the ground, trying to choke him out. The vampire, not subject to the normal things that kill a human, managed to fling himself over her head, landing face-to-face with her. He punched her in the gut and as she doubled over, he grabbed the lapel of her coat and yanked her back up, exposing her neck. He'd forgotten this party wasn't a twosome as Luke snuck up behind him and rammed the rudis up and under his ribcage until the tip found his heart. The vamp dropped like a sack of flour, exploding like one too.

The woman was coughing and gasping for air after the punch she'd taken. A human strength punch to the gut would leave a person wheezing for air; a vamp powered one left a normal person nearly incapacitated. The vamp dust wasn't helping the coughing situation, either. Luke put his hand on her shoulder and directed her away from the mess they'd made. Her wheezing and coughing quickly subsided.

"Are you going to be OK?" he asked her.

"Yeah. I think so. He just winded me a bit."

"He nearly made you into a meal."

"I had everything under control!" she retorted.

"You handled yourself with aplomb." Discretion sometimes was the better part of valor. She had handled herself well, better than anyone he'd seen in ages. She knew how to put down a vampire, even if she'd made a rookie mistake. "Just a pro tip to a fellow anti-vamp enthusiast; trying to choke a vampire might not be the best approach. They may look like they're breathing, but they don't need the oxygen."

"Yeah, I think I just figured that out." She gave a little cough and then straightened up. "Well, thanks for the help. Seven was a few more than I was expecting."

"I suspect someone objected mightily to your date."

"Ha! I guess so," she said with a light chuckle. "So, you just happened to be walking along and came upon a damsel in distress?"

"I'd hardly call you a 'damsel in distress.'"

"You're damn right I'm not. What were you doing here?" the woman asked.

"Apparently, the same thing as you."

"Hunting vampires?"

Luke nodded. "Yup."

"Yeah, I guess the 'vampire' cat is out of the bag. My name is Delilah." She stuck out her hand to shake, but Luke held up a finger to hold her off for a moment.

He could hear the last vampire scrabbling to get up. He whipped around, flipped his sword into a reverse grip, and launched his gladius like he was throwing a spear after the vampire as she ran away. The gladius flew through the air, striking the fleeing vampire in the back. While it didn't penetrate deep enough to kill the vampire, it knocked her off balance and to the ground.

"Pardon me for a moment." He sprinted over to the downed vampire and plunged the rudis into her ribcage and through her undead heart.

He knelt, placed his forehead on the pommel, recited the incantation, and felt the energy surge through the wooden sword into the vampire and back again. The throbbing in his forearm lessened from a dull roar to a quiet ache. Standing up, he pulled out the rudis, wiped it clean on the corpse's shirt, repeated the process on the gladius, then walked back to Delilah. He stopped at the vampire with the bisected head and sent it on its way with a quick stab from the rudis. "Sorry about that. Didn't want her bringing back uninvited guests to our party."

"Impressive. I didn't think you could throw swords like that," she said.

Luke blushed at the compliment, not used to the attention, but covered it up with a flourished bow. "It's not the most effective thing in the world, but it'll work in a pinch with some luck." He stuck out his hand to finally reciprocate her offer of a handshake. "Luke. You can call me Luke. We should probably get out of here. There are seven unattended sets of very stylish if soiled and holey clothes that might inspire authority figures to ask more questions than I feel like answering."

"I'm parked up by the Montage."

"I'll walk you to your car. I'm heading that way, anyway." They strolled up the block toward her older Honda Civic.

"Do you need a ride anywhere?" Delilah asked.

"No. I think I'll walk for a bit, but thank you. Would you like to meet up for a beer sometime? I'd like to talk about what happened here tonight at a more appropriate time and setting. I don't run into other vampire slayers too often."

"I can do that. When you thinking?"

"If you're free tomorrow evening, say seven? Howling Moon Brewing."

"Where's that? I'm new to town," Delilah replied.

"North Portland, just off Lombard Avenue. Take I-5 North and get off at the Lombard West exit. It's about a mile or so on the right. You'll see their sign, a howling wolf head inside a full moon. You can't miss it."

"Famous last words, but I'll probably just map it on my phone." She paused and smiled at him. "Hey, Luke, it was nice to meet you, and again, thank you for the assist. I wasn't expecting that many."

"No problem. I'm just glad I happened to be in the right place at the right time. It was very nice to meet you too, Delilah." He nodded and gave her a wave before turning around and walking off into the night.

SIX

"WELL, Alfred, I guess I should give you your evening meal before I head out." Luke dropped a scoop of kibble into the bowl as Alfred purred and rubbed up against his legs. He grabbed his backpack, headed out the door, and walked to Howling Moon Brewing. When he walked in the door, the place was already packed with the evening dinner crowd.

Pablo waved at Luke as soon as he saw him walk through the door. "Hey, Luke! I reserved the back booth for you like you asked. Can I bring anything over to you?"

Luke smiled and nodded. "Thanks, Pablo. I'll take the porter, please."

"Sure thing. I'll bring it over shortly."

Luke slid into the booth, taking a seat at the edge so he could watch the door. He set his backpack down on the bench. The back booth was in the far corner and provided excellent privacy. Pablo brought over Luke's porter and set it down on a coaster.

"Thanks, Pablo." Luke grabbed the glass and took a drink.

"Who are you meeting?" Pablo asked.

"I'm not entirely sure. Someone I met last night."

Pablo gave his new friend a knowing smirk with an eyebrow raised.

Luke chuckled at the implication. "No, nothing like that. I followed her and a vampire… Oh, she just walked in."

Luke stood up and waved to get her attention. Tonight, she was wearing the same coat, but underneath was a long black and white diagonal striped dress and a pair of reddish-brown boots that paired well with the wine red of her coat. Pablo turned back toward Luke and winked. Luke returned it with a friendly scowl.

Luke gestured toward Pablo. "Delilah, this is my friend Pablo. He owns the Howling Moon. Pablo, this is Delilah."

Delilah sat down opposite of Luke, and he slid deeper into the booth.

Pablo leaned over the table. "Pleased to meet you and welcome to the Moon. What can I get for you?"

"Do you have an IPA?"

"Sure do! We have our house Oregon-style IPA, a Double, and a seasonal West Coast IPA."

"I'll have a pint of the house, please."

Pablo nodded at her and walked back to the bar. They sat in awkward silence until Pablo returned with her beer.

"Enjoy! I'll check back in with you in a bit to see if you need anything else."

"Thanks, Pablo," Luke said. Turning to Delilah, he said, "Thanks for meeting me."

"Thanks again for the assist. I'm all for group dates, but seven was just a few too many for that party."

"I take it from your preparation that wasn't your first vampire?" He knew the question was awkward after seeing her skills in action, but he was grasping for topics.

She chuckled in response. "No, not my first. I've run into a few over the last few months. They're not hard to find if you're looking for them, at least not if you know what to look for, that is."

"No, they're not. They've mastered the art of hiding in plain sight, but that does leave them slightly vulnerable to those educated in the ways of the vamp." They sat in the awkward silence of two people who've just met because of weird circumstances and weren't quite sure where to go next in the conversation.

"How do you know this place?" she asked, indicating the bar.

"It's my neighborhood pub. They opened about a year or so ago. The beers are good and so is the food, plus I can walk from my house. Pablo runs a nice place, so it's become my regular watering hole. So, how about you? You said you're new to town?"

"Yeah. I've only been here a few weeks." She didn't elaborate.

They'd only just met. She didn't know who Luke was other than some guy she'd met on a dark loading dock who happened to be on the right end of a staked vampire, or at least that's what Luke guessed was causing her reticence.

She took a drink of her IPA. "I was thinking, after I got back to my place and the adrenalin faded, where did you come from? I didn't see you in the Montage or on the street."

"You didn't look up."

She looked at him with a skeptically raised eyebrow.

"I was walking over the Morrison Bridge when I saw you come out with the vampire."

"Wait… That's a long way to run in the wrong direction to catch up to us."

"I jumped."

"What?!" she exclaimed, her eyebrows climbing nearly into her thick, short, curly hair. "That's…that's like really high."

"It wasn't low. I did run down to a lower spot; I didn't want to jump too close to you and alert the vampire. I didn't realize there was another hunter on the scene, although, all things considered, it's a good thing I followed along. Speaking of which, one of the things I've been thinking about since last night. You said you just arrived a few weeks ago. Was this your first vampire encounter in Portland?"

"No." She didn't elaborate.

"I didn't think so. That would explain the evidence of vamp kills I didn't create." He took a sip and thought for a minute.

"Those weren't your first vampires, were they? You're too well equipped and too skilled to be a rookie," Delilah said.

"No. Lately, there've been too many, way too many. I haven't seen this many vampires in one place in a long time. That's worrisome, to say the least." He grimaced slightly.

"How long have you been killing vampires?" Delilah asked.

"A long, long time."

"You don't look that old."

Luke chuckled. "Thanks, I think. I'm a bit older than I look. I've been doing this for what seems like forever. How d'you pick up this hobby?"

"I kind of stumbled into it..." She trailed off as a brief wave of sadness flashed across her face. "It's not so much a hobby as a spiritual mandate. Let's just say I owe a specific vampire a very slow staking and leave it at that for now."

Luke nodded. He could appreciate the need for discretion. "You hungry? The food's pretty good here."

"Sure."

Luke flagged down Pablo, who promptly returned with a pair of menus. "Can I get you another round while I'm here?"

They nodded. When Pablo came back with their beers, they both ordered the burger.

"So..." Delilah said. "Did you go to college?"

"No. I joined the military."

"Oh, what branch?"

"The infantry." Luke quickly added, "Army," to forestall further questions. "How about you?"

"Yeah. I got my bachelors from NYU. I was working on my master's degree when I needed to take a sabbatical."

"What were you studying?"

"Psychology."

Their burgers showed up before they could delve deeper into Delilah's educational past. After they finished, they sat quietly and enjoyed their beers until Luke broke the silence.

"I've been thinking. Seven vampires in one block are a lot, even at a popular after-hours place like the Montage. Plus, it wasn't even closing time yet. What were they doing?"

"Yeah, that does seem excessive," Delilah replied.

"They were laying a trap. That's the only thing I can think of.

How long were you inside chatting with the vamp who escorted you outside?"

"Oh, a good hour or so. Plenty of time for him to summon his pals."

"How can you tell who a vampire is?" Luke asked.

"I'm not sure. They have a 'feel' about them. Once you pick up on it, you can pick them out of the crowd almost instantly. When I figure out who I'm looking for, I can usually flirt my way into their graces."

Luke nodded appreciatively. "How long have you been in town?"

"Oh, about three weeks."

"How many vampires have you encountered?"

"Not counting the seven from last night? Let's see…" She did the math in her head. "Ten."

Luke raised his eyebrows in surprise. "That many? Did you stake them all?"

"Well, nine and a half…"

Luke raised an eyebrow. "Half?"

"I staked him, but he deflected it away from his heart. I bet it hurt, but he hauled ass out of there before I could fix the problem."

"Which one was the miss?"

Delilah shrugged. "I don't know. I think he said his name was 'Chet,' or 'Chad,' or 'Chip,' or some other bro name."

Luke chuckled in response. "No, I meant which number."

She bobbed her head side to side as she thought about it. "Oh! I think he was number six or seven."

"So he got a good look at you?"

Delilah nodded. "Yeah. He did."

"I think your escapee set you up. I can't imagine vampires would want to let a known staker run around in their city."

Delilah pursed her lips and nodded. "I came to a similar conclusion myself. Things are getting more dangerous out there."

"Yeah, I haven't seen coordination like this in a while. Usually vampires are solo hunters out to get a meal. They like to get in and out without being noticed. I was afraid of this…"

"What? Afraid of what?" Delilah leaned in closer.

"Something big is on the horizon. I've never seen this much vampire activity in Portland in all the years I've lived here. You'd be lucky to find two or three in a year normally. Several in a week? Groups out hunting and laying traps? These aren't good signs." Luke frowned and shook his head.

"Luke, I'll just put it out there. Let's join forces. We handled those vampires pretty easily together. My dad always said that if you want to learn something or get better at it, you need to find someone great to teach you. If you've been doing this a long time, you've got to be good at it or you'd be dead by now."

"Your father is right, but I'm not a teacher—not anymore. I've been doing this long enough to know how dangerous it is and how people who try it die. I've met some people over the years who've tried to hunt. They may have a handful of successes, but eventually they run into a vamp that's more than they can handle, then they die. I've tried to help a few and even befriended some. That's the worst, to find your friend's corpse with all the telltale marks of a vampire kill. I've even teamed up with a few. Some I've managed to keep alive until they decided they were done with vampires, but most... most died horrible deaths at the hands of a vampire, some before my eyes. That's why I stopped helping people."

Luke shook his head. "Team up? No. I refuse to accept that kind of responsibility anymore. I can't split my attention between vampires and an apprentice. It'll get them dead and maybe me, too, and right now, with this city practically drowning in vampires, I can't have that kind of distraction. And I won't watch people who are my responsibility be brutally killed," Luke finished. He was breathing quickly and shallowly while his eyes had a touch of wildness to them. Delilah had shifted her body slightly away from him as his slightly frenetic energy built, then waned as he closed his mouth.

"Look, I'm not your responsibility. I can handle myself. You've seen me. I'm not offering to tag along and be some damsel. I'm offering to help hunt vampires. Could you have handled that many vampires?" Her expression indicated that she knew the answer was "probably not."

"The point is, I wouldn't have gotten into that situation. I don't let vampires escape. I don't get into street fights with seven vampires. The best I can do is offer you advice—get out while you can. Leave Portland before they hunt you down and finish you for real. They know who you are, and you've taken out a sizable contingent of their horde. After seven disappeared that were known to be hunting you, they're going to come after you even harder. I don't want to see you get killed. Killed by a vampire is no way to go." Luke shook his head.

Delilah didn't look happy with Luke's reply. The muscles of her hands, lying flat in front of her, flexed as she pushed against the hard wood of the table as she tried to control her anger. The muscles along her jaw quivered slightly. Finally, she took a deep breath, held it for a few moments, then released it slowly.

"Fine. I'm going to the restroom. I'll be right back."

She stood up and stalked off toward the back of the brewpub toward the restrooms. Luke felt bad that he'd hurt her feelings and angered her, but he couldn't handle the pain of watching someone under his care die, and he knew that's what would happen. He would come to like her, and they'd become friends. Then, she'd make a mistake, or he'd make one, and it would get her killed. It always worked that way. Luke wasn't sure if he could handle another death on his conscience. It might break him.

"Can I get you anything else?" Pablo's question pulled Luke out of his descent into the dark halls of his memory, where he stored all the deaths he blamed on himself.

"What? Oh? Um, no. I'm good. I'll take the check please. Put everything on it."

"No problem, Luke." Pablo walked off. On his way back to the bar, he caught Delilah's attention, and they exchanged a few short sentences. Delilah came back to the table and sat down. Her expression appeared to have mellowed some. Pablo brought the check and presented it to Luke, who slid his card into the check presenter and handed it back to Pablo.

"Thanks for picking up the tab," Delilah said curtly.

"No problem. I'm sorry I can't be more helpful, but I just can't..." Luke left it at that. They sat in silence until Pablo returned with Luke's card and receipts. Luke tipped and signed, then stood up. "It was very nice to meet you. I hope you take my advice."

Delilah stood up and shook Luke's extended hand. "I'll think about it. It was nice meeting you too."

Luke turned and walked out the door without looking back.

SEVEN

DAYS ROLLED into nights and back around as Luke continued his lonely routine. Days, he filled with exercise to increase his stamina and reading to stimulate his mind with periodic social media breaks to ensure he numbed it back down while keeping up with the latest memes and lingo. Nights, he spent wandering the neighborhoods of Portland seeking out those who fed from the city's late-night denizens. Some nights he went home covered in the blood of vampires, the others he came up empty.

While he was used to finding vampires in ones and twos, he increasingly encountered more and more working in coordination, canvasing a neighborhood for snacks. Largely, they'd either been sticking to catch and release or were finding creative ways of disposing of their more indiscriminate kills since the news had been strangely silent about new corpses found with few marks and even fewer blood cells.

Luke pulled his old Volvo onto one of the dark side streets in the Sunnyside neighborhood along Southeast Belmont Avenue in the hip and hipster-filled inner southeast of Portland. Popping the wagon's hatch, he pulled the plastic tub forward and opened it. He wrapped the heavy scarf around his neck and pulled his armor over it, snugging the leather laces together and sealing himself inside his tin can. Next, he slung his swords into their positions on his back before covering everything up with the oversized, black zip hoodie he'd bought to replace yet another one ruined by the claws of a vampire. Overall, the process took only a few moments. Luke had gone through variations of the procedure so many times over the centuries, he could do it in a near sleep and had a few times when a barbarian or vampire had breached the defenses.

Bundled up in his hoodie with a scarf, he looked like anyone else in the drizzly Portland fall, except with the physique of a linebacker thanks to the added bulk of the lorica segmentata. He wandered up to Belmont and strolled east looking like any of the nighttime pedestrians heading out to a bar or home from wherever. He wandered into the little market on 34th and bought a bottle of water before heading back into the night.

The bars along Belmont lacked the more fangy pub goers Luke was looking for, so he wound his way up 30th to Hawthorne toward the other popular bar districts in shallower southeast. He knew he had a good shot of finding vamps in the area with a large pub and movie theater and a small rock venue up near Cesar Chavez Boulevard. He wasn't wrong.

A show spilled its crowd onto Hawthorne and with it, the twinge that set off Luke's fanger alarm.

"Let's go back to our place. We can throw on some records, and we got fresh herb ready to spark up." A short, thin man with a cool, shaggy cut that was equally parts styled to within an inch of its life and perfect bedhead gestured to a small group to follow him. Several of the men and women had the telltale slightly glazed and infatuated eyes of the glamoured. Many had the slight stagger of the inebriated, and all seemed perfectly happy to follow along with the vampire's offer to keep the party going.

Luke blended into the back of the crowd, affecting a slight stagger of his own, nodding when it seemed appropriate, and agreeing with the kids that the show was either great or crap, depending on who was offering the opinion. No one noticed. The humans were all tipsy on booze and magic, and the thought of heading home was anathema. They worked their way through the streets and houses southwest of Hawthorne, which was an odd mix of punk flop houses, "trustafarians"—rich kids living a hippie-ish life on mom and dad's money—or the wealthy in their renovated old Portland homes. The house the vampiric pied piper led everyone to would definitely classify as the first of the three categories. The huge house in the Portland Farmhouse style featured old windows, peeling paint, and a surprising amount of shabbiness.

The group filed through the door and milled about the entryway and living room. The leader fished a set of keys out of his pocked and walked toward a door.

"Follow me. Beer fridge is in the basement along with the dank bud, buds." He chuckled at his own joke.

Luke hoped there weren't any more vampires lurking down there. His hands would be full with the three he'd followed here, not to mention the bystanders. Luke joined the parade downstairs and got in line to grab a cold tallboy can of Pabst Blue Ribbon out of the fridge.

"Fuckin' hipster vampires, of course they only have PBR," he mumbled to himself. He cracked the can open and took a sip, wandering over to check out the wall of records against one wall. If not to his taste, at least the beer was cold and refreshing. The vampire, however, had good taste in music. Over one shoulder, he noticed the lead vamp walking down the stairs. He'd probably locked the door before joining his all you can eat buffet. He looked over at Luke.

"Go ahead and put something on. Let's keep the party going." A selection of "woos" filled the basement as everyone chimed in their agreement with the host's idea. Luke continued flipping through the records until he found something he wanted. He pulled The Killer's "Hot Fuss" album down and fired up side one on the record player.

"Nice choice!" someone shouted.

Luke turned around to the gurgling sound of someone taking a large rip from a bong and the scent of marijuana filling the confined space of the basement. The woman passed it to the person next to her as she coughed out a lung full of smoke. More beers were passed around as the bong made its rounds. Luke found a place out of the way and leaned up against the wall to keep the scene firmly in front of him. Everyone was riding high.

The sound of the door opening and feet squeaking their way down the stairs, along with his tingly vampy senses, alerted him to more vampires joining the party. Two more, a man and a woman, joined their three fangy friends. The lead vampire tossed them a couple beers and grabbed one more for himself.

"Hey, you guys wanna see something freaky?"

The captive audience nodded. Luke switched from casual to hyper-aware as he watched the vampire's fangs slowly lengthen into needle sharp points. The vampire tilted his head sideways so the can in his hands could remain vertical, bit into the side of the can with his fangs, cracked the tab, and shotgunned the can, vampire style. Everyone in the room watched entranced while the other four vampires eyed their juice boxes. He finished the can in short order, then sketched an elaborate bow.

He slid into a spot on the couch next to a woman who had been staring longingly at him for a while, then latched onto her neck. A tiny dribble of blood wound its way down her neck. Her heavy breathing and the look of ecstasy on her face combined with alcohol, THC, and a heavy dose of vampire glamour tipped a few more people into a make-out session. More fangs came out. So far, the vamps were playing nice, but that could change any moment. Luke, however, was not really in the mood to play nice with fangers, not that he ever was.

Slowly and steadily, he reached up and slid his gladius out of its sheath. He casually lowered it to his side, shifting so his body and leg were between the crowd and his sword. He followed it up by freeing his rudis. With two blades and a wall to back him, he could command the room while trying to keep the vampires from tearing him apart. The only trick would be keeping the civilian casualties down.

A scream interrupted the opening bars of "All These Things That I've Done."

"He's got a knife!"

That killed the mood. More screams joined the first as everyone turned toward the large man with two swords. The sudden change in tone transformed the vampires from sexy to sadistic in the blink of an eye. Claws joined fangs as rage filled their eyes. The lingering arousal vanished as fear and adrenalin replaced the good times. One woman, the first to feel teeth, slumped over against the side of the couch. Luke hoped she had only passed out. He'd check her pulse when he had a chance.

"Well." He brought the gladius up to his forehead and saluted the vampires. "Here's to all the things I'm about to do..."

He waited until the humans made a break for the door and tripped up three of the vampires who were hanging back as two of their companions advanced on Luke. The intoxicated humans were too concerned with escaping up the tiny stairway to reach for their cell phones. By the time they'd shaken off the glamour and calmed down enough to think about calling 911, Luke hoped to be long gone.

He darted left, stabbing at the vampire's chest, who deflected the swing down and across Luke's body. Luke used the change of angles to bring a backhanded swing up and back across his body. The first vampire he'd attacked leaned back, but the second wasn't nearly as agile, and the gladius opened his throat. He went down, clutching his neck as thick black blood oozed from the gash. Distracted by the fate of his friend, the first vampire didn't see the rudis Luke plunged deep into his chest until it had destroyed his heart. Falling backwards and grasping the wooden sword protruding from his chest, he yanked the blade from Luke's hand. Luke kicked out, launching the vamp further away to clear his space and foul the crowd of vampires waiting their turn. Taking a moment to look at the other vampire, he brought his blade down, removing the vamp's head entirely.

Scooping the detached head with his foot and placing it in front of him, he took a step back, then kicked it at the remaining vampires, catching one in the nose. The sound of crunching cartilage brought a smirk to Luke's lips. Humming the chorus to the song, Luke launched his next attack, feinting a jab toward the center vamp, he used his momentum to place a big roundhouse punch on the vampire to the right, sending him sprawling over the couch. The one with the broken nose seemed preoccupied with his face, while the other one was tangled in the body of the hopefully unconscious and not dead woman on the couch.

The humans who could reach it were pounding on the door, while the others were crowded behind them, trying to get as far from the action as possible. Someone tripped, and several people tumbled down the steps, taking out the vampire with the broken nose and knocking the one still standing off balance. Seizing the opportunity, Luke struck, burying the gladius in the vampire's heart. He collapsed into the pile behind him and turned to dust.

The sound of splintering wood drew Luke's attention back to the stairs where the press of humans finally broke the door down. They were flooding out as fast as they could, tripping over each other and plugging the doorway. Luke directed his attention back to the two remaining vampires. The one with the broken nose was still tangled up with the people who hadn't made it up the stairs. The one on the couch was attempting to circumvent the pileup and get to the door.

Luke grabbed the back of his jacket, spun hard, and flung him up against the wall before administering a fatal stab. Since he was close, he pulled his rudis from the heart of the vampire corpse. Once the rudis left its body, it dissolved into a mess of goo. Luke turned and finished the beheaded torso with a kill shot to the heart. He spun around to address the last vampire, but only saw his back as he flew up the stairs and out the busted door. Luke sprinted after him, knocking down a guy who was trying to get out.

Emerging at the top of the stairs just in time to see the vampire throw his body through the big bay window like a stunt man going for broke, Luke didn't hesitate. He followed the fanger, clearing a few dangling shards with a sword as he jumped through and landed nimbly on the ground. He sprinted deeper into the dark neighborhood after the vamp who must have been a track star before he'd been turned, because he was quickly pulling away from Luke. Luke tried to turn up the speed but wasn't even keeping pace. The vamp took a right, and Luke lost sight of him.

Luke chased the vampire for a few blocks, turning corners just in time to see his prey turn another corner before eventually losing him. He slowed to a jog and concentrated on his vampire detection senses, hoping to get some clue as to where to look. He was so focused inward that he didn't notice the goo slick until he slid through it, almost falling. Catching his balance, he looked down and saw a set of clothes that perfectly matched the hipster vamp he'd been chasing.

Except for his boot print, the size and shape of the puddle, coupled with some hair, meant it had probably been a head at one point. Wiping the sole of his boot on the nearby grass, he turned his attention to the clothes and liquefying body inside them. Noticing an odd shape under the fanger's jacket, Luke used the tip of his sword to lift the edge of the coat. A stake. Another hunter had beaten him to the kill. The sound of sirens in the distance pulled him up.

"Well, fuck. Looks like someone objects to me crashing their party," he muttered to himself.

He stabbed the stake with his gladius, not wanting to leave any more unusual evidence, and jogged further away from the house and the oncoming police. Once he was a few blocks away, he ducked in between a bush and a brick wall. He propped the gladius up against the wall with the stake on the ground. With one hand free, he pulled out a rag and wiped down the rudis before putting it away in its scabbard. He popped the stake off his gladius and then cleaned and sheathed it, too. He rolled the stake in the dirt and grass, trying to get it as clean as possible before he picked it up with his cleaning rag so he wouldn't leave fingerprints, checked to see if it was clear, and continued on his way.

Luke walked further away from where he was parked, hoping to avoid any police making neighborhood sweeps. Once he'd judged that he'd gone far enough in the opposite direction, he angled back toward where he'd parked on Belmont. Along the way, he found a compost bin on the curb waiting for pickup the next morning. He shoved the stake deep down under the leaves and walked off into the night.

EIGHT

AFTER BREAKING up the house party, Luke had planned to take a much-needed night off. Every night, he'd roamed the streets of Portland, slaying vampires and rescuing those he could. He was only one man against an ever-increasing army of vampires. He hoped the souls of the victims he couldn't save didn't follow him around; he hoped they'd moved on to whatever afterlife they believed in. He didn't need any more baggage, but it still didn't stop him from dwelling on it.

He'd finished the boar burger and frites at Interurban on North Mississippi Avenue and was sipping his way through the Rye Manhattan he'd ordered for dessert when his vampy senses went off. Somewhere nearby, a sizable group of vampires was entering his sphere. He flagged down his server and paid his tab, then walked briskly outside to move his car to a more remote spot where he could put on his armor.

Luke's head perked up as he felt a vampire walk out of the alley into view near the I-5 sound barrier. Luke bent over, feigning tying his shoe so he could slide his gladius out of its scabbard.

"Excuse me, sir, can I—" the approaching vampire said.

Luke interrupted him abruptly, standing up and plunging the naked blade into his chest. The vampire looked down at the blade, then up at Luke, then down at the blade again before tumbling backward into a squelchy mess.

"I guess that's one way to start the night."

LUKE PANTED as he dashed down the abandoned streets of the Boise neighborhood. The bars on Mississippi Avenue had disgorged their drunken patrons into the night a while ago, and with it, a few vampires. The first few he'd tracked down had been dispatched with ease, with the first practically walking onto his sword of its own volition. The third one, not so much. The dark alley he'd stalked them down had more than just the vampire and its victim—another vampire feigning drunken infatuation with the handsome stranger who was supposed to be her liaison for the evening. When Luke had announced himself to the couple making out in an alley overgrown with hedges and trees, two gleaming sets of vampire fangs greeted him instead of one. Several more quickly joined their compatriots. They were all armed with blunt implements ranging from chains, to bats, to batons.

Luke carefully backed out of the alley, keeping a watchful eye on the five vampires stalking toward him with hunger and rage burning in their eyes. Clawed hands snatched for him as he emerged from the alley. He spun and lashed out with his gladius, eliciting a grunt. He dashed west down North Mason Street, the only option open to him now. He thought he heard someone shout "Get him!" as he chugged down the street and across Mississippi Avenue, then back into the darkness of the streets behind it. He barely caught the movement in front of him. Another pair waited in ambush. He lurched to the left, arms flailing as he tried to shift his momentum away from the new set of vampires, managing to stay upright and moving as he ran down North Michigan Avenue.

Unfortunately, he wasn't the only person running down

Michigan. Besides him and his newest tails, another pair was jogging toward him. Once they spotted him, they picked up speed. Luke needed to get somewhere where he could cut down their numerical advantage. He just hoped he'd be able to make it there before they boxed him in. He poured on a bit more speed as he turned right down Shaver Avenue. He was quickly running out of streets and if he wasn't careful, he'd be pinned with his back against the massive, concrete sound barriers separating I-5 from the neighborhood.

He angled his run so he could take the left turn onto Missouri as easily as possible without losing too much speed. Once he made his turn, he dug deeper and found a full-on desperate sprint as he made for the Failing Street Pedestrian Bridge that allowed people to walk over I-5 and get to a MAX light station. He rounded the corner onto Failing Street and saw the stairs and ramp that led up to the bridge. As his ragged breath burned in and out of his mouth, he continued his headlong sprint toward the hopeful safety of the bridge. Which would be better—stairs or the ramp? The ramp was longer and had a hairpin turn, but the stairs invited a trip and fall, which would tumble him into the waiting arms of at least eight vampires. Luke opted for the ramp. The sounds of shouting vampires behind him grew closer.

He launched himself up the ramp, and as he made the tight turn to continue up the bridge, he saw the vampires split, sending some of the horde up the ramp and some up the stairs. Luke chuckled mentally as one of the vamps tripped over a step and ate shit, slamming his head into one of the steps as he fell face first. It was a race at that point. Who would get to the bridge entrance first? Fortune smiled on Luke as the falling vampire tangled up his buddies.

Luke reached his left hand toward the pole that arched over the pedestrian bridge and used it and his momentum to swing himself into the entrance of the bridge. He slowed down slightly, trying to catch his breath but still put some distance between him and his pursuers. The sound of laughter brought him up short.

He slowed to a jog so he could peer over his shoulder. The vampires chasing him had stopped at the entrance of the bridge. The hairs on the back of his neck stood up as he became preternaturally aware that things were about to go from bad to worse. A second line of vampires solidified out of the darkness to block the other side of the bridge. Luke was trapped. The chain link fencing that arched over the bridge made escape over the side nearly impossible—the vampires would be on him and drag him down before he could get over the top. There was no flight, only fight.

Sighing, he pulled his rudis from its back sheath and tried to catch his breath and calm his mind and lungs for the fight that was about to wash over him like a riptide. Luke began rotating his shoulders and wrists, loosening up his joints while shifting his mind into battle mode.

"Mithras, guide your swords to their targets and watch my ass..." Luke mumbled the invocation as he strode into the very middle of the bridge, marking its distances and obstructions in his mind so he could know and command his battlefield.

"Well, hemogoblins, let's get this party started," he yelled.

The vamps advanced.

They didn't rush him; each group sent in a pair of combatants to avoid clogging the approach to Luke and interfering with each other. They each seemed to have some kind of blunt object to use as weapons. One even appeared to have a set of brass knuckles. Luke gestured with his swords to hurry them along into his killing field. It was knuckles who broke into a run first.

Using his vampiric strength and speed, he launched himself into the air, trying to direct Luke's attention up while he punched down at Luke's head. A vampire from the other side dashed in with a baseball bat swinging low at Luke's legs. Luke spun and launched a kick at the lower vampire's face, using his rotation to arc his gladius up and into the face and chest of the vamp flying over his head. A grunt of pain from both and a shower of blood from the airborne fanger rewarded his efforts. However, the bat caught him in the back of the knee of his plant leg and toppled him to his knees.

He swung his arms out to each side to present his blades to the attackers. The one with the bat slid toward him, his momentum carrying him into Luke's reach. Luke stabbed out, catching him in the gut. The vamp dropped his bat and tried to skitter back and away, shrieking in pain. Fortunately for him, a vampire advanced from the other side and swung her two-by-four at Luke's head, distracting him from finishing the gutted vampire. Luke ducked and used his gladius and the momentum of the swing to tip and deflect the lumber. Gathering his legs under himself, he launched up and back, using the steel barrier to stop his movement and prop him into a standing position further away from the remaining two vampires who backed off slightly to get out of reach of Luke's blades and superior fighting skill. Another vampire from each direction joined their forward positions to fill the spots vacated by the wounded vampires crawling back to their lines.

The advancing vampires were made wary by the swift violence already done to two of their number. The vampires plugging the bridge's two exits were shaking the chain-link fences and hitting the metal poles, raising a din to encourage their fighters. Luke quickly assessed the situation, trying to figure out his next move. One pair was armed with the baseball bat her buddy had left behind from the previous round and a chain its wielder was swinging menacingly. Though the chain was moving in a blur, he thought he saw a metal ball attached to the end. The other pair were armed with metal batons. The two with the batons looked nervous, while the one wielding the chain looked like he knew what he was doing as he carved complex patterns in the air around him like he was Gogo Yubari.

Luke broke to his right with lightning speed, sprinting straight down the middle of the bridge between the bat and the chain. A loud growl burst from his lips as his change from defense to offense caught the vampires off guard. The one swinging the chain lost his rhythm, his chain shooting off to side and tangling around the guardrail post. Luke made eye contact with the chain twirler, catching a panicked look, before quickly shifting his angle until he sprung off the metal pole of the guardrail toward the vamp with the bat. His move caught them completely flatfooted as he swept his gladius through the neck of the vampire with the bat, parting her head from her neck, leaving an ichor gushing stump. As his jump carried him forward, he brought his thigh and knee around and shoved the headless body into the chain wielding vampire. Their bodies tangled as both vampires collapsed in a heap. Luke landed on the pile and shoved his rudis into the chest of the vampire with the chain. He rolled off the pile of undead cadavers and rose to face the two baton-wielding vamps.

The savagery of Luke's counterattack left them slack jawed and trembling as they backed away. Luke put on his scariest "implacable murderer" face and stalked toward them, flaring his arms to look extra intimidating. As he picked up speed, the growl accompanying it rose in volume until the two fangers dropped their batons and sprinted to their lines. The vampires awaiting them booed and jeered. Luke reset his position, waiting for the next wave. It didn't come.

Instead, a few vampires jogged up the ramps leading up to both sides of the bridge, carrying large bags. The new vampires disappeared into the back of their respective crowds as most of the vampires turned to help themselves to whatever was in the bags. Luke couldn't see what they were doing through so many turned backs. Soon, about two-thirds of each group started slowly advancing down the bridge, eyes firmly fixed on Luke.

"Well, shit…" muttered Luke.

Each side continued their advance until they were halfway between Luke and the entrances of the bridge, while a few vampires stood guard. They stopped.

"Now!" went up the cry as the front rows of vampires cocked back their arms and let loose with a storm of rocks and bricks aimed directly at Luke. He threw up his arms, trying to protect his head as the projectiles streaked toward him, powered by the supernatural strength of angry vampire arms. The sound of rock hitting pavement, cotton covered armor, and flesh thudded and clanged. A snap and sharp pain in his left arm promised a deep bruise and a probable fractured bone.

"Again!" Another row of vampires stepped forward to take aim at Luke. This volley drove him to his knees. His arms felt like tenderized meat, but as yet, his head remained unscathed. Unfortunately, Luke's luck had run out.

On the third volley, a broken brick cut a deep gash in his scalp just above his forehead. On the fourth volley, a rock clipped the back of his head and sent him reeling to the pavement. Blood flowed into his eyes. His ears throbbed with adrenaline, pain, and the shouts of the vampires dashing toward him. He desperately tried crawling toward the barrier, although there was no escape or respite there. He grunted as a boot clanged against his armor covered stomach. While the armor absorbed most of the poorly landed kick, keeping it from hurting too much, it knocked him off balance. He curled into a ball, his arms wrapped around his head. Somehow, he'd managed to keep hold of his gladius and rudis.

A rain of kicks pummeled his body punctuated by the odd grunt or curse of pain as someone in softer shoes stubbed their toes on Luke's armor. The only thought that escaped his pain-addled and probably concussed mind was "Hold. Onto. Your. Swords." Someone tried to take one but drew back with a hiss of pain as their skin made contact with the silver and enchantments each was riddled with.

"Fuckin' silver. God damn, that hurts!"

Luke felt his hoodie being shredded as the vampires pulled out their claws, trying to tear into him. The sound of ripping cotton and claws raking over the steel of his armor swam through the foggy hearing of his throbbing ears. He felt his jeans shred and the burning of claws ripping into the flesh of his butt. The vampires continued pummeling him.

Luke lost track of how long he lay there. He couldn't tell if it was a minute or an hour. The sensations and the sounds became repetitive, blurring into one long symphony of pain. Over nineteen hundred years, Luke had walked the earth, and he was about to end his journey beaten to death on a pedestrian overpass in Portland, Oregon.

"Hey! Put the knife away. We want him alive. Enough!" someone shouted. "We've had our fun. The boss said we could fuck him up, but he wanted him alive enough to talk. Bind his hands and feet, we'll pry the—" The voice ended with the sound of snapping wood against skull. A growling howl joined a rough, high-pitched war cry. The kicks and punches stopped. Luke stayed balled up as the sounds of fighting battled with blood pumping through his ears. The edge of Luke's vision began to fade to black as he warred with unconsciousness. Consciousness lost.

LUCIUS II

ALL OF LUCIUS'S life after his father's arrival was spent with his father and his budding business. By the time Imperator Traianus ascended the principate's throne and orders to create two new legions went out at the end of his first Dacian war in 102 CE, Lucius could fight as well as any of the ex-soldiers in his father's employ and better than some. He'd grown up tall, and the hours laboring alongside his father and friends had built a strong body. All the time spent poring over books and assisting with the company's accounting had honed his mind and given him a practical set of skills that would serve him well as a legionnaire and help him advance more quickly up the ranks. His father, knowing the direction his son's life would take, used his connections as a former centurion of the auxiliary and his trading connections as preferred vendor to the legions to introduce his son at the forts he traded with along the northern Rhenus River. By the time Lucius neared his seventeenth year, his father had secured two recommendations—one from the Pilus Prior of the Second Cohort of the VI Victrix Legion and, most impressively, one from the Primus Pilus of the XXII Primigenia Legion.

When Gaius brought home, the news that a couple cohorts were being recruited and trained in the region before being sent off to join with the rest of the newly formed XXX Ulpia Legion in Brigetio in Pannonia Superior, Lucius eagerly received the news, excited for a chance to follow in his father's footsteps and seek adventure and fortune. Lucius could tell his mother was less than excited.

Although she fussed over her son, paying extra attention to him, he caught the sad look in her eyes more than once as she stared at him, thinking he wasn't paying attention. He was grateful for the attention and that she didn't try to talk him out of his decision. Verlia did her best not to cry as they said their goodbyes, but wasn't quite successful as she embraced her son before sending him off to Rome's war machine. Lucius, riding next to his father on the lead ox-drawn wagon laden with goods for Castra Vetera, turned as they crested the hill leading out of their village and saw his mother standing there, watching her son ride away.

Oxen are not fast creatures. Their usefulness lies in their strength, not their swiftness of foot. Each plodding step seemed to take forever. Lucius, who'd made the three-day journey many times before with his father, couldn't believe how alternately fast and slow the trip seemed to be going. He knew this was what he was supposed to do, it was what he wanted, but the shift from boyhood to adult, from living with his family to training to kill with strangers, was a momentous life change he could barely grasp. They camped a few miles from Vetera the second night, and after a simple road meal, Lucius, his father, and his father's friends sat around the cook fire.

"You ready, boy?" one of his father's employees asked.

"Not really," Lucius replied.

Several men chuckled at his answer.

"Smart answer. Follow directions, listen to your optio and centurio, and avoid the vine rod, although that'll be next to impossible unless you get a particularly kind-hearted centurio. The first time the centurio's rod kisses the back of your legs, that's when you'll know you're in the legions."

A few men nodded sagely.

"Were you in the legions? Not the Auxilia?" asked Lucius.

"Yup. VIIII Hispania at Eboracum. You'll do fine, boy. You've had more training with gladius and fighting than I did before signin' up."

Lucius hoped he was right. He didn't want to embarrass his father or his father's friends who'd helped train him and been his guides in the martial skills. He barely listened as the conversation drifted to memories of the older men's time under the Eagle. When it came time to rest, he was excused from his turn at the watch so he would be rested when adding his name to the lists. For all the good it did him—his sleep was fitful as his nerves kept him from achieving a restful sleep. When the camp stirred at first light, he rolled out of bed, sandy-eyed and groggy but ready to start his new life.

"NEXT!" cried out a man in chain mail sitting at a table, a helmet bearing the transverse crest of a centurion resting next to him.

Lucius stepped forward.

"Name?"

"Lucius Silvanius, Centurio."

"Proof of citizenship."

Gaius stepped forward and pulled out his military diploma—two bronze tablets bound with rings from a leather folio he carried. The centurio looked it over thoroughly before addressing Lucius's father.

"You're Ambeltrix Gaius Silvanius?"

"Aye. Served a full term with the Cohors I Tungrorum."

"Were you with Agricola at Mons Graupius?"

"Aye."

The centurion looked impressed as he eyed the giant Belgian Gaul standing before him. "Retired as a centurio?"

Gaius nodded. The centurion gave him a respectful nod in turn as he returned Gaius's citizenship diploma.

Addressing Lucius, "This seems to be in order. Place your hands on the table, Lucius."

Lucius placed both hands on the table as the centurion inspected his fingers and hands.

"Grip them... Now, touch your fingers with your thumbs."

Lucius followed his instructions as the centurion inspected his hands to ensure they were in good working order. Next, the centurion asked Lucius to read some symbols on a distant wall to ensure his eyesight was good. Finally, He asked Lucius to perform various movements to ensure his body appeared to be free of any lasting damage that would prevent him from meeting his future duties as a legionnaire of Rome.

"Very good. Do you have a letter of recommendation?"

Gaius pulled out the two letters. The centurio seemed surprised, his eyebrows working their way up his forehead to the short hair favored in the legions, as he inspected the signatures. His interest perked up, and he gave Lucius a more thorough inspection.

"Can you read and write?"

Lucius nodded. "Yes, Centurio. I can also do math and maintain accounting and inventory ledgers."

"An educated recruit, eh?" He scribbled some more notes on the parchment he'd been recording Lucius's information on. "Very good. Please report to the optio. He'll assign you to your contubernium. After you're settled, fall out into the forum where we'll administer your oath. Next!"

Gaius and his friends followed Lucius into the fort where a man in his late twenties holding the six-foot staff that marked him as an optio waited.

"Am I finding tents for all of you?" the optio asked.

"Just the lad, Optio," replied Gaius.

"Follow me, tiro."

It was the first time anyone had addressed Lucius as a recruit. The optio turned and walked deeper into the camp until he got to a series of identical small barracks. Walking down the lane separating them, he eventually stopped at one.

"You'll share this one with the rest of your contubernium, tiro. Say your farewells and assemble in the camp forum." The optio marched back to his spot near the gate.

Gaius's friends surrounded Lucius to wish him fortune and health. When the last of them got in their final farewell, they took off to allow Gaius a final moment with his son.

"Son, I know you'll do me proud, but see that you come home alive and in one piece or your mother won't forgive either of us."

Lucius nodded, giving his father a nervous smile.

Gaius reached out and laid his hand on Lucius's shoulder. "Listen to your centurio and optio. Learn everything you can from them. Earn the trust of your contubernium and centuria. And most importantly, learn who not to trust. That'll keep you alive. Understand?"

"Yes, Father."

Gaius smiled down at his son who hadn't quite caught up to his father's six foot five inches. Lucius, while broad of shoulder, had barely made it to six feet. As the silence hung between the two men, one past the twilight of his military career, the other at the beginning, Gaius pulled his son into a crushing hug. After they broke their embrace, Gaius walked away, giving Lucius one final wave before he disappeared behind a tent and out of sight.

"THIS IS your last opportunity to change your mind. If you take the oath, then decide to leave, you'll be guilty of desertion for which the ultimate penalty is death," the centurion who'd taken the small platform called out. A row of five other centurions and six optios stood behind him.

The recruits looked around at each other, nervously eyeing their future comrades to see if anyone would take the opportunity—a few hoping that someone would and give them the excuse not to be the first. Nobody moved.

The centurion pointed at Lucius, probably singling out him because of his position at the front and center. "Step forward, Lucius Silvanius, and raise your right hand. Do you swear by the gods an unbreakable oath that you will obey your commander's orders and leadership without question? That you will relinquish the protection of Roman Civil Law and accept your commanders' right to execute you without trial for disobedience or desertion. That you will serve under the Eagle for your contracted length of duty until you are discharged by your commander. That you will serve Rome honorably and will respect the laws regarding civilians and your comrades, even unto death."

"I do, Centurio!" Lucius replied, his voice carrying over the silence of the assembled commanders and recruits.

"Congratulations! You're now an official tiro of the Roman Legions." The centurion addressed the rest of the recruits. "Do you swear the oath you just heard?"

"I do!" came the enthusiastic reply.

"Congratulation, Tirones! Report to your contubernium for marking and enrollment."

The new recruits waited at their tents until their commander could get to them and record identifying scars, birthmarks, or moles which would be used to identify them if they deserted, or if the occasion arose, identify their corpse on a battlefield.

Over the following weeks, Lucius got to know the men he shared a tent with, the men he'd likely spend at least a few years with, maybe more. They gave their caligae, open-toed military boots, a heavy work out as their centurions strove to get their century in marching shape—twenty miles in five hours. If some lagged, a lick from the centurion's vine rod would liven up their step.

Time not spent on the march was spent with a heavily weighted wooden training sword, running stab and slash drills against a post.

"Start slow, be precise! Speed will come with practice," the centurion called out as he ran the tirones through the drills, critiquing technique.

Sword training was followed by scutum training using weighted versions to continue training their muscles. All the while, they kept increasing their marching distance until they could make forty miles in twelve hours. Each night, they poured themselves into their bunks, too tired to be thankful they weren't sleeping on the ground. A vexillation several cohorts strong from the VI Victrix had left plenty of space at the permanent fort at Vetera for the new cohort that would eventually be assigned to the XXX Ulpia.

"Damn, no wonder Romans are so short. They marched their legs right off," Cassius whined from his bunk.

"You're a Roman now, Cassius," Segomaros replied.

"Ugh. You know what I mean, Sego. Do you always have to be so literal?"

Several of their contubernium were already snoring, passed out from exhaustion.

"Enough with the bickering," said Lucius. "I'm too tired for this."

Sego and Cassius had enlisted together, claiming to be friends, although neither seemed particularly fond of each other. Cassius was tall and muscular with sandy brown hair, the prototypical Gaul. Sego, on the other hand, had just barely been tall enough and strong enough to be accepted, though he made up for it with endurance on the march. Lucius wondered how they'd fare the next day when they returned to the twenty-mile march but added in their full armor. He didn't wonder long as sleep quickly overcame him.

Lucius was the first one suited up the following day, the only one who'd brought his own well-fitted custom armor. His father had showed him all the tricks of gearing up quickly, a much-needed skill in case of emergencies. Some of his other tent mates weren't faring as well.

Lucius reached over and adjusted Cassius's scarf. "Set your focale like this. Then when you put on your lorica, it'll rest on it and protect your neck from the weight and chafing."

The others watched and adjusted their scarves to match. The rest of Lucius's tent had quickly learned his advice was good and followed his example. Although some of them had fathers in the military, few were as active as Lucius's father in teaching them the tips and tricks of an experienced soldier. Even fewer had access to the twenty or so military veterans who'd adopted Lucius as their young mascot.

Lucius helped everyone put on their armor, making sure it settled properly so it wouldn't cause problems on their first armored march. Soon, the young men were pounding each other on the shoulder and bumping into each other to hear the clang of metal on metal, excited about their new armor. Lucius stood back, enjoying his comrades' horseplay.

He'd had a few cousins but hadn't spent much time with boys his own age when he was growing up. Then when his father returned,

Lucius spent most of his time with Gaius and his adult friends. He liked having companions his own age, even if they'd simply been tossed into the same tent together. This was his chance to earn friends as well as a career.

"Nicely done, Tiro Silvanius. Let's see how enthusiastic they'll be after our march today," a quiet voice said. Lucius turned slightly to see Optio Brabo standing behind him. He gave the optio a salute before answering.

"Yes, Optio. Thank you."

"Get them to the mess before the porridge gets cold, Tiro."

"Yes, Optio," replied Lucius, saluting again as the optio walked away.

Exhausting training and lessons with a variety of weapons filled the young men's lives over the next several months. Soon, the other contubernia began to follow the lead of Lucius's tent. Lucius often felt the eye of Optio Brabo—and overheard his Optio say Lucius was helping his century increase its skill at a quicker rate than the other five centuries. Brabo's century was catching the eye of the other officers, even if their own cohort's centurion seemed oblivious to the excellent crop of recruits he'd been assigned and the high marks the tribune was giving them. Centurion Antoninus ruled their century, but it was Optio Brabo who led the recruits.

When it came time to finally leave Vetera, Lucius's contubernium was the first contubernium of the first century of the cohort. They'd have to wait until they joined up with the rest of the cohorts from their legion to learn how they ranked overall. They marched south and joined the vexillation from the XXII Primigeneia and the VIII Augusta on their march toward Pannonia and Moesia and the next round of war with the Dacians.

NINE

"LUKE... LUKE..." a woman's desperate voice yelled his name.

It sounded like he was underwater. Why was he underwater?

"Luke...get up. Fight!" Each word cut to his brain a bit more clearly. A sliver of light returned to his eyes. "Get up, damn you!"

His mind slow from the concussion, Luke thought he recognized the voice of Delilah. He felt someone nudge him with a foot. Unwillingly, his body uncurled and fought its way to his hands and knees. He reached to the metal rail to pull himself up, but slipped and fell back on his hands. As he slid his hand toward the pole, his fingers ran over the hilt of his gladius. He picked it up. Once more, he swam up toward the railing, locking his wrist behind the back of it while holding onto his sword. Using his forearm and elbow to stabilize himself, he pulled himself to his feet. As he rose, he rammed his head into the railing, sending searing pain through his head as a fresh wave of blood tinged his vision red.

Luke roared in pain and rage, staggering to his feet. Someone threw a fist at his face. His body automatically moved to counter it and blocked it with a blade that bit deep, nearly taking most of the forearm off. The assault and the sound of someone else's pain flicked a switch in his brain. Luke plunged a blade forward into the chest of his assailant. Over swinging, he fell forward into the faceless vampire, shoving the blade deeper. Their fall stopped as the vampire bent backwards over the railing, her back slamming against the chain link fencing. The body softened around his blade as it started its final journey to true death.

His enemy's death brought with it a taste of victory as Luke, vision red and guided by his reptilian brain, went into automatic mode. Centuries of swinging a blade against the forces of fanged darkness had honed his body and mind into a weapon, one that didn't need a pilot to guide it. A breath shuddered through him as he gasped in sweet air and released it as a brutal roar of anguish and rage. He swung his gladius. He stabbed at whatever moved. Enemies fell before him like wheat to the reaper. He was the reaper. Death to the undead. His fury was boundless. His bellicose shouts cowed the victorious fangers as his friends fought to save him.

The brutal efficiency of Luke's slaughter both buoyed and terrified his rescuers. The werewolf and woman continued their advance, keeping a good distance between them and the battle-maddened Luke. Gradually, with each vampire wounded or killed, the rest began to retreat until finally, the bravery of the last few standing against the two humans and the werewolf broke ranks and ran. Luke, still mired in his foggy fight brain, tried to chase them down.

"Pablo! Stop him!" the woman shouted. A massive set of hairy arms wrapped around Luke's chest, pinning his arms to sides. Luke tried to pull away and run after the fleeing vampires, but Pablo just lifted him off the ground. Luke kicked out with his feet but was coming down off his battle high and quickly losing his strength and coordination. Delilah cautiously walked up to him, staying out of reach of his legs and his sword.

"Luke, it's OK. They're gone. We're your friends."

Luke continued to thrash weakly and ineffectually, the familiarity of her voice slipping through the haze of his brain.

"It's me — Delilah. Pablo will let you go if you relax."

Delilah continued making soothing sounds and reassuring him they meant him no harm. Her words finally penetrated Luke's foggy brain; he stopped struggling and went limp, dangling like a rag doll in Pablo's arms.

"OK, Pablo. I think he's calmed down. You can set him down now."

Pablo set Luke down gently, propping him against the steel rail that separated the chain link fencing from the walkway. Luke wobbled as he placed his hands on the rail to hold himself up. He bent over the railing and vomited. Once he finished heaving, he tried to turn around but nearly fell. Pablo darted in and stabilized him.

Delilah scrunched up her nose. "That's nasty! Let's move him away from the puke."

Pablo wrapped his arm around Luke's back and helped Luke stumble to the other side of the bridge where Luke sagged against a pole and slid down to the ground breathing heavily.

"Let's give him a moment to catch his breath. I think we're OK here for a minute, but we better get out of here in case the popo decide to stick their noses where they don't belong. You better change back." Delilah reached into a small bag slung across her shoulder and pulled out a bundle of cloth and handed it to Pablo. She turned her back and folded her arms across her chest.

Luke took shallow, short breaths, trying to keep his mind clear enough to stay conscious. A few moments later, Pablo rejoined them in his human form, wearing a T-shirt, shorts, and a pair of slip-on sandals.

"Can you help him back to your truck?"

"Yeah, I'm still way stronger than a normal human, even in my human skin."

"OK." Delilah turned to Luke. "Luke, Pablo's gonna help you up and get you back to his car. We'll get you somewhere safe and get medical help." She reached down and took the gladius from his weak fingers. "Shit, where does he keep his swords? I don't think a Black woman and a Latino man carrying an obviously injured white man should be seen carrying a huge sword." Spying his rudis on the ground, she walked over and picked it up.

"Yeah, that might not go over well with the authorities. I think he sheathes them on his back. Luke, I'm going to tip you forward a bit so Delilah can put away your sword, OK?" Pablo asked.

Luke nodded in response.

Pablo knelt and making sure Luke was securely propped up, located. his back scabbard. "Yup, it's right here."

Delilah slid the gladius into its scabbard. "OK, now the wooden one."

"No…" Luke fought weakly to reach it. "Ne…need it." He swallowed and struggled to form his next sentence. "Need…it. Body. Take me…to…" He was gasping for breath. "Body. Vampire…" His head sagged onto his chest as he panted.

Delilah looked at Pablo, who shrugged in response. "Let's get him up, Pablo."

"Damn, he's heavy. All that armor…" Pablo commented as he squatted and lifted Luke by the armpits. He worked his shoulder under Luke's arm so he could help him stumble out of there.

"Please…Pablo…body…"

Pablo looked at Delilah. She shrugged and nodded. Pablo walked Luke over to a vampire missing a head. He helped Luke down to his knees next to the body. As Luke settled onto his hands and knees, he grunted, taking the weight off his left arm. He rolled onto his butt and held his arm.

"Arm. Broken?" Luke gasped out.

Delilah looked at Pablo and shrugged. "I know some basic first aid, but I'm not a doctor."

Pablo bent down and gently took Luke's arm and felt up his forearm. "Is this it?"

Luke grunted and nodded as Pablo touched a spot in the middle of his left ulna.

"It doesn't feel broken, but he could have some hairline fractures or a serious contusion. He probably needs an x-ray."

Luke nodded and leaned over the vampire body next to him. He propped himself up with the rudis. "Help. Heart."

Pablo pulled aside the vampire's jacket and helped Luke move the point of the rudis over to the vampire's heart. "Can you do it?"

Luke shook his head and nearly toppled over. Pablo caught Luke and righted him before he completely lost his balance. Pablo placed one hand over Luke's clenched hands and the other on the pommel of the sword. With a grunt, he shoved the blade down into the vampire's ribcage. Ensuring Luke was stable enough, he stood up and backed off a step as Luke placed his forehead on the pommel. It took Luke several stuttering starts and stops until he finally muttered the proper incantation to activate the rudis, sending threads of light winding down and back up the rudis's silver filigree. The trembling that had been running through his body lessened. He raised his head and looked at Pablo.

"Another," he said, his voice sounding firmer and stronger.

He offered his free hand to Pablo, who helped him up and guided him to another vampire body. This time, Luke managed to punch the wooden sword through the vampire's ribs without any assistance, although the extra effort nearly made it too difficult for him. This time, the process went faster.

All three of their heads perked up when they heard the distant sound of sirens off to the east, getting louder as they approached their position.

"Uh, guys. I think we better get the hell out of here…" suggested Delilah.

"We have to stab the rest of these bodies or there's a chance they can heal," Luke said.

"Fuck! Um, you're not going to be fast enough. Can Pablo and I do it with your swords? Do we have to say something to make it work?"

"Here." He grabbed his gladius and offered up his swords. "No, just stab them through the heart. The wood and silver will take care of the rest."

Pablo and Delilah rushed about stabbing the remaining bodies while Luke crawled over to the railing and pulled himself to a standing position. He worked on catching his breath while Pablo and Delilah finished up.

"I don't think I'm going to be able to walk out of here on my own…" Luke gasped out.

Pablo nodded. "Alright, between the two of us we can get you out of here."

They handed Luke his swords one at time so he could resheath them.

"Delilah, you get under the right arm, I'll do the left." Pablo slid under Luke's left arm.

With Delilah and Pablo's help, they quickly walked, half dragging Luke west and off the pedestrian bridge as the flashing red and blue lights pulled onto Failing Street and moved toward the bridge's east side.

"We're up the block and around the corner. We had to park far enough away that the vamps wouldn't see us," Pablo said.

Pablo and Delilah were breathing heavily as they lugged Luke toward Pablo's truck. Luke tried to keep his feet under him to take some of the burden off his rescuers. They rounded the corner onto North Montana Avenue.

Delilah, panting, said, "I think it'll be faster if we just put him in the bed of the truck."

Pablo drove a black Toyota Tundra crew cab with a canopy. As weak as Luke felt, he wasn't sure he could climb into the back seat without a lot of help, and time was burning.

Delilah fished the keys out of her pocket. "Pablo, let's turn him around so he can sit on the tailgate." After they turned around so all three of their backs were pointed toward the tailgate and canopy door, Delilah added, "OK, keep him standing, I'll unlock it and open everything up."

"OK, back up slowly," Pablo said.

They each took a hand and helped Luke sit back, then stuffed him the rest of the way in, shutting the tailgate and canopy behind them. Delilah tossed Pablo the keys as they headed to the front of the Toyota. A few seconds later, they pulled cautiously onto Failing Street and headed to Interstate Avenue and back home.

LUKE DOZED FITFULLY as they made their way through the dark and nearly abandoned streets of North Portland. He startled awake when he felt the truck climb a curb and flop back onto the street as the driver parked sloppily along the street side. Two doors shut, shaking the truck, before the canopy and the tailgate were opened.

"We're here, Luke," Pablo exclaimed. "Swing your feet around and we'll pull you out."

Luke didn't know where he was. They were still a few hours from sunup and the cloudy winter sky blocked any moonlight. The fact that Pablo's canopy windows were tinted nearly black didn't help either. When they finally got him out of the back of the truck and on his feet again, he saw that he was in front of his house.

"How do you know where I live?" Luke asked.

"Well…" Delilah said awkwardly. "I kind of followed you home after we met at the brewery." She wasn't making eye contact and looked embarrassed.

Luke sighed. "Whatever. We can talk about that later."

He fished a pouch on a cord out from under his armor and pulled out a key and handed it to Delilah. She and Pablo helped him to the door and walked him inside.

"Light switch is to the side of the door. Take me into the kitchen, please." They complied and set Luke down in an armed dining chair. He sagged against the back and closed his eyes, releasing a sigh from the exertion. "There are some clean dishrags in the drawer. Use the red ones, please. You'll need to clean my scalp and see if it's closed itself up."

Pablo grabbed a rag out of the drawer and got it damp, then dabbed gently at Luke's blood-matted hair and scalp. "Holy shit, man. It's completely closed! There's an angry red scar, but no cut. How about the arm?"

Luke pressed the fingers of his right hand into the tender spot where the suspected fracture had been. "The arm is tender but feels a lot better. I think it started knitting."

"There's no way you could have healed that quickly," Delilah stated. "What the fuck?"

"I don't have the energy or brain power to discuss this tonight. This is embarrassing, but I'm going to need some help. Can you snag me a coconut water from the fridge? There's beer in there; help yourself to whatever. In the left most cabinet on the second shelf is a box of candy bars. If you want one, you're welcome, but I need two please. And can someone please feed the cat? Alfred!" he called, raising his voice so the cat would hear him. "It's OK, you can come out. They're friends."

The giant, orange tabby sauntered out of the hallway that ran back to the laundry room.

"Aren't you a big, handsome fella!" Delilah said as Alfred rubbed up against her legs before walking over to check out Pablo. He was a bit more wary of the werewolf, but still let Pablo scratch under his collar after he'd had a good sniff of Pablo's hand. "I'll take care of the cat. Where's his food?"

"Just follow him. You'll see his bowl and the food container next to it." Alfred mraowed in response and jogged back to his food dish.

"You want a beer, Delilah?" Pablo called.

"Sure! No candy bar though."

Pablo grabbed two candy bars, handing one to Luke and setting down the other. He opened cabinets until he found the glasses, then got two beers and a coconut water out of the fridge. He opened the coconut water and placed it in front of Luke before pouring his and Delilah's beers. Luke, his hand and arm trembling, knew he needed sustenance to keep healing. Pablo sat down at the table next to Luke and pushed the glass toward Delilah as she sat down. Pablo and Delilah drank their beers in silence while Luke slowly worked through his candy bars.

"Good beer," Delilah commented.

"Yeah, Pfriem's a great brewery. Can never go wrong choosing their beer," replied Pablo.

"Even over Howling Moon's?" teased Delilah.

Pablo chuckled. "I wouldn't go that far." Noticing Luke was finished, he added, "What can we do for you now, Luke?"

"Um," Luke said as he forced his attention back into the present. "I need to wash the blood and grime off before I crawl into bed and pass out. In the back of the coat closet in the entryway, there's a wooden stand. I'll need that. Then I'll need to get these clothes off."

Luke fumbled with the zipper of his hoodie, unable to get it moving.

"Here." Pablo removed Luke's hand and got the zipper started. "Let's get you standing."

He propped Luke up against the counter while Delilah set up the wooden stand with the t-bar at the top she'd gotten from the closet. Pablo finished unzipping the shredded hoodie.

"That's ruined. Just throw it in the garbage can. I should buy those things in bulk." Luke shook his head.

Delilah whistled appreciatively. "That's some mighty fine armor."

Luke nodded weakly while Pablo unbuckled the tactical straps holding the swords, then handed them to Delilah, who set them on the table.

"The thong should pull like a shoestring."

Pablo untied the leather thong holding the front of the armor closed and pulled it free of the brass loops. "The back one too?"

"No, leave it. Throw the one in your hand up on the shelf or the cat will eat it."

Pablo carefully worked the armor over Luke's shoulders and down his arms. He walked over and set it up on the stand where Delilah ran her fingers over it, checking out the detail. Luke unwrapped the scarf from around his neck and tossed it on the table.

"What's the scarf for?" asked Delilah. "It's not that cold."

"It protects my neck from the armor. I think I can shower myself but wouldn't refuse some help to the bathroom." Pablo helped him down the hall, stopping at the open door to the guest bathroom. Delilah followed behind.

"Hey, the cuts on your butt and legs have healed up too!" Delilah remarked.

"Checking out his ass?" Pablo snickered.

"No, his pants are shredded and covered in blood. It's kind of hard to avoid it."

Luke sighed, adding one more embarrassment to the evening's

tally. "Thanks. Make yourselves comfortable. Have another beer. I won't be long."

Luke shut the door as he hobbled into the bathroom and somehow managed to get undressed and in the shower without falling over. Leaning against the shower wall, Luke let the steaming hot water cascade over his head and body, washing the blood and dirt away. If only the soap could wash away the humiliation of nearly dying along with the physical grime...

When Luke shuffled out of the bathroom wearing a robe, he saw Pablo sitting in a chair with a fresh beer. Delilah had taken off her boots and fallen asleep on the couch. Alfred had decided that sprawling out against her stomach seemed like a good idea.

"Pablo, there's a blanket for her in the coat closet. You can crash in the guest room if you want. I'm about to pass out here, so I'm going to bed. Goodnight." Luke didn't look back as he stumbled into his room and passed out on top of the bed without even crawling under the covers.

TEN

LUKE SLEPT until nearly noon the next day, far later than he usually did, but not late enough for his body's needs. His feet were cold. He'd fallen asleep in his robe, but his feet dangling over the edge of the bed were ice cold. Grunting, he forced his way to his feet and dressed in a T and flannel pajama pants. His favorite pair of slippers seemed the ideal solution to his cold feet problem. After using the bathroom, he followed the smell of coffee and sound of conversation to the kitchen.

Pablo smiled and waved at Luke. "Hey, Luke. The carafe is full of coffee. Sorry, had to rummage through your cabinets to find everything."

"Coffee," Luke grunted, fumbling to open his vintage aluminum cabinets and retrieve a coffee cup. With a filled mug in hand, he made his way to the table and sat down. Silence reigned as Luke slowly worked his way through the cup of coffee. By the time he'd finished refilling his cup, the front door opened.

"Is he awake yet?" Delilah called from the entryway.

"Yup, just finished his first cup of coffee," Pablo replied, then directed his next comment at Luke, "She walked over to King's to grab burritos. I hope you like chorizo!"

The first genuine smile cracked Luke's lips. "They do make a fine chorizo breakfast burrito. Hey...if Delilah just got back, who were you talking to?"

"Um. Just the cat." Pablo looked embarrassed as he stood and grabbed plates from the cabinet and set three spots before grabbing the carafe and sitting back down. "Thanks for getting the burritos! Turns out our boy here has good taste."

"No worries. I needed to stretch after sleeping on the couch all night." Delilah turned to Luke. "I'm not a tiny lady, but that cat of yours managed to take up most of the damned couch last night."

Luke shrugged. "I guess he likes you. He's usually pickier about who he befriends."

They all dove into their burritos, leaving nothing but greasy paper wrappers.

"That hit the spot," Pablo said, patting his stomach. "How are you feeling, man?"

"Taken up for hawks," Luke replied.

Delilah and Pablo stared back at Luke with puzzled expressions.

Luke shook his head. "Not into antique English phrases? Shit. I feel like shit. I feel like I've been whaled on by a whole gym full of meathead bros with kettle bells."

Pablo and Delilah looked over the exposed skin of Luke's arms. They were covered in deep, nasty looking bruises. Delilah cringed.

"Does the rest of your body look like that?" asked Delilah.

Luke nodded. "It's colorful. The armor protected my vitals, more or less, but a kick from a vampire still applies a lot of force to the body. I've got a few tender ribs I'm wondering about as well."

"Alright, healed cuts, mysterious ribs. Judging from the beating we walked in on, you should be in the hospital in critical care. Dish." Delilah's face looked like she'd brook no more equivocation.

Pablo looked amused—he knew a bit more about Luke's secrets than Delilah, and that "bit" was a hefty bite of secret to have. He also looked curious since he knew what Luke had offered him the night they'd discovered some of each other's secrets was only the tip of a very large iceberg.

Luke kept his face emotion free. "I'm a fast healer."

Delilah stared at him deadpan, clenching her jaw slightly. "Try again."

Luke sighed. "You're going to insist, aren't you?"

Delilah pursed her lips and gave him a slow nod.

"You're not going to let this go?"

"No. We saved your ass last night. And judging by the cat that ate the canary look on Pablo's face, I'm guessing he knows more than he's told me." She turned her glare on the werewolf, who put his hands in the air in protest.

"They're not my secrets to share."

Luke refilled his coffee cup, shook his head, then started in on his tale. Delilah's expressions ranged from incredulous to shocked to disbelieving.

"You're full of shit! Entertaining, but full of it up to your brown eyes." Her words were more confident than her tone of voice or her facial expression.

"What did you do last night?" Luke asked.

Delilah looked at him, not sure what answer he was seeking.

"You killed vampires alongside a werewolf. I'm just one more oddity of the world you didn't know about until this morning. Look at my gear. It's not an affectation," Luke said.

Delilah eyed the armor sitting off to the side of the kitchen and the swords sitting at the other end of the table. She still looked unconvinced but seemed to be drifting further away from her espoused certainty. "You're a two-thousand-year-old Roman guy? Whose job is killing vampires?"

"Almost two thousand; just over nineteen-hundred. And Gallic Celt is probably a better description of my heritage. As to slaying, well, it's more of an all-consuming hobby. It doesn't pay well; I don't even get a W2."

Delilah rolled her eyes at him, her face settling into a pensive expression. She looked at Pablo. "What do you think, wolfboy?"

"I believe him. It's a pretty crazy story to make up." He shrugged. "It all fits. I've never seen anyone fight the way he does. I think he's authentic."

Delilah still looked unconvinced. "It's just..." She sighed and shook her head.

"You can believe it or not. I am who I am, regardless," Luke said a bit testily. He cringed at his impoliteness. "I'm sorry. That was rude of me. I'll settle for a polite suspension of disbelief."

Delilah nodded her assent.

"What do I owe for the burritos?" Luke asked.

"Nothing. My treat, Luke," Pablo replied. Seeing Luke's confusion, he added, "I buys, so Delilah flies."

"Thank you." Luke looked over at his armor and grimaced. "I hate to keep imposing on your kindness, but I need to move my stuff downstairs so I can clean it. I don't think I can quite handle it yet."

"I'll get the armor!" Pablo said.

"I can carry it. It's not that heavy," Delilah replied.

"It's not the weight, it's the silver in the swords," Luke commented.

"It burnses, Precious..." Pablo joked, affecting his best Gollum voice. Delilah chuckled and grabbed the swords.

"The scarf too?"

"Nah, leave it. I'll run it through the wash." Luke shuffled gingerly to the hallway leading to the laundry room and opened the office door. "OK, hang out here for a moment."

Luke walked in and activated the switch that opened the bookcase door. "Alright. It's clear."

"Holy shit, man! A secret doorway? That's pretty effing cool," said Pablo.

"Watch the steps as you go down. It's a spiral staircase."

"Hey, uh, Luke, before I walk down into your basement. Let me ask you a question. How do you feel about lotion baskets and pits?" Delilah asked.

Luke chuckled in response. "I give you a one-hundred percent pit free promise, although moisturizing is always a good idea."

Pablo led the way, followed by Luke; Delilah brought up the rear, so she could escape back up the stairs if it turned out there was a pit. Luke slipped past Pablo and opened the cabinet with the armor stand, then sat in the chair in front of his work area. Pablo set the armor on the rack.

"What's behind the door? A closet?" he asked.

"Why don't you take a look. Switches are on the wall to the left."

"Switches?" Pablo opened the door and flipped on the switches. "Holy. Mother. Of God! This place is HUGE!"

Pablo disappeared into the room, and Delilah and Luke followed. Weapons racks containing a variety of swords, spears, axes, and more lined the walls. A selection of fighting dummies and work out equipment were neatly set up around the outer edges. The center-piece, literally and spiritually, was the massive sparring area.

"Daaaaamn!" Delilah finally found her voice. "This is tight!"

She walked over to a wooden Kung Fu dummy and ran through a few series of moves, sending up a clatter of wood as the protruding wooden arms rattled in their joints. As she progressed, she sped up, working through a series of blindingly quick punches and blocks that crescendoed into a staccato slap with the heel of her palm to what would have been the dummy's face. She walked back over with a touch of strut in her stroll, obviously enjoying the stunned look of surprise on Pablo's and Luke's faces.

"What? Can't a lady know some Wing Chun Kung Fu?" She turned to Luke. "So this is your playroom, eh?"

Luke shrugged. "I don't know if 'playroom' is accurate. It's my gymnasium, my training center. I have to keep my body honed and my technique good. You don't live this long if you let your skills dete-riorate."

"It wasn't skills that were your problem last night. It was going solo. You almost become a 'Pride goes before the fall' motivational poster. If we hadn't been there, you'd have shuffled off your ancient ass's mortal coil."

Luke clenched his jaw, breathing heavily through his nose. His fists were balled up tightly.

"Don't get mad at me. It's the damned truth," Delilah added.

"I know. I'm not mad at you. It's just... That's the closest I've come to dying in a long time. It's a bitter pill, and I'm having trouble swallowing it."

"Maybe you should rethink my offer of help?" Delilah tilted her head to a saucy angle.

"It's been a long time since I've teamed up with anyone, and when I do, they always end up dead, and I keep going. Do you know how many deaths are hanging over my head? How many debts you accrue in a life that never ends? How many times you watch the light go out in a friend's eyes as the last breath slips between their lips? It's too much. Too much. I need to sit down."

Luke's knees were wobbling. The burrito had done him a world of good, but his body desperately needed more time to heal. There was no escaping the beating he'd taken the previous night. Luke made it into the other room and settled back into the chair in front of the workstation.

"I need some music. Slide back those wall panels and grab a record to throw on the player." Luke turned to the workstation.

"More coffee?" Pablo asked.

"Yes, please," replied Delilah.

Luke nodded. Pablo headed upstairs.

"You have '36 Chambers' on vinyl? Original Vinyl? And the 180 Gram re-release? Man, that's dope. My dad would have loved this collection." She slid the records back into their spot on the shelf. Luke was trying to pry the swords out of their high-test nylon sheaths. Finally, he worked one of them free of the gore-encrusted scabbard. Delilah noticed his struggles.

"Sorry about that. We were kind of in a hurry last night."

She continued looking through the records while Luke cleaned the weapon, checking for damage, and returning it to a state of readiness. Finishing with the gladius, he worked over the rudis. He was nearly finished when he heard the needle drop, followed by the sound of piano, drum, and bass. They were soon joined by the sound of Miles Davis's trumpet in the iconic start of "So What."

"'Kind of Blue?' Good choice," Luke said.

Delilah nodded, acknowledging Luke's compliment. "Yeah, this doesn't seem like a Wu-Tang kind of conversation."

Luke chuckled in response. "No, not quite."

"You're quite the vinyl enthusiast."

"Yeah, music has been a hobby for a while." Luke rubbed the back of his neck, trying to get it to release some tension.

"You start out jamming to lyres and pan flutes and super old shit like that?" Delilah smirked.

Luke rolled his eyes but smiled at the young woman's joke. "No, I was largely indifferent to music for most of my life. It made for a good background or a good beat for a dance. Although there have been moments throughout my life where the beauty of music has transfixed me, it wasn't until the first time I saw Beethoven play the piano that I truly fell in love with music."

Delilah's eyebrows jumped up. "Wait, what? THE Beethoven? 'Moonlight Sonata?' 'Ode to Joy?' You saw Beethoven play? Like for reals?"

Luke nodded. "Yeah, Ludwig van himself."

"Damn! That must of have been something to see." Delilah's eyes twinkled with excitement.

"Ludwig started my love of music. It's been a life saver over the last two centuries."

"What now?" Pablo remarked as he returned with coffee for everyone.

"Yeah, the way he casually throws around 'centuries' like it's nothing. I'm almost thirty and feel positively ancient some days." Delilah shook her head, folding her arms across her chest.

Luke and Pablo both looked amused at the double-digit number she'd cited.

"What?" Delilah asked, looking skeptical.

Luke lifted his chin toward Pablo. "How old are you?"

Pablo scratched at the stubble on his chin. "About three hundred."

"Jesus," Delilah swore. "You are a couple real old dudes."

"Some mornings I feel it more than others," Luke commented.

"Speaking of which, how the hell are you even moving around? When we found you, I expected we'd be taking you to the emergency room, or more likely, the morgue. No more distractions." It wasn't a request.

Luke turned around and grabbed the rudis from its stand, handing it to Delilah handle first. "Watch the blade, it's sharp."

Delilah looked over the exquisite workmanship as the light reflected off the silver inlay and set the light and dark tones of the wood dancing. Pablo examined it closely without touching it.

Luke rested his elbows on his knees. "That's the secret to my success."

Pablo and Delilah looked back and forth between Luke and the rudis with blank expressions.

Luke stared at the rudis in Delilah's hands with a mix of adoration and revulsion. His jaw worked as his forehead set into a pensive expression, thinking about how best to reveal his secret. "It... It siphons the life force of a vampire and transfers it to me. It heals me and keeps me young. It gives me an edge. I'm faster, stronger, tougher, sharper. It gives me the powers of a vampire so I'm able to counter them."

"Does it work for everyone?" asked Delilah, a gleam in her eye as she stared at the rudis.

Luke shook his head. "No. It doesn't. I've tried it with others before. It's tuned to me alone."

Delilah handed the rudis back to Luke, a slight look of disappointment in her eyes.

"It's the secret to my immortality, my cruel master..." The sound of loathing in Luke's voice matched the haunted look in his eyes.

Not wanting to get too deep into his past and its complications, Luke begged off as tired and escorted Delilah and Pablo out of his house with a promise to speak again soon. Even though they'd saved his life, they were mostly strangers, and he wasn't ready to get that deep with them, not when he still felt physically and mentally drained from his beat down. With them gone, he could return to his quiet, lonely life, except for Alfred, who insisted Luke needed to exercise his arm by petting the orange tabby. Maybe he'd be ready to let them in a bit more when he felt better.

ELEVEN

LUKE DIDN'T SEE Pablo and Delilah for a week after his near fatal brush with mortality. Except to pick up his car or the occasional excursion out for supplies, Luke didn't leave the house. He spent the nights passed out and the days napping on the couch. Alfred, always the opportunist, used this to his favor and demanded near constant cuddles and attention. Luke enjoyed his furry companion; the comfort his feline friend brought helped settle his mind and soothe his wounded heart. By the time Delilah and Pablo came knocking a week after their last conversation, Luke was more ambulatory but still nowhere near top shape.

"Hey, Pablo. Delilah. Come on in." Luke led the way into the kitchen, grabbing beers for everyone.

A palpably awkward silence drifted between them as they drank their beers.

Luke broke the silence. "I'll just say it. I can't do this alone tonight. I need your help. I'm still too weak, and if I'm not out on the street, that's more people disappearing. More people dead."

"Just tonight?" Delilah asked, a snarky expression on her face.

"Let's try out tonight and see how it goes. That's the best I can promise for now. I'm still not thinking straight with this concussion."

"What can we do to help?" Pablo cut in.

"We'll need to find a solo vampire. That's been harder and harder to find lately, as you saw last week. I'm not going to heal fast enough if I can't get my rudis into a vampire, and I'm in no shape to handle one myself." Luke sighed, looking down at his hands folded together on the table. "I'm going to need you to catch one and hold them down for me. Damn it, this is so fucking embarrassing."

"Hey, man. It's OK. You can ask your friends for help when you need it," Pablo replied.

Luke raised an eyebrow. "We're friends?"

"I can't speak for Delilah, but you and I are headed that way."

"Speaking of which, how are you involved in this? I know Ms.... I don't know your last name," Luke said to Delilah.

"Johnson."

Luke nodded his thanks to her. "I know Ms. Johnson followed me home after our meeting. I can only assume she's been following me as I go out hunting."

Delilah looked straight into Luke's eyes with a mix of mild embarrassment and boldness. Luke smirked at her and turned his attention back to Pablo.

"But you, Mr. Pablo the Werewolf, how are you mixed up in all of this?" Luke tilted his head to the side.

"My last name is currently Sandoval, by the way, since we're getting to know each other. I have a bad habit of eavesdropping on my customers. I caught Delilah when she got mad at you and left for the restroom and informed her I was also interested in joining you for some late-night stake capers after we'd sent the ones behind the pub on their mushy way. We've been hunting together over the last few weeks." Pablo said.

"Stake capers?" Luke asked.

Pablo shrugged. "You know how it is. You live long enough, you get bored with the normal routine. Besides, how often do you get to hang around with someone older than any werewolf I've ever met?"

"So what you're telling me, Pablo, is that you're an old guy looking for kicks?"

Pablo shrugged and smiled at Luke.

Luke shook his head. "So I have a thrill-seeking werewolf and a human with unknown motives who want to join me in killing vampires?"

Pablo and Delilah looked at each other, then nodded at Luke.

"That about sums it up," Pablo confirmed.

Luke looked at them, then sighed.

"OK," Luke started. "If we're going to do this, we need to make some things clear. I'm in charge. I've been doing this for many times longer than either of you has been alive. From the bodies I've come across, it's apparent you've had some success, but things are getting a lot more serious, more serious than I've seen in a long time. Can you take orders from me?"

They mumbled their assent.

"Good. We'll need to start training together to see what we each bring to the table and how to integrate it so we can keep each other alive. I don't fancy a repeat of the other night."

"Yeah. You're lucky you didn't get killed," Delilah chimed in.

"I was. I've been thinking about it though… Seems like that's all that's been running through my head lately." Luke paused, looking down at his folded hands. "I don't think they were trying to kill me. They were only using blunt weapons and mostly avoided my head. Also, just before you showed up, one of them was trying to call the others off. I think I heard something about binding my hands and feet and taking me to their boss. I'm not sure though. It's all very hazy."

Pablo chuckled. "I bet it is. Hazy, that is. That was one hell of a beating you took. So what next?"

"Let's see if we can find some lone vampires. Pablo, do you mind driving? I'm not sure I'm strong enough or quick enough right now to hop in and out of my car and put my armor on." Luke stood up.

"You'll fit in the back seat easily enough," Pablo replied.

Luke gave a closed-mouth smile. "Help me suit up, and we'll go hunt us down a fanger."

THEY DROVE around the more popular bar districts of Portland for several hours before Luke felt comfortable the circumstances were right—either there'd been no vampires, too many human witnesses, or too many vampires. As Luke signaled he'd sensed a potential target, they saw a man walk out of a bar on NE Forty-second Avenue and walk north before turning west onto NE Tillamook. A moment or so later, a woman dressed in motorcycle boots and a leather jacket popped out of the same bar and followed the man. While his walk was casual with the slightly off-balance gait of intoxication, hers was steady, determined, yet quiet.

"Bingo!" Luke muttered. "Follow that man."

Pablo turned left on Tillamook. "I'm going to turn into the neighborhood up here. We can park and use the trees and bushes to hide."

"Good plan."

Pablo turned right onto NE Forty-first Avenue and parked alongside the curb about halfway down the block. They exited Pablo's truck, holding the handles and gently pushing the truck's doors in to keep them from making a sound as they shut them. They slunk around the trees back toward Tillamook when they saw the man cross Forty-first with the woman just behind him, still seemingly unnoticed by the intoxicated man. He continued, unaware of the danger stalking him, while she closed the gap, oblivious to the danger about to find her.

Trying to step up onto the curb that wasn't there, the man's foot dropped onto the ramped curb and twisted, sending him sprawling to the ground. The woman seized the opportunity.

"Oh! Let me help you up." She bent over to offer him a hand as he rolled onto his butt.

He went completely still as his eyes made contact with hers, and her vampire magic easily overcame his intoxicated brain, glamouring him. He rose with her help and followed her into the nearby sheltered alcove entrance of the Hollywood branch of the Multnomah County Library. She hauled him to the back corner of the alcove and latched on to his neck. To anyone passing, it would look like a young couple simply couldn't wait to make it home and stopped for a bit of passionate necking. The look of ecstasy and arousal on the man's face would confirm that assumption.

Luke motioned for his companions to move out. They stalked forward until they reached Tillamook. Luke signaled Pablo to walk down the block to the right and approach from that side. Delilah looped to the left and came back at the alcove the other way. Luke stood in the shadows of the bushes on the corner while his friends got into position. Once they were in their respective corners, Luke waved them both to a halt. He strolled across the crosswalk until he was behind the huge brick pillar that blocked his view of the vampire and her meal.

So far, they'd remained undetected. She must be a young vampire to be so involved in her snack that she didn't pay attention to her surroundings. Her vampiric survival senses weren't yet honed by years of hunting and stealth. Standing at the corner of the pillar so he was visible to Delilah and Pablo, he waved them in. They darted around their corners and caught the vampire completely by surprise. They dragged her backwards until her back was pinned up against the pillar and her arms pinned back on either side. Though she was young, she was vampire strong. The only option Delilah and Pablo had was to take her straight back. At least with her arms pinned that far back, it reduced her strength significantly. She still kicked and thrashed, but she couldn't break the werewolf's hold. Delilah, though not as strong as the werewolf or vampire, used all her ability to keep the arm pinned, so that she had leverage and the advantage.

Luke shoved his hands in his pockets and sauntered around the corner.

"Hello, my blood sucking friend. Sorry to interrupt your tasty snack," Luke said, tilting his head toward the passed-out man who'd slumped to the ground, his chest rising and falling with the rhythm of life. "I'm afraid this is your last night among the living and the undead."

The vampire focused her intense stare on Luke's face, trying to glamour him.

"Sorry. That shit ain't gonna work on me. Let's get this over with." Luke slid his rudis out of its sheath. The vampire's eyes widened when she caught sight of the wooden blade with its silver inlay. She renewed her thrashing. Pablo and Delilah were using every ounce of strength and determination they could muster to keep her still.

"Fuck you! I'll rip your fucking throat out and drink you dry." She continued using her unattended legs to try to kick Luke.

"It's nice to die with delusions." Something about her face tugged a string of memory in Luke's mind. He hesitated for a moment, trying to figure out why.

"Bruh, just fucking finish it already," Delilah grunted as she struggled to keep the vampire's left arm contained.

Luke tried to position himself to get in, but a steady barrage of flailing kicks, combined with his greatly reduced speed and flexibility, were stymieing his attempt to get a clean kill. Delilah and Pablo had her arms firmly pinned against the brick column, essentially gluing her back into position. She used it to her advantage to keep Luke from closing within range of her heart.

Switching the rudis to his left hand, Luke reached over his shoulder and pulled out his gladius. He was hoping for an easier kill, but this was turning out to be a bit of an unintended mess. Delilah's face glistened with perspiration as she strained to keep the vampire's arm restrained. Luke could see cords rising in Pablo's neck as he held onto the other arm. As soon as the vamp unleashed a kick with her left leg, Luke darted around to the side and brought his gladius down and through her femur before rotating and thrusting the rudis into her heart. The movement left him winded, his poorly recovered muscles protesting the sudden exertion. He left the rudis in the vamp's chest as he stepped back to catch his breath.

"Should we lay her down?" asked Pablo.

"Yeah. Drag her a bit further back in the shadows and lay her out," Luke replied.

"Sure." Pablo pulled her around to join Delilah on her side of the post. Together they laid her flat, the rudis still sticking up from her chest. Pablo straightened up. "You were struggling a bit there, buddy."

"Yeah, still not recovered."

Delilah walked over and checked the victim's pulse. "He's alive. Pulse seems strong."

Luke clumsily lowered himself to his knees, wrapped his hands around the hilt of the rudis, placed his forehead on the pommel, and spoke the words that activated the weapon's ancient enchantment. The silver inlay glowed white, disappeared into the vampire's chest, then ran back up the blade into the pommel and into Luke. He shuddered and released a euphoric sigh.

Luke got up, feeling steadier than he'd felt since before his epic beat down. He walked over to the slumped almost-victim.

"He probably just passed out from a mix of booze and vamp glamour. Well, and a bit of blood loss too."

All three of their heads perked up as they heard the distant sound of sirens.

"I think your handiwork is drawing some attention," Pablo said.

Luke nodded. "We probably better get out of here. He'll be OK."

"What about…" Delilah gestured over the liquefying vampire.

"It's unknown goo and some clothes. Cops and police labs aren't equipped to handle vampire remains. The dissipating magic is destroying any biological traces of her former humanity. Let's go."

Delilah and Pablo looked at each either and shrugged, then followed Luke as he stepped over the goo and crossed the street. Once he was in the shadows of the trees, he picked up his pace into a light jog until all three were back in Pablo's truck. They pulled out onto the street and drove slowly through the dark neighborhood and away from the scene of the crime.

Delilah turned around in the front passenger seat to face Luke. "Bruh, what the hell took you so long?"

Pablo nodded his head in agreement.

"I was having trouble getting around her kicking. I'm not as recovered as I thought," Luke replied.

Delilah shook her head. "I wasn't talking about that. At the beginning, you hesitated."

"Yeah, you kind of stared at her," Pablo added.

"I knew her," Luke replied.

"What?" Delilah and Pablo exclaimed in stereo.

"I've seen her before, before she was turned." He stared out the window as Pablo drove toward NE Broadway.

"Where? Was she a friend?"

"No. I'm not sure I even knew her name." He turned to make eye contact with Delilah. "She used to live at a houseless camp up on Greeley. I was afraid of this."

"Dude, you want to quit vaguebooking us?" Pablo interjected.

"Sorry. My brain is still not running at full speed. I'm trying to gather my thoughts." After a moment, he continued. "Vampires prey on the weak and the voiceless. They hunt victims who won't be missed or won't be believed—the sick, mentally ill, poor, marginalized, and the houseless."

Delilah looked sad.

"Portland makes for a tasty hunting ground for vamps. A lot of dispossessed people have washed up in Portland. There are transients working their way up and down the west coast. People don't pay attention to them while the cops harass them. They're the perfect victims. Vampires kill some, turn others. No one's looking for them. Who's going to figure out they're now bloodsucking monsters?"

Silence shrouded the cab of the truck as they pulled onto I-5 North.

Pablo looked at the clock on the truck's dashboard. "It's about closing time at the pub. You want to stop in for a few quiet after-hours beers?"

DELILAH AND LUKE tucked into the back booth while Pablo helped his bartender close up for the evening. They enjoyed a couple pilsners while they waited for Pablo to finish and usher his employee out into the night.

Luke finally broke the silence, making eye contact with both of them. "Thanks for helping out tonight, and thanks for listening to my instructions."

Delilah and Pablo nodded and continued sipping their beers.

"It's been a long time since I've hunted with anyone. It's…a bit weird, but not bad." Luke drank from his beer and let the silence stand while he finished his first beer.

Pablo got another round before Luke continued. "It's going to take us a bit of time to get used to working together, but I'm willing to see where this partnership goes."

Delilah and Pablo relaxed but still were uncertainly eyeing Luke after the night's events.

Luke continued, "Vampires are powerful and cunning creatures. I feel like..." He halted, took a drink, and sighed.

"How are you feeling?" Delilah interrupted.

"Still not one-hundred percent but much better. I think I'll be fine as long as we don't attempt another full gang fight. If we're careful picking our engagements, we'll be able to take care of business while I get fully recharged."

"How many vampires will it take to juice you back up?" Pablo asked.

Luke shrugged. "I'm not sure. That's the closest I've been to death in a long time. I'm hoping not too many. I don't want to be at a disadvantage if we run into a big group, especially with you two still so green."

Pablo and Delilah started to protest. Luke held up his hands to calm them.

"Look, I know you've both killed some vampires, and you saved my life. For that, I'm most appreciative, but I've been doing this for almost nineteen centuries. Trust me when I say I'm not insulting you. If we're going to work together, we have to make sure all your skills are fine tuned. Most importantly, we need to learn to coordinate together. If we're getting in each other's way, that'll be almost as dangerous as going it alone."

They accepted his explanations and seemed mollified for now. Pablo pulled out his cell phone to select something to play over the pub's sound system. The soundtrack to Crouching Tiger, Hidden Dragon started playing. "I figured if we were going to be talking about fighting, we might as well have a good soundtrack. It was either this or Carl Douglas, and I didn't know if either of you cats were fast as lightning."

Delilah shook her head while Luke tried to stifle a laugh.

"Wait here. I have something special I want you to try." Pablo disappeared behind the bar.

They heard the walk-in cooler door opening and shutting.

"Where does he think we're going?" Luke asked.

Delilah shrugged and went back to drinking her beer in silence. The walk-in door opened and closed again. Luke peered out of the booth and watched Pablo grab a pitcher and clean out one of his beer lines. Soon, he returned with three footed tulip glasses filled with a thick, black beer with a rich brown head.

"And voilà! You get to be the first to try the new Imperial Stout. It's a classic English-style Russian Imperial Stout. Although, I should call it a Roman Imperial Stout, eh?" Pablo winked at Luke. He raised his glass. "I want to propose a toast. To new partnerships and new friends!"

Luke, Delilah, and Pablo tapped their glasses together and said, "Cheers!"

The Russian Imperial stout was big and tasty with an air of danger thanks to the high alcohol level. Luke chuckled mentally. Tonight had an air of danger about it as well, relying on people for the first time in a long time, but it had gone smoothly, even considering his poor performance killing the vamp quickly. Maybe Delilah and Pablo would work out and be a good addition to his life. He just had to ensure they stayed alive long enough to get experienced enough to be truly dangerous hunters. Hope and the responsibility—two things he'd avoided for a long time—flared to life inside him.

TWELVE

LUKE SAT at his table with a cup of coffee as he watched the birds flit about his backyard. He'd stayed at the pub with Pablo and Delilah later than he should have. It'd been a long time since he'd joined with others in convivial companionship. It felt good. He heard the cabinet open behind him and turned to see Delilah grabbing a coffee mug out of the cupboard. She was wearing an old T-shirt and a pair of Luke's shorts that showed off her surprisingly muscular and toned arms and legs. She poured herself a cup of coffee from the carafe and sat down opposite of Luke.

"Thanks for letting me use your spare room last night. That Roman Imperial Stout really kicked my ass." She blew on her steaming coffee to hasten its cooling so she could dive into the healing potion's caffeinated goodness.

Luke got up and rummaged around. "Breakfast?"

"That sounds wonderful!"

Fifteen minutes later, Luke set two plates down on the table—each with two poached eggs perched on top of a stack of sliced avocado, tomato, and a toasted English muffin. He put a couple basil leaves on top of each stack and finished it with a drizzle of balsamic vinegar and olive oil and a couple twists from the salt and pepper grinders.

"Damn, that's some good-looking breakfast."

"Top off your coffee?" Luke asked.

Delilah nodded. "Please."

Luke refilled both cups before sitting and digging in.

As Luke cleared the dirty dishes, a knock came from the front door.

"Delilah, do you mind letting Pablo in while I throw these plates in the dishwasher?"

Delilah stood up and disappeared into the other room. A moment later, she reappeared with Pablo.

"Hey Luke! How you holding up?" He grinned at Luke mischievously.

"Pretty well, considering. That imperial stout had some kick. It was good, but one probably would have sufficed. I'm going to go put on some workout clothes."

Luke disappeared into his room. When he emerged a few minutes later, Delilah had changed back into her clothes from the night before and was chatting with Pablo in the kitchen.

"Shall we adjourn to the Batcave?" Luke walked into the office with Alfred on his heels. He flipped the mechanism before either Pablo or Delilah got into the room, then headed downstairs. Luke sat in his desk chair while Pablo and Delilah took the easy chairs.

"I guess we should figure out what everyone knows and what kind of training we've had. I'll start... I've studied most forms of western martial arts over the years, by default. I've studied several forms of eastern martial arts as well, mostly Japanese forms—katana, aikido, judo, etc. A little kung fu as well."

"Why do you still fight like a Roman, then? If you know all these other martial arts?" Pablo asked.

"You use the forms that work with the equipment you have. My original gear was specially created to fight vampires. A katana will do just as much physical damage and a simple wooden stake will handle the fine print details, but in concert, my gladius, rudis, and lorica turn me into something more. I'm not just using weapons; I am a weapon. Delilah, what about you?"

"I guess the one I've been studying the longest is Wing Chun Kung Fu. My dad loved Bruce Lee movies. He always used to say, 'That Chinese cat is the baddest little mofo.'" Her voice slipped into a deeper register with a hint of an African accent Luke couldn't quite place. The corners of her lips turned up in a gentle smile that ran counter to the sad look of longing in her eyes. "We always watched the old kung fu movies on Saturdays and Sundays. 'Enter the Dragon' was his favorite. He was a big Jim Kelly fan, so having him and Bruce in one movie made him happy. After my mom passed away, he started taking me with him to his school. They thought Wing Chun would work well for me since I was small at the time, but quick. So that's what I started with."

"I'm sorry to hear about your mom. Do you mind if I ask how she passed?" Pablo asked.

"Breast cancer. By the time the doctors listened to her and diagnosed it, it was too late." She paused for a second, taking a breath and letting it out slowly. "Anyway, going to my dad's 'school,' as he called it, helped with my anger and brought us closer. I've kept up with my studies. I'm proficient in unarmed fighting but could use some more work with weapons. I've also studied some Krav Maga." She looked back at Luke.

Luke turned to the werewolf. "Pablo?"

"Damn. Now I feel all inadequate. I'm pretty much a scrapper. I'm a werewolf, so I'm stronger than your average human, and I can take a lot of punishment. I usually just punch them hard until they stop fighting back. I haven't had to do much fighting lately. Not much need when you have a good community around you, but when I needed to, I could handle my own. Being a gay Latino made me a target for meatheads looking to prove how tough they were. It never worked out well for them. I never looked for trouble, but I wasn't going to take shit from anyone if they brought it to my doorstep."

"OK. That gives us a starting point. You up for a little sparring?"

Pablo and Delilah looked wary but excited as they moved into Luke's training cavern. Luke had them do some calisthenics before stretching. Once they were warmed up, Luke addressed their first lesson.

"Pablo, we should start with one of the most important lessons of martial arts. It'll be a bit basic for Delilah, but it's a good place to start, especially to keep everyone healthy. Lesson one — falling."

Pablo snorted in response. "Dude, I know how to fall. Gravity pretty much does all the work."

"There's falling, and then there's FALLING, or perhaps I should say landing. Learning how to take a fall and land safely will hold you in good stead in all forms of fighting. Delilah and I will do some demonstrations." Luke led them to the large, padded mat in the back corner.

"Delilah, I'm going to start with some basic hip throws. Pablo, don't watch me for now; watch what Delilah does as she falls." Luke looked at Delilah and asked, "Ready?"

Delilah nodded as she and Luke locked into a grappling position that would set her up to be thrown. Luke stepped in, put his hip against Delilah's and brought her around with a textbook throw to the ground. Delilah popped up, and they ran through it a couple more times.

"OK, that was slower than it would be in a real situation, but what did you see?" Luke asked.

"Well, she tucked her head and loose arm."

"Exactly. You want to protect your wrists and head. If you try to break your fall with your wrist, you can sprain or break a wrist. And you definitely want to keep your brain from getting rattled in a fight. I'm going to come at Delilah, and she'll take her pick on how she wants to throw me. Again, don't worry about what the thrower is doing; watch how I'm landing. Delilah, I'll try to present some different approaches so you can throw me in different ways. That should give Pablo a good idea of what we're trying to do."

Luke repeatedly presented different attacks to Delilah, which she used to throw Luke all over the mat. They ran through several variations for a few minutes until Luke and Delilah were breathing heavily with sheens of sweat glistening on their foreheads.

"That's probably enough for me for today," said Luke, letting Delilah work with Pablo while he watched.

They'd all worked up a good sweat throwing and falling and getting to know each other a bit more. Luke poured everyone glasses of cold water from the sink near the training room door. Relaxing into the chairs in Luke's studio, they drank their water and cooled down.

"That was a good start," Luke said as he polished off the last of his water. "I have a project for us this afternoon if you guys want to meet me back here at four?"

"I'm off today, so that works," Pablo replied.

"I'm unemployed and living on a friend's couch; I'm available," answered Delilah.

Luke nodded and smiled. "Good. Go home and shower. Be back at four. Oh! You might also want to bring back a stash of workout clothes to leave here. It'll be more convenient for our ongoing training."

Luke escorted them out of his home, then took his own advice and showered before heading out to run some errands. He hoped the training would be enough. He didn't have any non-feline friends, and now that he was making two new friends, he had to do whatever he could to keep them alive.

PABLO AND DELILAH arrived promptly at four. Instead of inviting them in, Luke grabbed a big Rubbermaid tub next to the door and moved it outside, closing and locking the door behind him.

"What's in the tub, dude?" Pablo asked.

"That's my gear."

Pablo's eyes shot open wide. "What?! You keep your magical swords and armor in a plastic tub? Aren't you worried someone will smash your window and jack it?"

Luke slid the tub into the back of his Volvo which was already filled with cardboard boxes and a hand truck.

"I'm usually wearing it or driving around. It's always been fine."

Delilah massaged her temples as she shook her head; Pablo looked shocked at Luke's seeming naïveté.

"What?"

"Dude. I'm taking you to see my nephew tomorrow," Pablo replied.

"What is your nephew going to do? Install a car alarm?"

Pablo folded his arms across his chest and shook his head. "Nah, well, I mean, he can if you want him to, but he does custom work on cars. We sent the little squirt to college for an engineering degree, but he loves cars, so that's what he uses it for. You ever see those custom car shows where they soup up the cars into works of art?"

"I'm familiar with the concept," Luke replied.

Pablo nodded. "That's my nephew, except he's better at it and doesn't have a TV show."

"I'm not sure 'hotrod Volvo' was what I was going for when I bought this beast."

"What were you going for? Aging hippie soccer mom?" Delilah interjected.

"Laugh all you want, but watch the sides of the streets as we drive through town. I wanted a car that was reliable and nondescript. Old Volvo fits the bill." Luke closed the hatch and got into the driver's seat. "Let's go."

Luke backed out of the driveway and wound his way through north Portland until they got to the bottom of the hill on Mississippi Avenue. He took a right toward North Interstate, then left onto Greeley to head back north, but before he drove too far, he pulled off on to the shoulder, parking just off the shoulder in the dirt next to the road.

"Man, you weren't kidding. Old Volvos everywhere. I never noticed until I was looking for them." Pablo chuckled.

"And that, Pablo, is why I have one. They're practically invisible. I guess I could upgrade to a Subaru Outback or a Prius and get the same effect, but I like the Volvo." Luke walked around to the back of the car.

Luke stacked the boxes on the hand truck and walked up the bike path that ran parallel to the road. The path led up the hill below

Overlook Park. Piles of garbage in bags were stacked along a fence not far from a few scattered tents. Further along the path, the tents turned into more robust structures, including several mini-houses.

"What is this place?" Delilah asked.

"Hazelnut Grove. It's a sheltered community for houseless people. They've built this themselves."

Delilah frowned. "That's impressive but sad that there isn't a better solution."

"People make do and survive. What other choice do they have? This country's systems aren't exactly robust when it concerns helping the poor or disadvantaged." Luke shrugged and stopped walking. "OK, we're meeting with my contact. He leads the council here."

"There's a council?" asked Pablo.

"Yeah. They have their own government and by-laws set up to protect and guide the community," said Luke.

Pablo replied with an impressed expression and a nod.

"Max is a good guy. He does his best to look after the community here. Stick close to me. There's nothing to worry about, but strangers make people here nervous. You don't look like cops, but people are still wary. They're getting used to me and know Max trusts me a bit. Ah, here he is." Luke nodded at Max as he approached.

"Hey, Luke. How you doing?" Max was tall and thin with shaggy, brown hair. He wore a heavy jacket and slightly baggy jeans.

"Hey, Max. Pretty good. How about you?"

"Oh, got a bit of a cold, but can't complain." He eyed Delilah and Pablo.

Luke gestured toward his two friends. "These are my friends, Pablo and Delilah. Pablo, Delilah, this is Max. I've got some of the stuff you asked for."

Max smiled. "Thanks! This is much appreciated. Next time you come out, we could use some more feminine hygiene products, if it's not too much to ask."

"Sure thing. I'll add it to the list.

Max smiled and nodded his thanks before directing them to a nearby picnic table.

"How have things been here lately?" Luke asked.

"The usual. We try to keep things quiet," Max replied and looked around the table at Luke, Delilah, and Pablo.

"Any unaccounted-for disappearances? Strangers lurking about at night?"

"I don't know. It's hard to tell. We have a fairly stable population here. A few of the people on the outskirts come and go," Max replied.

"Any abandoned stuff? Tents, good clothes, sleeping bags?" Luke asked.

"Yeah, we have been getting a bit more of that lately. Normally, we chalk it up to people getting picked up by the cops, so we set it aside until it's reclaimed. They usually show back up in a few days. Lately, we've had a few lots of gear that still haven't been claimed." Max shrugged. "In those cases, we assume they moved on or are residents of the county, so we sort out their stuff and move on."

"What about the lurking strangers?"

"Look, Luke, I'm not sure what you're looking for. I appreciate what you do for us. The council appreciates it, too. The stuff you bring us helps out immensely, but we also have to protect the people who live here and rely on us."

"I can understand that. Believe me, I know what it means to protect a community from outside threats, especially threats they don't know about and are ill-equipped to handle. That's why I'm here. The first people those sort target are the most vulnerable, the most likely to not report or not have their stories believed. It's generally—and it's shitty to say this but unfortunately true—those who won't be missed."

Max grimaced but nodded. "Yeah. Unfortunately, that is too true." He sighed and shook his head sadly.

"I know we've only known each other for a little while, but..." Luke sighed and made direct eye contact with Max. "I have the same goal you do. I'm not here to mess with your community. I'm not here to police it. It's probably too much to ask for, but trust that I'm not here to hurt those you're looking after. We're doing the same thing, ultimately—keeping predators away from vulnerable communities."

Luke let the silence hang in the air until Max nodded and replied, "I can go with that, for now."

Luke smiled at Max.

"Just keep an eye on the edges of your community. Try to bring them in closer, not so isolated." Luke looked around at the tree-covered hill. "This is a great community, but it's too easy to creep up on the outskirts at night."

"The isolation has its advantages, but it also has its issues. I'll take your advice and alert the council. Ultimately, it's a group decision, but we'd be foolish to disregard any information that could prevent harm to our people." He stood up, effectively ending the conversation.

"Thanks for your time, Max. I appreciate it. I'll see you next time." Luke indicated that Delilah and Pablo should follow him.

They walked back down the bike path that led out of the camp, the only sound the wheels of the hand truck on the path. The silence lasted until they were all buckled into Luke's car. Luke was waiting for a spot to pull into traffic when Delilah finally spoke.

"How often do you bring supplies to Max?"

"About once a week, but it's only been a couple months or so. I screwed up, got lazy." Luke pursed his lips.

"Lazy? What do you mean?" asked Pablo.

"I should have been building these relationships years ago. Vampires always seek the most vulnerable as their prey. I know that, but I got complacent. A few vampires would pop up here or there, and I'd easily dispatch them and return to life as usual. Now the city is neck deep in fucking vampires, and I'm scrambling to lay the groundwork to fight them. I should have been building my network regardless of the threat level." He sighed and shook his head before pulling out into traffic. "Now, I've killed a few dozen vampires recently, and they're coordinating on a very high level. I found that out the hard way the other night. It's probably only the tip of the iceberg."

THIRTEEN

LUKE, Delilah, and Pablo tracked a quartet of sophisticated young vampires through shallow southeast Portland. They'd been trying to home in on their location since Luke felt the tingle indicating they'd run across his favorite prey, ultimately stumbling upon them as they left one of the city's new brewpubs. The quartet blended in perfectly with the young hip set that liked to wander around Southeast Belmont on a Saturday night. Sporting a mix of black, ripped skinny jeans, cool band shirts and appropriately "I don't care about fashion" fashionable jackets, they looked just like anyone else wandering around. Luke, Delilah, and Pablo held back to see where they'd head to next, hoping for a less populated dark street to conduct their business.

The trio continued to hang back and keep a casual distance as they followed their fanged quarry east along Belmont. Catching a lull in traffic, the vampires darted across the street toward Audacious, one of Portland's more popular and long-standing strip clubs.

"A strip club?" asked Delilah cynically.

"They're popular in Oregon. It's one of the few states that allows full nudity and a full bar," Pablo responded. "Plus, the Oregon Supreme Court ruled that exotic dancing qualified as free speech.

That, coupled with Oregon's friendly liquor laws, makes for an ideal business environment for strip clubs to flourish. It's a pretty popular tourism draw."

Delilah pursed her lips. "I've been to Vegas with girlfriends. I've seen the roving bands of skeezy bros. No thank you."

"Don't get me wrong, there are definitely those guys and the kinds of clubs to match, but there are also more respectable establishments like Audacious. I know the owners; I've sold them beer on occasion. Audacious is a fairly popular date spot."

"You're shitting me," Delilah replied skeptically.

Pablo crossed his heart and raised his hand, holding up his forefinger and middle finger and giving Delilah scout's honor.

"Seriously?" Delilah's eyebrows lifted.

"Yeah. Portland has a unique culture around them. I guess it's one of those things that contributes to keeping Portland weird, as the bumper sticker says," Pablo replied.

They crossed the street and got in line at the door of the purple brick building where a tall, bald man covered in tattoos was checking IDs. When Delilah fished her driver's license out of her wallet, Pablo peeked over her shoulder.

"New York, eh? Oh, those are some awesome locs. What happened to them?" Pablo asked.

Delilah ran her hand over her teeny-weeny afro and covered the license's picture with her thumb. She sighed. "I'm still pissed off about that. I'm not sure I'm ready to talk about it yet." Her face set into a mix of anger and mourning.

The bouncer checked Delilah's and Pablo's IDs before moving on to Luke's. "You're probably fine, pops, but got to check everyone."

Luke's jaw dropped as he handed his license over to the bouncer; Pablo and Delilah snickered with amusement. The bouncer returned Luke's ID, letting the trio enter the club. They were greeted by the sound of loud alternative music and flashing lights. Selecting a table in the back, they settled in to keep an eye on the vampires.

"Pops? Do I really look that old?" Luke asked.

"Nah, dude, you look great for a two-thousand-year-old guy. You don't look a day over seven hundred," Pablo teased.

The situation had reversed Delilah's earlier bad mood, and she smiled at her companions. Luke, put out by the direction the evening had taken, crossed his arms and slouched into his chair.

"I know I don't look like I'm in my twenties, but I'm not sure I warrant a 'pops.'"

Pablo was trying to contain his laughter as Delilah finally took pity on Luke.

Delilah looked at Luke. "It's not so much that you look old; it's the presentation. You're wearing baggy, faded, dad jeans. Also, your haircut is a bit…"

"Suburban dad trying to cling to his youth?" Pablo interjected between snickers.

"Well, I wasn't going to phrase it that way…but yeah, the bit of salt creeping into your pepper at the temples kind of accentuates that vibe with your longer hair."

Pablo was trying to contain his amusement and failing miserably, although he managed to keep from making a spectacle of himself in the close quarters. Delilah inspected Luke's face carefully.

Delilah leaned closer. "The beard's solid but could use shaping. The lines at the corners of your eyes give you a bit of gravitas. When did you stop aging? I'm not sure how your whole deal works."

"I was in my late thirties the first time I used my rudis. It pretty much halted my aging at that point."

"And your appearance has stayed like this ever since?" Delilah asked.

"Yeah, basically. If I go too long in between…" Luke looked around to make sure no one was eavesdropping, but the wall of sound coming from the speakers drowned out their conversation before it could leave their table, "…rudis uses, I start to age, but it never gets beyond a few years of appearance before I'm forced to seek a member of the living challenged community."

Their server brought their drinks, and they settled back to watch the crowd. Pablo's words rang true. There were far more women in the audience than either Luke or Delilah expected. Some were in groups with friends, while others appeared to be on dates. Luke, having marked the location of the vampires they'd followed in—two were at the bar while the other two sat at the rail, placing dollar bills on the ledge for the dancer—sipped his beer and thought about what his friends had said. He looked down at this clothing.

"I guess I have let my fashion sense slip a bit. Do you think you could help me out?" He fidgeted with the drawstrings of his hoodie while looking down at the table.

"Sure. That sounds like fun. I'll ask my friend if she's got a good recommendation for a stylist then take you shopping at Nordstrom so we can update your wardrobe. I'll have you looking fly in no time." The song changed, and Delilah's eyes shifted to the stage. "Daaammmmnnn!"

Pablo and Luke looked toward the stage to see what Delilah was commenting on. A tall, slim, athletic woman covered in elaborate, beautiful tattoos and sporting a bright green, immaculately groomed double mohawk descended the two-story pole with incredible grace and athleticism. For the length of two songs, she kept the entire club entranced as she worked through her routine, an artful display of seductive gymnastics that harmonized ballet, hip hop, and burlesque into a symphony of physical control and beauty. The dollar bills were falling onto the stage like autumn leaves. As her last song ended, she strode off stage to thunderous approval. When the applause and whistles slowed, someone darted out to collect her tribute.

"That...was impressive," chimed in Pablo after the clapping died down and people retook their seats.

Delilah nodded along. Luke looked dumbstruck.

"You OK there, buddy?" Pablo grinned.

"Luke... Luke... Pablo was talking to you." Delilah tried to contain her laughter.

"Oh. Sorry. That...that was magnificent." He exhaled and gathered his thoughts. "That was artistry. I was not expecting that."

"Do you frequent strip clubs?" Delilah asked, an eyebrow arched.

"I've been around a few. It's sometimes an occupational hazard; vampires tend to congregate at such places," he gestured toward the quartet of bloodsuckers, "as evidenced by their presence here tonight."

"Sure..." Pablo teased. He had a big grin on his face as he winked at Luke.

Luke rolled his eyes.

"A lot of these places can be exploitative, which fits the M.O. of vampires. Also, the late-night nature of such businesses is ideal for the solar averse. When you're in the business of freelance fang extraction, you go where the clients are." Luke shrugged.

The club settled into a more normal rhythm as songs changed and the other dancers took their turns. The vampires seemed to be settling in as normal patrons. They mingled with the crowd, occasionally breaking off for a private dance or to "flirt" with a patron. Delilah had been watching them as well but periodically scanned the room, perhaps hoping to catch a glimpse of the mohawked dancer.

Delilah turned back to Luke. "Uh, question, Luke."

"Yes?"

"I haven't been doing this as long as you, but does it seem like most of the vampires we've encountered have been male? I mean, there've been a few women, but the sizable majority have been dudes. What's up?"

"I mean, I've not spoken to the vampires' human resources —"

"Human resources! Doesn't that mean lunch?" Pablo interrupted, laughing at his own joke.

Delilah and Luke rolled their eyes at each other and continued with their conversation as if the joke had never existed.

Luke continued. "But vampire hierarchies are based largely on age. The older you are, the more powerful you are. Older vampires tend to come from more patriarchal cultures and have rebuilt that ethos into vampire culture. They tend to view women as a commodity. Although, I've come across some extremely powerful female vampires. They're not as prevalent, but they do exist."

Delilah nodded. "Huh, interesting."

"Another round?" asked Pablo, surveying their empty beers.

"I guess so. Doesn't seem like the vamps are in a hurry," Luke replied.

"Oh, look. It's her!" said Delilah, pointing out the woman with the twin mohawks.

She wore black leather pants, a sheer black shirt with a red bra underneath, and had a black leather jacket slung over her shoulder. She capped off her look with a pair of short, black Frye boots with a silver loop at the ankle anchoring a series of straps. The vampires at the bar slid off their stools and strolled up to her. One of them said something funny enough to elicit a laugh from her. The other two vampires were surreptitiously keeping an eye on the situation from their table near the main stage.

"Is she a vamp?" Pablo asked. "It's hard to tell by smell in this crowd."

"No. She comes by her grace and magnetism honestly," Luke replied, all business again. "No next round. Delilah, head outside, hang a left, and station yourself about halfway down the block. Pretend to make a call or something. Pablo, you go to the right. I'll hang back and follow them out. Use the group text to communicate."

They gave Luke fake goodbyes, pretending they were heading home and leaving Luke at the club. After Delilah and Pablo left, Luke refocused on the two sets of vampires and the dancer. He hoped they all left together; he didn't want to have to split up and track two groups, especially not with Pablo and Delilah's inexperience. After another moment of conversation, the vampires and the dancer migrated to the table with the other two vamps. The dancer signaled to a server who strode over to the bar where the bartender was already filling five shot glasses. Apparently, she had a "usual" and was letting the vampires pay for it. Their table was too far away to tell if she'd been glamoured or was just being hospitable.

One of the vamps paid for the shots when the server returned with her loaded tray. The vampires and dancer picked up their glasses and clinked them together while making eye contact. The four vampires knocked back their shots while the dancer's hung in the air for a few moments as if she'd been frozen.

"Damn, they got her with the toast and eye contact," Luke mumbled to himself. He shot a text to Pablo and Delilah.

The dancer finally drank her shot and set the glass down. As one, they stood and headed toward the exit. Luke prepared to follow suit. On the way through the door, the dancer paused and whispered to the bald, tattooed bouncer. The bouncer's gaze shifted to Luke. He nodded at the dancer as she followed her quartet of fanged escorts. The bouncer cruised through the crowd to Luke's table.

Luke fired off another text, *Fuck, I've been made. Follow them. Keep me posted.*

The bouncer loomed over Luke. "So, pops, Natalia says you could use a little company…"

"Not particularly, but I assume you're going to insist," Luke replied.

The bouncer gave Luke a smug nod and pulled up a chair. He settled in, keeping an eye on the crowd and Luke. Deciding to take a different approach, Luke started to stand.

The bouncer put his hand on Luke's forearm. "Where do you think you're going?"

"I need to take a leak. You don't buy beer, you only rent it. Am I right?"

The bouncer rolled his eyes at Luke and released him. "I guess you can't get out that way."

Luke understood why as he walked down the hallway to the restrooms. The men's room had no windows to the outside. He relieved himself, then headed back out. The bouncer was waiting near the end of the hall, surrounded by the flashing halo of a strobe light going off in the background. As Luke neared him, the bouncer reached out and placed his hand on Luke's artificially broad shoulders.

"What the…"

Luke took the bouncer's arm, yanked it down and spun behind him so Luke's body blocked the hallway from the view of the room beyond.

"Hey, asshole, I guess we'll have to stomp your ass after all," the bouncer threatened.

Rolling his eyes, Luke silenced him, banging the bouncer's head into the concrete wall and knocking him out cold. Luke supported him as he dragged him into the men's restroom. The open stall looked like a good place to stash him. Luke propped him on the toilet seat and left him there, closing the stall door behind him. He checked himself in the mirror on the way out the door to make sure he didn't look like he'd just knocked out a bouncer.

His phone buzzed, vibrating the back pocket of his jeans. The text from Delilah had a maps link to their location and one message.

Hurry!

LUKE SPRINTED down the abandoned residential streets toward Delilah and Pablo's location, the urgency of her word gnawing at his insides and speeding his feet onward. Despite all his violent and bloody experience, Luke wasn't prepared for what he saw when he finally found Delilah and Pablo. Delilah, sobbing, was crouched over Natalia's body, holding her hand with both of hers. Pablo, naked, crouched over Natalia, his hands pressed to her throat as blood oozed out between his fingers. Tears ran down his cheeks as well. Two abandoned and gooey sets of clothes marked the location of half of the vampire posse; the other two must have gotten away. Natalia's heels thrashed weakly against the alley's ground; the hand not held by Delilah grasped Pablo's thigh. Luke stared at the scene before him, jaw clenched in rage.

Natalia's hand fell to the ground, bouncing slightly. Her heels stopped moving. Her chest stopped rising.

Luke wasn't sure how long they stood there, motionless—Luke staring blank eyed, Delilah holding Natalia's hand, crying, and Pablo with hands trying to hold in the blood that had finally stopped flowing. The sounds of sirens finally pulled Luke back to reality.

"Shit. We got to get out of here. Fast. Delilah, gather up the shreds of Pablo's clothes. Watch out for the pool of blood. Pablo, can you go full wolf? You're covered in blood. Maybe wolf tracks will fool them into thinking a big dog went through here. I doubt the Portland Police would know a wolf track if one walked up and bit them."

They nodded. Delilah gave Natalia's hand a final squeeze before placing it gently across her stomach. She grabbed the ragged shreds of Pablo's outfit. Pablo was about to take a step back before realizing he'd leave a human footprint.

"There's a park nearby. It's got a pond. I'll meet you there," said Pablo quietly. "Do you know it?"

"Yeah. We'll get there as soon as we can without being direct," Luke replied.

"Good. Delilah has a spare T-shirt and shorts in her purse." He blurred into a full wolf and trotted out of the alley, leaving large, bloody paw prints on the ground as he left.

Luke watched him go before inspecting the alley for any evidence of their presence. He bent over to pick up a small strip of cloth that looked like part of Pablo's T-shirt.

"Looks like we got it all. You ready to move?" Luke asked. "Did you two touch anything? Anything we might need to wipe for prints?"

"Just the stakes." Delilah's voice was flat and empty of emotion.

Luke picked them up, careful to avoid touching anything else. "We'll ditch them in a yard debris bin somewhere."

Delilah nodded, staring at the body cooling on the ground.

Luke gave her shoulder a reassuring squeeze. "I know. I do. But we need to get moving or we're going to be in a pile of deep shit when the cops get here."

Delilah nodded again, forcing her head to turn away from Natalia. She walked out of the alley.

Luke took one last look at Natalia and said, "I'm sorry…"

He sighed, shook his head, and followed Delilah out of the alley into southeast Portland. They dodged in and out of the light of the streetlights and back into the shadows of the trees, trying to move quickly but inconspicuously.

LUKE TOSSED and turned all night, plagued by bad dreams he'd not had in years and years. With each dream, he woke shivering and filled with despair at how much blood he'd witnessed and how very helpless he was to stop it all. Each time he startled awake, his anger grew. Finally, he threw his blankets off and put on some workout clothes.

He headed down to his training center and mounted the treadmill. He started out slowly, hoping to work out the tension. Instead, he kept picturing Delilah holding her hand, Pablo trying to stop the flowing blood. And each time he saw her terrified eyes slacken and go dead, he hit the up button.

After five miles, he was flying. After ten, he was practically sprinting at a dead run. Nothing was cleansing the vision from his head. He wasn't sure who would break first, him or the treadmill. He smashed his hand into the stop button.

The heavy punching bag was his next victim. Jab, jab, jab, uppercut, uppercut, jab, jab. Soon, that devolved into a brawl with the inanimate object as Luke unleashed uncontrolled haymaker after uncontrolled haymaker. Every face he'd failed flashed through his mind. Every massive punch was a vampire who'd destroyed some piece of the world in their relentless lust for blood. Sweat streamed down his face, stinging his eyes. Tears, running freely, joined the beads of sweat rolling down his cheeks.

No relief came.

His punches got slower and weaker, until Luke propped his head against the bag as he continued to pummel it pathetically, his knees wobbling with exhaustion.

His body had had enough. He still wasn't up to full speed, and tonight's exertions had pushed him past what little physical reserves he had left. He slumped to the ground, pushing off the bag so he landed with his back against the wall, his knees up in front of him, elbows propped on his knees, and his head in his hands. Tears streamed down his face as he gasped for air.

As his breathing calmed, the sound of music penetrated his foggy head. Someone had put on a record and flipped the switch that tied the system to the gym's speakers. Through his red, swollen eyes, he saw a silhouette approach. It resolved into Pablo.

Sitting next to Luke, Pablo wrapped his arms around his knees. Luke sniffed and rubbed his cheeks dry with the heel of his palms and wiped his nose on his sleeveless arm.

"I thought I'd check in on you before heading into the brewery," Pablo said.

"I had trouble sleeping, so I thought some exercise would help." Luke's voice sounded empty, even to his own ears.

"I didn't sleep well either."

"I just... I can't get the image out of my head." Luke shook his head. "Her body, laying in a pool of her own blood. I've seen an ocean of blood and caused another. Why her? Why now? Why is this death lingering? I don't... I couldn't stop it. I failed."

"I haven't seen what you've seen, nor lived as long as you, but I've seen friends die violently. I'm fairly jaded after this long, but this is affecting me more than I would've thought. For a few minutes, we got to witness something special, something almost otherworldly, and then it was brutally snuffed out by the ugliness of our world." Pablo sighed.

"I could have gotten there faster. I could have bounced the bouncer's head off the table and run by the other bouncer before they knew what was up. I thought about it..."

"It wouldn't have mattered. As soon as we jumped them, one clawed her throat out and ran with the other one while the other two stayed to hold us off. It would've been the same story if you'd been there. You can't save everyone all the time." Even though Pablo's words were logical, he still sounded as frustrated as Luke.

"It feels like I've saved so few. A person here, three there. Yet we're drowning in vampires. I can't keep up. I just can't..."

"How long have you been doing this? Like nineteen hundred plus years? How many have you saved in all the time? How many vampires have you dispatched?" Pablo asked.

Luke shrugged shallowly. "Countless vampires, but for every one I kill, more crop up. It's like trying to smash mercury with a hammer. It just squishes and moves. You just can't get it."

"And you're just one man. One man against a horde of hungry undead monsters? How do you keep going? I'm honestly impressed," Pablo said.

Luke laughed bitterly. "I don't have a choice. It's like an addiction. I'm incapable of stopping. It's not just that I start aging. I go through withdrawal. Brutal withdrawal. I've tried to quit, to 'retire,' but I can't. He won't let me…"

Pablo's head tilted as his brows furrowed. "Withdrawal? Like drugs?"

"Yeah. Like heroin or alcohol. It's painful, horrible. I get the shakes, the sweats. If I let it go long enough, hallucinations. Eventually, the compulsion will take me over and drag me out to a vampire. It's…" He struggled for the words. "It's like an out-of-body experience. I see myself through a fog, hunting, stalking. I'm honestly amazed I don't get killed in such a state."

"Wait. He? Who won't let you?" Pablo asked.

Luke sighed, collapsing in on himself even further. "Mithras…"

"Mithras? Who's Mithras?"

"My patron. The wellspring of my power. He is my master, and I can't escape from him."

"I still don't understand," Pablo replied. "Who's Mithras?"

Luke didn't respond, and silence hung heavily in the air.

"I'm exhausted, Pablo. So damned tired." Luke put his head in his hands and shook it slowly.

Pablo put his arm around Luke's shoulders.

"I know, buddy. I can see it in your eyes, the slump of your shoulders. You're carrying the weight of the world. You've been doing it alone for a long time. It's draining." Pablo gave Luke a reassuring squeeze. "I can't say I know your burden, but I've had times in my life when I've been done."

Pablo stared into the middle distance.

"I was drifting for a long time, packless, alone. I'd disappeared into the California surf culture of the '60s. I was already old by then, but it kept me distracted. It was fun for a while. After a time, I just felt empty. I started wandering. Eventually I heard about a pack forming up in Portland. A gay woman was starting a queer wolf pack and inviting anyone to join.

"For the first time in a long time, there was a spark of hope in my life. I worked my way north until I landed in Portland and looked up the packleader. That's when I met Holly. She was the youngest wolf I'd ever met who had that 'packleader' vibe. She was impressive.

Then I met her wife, Sam, and you know Sam. She's one of the most welcoming people you'll ever meet. For the first time in a very long time, I had a home. I poured myself into the pack, helping Holly get it off the ground and make it a refuge for the outcast wolves of America…"

Pablo's smooth and gentle tone helped soothe Luke as he set aside his sorrow and disappeared into Pablo's story.

"Then, a few years later, Tony showed up. It was like being reborn. Colors were crisper. Food tasted better. It was like I'd been existing as a two-dimensional being and Tony's love inflated me into a three-dimensional man. The joy in that man's soul makes me feel truly alive."

"I don't have a Tony." Luke sounded petulant, even to himself.

"No, but you do have a Pablo and a Delilah, and friends are a good place to start."

"Yeah." Luke chuckled. "Although, I'm not entirely sure Delilah likes me."

"I'm pretty sure she considers you a friend at this point, or will after a bit more time, but she's got her own burdens. She's got some fresh grief she's managing."

Luke perked up a bit. "Has she talked to you about it?"

"No, but I can tell. She's good at walling it up, nearly as good as you are at hiding your pain." The word "pain" caused Luke to cringe. Pablo felt it.

"Is it that obvious?"

"Well…you've let your guard down a few times. But there's a reason I'm Holly's second. I can read people very well. It lets me get ahead of trouble and figure out what needs to be done."

"I used to be so good at bottling it up, but I've been alone for too long. Rambling to a cat all day doesn't really make for quality human contact. Not to slight Alfred. His companionship has been lifesaving, but I guess I underestimated how much I needed a friend." Luke laid his head on Pablo's shoulder as they sat silently, letting the sounds of Future Islands' "Fall from Grace" wash over them.

After the Twin Peaks theme-like intro to the song, the primal scream of the singer at the chorus shook something loose in Luke.

"I'm fading away…" Luke said, almost too quietly to hear.

"What?" Pablo asked.

"Like the song says, I'm slowly fading away…"

"What do you mean?"

"Since I've been dredging up my ancient history, I've been having vivid memories of my younger days, before all this." Luke gestured vaguely with his hand.

"I guess that's only natural."

"They're somebody else's memories. I don't recognize that person. He's not a part of me anymore."

LUCIUS III

LUCIUS'S first campaign season was drawing near its end. The Romans' bloody advance into the mountains of Dacia had been countered with a series of hit-and-run actions as the Dacians tried to avoid a direct set piece battle with the Imperator's twelve legions. The Dacians used the terrain to their advantage. To counter it, Traianus and his legates sent out vexillations into the hills and forests to hunt down the Dacian raiders. Lucius and his century had been detached from their cohort and assigned to X Cohort, the second ranked cohort after the I.

"Fuckin' idiot kid tribune," Centurion Antoninus said. "Let himself get drawn into an engagement on ground they chose. Just because he's some senator's nephew, we're gonna get our asses killed."

"What can we do?" Optio Brabo replied. "Ours is not to reason why, ours is but to do and die."

"Shut it, Brabo. You've got a smart mouth, and it's getting on my nerves. We should have heard back from the messengers by now."

Cassius, standing in his usual place to Lucius's left, snorted. The centurion, not even bothering to turn all the way around, flicked his vine rod across the back of Cassius's legs, eliciting a yelp. Lucius did his best to keep the smirk off his face, not wanting to draw the centurion's ire or add insult to the injury of the man who'd become his closest friend since joining the legions. Cassius had trouble controlling his mouth, and Lucius liked to remind him how it always got him in trouble.

The optio had stepped out of their marching fort to consult with the centurion. While the other five cohorts had marched out with most of their cavalry and archer auxilia, the inexperienced I Century of the VI Cohort, the cohort made up of the best of the new recruits and younger legionnaires, had been left to guard the marching camp. Half of the century had been posted inside the fort while the other half stood in their open formation battle line, eight wide and five deep.

"Hades cursed, damn tribu—"

The centurion's vitriolic rant ended abruptly as a large arrow sprouted from the side of his head. Arrows plunged into the signifer and cornicen as well, sending them tumbling to the ground. Lucius ducked as a fourth arrow shattered against the side of the optio's helmet, spraying shards. The optio slumped to the ground. In a matter of seconds, the entire command structure of the century was down. That's when the arrows began raining thick. Staring at his fallen officers, Lucius snapped into action.

"Close ranks! Testudo formation to the front! Sego, get that signum off the ground," Lucius commanded in a hoarse bellow.

Sego dropped his scutum and dove to the ground, yanking their Centurial Signum out of the dirt. The half century, reacting to the command, collapsed their formation into close ranks as shields locked side by side, and the back rows lifted theirs to form a lid and cover the formation. The sound of arrows thudding into the leather covered wood of the scutums was accompanied by the occasional scream as iron arrowhead found flesh. Lucius peeked over the steel-rimmed edge of his shield, surveying the tree line to see where the attackers were coming from.

"Tighten up! Incoming arrows."

The legionnaires pulled in closer, ensuring there were as few gaps in their shield tortoise as possible. A roar of battle screams emerged from the tree line as a band of Dacians burst from the cover of the forest. Fearing hitting their own warriors in the back, the concealed archers halted their arrow flights.

"Front lines, open formation! Loose pila," yelled Lucius.

The first two lines broke out of the testudo wall they'd created and trotted forward, hurling their light-weight, longer-distance javelins into the oncoming crowd of Dacian warriors. The pila arced into the air and descended, forming a deadly rainbow. The javelins ended their flight meeting shield, armor, and flesh. When they met shield, the hard iron tip punched through seeking the flesh underneath while the softer iron of the shaft bent, rendering the pilum useless to throw back and making the shield an unusable dead weight. Where they met flesh, they felled the warrior, who in turn took down anyone failing to avoid their fallen comrade. Before the Dacians could recover, the first two lines of legionnaires sent their heavier-weighted pila soaring into their enemies. The Roman back lines were falling in behind the advanced lines and started sending up their lighter pila.

After sending his second pilum flying, Lucius yanked his gladius from its scabbard on his right hip and bellowed, "Charge!"

The Romans let loose their war cry as all down the line swords left sheaths and caligae-covered feet sprinted toward the advancing line of opposing warriors. The Dacians' line had become ragged as warriors were cut down by pila and those still alive broke rank. Their line was mixed between sword and shield wielding men and warriors wielding the deadly falx, which was most effective when wielded with all the power two arms could provide. As the lines drew near each other, the last of the unflung pila were cast aside and replaced with Roman gladii thirsting for Dacian blood.

The thunder of shield meeting shield rocked ears and sent birds flying from distant trees. Lucius deflected a falx before plunging his short sword into the exposed armpit of the Dacian facing him. With a rough twist, he yanked it free before sinking it into the gap between neck armor and helmet, slicing the arteries concealed within. He kicked the dying man off his sword and parried an incoming sword with a backhand slash. He swung around and caught a Dacian hard in the side with the edge of his scutum, sending him careening into the waiting sword of whoever had stepped up on Lucius's right side.

That enemy handled, Lucius raised his shield in time to catch a downward arcing falx. It tore into Lucius's scutum. Lucius gave his shield a hard twist, hoping to lodge the weapon in the compromised wood. It had the added benefit of pulling the warrior slightly off balance, preventing him from removing the falx and finishing the work he'd started. The two men were locked in a deadly dance as Lucius tried to keep the man from freeing his falx while bringing him close enough to get in a solid attack. A second Dacian rushed at Lucius, falx raised and poised to strike. Lucius yanked on the scutum, pulling the first Dacian off balance before shoving out with his shield with all his strength. The first Dacian, falx still wedged in Lucius's rapidly crumbling scutum, tipped back toward his oncoming comrade, tripping him up enough that he lost a lot of the power in his swing. The second Dacian missed his comrade but struck Lucius's shield, tearing another deep gouge into it.

Lucius's shield, held wide side up, was losing its structural integrity with two falxes stuck in it. Lucius slashed under the bottom edge of the scutum, hoping to make contact with flesh. He felt the slight tug as the tip bit into something as it passed by. A grunt from one of his opponents rewarded him as he dug his hob-nailed boots into the soil and tried to keep from being overwhelmed by the two enemy warriors.

"Lucius, knees, now!" came the cry from behind him.

He responded instantly, dropping to his knees and yanking the two warriors off balance. One fell within reach of his gladius as Lucius stabbed it hard into the face of the first warrior. Out of the corner of his eye, he saw the edge of a scutum fly over his head and punch into the face of the second Dacian0 who staggered back with a broken nose and probably more. A second scutum flew toward the first warrior, sending him falling away from Lucius. He used the opportunity to shove away his ruined shield, both falx still stuck in it. As he stood, he saw Cassius standing in front of him, a scutum in each hand, protecting his friend as he stood.

Cassius handed Lucius the shield in his right hand. "You looked like you might need a spare." Cassius pulled his gladius free of its scabbard. "What next?"

The line had advanced beyond them as they caught their breath in a small pocket of quiet. Lucius looked around. The meager forty legionnaires had opened their line trying to keep the more numerous Dacians from flanking them but were starting to lose the integrity of their battle line. The fighting was breaking up into pockets. Occasionally, an arrow would fly out from the woods, picking a safe target. The few Roman archers left with the camp were likewise seeking targets of opportunity from their vantage points on top of the fort's walls. Lucius gestured for Cassius to follow him as he broke into a trot. Seeing where Lucius was headed, Cassius caught up and flanked him to the right. Together, they began taking out Dacians engaged with their fellow legionnaires. With each one they freed, Lucius pulled into formation as they worked their way down the line. As they liberated more legionnaires, they gained more momentum and were starting to roll up the left flank of the Dacians.

Lucius and his legionnaires were running on pure adrenalin, pushed long past the point they'd have been relieved by a fresh line. As they puffed for air and slashed with gladii, the sound of the camp's gates banging open was followed by the harsh cry of twenty legionnaires charging out to join their comrades. They quickly flared into a charging battle line and hit the Dacians hard in their right flank. The engagement, which had been slowly tipping toward the Romans, turned into a full rout. Those Dacians who could disengaged and made a break for the tree line where their archers were providing cover fire to dissuade pursuit.

As the fresh troops put down the last few Dacians, Lucius propped his shield on the ground and leaned into it, catching his breath. Petrocles—a short, stout, and swarthy man of Athenian heritage—strode toward Lucius.

"Lucius!" Petrocles raised his right hand in greeting. "That was a bit touch and go there for a moment."

"For more than a moment..." Lucius replied, his breath slowing as his young body, drilled into excellent shape, recovered quickly.

"What's our next move?"

"Um, take twenty men and form a line parallel to the tree line the Dacians came from. Open formation. See if you can find a few pila. Stand plenty far from the tree line, but I want a deterrent to keep the Dacians from getting brave and falling on us again. I'll take the remaining men and sweep the field for survivors."

Cassius walked up to them, setting his shield down. "What about the Dacians?"

"Kill them. We don't have the numbers to deal with them, unless you find a cap-wearer in decent shape. A noble might be worth interrogating."

Cassius stood up and saluted Lucius like he was a superior officer —his right fist banging into the armor over his heart, followed by extending his arm with an open hand—before turning around and working his way through the bodies writhing on the ground. He wasn't sure if Cassius's salute was genuine or ironic; it was hard to tell with the sardonic expression Cassius always wore. He seemed more interested in dispatching the Dacians than checking on his comrades. Lucius left him to it. Someone had to do it.

Sego, squatting over a body, looked up and yelled toward Lucius. "Silvanius, the optio is still alive."

Lucius ran over and confirmed that Brabo was indeed still breathing. The arrow that shattered on his helm had knocked him unconscious. If he woke, he'd have a hell of a headache and some nasty bruising, which was already spreading across the right side of his face.

"Lucius, incoming!" Petrocles yelled.

The rider must have given Petrocles the proper pass code as he was waved through, one of Petrocles's legionnaires pointing to the group of people where Lucius stood. The rider, one of the auxilia cavalry that had marched out with the rest of the cohort, yanked the reins, forcing his mount to a sliding halt. He leapt to the ground and walked to the legionnaires clustered around the fallen command officers. Cassius sauntered over to join the group.

"Where's your centurio?" the rider asked.

Lucius pointed to the corpse with an arrow sticking out of its face below the rim of the helmet with the transverse crest that marked its owner as a centurion.

"Who's in charge then?" the rider asked.

Everyone looked around before Cassius, Sego, and a couple other men pointed at Lucius.

"I guess I am. Decanus Lucius Silvanius."

The rider looked around, his eyes drifting over the bodies of legionnaires on the ground. "Looks like you were hit pretty hard. How many can you field?"

Lucius looked at his people, doing some quick math in his head. "I think forty, maybe fifty. I've got twenty fresh men still in the fort. I'll pull them and leave some of the more ambulatory injured to take in the wounded and hold the fort."

"Gather them. The tribune led the cohort into a trap. Last I saw, they're boxed up and doing their best to hold off the Dacians," the horseman said.

"What about the reserve centuria they took with them?" Lucius asked.

"The Dacians split them off and likewise have them surrounded."

"Shit. Cassius, grab Petrocles. Sego, gather the men in the fort. Also, I'll want the cavalry and archer auxilia. Tell them to leave four horsemen and five archers to help with the wounded and hold the fort," Lucius ordered. "That'll give us seventeen riders, including you, twenty-five archers, and half a centuria, maybe more."

Lucius organized his force while servants brought water and dry rations for the legionnaires about to march out. The less wounded soldiers and servants began bringing in everyone who couldn't walk on their own. When all was said and done, there were few grievously injured and even fewer Romans dead. With his men watered and fed and armed with a fresh supply of pila, Lucius marched out his small relief force.

FOURTEEN

THEY PULLED the last box out of the bed of Pablo's truck and stacked it on one of the three hand trucks they'd brought with them. Pablo locked his pickup and followed Luke and Delilah up the path, each of them pushing a hand truck toward Hazelnut Grove. As they crested the gentle slope leading into the camp, Max strode purposefully toward them, concern and concentration written loudly across his face. Before Luke could even greet him, words tumbled out of Max's mouth.

"There's something you need to see. Set those down by my place; someone will take care of them." He turned and walked into the camp.

They followed Max to his mini house and stacked the goods against the wall, then followed him through the tents and mini houses toward the back of the camp. They climbed the grassy slope toward a more isolated tent standing alone under a Doug Fir tree.

As they walked, Max filled them in on the situation. "Last night, one of the residents was up late and walking around camp when they heard a scream toward the edge of the camp. When they got up here, they saw people moving up the hill. They weren't sure, but they thought they might be carrying something."

"Has anyone inspected the scene?" Luke asked.

"No. When they woke me up, I got the council to cordon off the area around the tent and tree. Since you were coming today, I thought you might want to inspect it. We organized a search and swept the hill but couldn't find anything." Max's brow furrowed.

"Did anyone call the police?" Delilah asked.

Max shook his head. "No. We don't want to involve the police in our community. Rarely does any good come from the police interacting with the disadvantaged in this city."

"OK. Everyone hang back a minute," Luke said.

Luke walked a circle around the tree and tent, bending over periodically to look at the ground, occasionally shifting aside a leaf or branch to peer under it. He made another pass in a tighter circumference, repeating his inspections. Finally, he walked up to the entrance flap of the tent, pulled his hand inside the sleeve of his black hoodie, gripped the zipper, and opened the flap. Before entering, he bent over, peeking into every corner of the tent he could see. Pulling his other hand inside its sleeve, he crawled into the pup tent.

"They slashed the back of the tent open along the ground. Shit. There's blood. It's not a lot, but is reasonably fresh."

He crawled back out and gestured for everyone to follow him. They stopped at the back of the tent. Luke bent over and stuck his hand, still covered in his sleeve, into the barely visible slice just above the seam next to the ground. The others squatted down to look inside.

"It looks like they sliced into the tent and dragged the person out. You can see they roughly stuffed the sleeping bag back in." He lifted a Doug Fir branch laying across the ground in the path from the slit. "The drag marks are visible here. They did a quick cover up, but not thorough."

He stood and walked up the hill, periodically squatting to inspect the marks on the ground, most of which showed obvious signs of half-assed efforts to conceal them. Needles or leaves had been hastily swept over the drag marks but left signs where they'd been moved. After about thirty feet, Luke stopped and turned toward Pablo, Delilah, and Max.

"They picked up the victim here. The drag marks stop, but the footprints are much deeper in the rain damp ground." Luke, Pablo, Delilah, and Max struggled as the ground got increasingly steep the closer to the top of the rise they got. "Looks like they slipped and dropped the victim a time or two before they crested here."

The four of them climbed over the ridge—Max sweating and puffing heavily, the others to a lesser degree—into a nicely manicured park next to a large parking lot. They followed the tracks to the edge of a parking lot next to a medical center. Pablo pointed down at a set of tread marks on the pavement.

"Looks like they peeled out. Must have been in a hurry. I'm guessing a larger truck or box van of some sort," Pablo said, staring at the two sets of side-by-side dual tire tracks.

"The marks could have been anyone, but they're right at the end of the footprints and perpendicular to the flow of traffic. You're probably right," Luke replied. "Max, is this the first disappearance since the last time we've talked?"

"Yes. Well, I'm not sure. This was the first obviously violent one. We've found some empty tents the last two mornings before this one, both along the edges of camp, but we haven't really looked into it. People come and go." Max shrugged.

"Do you think anyone saw your search party or the person who reported it?" Luke asked.

"Probably not the search party. It didn't take us long to get up here, and we were walking. If they did have a truck, they'd have been gone before we even assembled the search party. Who knows about the witness?" He shrugged. "He doesn't think they saw him."

The corners of Luke's lips tipped downward as his brows furrowed. "OK. Can you show me the other tents?"

"Sure? But can we walk down Interstate? I'm not sure I want to scramble down that hill. A sidewalk sounds like a better idea."

Luke smiled. "No problem, Max."

They turned onto the sidewalk leading out of the park toward Interstate Avenue.

"Luke, what's going on? Who's doing this?" Max asked.

"That's a lot to explain, but suffice to say, some very bad people who intend nothing good. I have a feeling your uninvited guests might be back tonight."

Max's eyes widened as he hung his head and shook it, sighing.

"I have an idea. Can I borrow some of that gear you're storing? A tent, sleeping bag, a few other appropriate things to set up a new camp? I can pay for anything that gets damaged," Luke said.

Max nodded, thinking. "I think I understand what you're planning. I'll have to run it by the council, but I'm pretty sure it'll fly."

LUKE YAWNED, bored with laying still pretending to sleep. The ground underneath him was lumpy and cold. Somehow, despite wearing armor, the lumps and rocks where he'd pitched the tent Max had lent him dug into his back. His breath fogged above him in the cold autumn air. He tried to keep the yawn as silent as possible while maintaining the illusion of sleep. It was well after midnight; the MAX light rail had stopped running a while ago. The sound of the camp had quieted to nothing. Only the occasional car separating from the constant traffic noise of I-5 and exiting onto Greeley Avenue added variation to the sounds of the city at sleep.

Luke hoped he wasn't wrong and that the vampires would be back to separate another sheep from the herd they'd been preying on. The irony of the image of a wolf preying on sheep caused him to chuckle silently since a real werewolf hid not far away.

"Zero-one-hundred hours, all clear," came Pablo's whispered time check through the earpiece attached to the FRS radios Luke had picked up a few days ago. He'd figured they'd be useful at some point now that he was working with other people. They couldn't always be on top of each other and might need to coordinate over a short distance. The compact but powerful personal radios would do the trick. Tonight was their first live run. Luke keyed the button on his radio to indicate he'd heard.

The snap of a branch preceded the sound of someone tripping, which elicited a muffled, "Fuck!"

Luke, adrenaline pumping, maintained a steady sleep-like

breathing rhythm, sliding his hand slowly and silently along the bottom of the tent until his fingers grasped the hilt of his gladius, blade naked and ready for action. Feet shuffling across fir needles and dried leaves alerted him to the proximity of predatory vampires approaching. What little light there was cast shadows as a trio of bodies loomed over the small tent.

"They keep setting up right out in the open. This is too easy."

"Shhh," another voice said.

The next sound Luke heard was a knife stabbing into the back right corner of the tent, slicing gently and slowly along the bottom. The blade briefly whispered along his hair, a finger's breadth from his scalp, as it continued its journey to the other corner of the tent. Hands slid into the tent and worked their way under Luke's shoulders. Pulling back, the vampire was barely able to budge him.

"Damn. This one's heavy."

Two more sets of hands slid into the tent, one on each side. With the three of them gripping Luke's shoulders, they slid him out the back of the tent until the cut fabric of the tent bisected him just below his ribcage, his hands still hidden inside the tent. Luke's eyes opened slowly, feigning grogginess.

"He's awake. Dazzle him with your glamourous self and let's get out of here," the vampire to the left said. The middle vampire made eye contact with Luke and poured forth his magic. Luke responded with a wink before whipping his right hand up, the tip of the gladius slicing out of the tent, followed by the rest of the sword. The vampire's eyes flashed open in surprise as he tried to pull away. Unfortunately for the fanger, pulling back opened up the vampire's chest perfectly. Luke plunged the gladius through the vampire's ribs and into his heart.

The vampire exploded into a torrent of goo and landed all over Luke's head and torso with a giant splat, his gladius tangling in the vampire's jacket. The other two had fallen on their asses and were scrambling away from Luke as he extricated himself from the ruined tent while sliding in the sludge of his victim.

"I'm coming, buddy," Pablo said through the earpiece.

Luke finally got his left hand free and swiped as much of the vampire's remains out of his eyes and off his face as he could. He rolled to his stomach and managed to almost get up before one of his feet slipped in the spreading slick that was his attempted kidnapper. He crawled out of the vamp puddle and got to his feet. Two vampires were sprinting up the hill as fast as they could. Their panicked desire to flee caused them to slip and fall a few times on the wet grass. Luke sprinted after them, careful to avoid another fall.

A blur of motion to his left became Pablo as he burst through the trees after the vampires. He kept to their left while Luke stayed on their right, trying to keep them from splitting up. The vampires reached the top of the hill and leapt through the hedges bordering the parking lot. One made it through a gap in the barrier while the other missed its mark, tripping over the metal fence and tipping ass over teakettle onto the ground. He scrambled to his feet and dashed after his friend, sprinting with all his vampire speed to catch up. Luke made for the gap the first vampire had leapt through while Pablo solved the fence problem by simply leaping over the hedges and the barrier, landing gracefully to continue pelting after their quarry.

The vampires made straight for an open box van and tumbled into the back, shouting, "GO, GO, GO!" The van peeled out, fish-tailing as they hauled ass out of the parking lot. Pablo's black Toyota screeched to a halt where the box van had just been. The passenger door popped open, then the back door behind it. Pablo jumped into the front seat as Luke dove into the back; Delilah mashed the gas pedal and tore after the vampires. Luke scrambled upright and reached out to slam his door as they caught up to the van.

The van flew out onto Interstate Avenue, launching onto the curb blocking the light rail tracks. It bounced violently over the tracks, taking out one of the signs between the south and northbound rails and spraying gravel behind them. The headlights from the pickup lit the inside of the box, illuminating the vampires clinging desperately to the bars of a cage inside the cargo bay and struggling to stay upright. One of the vamps lost his grip and tumbled toward the open door of the box. The other vampire grabbed a chain that was attached to the bar and dove after his companion, catching him with one hand as the van flopped off the other curb and swerved onto northbound Interstate Avenue.

"Oh, shit..." Pablo called as Delilah wrenched the wheel over, tires screaming as she turned the truck north into the southbound lane.

"Fuck, fuck, fuck," chanted Delilah.

Everyone saw why as a set of headlights bore down on them. The semi-truck blasted its air horn at them. Delilah slammed her foot down on the gas and whipped to the right into the intersection just as the semi ripped past them. She settled Pablo's pickup into the north-bound lane, releasing an audible sigh of relief. Pablo muttered something in a language Luke didn't know.

"That was some fancy driving," Luke commented.

"Yeah, not sure I want to do that again anytime soon," Delilah replied, trying to calm her breathing. She edged her speed up a bit to gain some ground on the van. "I just hope there aren't any cops looking for someone to pull over. I might have to run some lights, so you two keep an eye out for cross traffic."

"Oh, man! Just don't hurt my baby! I haven't had this truck that long," Pablo pleaded.

Delilah sped up Interstate. The roads were practically devoid of traffic this late at night. Most of the bars were closed, and people were safely tucked in bed. Luke hoped they didn't run into any trouble around the late closing bars.

"Crap! The Alibi just closed," Pablo called, pointing to a brightly lit building with a giant lighted "ALIBI" sign and numerous Tiki decorations. A sizable crowd of drunk karaoke singers spilled out onto the street and started crossing. The van gunned it and laid on the horn before blasting through the red light. People scrambled out of the way. One poor sucker didn't make it quite in time, the passenger side mirror punching into his back and spinning him into a car parked on the side of the road. The mirror crumpled, glass exploding from its frame, and dangled on the door, flapping in the wind of the van's slipstream. People yelled at the van, gesturing rudely and shaking fists after it. Several people were standing in the middle of the road flipping the bird toward the back of the van's now shut roll-down door. A few people took out phones and tried to get pictures of the van disappearing in the darkness.

Delilah locked up the brakes, throwing everyone forward in the cab as the wheels screeched and smoked. The pickup came to a stop in the middle of the intersection just short of the crowd in the crosswalk. The bar patrons scrambled out of the way as Delilah smashed her palm into the center of the steering wheel, blaring the horn and revving the engine. The pedestrians got the hint as Delilah floored the gas pedal and sped after the van. They caught the brake lights ahead as the van slowed to pull off Interstate onto North Maryland.

"They're heading toward the freeway!" Pablo yelled, pointing.

"I don't know what that means, Pablo. Remember, New York. Not from here," Delilah replied, sounding slightly panicked.

"Follow them. You've got about three blocks then a hard right onto Going Street toward the freeway on-ramps. Southbound is the right lane and is a reasonably gentle straight down. The left lane is a tight clover loop to the right."

"Pablo, can you turn the lights off on this thing or are they automatic?" Luke asked.

"They'll turn off."

"Delilah, turn the lights off. Let's see if we can sneak up on them. They may slow down thinking they lost us in that crowd."

"O-O-OK..." Delilah nodded nervously.

Luke reached up and patted her on the shoulder. "You're doing great, Delilah. One might think this wasn't your first car chase."

"Well, it is," she replied tersely. "Now stop distracting me."

She flipped the lights off and turned off Interstate just as the brake lights of the van flared on and the van took the anticipated right turn toward the on ramps. Delilah accelerated, trying to make up a bit of distance. She flew through the abandoned intersections and slowed just enough to take the right onto North Going Street. She'd caught up just enough to see the last edge of the van's right rear brake light turning onto the southbound on-ramp. She goosed the gas pedal to eat up a bit more distance as she took the right turn toward I-5 and I-405 South.

"Let's get those lights back on before we merge onto the freeway," Pablo said.

Nodding, Delilah turned on the headlights. Even that late at night—or that early in the morning, depending on how one wanted to look at it—there was traffic. Fortunately, the van had pulled into a traffic lull, making it easy to spot its next move; it stayed in the right lane that would lead it up the split to I-405. As the van pulled onto the Fremont Bridge, it joined traffic coming from northbound I-5, weaving around cars before pulling in front of a semi-truck with a box trailer and settling into the flow of traffic.

Delilah pulled into traffic. She deliberately worked her way forward, keeping an eye on the van. She eventually settled in behind a car that was holding steady next to a semi-truck. They kept up that pace until the semi took the exit for Highway 26. The car they were following pulled behind the vampmobile, so Delilah eased the pickup behind it, leaving enough space to avoid tailgating and to have room to maneuver if she needed it. So far, it appeared the vampires hadn't noticed them, staying in their lane and traveling with the flow of traffic.

They followed for several minutes, keeping their distance as the van wove through traffic, trying to move quickly but escape notice.

"Looks like he's signaling to turn onto the exit to I-5 south," commented Pablo.

Delilah pulled in behind another pickup in the I-5 south exit. The pickup in front of them was tailgating the vampmobile when it jammed on its brakes, causing its tailgater to reciprocate before swerving off to the right where a car smashed into its rear-end. Taking advantage of the mayhem, the van pelted across the lines, narrowly missing the divider and oncoming traffic onto the I-5 North ramp. Delilah flipped on the turn signal and got over before it was too late.

"Looks like they made us," Luke chimed in from the backseat.

"Ya think?" Delilah replied. "Well, no need to be subtle..."

Delilah sped up, weaving around traffic to catch up to the speeding van. With each oncoming exit, they panicked that the van would make more erratic decisions and endanger more civilians.

However, the vampires seemed to have given up subterfuge and were using whatever speed they could muster out of the beat-up delivery van. Fortunately for the vampires, the engine was designed to carry a heavy payload, not the few humans and vampires they had stashed in the back, so they had plenty of power to spare. Delilah matched suit with Pablo's new pickup and its powerful engine.

They cruised up I-5 north, returning to north Portland. They passed the Rosa Parks exit. A car was accelerating down the next on-ramp when the van swerved to the right clipping the car's bumper and sending it careening into the concrete barrier where it bounced off with a deafening screech of metal on concrete and spun out of control back into traffic. Delilah, almost preternaturally, jammed on the brakes, keeping the truck safely in its lane, narrowly missing the car as it spun in front of them. Delilah used the speed dump to safely get in the exit lane to follow the van as it ripped up the off-ramp to eastbound Lombard Avenue. At the top of the exit, the vampires sped into traffic in a huge, barely controlled arc that sent them into the oncoming lane where they nearly ran headlong into an approaching car. The vampires swerved back into their lane and gunned it. Delilah took a more controlled approach and was soon gaining on them.

Delilah, Luke, and Pablo flew through the red light at the Vancouver intersection and burned down the road, dodging the few cars that were out at that time of night. The van ran the red light at MLK. As the cars locked their brakes to avoid the van, one didn't stop in time and rammed into the rear end of another vehicle. Delilah, using some sharp driving to avoid getting tangled in the mess the van had made, cleared the intersection without causing more chaos.

"You can open it up some. There's only one light coming up, but there won't be any traffic out here this time of night. It'll be green," Luke said.

They pulled around the gradual curve and saw the green light in front of them. The van barreled east down Lombard in the right lane, then jammed on the brakes and took a hard left at the light.

"Holy shit! They're going to try to beat the train!" Pablo yelled.

The red lights at the intersection were flashing as the crossing arms lowered to block the street. The freight train chugged along at a steady pace. It didn't look like the van was going to make it. It slammed into the first arm, sending it splintering into the air, bounced across the rails, and smashed through the second arm as the train flew past, blasting its air horn and cutting off their pursuit. Delilah locked up the brakes sending the smell of burnt rubber and the sound of screeching tires into the air. The speeding freight train blocked all hope of seeing where the van was headed next.

She slammed her hands onto the steering wheel, cursing under her breath. She pulled off Lombard onto NE 11th and parked. "Now what?"

Pablo and Luke looked at each and shrugged.

"Tonight's score—Fangers: one. Us: zero," Luke said.

"Beers?" Pablo asked.

"Beers," Luke agreed, quelling the rising bitterness that accompanied yet another failure.

FIFTEEN

LUKE WOKE up and checked his phone. He had a text, something that was becoming a regular occurrence now that Pablo and Delilah were becoming fixtures in his life.

Got you a hair appointment with my friend's stylist. 12pm. Bring coffees. Soy Latte and a nonfat Mocha.

He brought up the attached address. It was up on Alberta Avenue; it'd take him about twenty minutes to get there. He had just enough time to shower and grab the coffees and a scone to break his fast.

The tinkling of a bell announced his presence as he walked into the salon. Spying Delilah sitting next to a salon chair, he walked over. He set the cardboard coffee carrier down and handed the Mocha to Delilah. He pulled out his triple shot Americano and left the Soy Latte for the stylist.

"Thanks, Luke. I needed a little pick-me-up," she said as she took a drink. "Ananya will be out shortly."

Luke sat down next to Delilah. It was only a moment before a plump brown woman of medium height in a black smock emerged from the back room. Her black hair swept down just below her ear on the right side while the other side was buzzed, leaving just enough length to contrast with the intricate design shaved into it.

"You must be Luke. I'm Ananya. Have a seat, please."

She picked up her latte and assessed Luke's hair. "I see what you mean. He could use an updated cut." She took a drink. "So, Luke, Delilah says you can't have any input, and you're to trust me. That work for you?"

"Let's do what the lady says."

Ananya set the coffee down and went to work, sending long hunks of hair flying. Once she'd thinned the top out enough, she broke out the clippers and shaved the sides and back before finishing styling the top. When she determined his hair was done, she shortened and shaped his beard. After giving him a rinse and adding some product to his hair, she revealed her work.

Luke's hair was swept forward with gentle curls sticking up artfully in places. The gray at his temples gave a nice salt and pepper effect. His beard was shorter and neater.

He moved his head to different angles so he could look at his new cut. "This looks really good! I like it."

"Excellent! I'm glad to hear it." Ananya smiled.

"I'll take a tube of that gel, too. If I'm going to pay for a new style, might as well put the effort into keeping it going." He paid for everything, leaving a generous tip for Ananya's efforts, and grabbed a business card so he could get an appointment for his next cut.

"Thanks, Ananya," said Delilah.

"It was nice to meet you, Delilah. Say 'hi' to Clarvetta for me!"

Delilah nodded and waved. Looking at Luke, she said, "Next stop, new threads!"

LUKE STOOD at his front window, watching finches flit about on the bird feeders hanging from the large Japanese maple that dominated his front yard. The sound of a closing car door drew his attention to Delilah striding up the sidewalk to his front door. Before she could knock, he opened the door and invited her in.

"Hey, Delilah. Thanks for meeting me here. Mind helping with a few boxes? We'll load up and then go pick up Pablo." Luke bent over and picked up a large box.

"What are these?" asked Delilah. She grabbed the other box and followed Luke out, putting the box in the back of his Volvo wagon.

"A little project I've been working on for the last several days. After we grab Pablo, we'll head up to Hazelnut Grove."

"Mind if we get a coffee on the way? Mama needs caffeine." Delilah yawned.

"Sure, my regular shop is on the way," Luke replied.

Standing on Pablo and Tony's porch, coffees in hand, Luke rang the doorbell while Delilah sipped her nonfat mocha. After a few moments, Tony opened the door and invited them in.

"Hey, Tony!" Luke said.

"Hi Luke, Delilah. Come in."

"Is Pablo ready?"

"Not yet; he's upstairs changing. Something about a new outfit. I'll run up and check on him." Tony disappeared upstairs.

Luke addressed Delilah, "Your talk of new clothes for me got Pablo in the mood, too."

"I guess. He's a pretty solid dresser, though," Delilah replied.

They waited in the entryway, drinking their coffees. A door slammed, followed by Tony storming down the stairs. His eye catching on Luke, he stalked over and pointed a finger at him.

"I put this nonsense on you! When he said he wanted to help you chase down vampires, I went along with it because he needed a friend and a hobby outside the pack and, for whatever reason, you're it. But this is too far!" He spun around and walked across the room, leaning up against the wall.

A moment later, Pablo came bounding down the stairs. Instead of his usual dark jeans and T-shirt, he was wearing what looked like a basketball warm up suit in the signature black and red of the Portland Trail Blazers. Pablo, grinning broadly, stopped in the middle of the room, arms extended out from this torso, and spun slowly, showing off his outfit.

Luke looked Pablo up and down. "That's not too bad, Tony. He kinda looks like a bench warmer for the Blazers."

"That's not the worst of it," Tony replied.

Pablo turned and faced Tony. "What? You didn't want me coming home with any more ruined clothes. I came up with a solution." He bent over, grabbing the seams at his thighs and ripped the pants forward. Popping snaps filled the room like firecrackers going off. Pablo wasn't wearing any underwear.

Next to Luke, Delilah was struggling valiantly to keep her laughter in, snorts and snickers escaping from her nose as she tried to keep her lips tightly clamped. Pablo stood there, pants in one hand and his light brown butt hanging out from under his matching long-sleeved top.

"See, Tony..." He gestured with the split open pants. "They rip right off, and all I have to do is button them back up when I'm done. No more ruined clothes. Besides, the shorts took too long to take off, and the weather is getting colder."

Tony's lips were tightly pursed as he shook his head in disgust at Pablo's outfit. Pablo turned to face Luke and Delilah.

"Uh, your twig and giggleberries are hanging out..." Luke trailed off awkwardly.

At that point, Delilah lost what little composure she had left and slid down the wall behind her, laughing uproariously.

"Well, it wouldn't be a very good solution if I had to stop and take off my undies before transforming. This way it's rip and roar." He nodded his head, a smug look on his face, giving them the visage version of finger guns—a cheesy grin and waggly eyebrows.

"Oh, god. You've been waiting to use that line, haven't you?" Tony asked. He exhaled with an "ugh," shook his head, and disappeared into the kitchen.

Delilah was struggling to catch her breath as she slapped her thigh, laughing uncontrollably.

"Hey, I like the new haircut, Luke." Pablo gave Luke a complete once over.

Luke shifted in his dark-wash, designer skinny jeans, tight black t-shirt, and stylish jacket Delilah had helped him pick out after his haircut, one of the many, many outfits he'd assembled with her aid.

"Damn, buddy! Looking good." Pablo nodded in approval.

"Thanks. You, uh, ready to go?"

"Gotta snap my pants back on, unless you want my bare ass riding shotgun." By way of emphasis, he moved his hips back and forth, pantomiming rubbing his ass on Luke's car seats.

Delilah, inhaling a huge gasp of air, let out another gleeful cackle.

"HEY, Max. I got a present for you!" Luke called as they walked up to where Max was sitting at a table talking with a couple people.

"Oh, hey, Luke. This is Pam and Jim; they're part of the camp's council. This is Luke and his friends Delilah and Pablo."

Luke, Pablo, and Delilah sat down. "I've been trying to come up with a way to keep in better communication." Luke opened the backpack he'd filled from the boxes in the car and pulled out a cell phone and a small plastic box with a solar panel built into the top. He set them in front of Max. "I've programmed my number in here. It's activated and charged up. If you need to recharge it, just plug it into the solar charger."

The Hazel Grove residents looked over the phone and solar charger.

"There's not a lot going on with the phone, but it's the best I can come up with for now. It'll at least let you get a hold of me if something bad is going down." Luke shrugged.

Max nodded. "Thanks, Luke. This is thoughtful."

"I do have a favor to ask. How well do you know the people at some of the other camps? I haven't had time to introduce myself anywhere else," Luke said.

"We try to keep communication open with most of the other larger, more-permanent camps. Between the three of us, we probably know most of the key people. What do you have in mind?" Max asked.

"I have several more setups like this," he said, showing the phone and solar charger. "But I need someone to make introductions to the right people. I'm pretty sure Hazelnut Grove isn't the only place with missing people. When we chased that van out of here the other night, they already had people in cages in the back of their van. This wasn't their first stop of the night."

"Who would do this?" Pam asked. "People are getting scared."

"Some very bad people. They like to exploit marginalized communities for their own gain. I've encountered them before. This is more organized than I've seen in a long while, though."

"But who are they? Why can't we go to the police?" Pam frowned, her brows pinched together in worry.

"You should report anyone missing to the police. It never hurts to have eyes out for those in need. The police, however, aren't equipped to deal with these people. I've been tracking and dealing with this group for a long time. Unfortunately, they've gotten a little too estab-lished in Portland, and I'm forced to react until I can get ahead of them. We almost had them the other night, but they got away. I'm hoping by setting up a network of eyes, you can help me stop them before any more people go missing."

Pam and Jim made eye contact. Something passed between them. They turned to Max and nodded, indicating they were on board with the plan. Max turned to Luke.

"OK. Let's start with the camps in North Portland." He stood and grabbed the phone. "I'll program numbers in as we go."

"Pam, Jim, it was nice to meet you. Thanks for helping," Luke said.

"We're just looking out for our community. I hope this works," Pam said.

SIXTEEN

LUKE, Delilah, and Pablo sped down I-5 in Luke's Volvo, well, as much as an old Volvo wagon can speed. A camp in southeast Portland had reported sightings of strange people lurking in the evenings, along with a few of the outer tents being slashed. Fortunately, no one had been abducted. The camp was on the alert thanks to Luke's and Max's efforts. The camp had started patrolling at night, successfully, it seemed. After several nights in a row of apparent vampire activity at the camp, Luke wanted to see if he could lay another trap.

"The app says I-5 to I-84 to I-205 to Powell Boulevard east. No traffic," Delilah instructed.

"That's the nice thing about vampires. They tend to come out during the low traffic times of the day," Luke replied.

"Mighty thoughtful of them," Pablo quipped.

"This is a long ass haul, though. It seems way out of their usual range," Delilah said.

"Maybe we're forcing them further out as we lock down the central part of Portland?" Pablo looked hopeful.

"Maybe…" Luke said. He'd like to think that was the case, but they'd been one step behind the vampires the entire time, probably more. It just didn't feel right, and that made him even more anxious.

"Delilah, can you text the Johnson Creek camp and let them know we're on the way? Rosario is the contact there. Also, tell them to keep their patrol up for now."

"Sure thing."

Listening to Fleetwood Mac's "Landslide" on the radio, they sat in silence as Luke navigated them through Portland as quickly as he could without drawing attention to themselves.

"Damn, this is way the hell out here," Delilah said as she popped open the door and stepped out.

They'd parked alongside the street a little way out from the camp. Pablo helped Luke on with his gear while Delilah let Rosario know they'd arrived.

"OK. They know we're here," Delilah said.

Luke zipped up the oversized hoodie over his armor. "Let's head out. We should do a radio check before we go silent."

They keyed in their FRS radios and ensured they were all on the same channel.

"You all know the plan. Don't drift too far, though. These hills and trees will cut down on the radios' range. I don't want anyone getting in trouble and not being able to call for help."

Pablo and Delilah acknowledged Luke's instructions with nods.

"Make sure your cell phones are on do not disturb. Leave them in your pockets. The screen light could give away your position, plus it'll mess with your night vision. The jog to get into place should give your eyes plenty of time to adjust. Let's keep quiet from here on out."

They followed Luke as he jogged up the bike path that would lead them into the Johnson Creek area just east of Powell Butte Nature Park. The sound of Johnson Creek gurgling beside the trail was a pleasant accompaniment to what promised to be an unpleasant evening. They'd caught a break in the usual fall rain and had a clear night and a nearly full moon to work with, but the thick, angry looking clouds to the west promised only a short reprieve before the rain came back with a vengeance.

Luke halted along the path, allowing Delilah and Pablo to catch their breath. He gave them each a questioning look. They nodded their readiness . Delilah opened the backpack she'd been carrying and withdrew a belt with loops loaded with wooden stakes. She strapped the belt around her waist. Next, she pulled out a machete in a black canvas sheath. She hooked it to her belt and snapped the nylon strap at the tip of the scabbard around her thigh. She grabbed the hilt and pulled the blade a few inches from its scabbard to loosen it. The blade was made from black steel with a glint of silver along its slashing edge.

Luke raised his eyebrows and tilted his head at the new addition of the machete. Delilah shrugged and winked. Pablo chuckled silently and shook his head. Reaching back, Luke slid his gladius out of its scabbard. They split up, Pablo to the right, Delilah to the left, Luke straight down the middle. The wooded hill separating them from the camp would work perfectly to screen their advance so they could approach the vampires in secret. After their earlier text, the camp had pulled back their patrol, leaving a few outlying tents tantalizingly unprotected. Luke hoped the vampires would try to take the bait.

Pablo, an experienced wolf, slid into the dark, disappearing silently; city-raised Delilah wasn't doing as well. Eventually, she got the knack, and Luke stopped hearing the crack of twigs and rustle of leaves. He needed to hold back a bit longer to give them time to advance into position. After he'd counted to one hundred, he started his advance up the hill, a wraith stalking its prey. Once he crested the hill, he worked his way down until he was a few trees back from the tree line. He posted up behind a particularly large Douglas Fir and clicked the radio button once, sending a brief bite of static into his earpiece. Three answering pops indicated Pablo had reached his position. Delilah didn't respond.

Luke counted one hundred again and gave the radio another pop. Pablo replied immediately with three pops. Again, no Delilah. Luke was getting worried. He was up to fifty on his next count when two pops of static halted his counting. He replied with a pop from his radio. Pablo replied with three and Delilah's repeated two clicks of static confirmed she was in position. He crept up to the tree line, darting behind another sizable tree, and peeked out. Focusing in, he saw a couple bodies moving slowly through the tall grass, occasionally popping a head up to look around. Vampires. They'd set off Luke's vampy senses.

He hoped they'd keep their attention on the camp and not pick up the danger to their rear. He figured Delilah had had enough time to catch her breath, so he keyed in the signal for the next advance — one long static burst. The two and three pops back indicated order received and acknowledged. Luke smiled, proud that his team was starting to gel. They hadn't been working together long, but they were already starting to anticipate each other. If he could get them through this alive, he had high hopes for their continued development.

Luke ducked out from behind his tree and entered the tall grass that separated the tree line from the back side of the camp. Moving at a quick jog while crouching and keeping a low profile, he'd periodically stop and raise his head above the grass, checking the position of the vampires. He chuckled as he mirrored the fanger's earlier actions. He also saw Pablo and Delilah coming in from their respective sides. If everything kept going as planned, they'd cut off the vampire's incursion into the camp and force them back toward Luke.

Luke advanced, anticipation of the imminent fight and the chance to strike back at the fangers bubbling up. He didn't see the trip wire until it was too late, and he pitched face forward into the ground. A bell rang, breaking the night's silence. The vampires jumped out, spied Delilah and Pablo closing in, abandoned subterfuge, and took off in a mad dash. Cursing, Luke disentangled himself from the tripwire and burst into a sprint as soon as he got standing. Delilah and Pablo were doing their best to keep up with the vampires.

Luke flew out of the grass into the camp, jumping over obstacles strewn about on the ground. People were sticking their heads out of their tents to see what the commotion was as five people hurtled through their camp. Once they emerged on the other side and onto the bike path, the vampires turned toward the main road. Using the unobstructed pavement to its full advantage, Luke poured on more speed. He was starting to catch up to Delilah, Pablo had raced ahead to keep up with the runners, when Luke caught movement in the grass off to his right. Three vampires ran toward him, trying to get behind Luke's small team. Screams from the camp alerted Luke to another problem. He skidded to a halt as two vampires violently shoved their way through the crowd of camp residents that had gathered to see what was going on.

"Shit. This isn't good," he said to himself. He keyed the talk button on his radio. "Delilah. Stop. Vampires behind us. Come back to me. Pablo, keep on the first two. You're on your own for now."

He heard Delilah's feet slapping on the pavement as she ran up behind and stopped abruptly, breathing heavily.

"Damn," she huffed, holding an arm across her chest, "I need a better sports bra. All this running is about to bounce my damned tiddies off."

Luke didn't acknowledge the comment. He was tracking the five incoming vampires as they fanned out to surround him and Delilah.

"Delilah, get that machete out. You're going to need it." He turned toward her while keeping an eye out around him. "We're going to keep moving away from the camp. Let's make a light jog down the path. There's five of them. If they start coming in on your side, shout out; we'll stop and go back-to-back until we can break free. I want to keep behind Pablo in case they've got more waiting ahead."

Delilah nodded and pulled the machete from the scabbard strapped to her thigh. She jogged down the path. Luke caught up to her and paced her on her right side. "You watch the left. I'll take the right."

They ran along, watching the vampires that seemed to be keeping their distance, biding their time.

"Stop!" Delilah cried out. Two of the vampires from the back were moving up on them. They'd produced weapons from somewhere. One had a short knife while the "L" shape the other one had looked like a tire iron. Luke brandished his sword and stalked toward them. Delilah kept pace with him, watching his back. The vamps thought better of it and returned to their previous positions. Using the temporary distraction, the two lead vampires had moved ahead. Delilah and Luke were caught in a circle of fangs.

Delilah slid a stake out of its loop with her left hand. Luke freed his rudis from its scabbard as they went back-to-back. Between them, they presented a wall of sharpened steel and jagged wood that should give the vampires pause. Vampires, especially newly turned ones, often became infatuated with their immortality and were very cautious about putting it on the line. Luke hoped the huge number of vampires he'd staked recently would add an extra sense of trepidation to this lot's attacks. A moment's hesitation on their part would give Luke all the advantage he needed to send them permanently on their way.

"Just like we've trained. Engage the group, not an individual. Keep them off you and take advantage of their mistakes."

"Uh huh," Delilah replied.

Luke swept his eyes over the vampires within his range, keeping a close watch on their eyes; it was always the eyes that gave away an inexperienced fighter about to launch an attack.

"Ah, shit! Two more coming up on my side," Delilah called.

"Same deal. They can't all attack at once, they'll be more likely to trip each other up." Luke could tell Delilah was extremely nervous as her voice rose and her head swiveled around, trying to keep everything in sight.

This was the first larger group they'd come on since she and Pablo saved him from the ambush on the pedestrian bridge. With the few smaller groups they'd encountered since, they'd pursued the vampires and been in charge of the engagements. Luke was sure Delilah would handle her own end as long as she didn't get too far into her head.

Luke watched as the vampires looked at their comrades, trying to figure out who'd go first. Eventually a decision was made, and the vampire directly in front of him widened his eyes and took several deep breaths. On his last exhalation, he let out a less than confident shout and charged.

"One incoming," Luke said.

"Two here," Delilah replied.

The vampire running at Luke was coming in fast and out of control. Luke sidestepped just enough to miss his wild swing, put a shoulder into the vamp to deflect him away from Delilah, and followed with a slice to his back, sending him sprawling to the ground.

Delilah kept her back aligned with Luke and waved her machete through a series of defensive forms to give pause to the two stalking in closer.

"Delilah, rotate." They rotated around so Luke faced the two fangers who'd been coming up on Delilah. The one closest to the first failed attacker glanced down at her friend writhing on the ground with a giant, oozing slash across his back. She moved away while her co-attacker came in with a branch he'd snagged off the ground. Luke backhanded it with his gladius, knocking it aside, then followed through with the rudis directly into his sternum. The vamp dropped the limb, grasped at the hole in his chest, and collapsed to the ground in a shrieking heap. The female vampire crept away, joining her friends in the outer circle.

Turning slightly, Luke quietly said, "Stay there, be right back."

"K."

Making eye contact with the nearest vampires, he poured all the contempt he held for their kind into his gaze as he walked up confidently to the downed vampire that was trying to crawl out of the killing zone. Luke placed a boot firmly on the vampire's ass and plunged his rudis down into its ribcage and into its heart. The vampire ceased moving. Keeping eye contact with the vampires that were shifting their eyes to their former companion—currently turning to goo—and back to Luke, he reversed until he was once again back-to-back with Delilah.

"Delilah, I want to see if we can get the group moving toward Pablo. Let's start jogging down the path," Luke said quietly.

"Got it."

They shuffled down the path, moving on the two vampires that were blocking the path Pablo had disappeared down a few minutes ago. Instead of engaging, the vampires retreated, not turning away from Luke and Delilah.

"Now!" Luke shouted.

He and Delilah charged the fangers in front of them. One turned and ran away while the other ran smack into the waist-high pole that blocked larger vehicles from entering the path and fell over back-wards across it. Delilah darted to the side and plunged the wooden stake into its chest, then jumped back onto the path next to Luke. She fumbled at her belt, trying to grab a new stake, and dropped one before securing another stake in her left fist.

Three static pops filled Luke's and Delilah's earpieces followed by another two in quick succession. They skidded to a halt where the path met the parking lot and went back-to-back. Luke glanced around but didn't see Pablo, so he returned his attention to the four remaining vampires, knowing Pablo was nearby.

Luke smiled at the vampire blocking the way off the bike path as Pablo, sneaking out of the bushes, ended the vampire's blood sucking career with a jagged branch through his chest.

"Go, now!" Luke called.

Delilah charged the vampire to her left, catching the fanger completely off-guard as she stared at her friend who'd just sprouted a tree limb from his ribcage. Delilah raked her machete across the vampire's face, plowed into her with her shoulder, knocking her to the ground, then finished with a stake to the chest. Luke aimed for the vampire on his left, sweeping his leg out from under him with a vicious slice from the gladius. He rotated and plunged the rudis into the vamp's heart before it hit the ground. The last vampire broke and sprinted back toward the camp as fast as his vampire legs could carry him. Luke wiped off his swords on the T-shirt of vampire that had dusted out instead of turning to goo before turning to Pablo, who was limping a bit.

"Should we follow him?" Delilah asked.

"Let's head back to the camp in case he tries to cause in mischief. As fast as he's going, we won't catch him. He's probably looking to escape," Luke replied. He turned to Pablo. "You OK, dude?"

"Yeah, assholes got away. Got into their van and hauled ass out of here. I tried to jump on the back but bounced off. They dragged me for a bit. Got some road rash." He turned to show Luke where his button-seamed warm-up pants were shredded, along with the bloody scrapes under it. His enhanced werewolf healing was pushing out the bits of gravel that had embedded in his skin.

"Oof, so much for not going home in shredded clothes," Luke said as Delilah cringed. "Did you get the tracker on the van?"

"Yeah, that's how I got the road rash. I was dangling from the bumper like a set of truck nuts. Slid it under the bumper and fell off."

Luke smiled. "Excellent! At least that part of the evening went well. You going to be OK to keep up?"

Pablo rolled his eyes at Luke and started jogging down the path. They were almost back to the camp when Luke's phone went off, vibrating in his pocket. Dread filled his stomach. He'd set the other camps to get through his do not disturb. He pulled out his burner phone and saw he had a voicemail.

"Help! So many of them. He —" The voicemail cut off.

Luke shook his head. "Fuck. Check your phones."

"What about the last vamp?" Delilah asked.

"He's gone by now. They were here to set a trap for us, not mess with the camp."

Delilah and Pablo nodded at Luke's assessment and peered at their phones, then looked at each other.

"Portsmouth Women's Village."

"CAN'T YOU GO ANY FASTER?" Pablo asked from the back seat of Luke's Volvo.

"I don't know. I've never raced this thing. This car is older than Delilah."

"It's true," Delilah agreed.

"We have GOT to go see my nephew," Pablo said.

"Let's worry about that after tonight." Luke pushed the gas pedal down further. The speedometer edged toward ninety-five mph. A worrying shimmy vibrated the car. "I don't think I can get it up much further and still get there...at least not in one piece."

Luke hoped there weren't any Johnny Law types out past their bedtime. He slowed the car enough to make the exit from I-84 to I-5 North and started to accelerate when Pablo yelled, "Brakes, NOW!"

Luke jammed on the brakes, checked the rear-view mirror to make sure there wasn't anyone behind him, and brought the car down to the speed limit.

"What's up, Pablo?" Luke asked.

"There's a cop on I-5. Just tuck in behind him, and we'll see where it's going."

"Gotcha."

Luke carefully merged onto the freeway behind the cop and stuck to the 50 mph speed limit. He was hoping the cop would get off at the Broadway exit, but no such luck. Luke was getting antsy.

"Hey, just calm it down there, Luke," Delilah advised. "You're getting a bit jittery, and we don't need the cop pulling you over because he thinks you're driving under the influence."

Luke took several slow, deep breaths and collected himself; better slow than not at all. Irritatingly, the cop continued down I-5.

"Look, man. Just stick to the freeway. Fifty-five and steady to the Columbia Boulevard exit is still going to be faster than getting off the freeway and taking surface streets."

"Yeah, you're right." Luke knew Pablo was but couldn't help being frustrated with the delay. Luke's patience was rewarded when the cop pulled onto the Going Street exit. As soon as he was halfway up, Luke depressed the gas pedal. Without further interference, they made it to the Columbia exit and slowed down to take the clover loop onto Columbia. The boulevard through the industrial part of North Portland was virtually abandoned this late at night.

Luke passed the Portsmouth Women's Village and turned off Columbia, finding a parking spot near a park a safe distance away. They piled out of the car and grabbed their gear. Luke pulled a black vest from inside a bag tossed in the back of the Volvo.

"Sorry, I forgot about this in the rush to get up to Johnson Creek, Delilah. I hope this fits." He handed her the heavy black vest.

"Bulletproof vest?"

"Stab vest. It's made specifically for bladed weapons. It's got some bullet rating, but don't take that chance. If you see a gun, duck." Delilah shucked her coat and put on the vest.

"A bit tight in the chest," she grunted as she worked to get the zipper all the way up.

"Sorry; it was the best I could do on short notice. We might have to look into getting you a custom fit."

"Ya think?"

"Don't I get a fancy vest?" Pablo pouted.

"Pablo, you're a werewolf. You are *a* bulletproof vest. Alright. I'm not sure what's going on, but keep your eye on the ball. It's tight confines down there and a lot of civilians. I don't want any of the women to get hurt, and I especially don't want either of you to get hurt. Let's watch each other's backs and stay alive."

SEVENTEEN

THEY CREPT DOWN THE HILL, sticking to the shadows and ducking behind bushes when the occasional car drove by. Darting across the street into the shadows of a newly built brick building that belonged to the city, they halted to plan their next moves. Pablo looked at Luke, exchanging a loaded and knowing look.

"You feel it?" Pablo asked.

"Yeah," was Luke's staccato, whispered reply. "Lots of fucking vampires. I can't get any sense of numbers. It's kind of overwhelming. There's too many to track."

"Come here. I'll give you a boost." Pablo cupped his hands, offering Luke a place to stand. "Tell me when."

Luke grasped the top of the eight-foot-tall brick wall that surrounded the building and stepped into Pablo's hand for a boost. Pablo lifted him up slowly.

"OK," Luke whispered, and Pablo stopped. Luke could only see part of the village from this angle; the brick building was blocking part of the camp. There was no movement. The village was a collection of mini houses, repurposed shipping containers, and other semi-permanent structures. Narrow walkways and alleys separated the buildings and formed a maze of blind turns, hidey-holes, and dead ends—the perfect place for an ambush. "Down."

Pablo lowered him, and Luke cursed under his breath, pacing a short path. He calmed down and waved Pablo and Delilah in for a huddle.

"It's a fucking death trap in there. Sharp turns, dead ends, and all kinds of killing fields. Pablo, I'm gonna need you to go wolf. Can you jump up onto the wall and then the roof?"

"No prob." He pulled out the earpiece and stripped. Delilah took off her coat and removed the near empty backpack she'd been wearing under it. She opened the top zipper, and Pablo shoved his clothes in.

"Can you keep it quiet?" Luke asked.

"Come on! It's me you're talking to," he replied, giving his best Han Solo innocent shrug.

"Have you seen the movies? Cause it never worked out when Han said that," Delilah said.

Pablo stuck his tongue out at her.

"Pablo, if you can, keep to the roofs. Attack from above. Keep an eye on us, make sure we don't get ambushed. Delilah, stick close to me. Let's keep each other safe."

Delilah nodded. Her eyes were wider than normal and her nod tight. Pablo waved his hand and motioned they should turn around so he could go wolf, preferring a bit of privacy if the time and location allowed. He tapped them on the shoulder with his pointy wolf claws. They turned as he nimbly jumped onto the high brick wall and then carefully crawled onto the roof of the building overlooking the village. He didn't make a sound.

Delilah and Luke looked at each other with eyebrows raised and impressed expressions on their faces.

"Like a cat," Luke whispered to Delilah.

"I'm sure a werewolf would just love being compared to a feline." Delilah snickered.

"Alright, put your game face on."

"We just walking in?" Delilah looked incredulous.

"They know we're coming. We know it's probably a trap. They'll try to get the jump on us thinking we're unaware. We stroll in like we're oblivious and spring their trap." Luke shrugged. "Keep moving, watch your back, and call out if you need help."

Delilah loosened her machete in its scabbard and patted her wooden stakes nervously. Together, they strode confidently out of the shadows and walked down the sidewalk and around the corner of the tall, brick wall toward the entrance to the Portsmouth Women's Village.

Once they could see the village, Luke began assessing all the information he could gather. The gravel, some of which was strewn out onto Columbia Boulevard, was evenly spread out across the entryway to the village. It was too even. When Luke had visited a few days ago with Max, it had shown signs of use and weather and was unevenly packed. Now, everything was smooth. Some pieces were muddy with dirt lines, giving evidence they'd been churned up from the bottom layer that met the packed earth. Something had torn up the gravel, flinging some out into the street, and then gone to a great deal of trouble trying to erase the evidence.

A few doors looked slightly askew, a hinge displaying a bit too much gap, a screw dangling precariously from a screw hole, and one door propped against its door jamb, leaving a gap at the top and a sizable angle at the bottom. Luke spotted a few streaks where the light glinted off a dark, smeared, sticky liquid. The raid on the camp had been fast and violent, and then just as quickly erased in hopes of fooling the less aware.

Luke pulled the gate open. Unlocked. At this time of night, the gate should have been locked. The sound of the metal gate swinging shut rattled the chain-link fence surrounding the village. Summoned by the noise, the leader of the camp exited one of the small shelters and stopped in the shadows separating her from Luke and the light thrown by the streetlights.

"Tresa, right?" Luke asked.

She shifted her head, a look of confusion passing over face as she shook her head slightly. Her hair, which had been covering half of her face, shifted, allowing Luke a glimpse of a swollen eye on the way to a serious bruise. Once the confusion passed, her visible eye settled into a dazed, half-dead stare.

"Yeah. Tresa. That's me. You're Luke." Her body stood motionless, the only movement that of her mouth when she spoke.

Delilah shifted nervously, her feet kicking up a grinding noise as her shoes crunched the loose gravel. Floorboards straining and creaking broke the silence that hung between Tresa and Luke.

Finally, Tresa spoke again, "Sorry about the voice mail. I hope it didn't cause you any inconvenience. Um, someone got the phone and thought it would be amusing to play a prank."

"I see..." The sound of a pebble skittering was the only warning Luke got that something was happening behind them as a chain flew through the gate and was quickly wrapped around the gate post. The click of a padlock sealed them in. The sound of Delilah's machete being drawn sent his hands to his own weapons. He yanked out his gladius and rudis.

"There's no cause for alarm..." Tresa droned on.

Doors were kicked out of their frames as vampires emerged into the courtyard. A tall, lanky female vampire strode out of the building Tresa had appeared from. She turned to Tresa, stroked her cheek, and said, "You may go hide now, my pet." Tresa turned and walked woodenly back into the little house.

"So you're the one who's been interfering with our plans. It looks like your adventures in slaying end tonight." She lazily raised her arms and gestured toward Luke and Delilah. She looked around at the vampires, all champing at the bit to chomp on the humans. "I do so enjoy my job."

She snapped her fingers and pointed aggressively at the humans as if giving commands to an attack hound. Responding to their mistress's order, the vampires edged toward Luke and Delilah, looking cautious and, in some cases, trepidatious. Luke scanned the crowd, looking for signs of who'd be first. Homing in on a couple of vampires exchanging glances, he exhaled, his muscles relaxing into readiness as their eyes shifted from questioning to decided.

Luke exploded into violence. Where his gladius landed, limbs fell and blood flew. A head, an arm, a back slashed, a gut opened, four vampires down and crawling away or writhing on the ground holding stumps. Delilah darted out from behind Luke and dispatched one of the downed vamps with a precision stake strike before tucking in just behind Luke and to his left. The rest of the vampires, seeing the vanguard so efficiently and brutally handled, halted their progress, eyeing each other and hoping someone else would be ballsy enough to advance on Luke. Their attention was so firmly fixed on Luke, they had no idea a hulking werewolf was about to drop on them like a ton of angry bricks.

"You assholes got anyone here that can actually fight?" Luke taunted them loudly, hoping to distract them from any noises Pablo might make. "What a bunch of clowns. Just a friendly piece of advice. You should probably flee while you have the chance, or you'll end up one more pile of vampire sludge oozing into the gutter and winding your way to the sewage treatment plant."

They ignored his bravado and returned the scowls and snarls to their faces. Pablo dropped down into a narrow alley between two of the tiny houses and began tearing into the vampires. As the dismembered head of one vampire struck another vampire in the head, the vamps realized they might be in more trouble than they wanted.

"Oops. Too late…"

Nobody paid attention to Luke's banter as all hell broke loose. All eyes were on the werewolf ripping bodies to shreds. Pablo had grabbed one vampire by its arms and kicked it in the chest so hard that he was left holding a pair of arms. Doing a passable imitation of Luke's sword work, Pablo smacked vampires in the heads and bodies with his arm cudgels. Using the distraction, Luke charged into battle, Delilah racing after him.

Not sure what to do, the vampires scattered, running through the tight alleys and darting into various buildings. A few of the more valiant ones engaged Luke or tried to face off with the raging werewolf. Luke closed with his first vampire, getting inside its clawed reach, and delivered a wicked slash to its face. The fanger stumbled backwards until it reached the perfect distance for the incoming stab from the wooden sword in Luke's other hand. The vampire went rigid, then sloughed off the rudis into a vampire standing behind it.

Delilah, using the distraction, darted around Luke and staked that vampire, quickly withdrawing and pulling another stake from her belt.

Pablo, done playing with his arms, had tossed them aside and was busy wrenching the head off another vampire. He chucked it straight at Luke, who ducked to avoid it as it smashed into the vampire sneaking up behind him. Delilah raked a backhanded slash of her machete across the face of the vampire before pivoting in with a stake to its heart. Straightening, Luke nodded his thanks to Delilah.

The last of the braver—or stupider—vampires had finally broken and run, leaving the tiny courtyard deserted. Behind Pablo, a set of shadows in the window of a darkened home jostled, trying to get as far as possible from the door. Luke caught Pablo's eye, nodded his head toward the tiny house, and pointed with the tip of his sword up to the roof of the house next to it. Pablo jogged over to the second house, leapt onto its roof, reached across the foot-wide gap, and ripped off the corrugated tin roof, chucking it aside and jumping in. The sound of vampires screaming serenaded Luke's ears as he kicked in the door of the shelter closest to him.

"Delilah, watch my back." Luke shot inside, leading with his gladius. As he pulled his other arm in, he stabbed to the left with the rudis. His eyes, already used to the low light outside, quickly adjusted to the dark space of the interior. Empty. "Coming out."

"Thanks for the heads up." Delilah looked around the empty courtyard nervously.

"You'd feel pretty bad if you stabbed me by accident. On to the next."

Luke peaked into the gap left by a door hanging off one hinge but couldn't tell if anyone was inside. There were still too many vamps for him to be able to sense where they specifically were. He kicked the door just next to the hinge and sent it flying. He repeated his previous maneuver, leading with his sword. Unlike last time, someone was there. A body flew out the window. Reacting on pure reflex and nerves, Delilah chopped down with her machete, nearly taking off most of its left arm. The vampire landed on the ground in a heap. As it struggled to get up and away, Delilah finished it.

A vampire, taking a cue from Pablo, had gotten to the rooftops and sneaked onto the building Luke was in. Luke stepped out, and the vampire sprang. Delilah called out as the roof squeaked and cracked under the vampire's leap. Luke spun and caught the vampire, impaling him with both swords. He rolled to his back, coiling his legs between himself and the falling vampire, and kicked out, launching the vampire over him and onto the ground behind him. The vampire hit the ground hard, the impact shattering it into dust. One of Luke's blades must have pierced its heart.

Delilah hacked her blade into the doorjamb, sticking it in the wood. She reached down, grasped Luke's forearm, carefully avoiding his blade, and helped him up. She reached out and yanked her blade free. Luke raised his eyebrows at the casual maneuver with her blade but didn't comment. He turned and slipped into the shadows of one of the narrow alleys.

Somehow, a vampire had wedged itself into the tiny space between two of the buildings. As Luke passed, it stabbed out with a knife. Luke jumped out of the way as the vampire's sleeve snagged on a nail, then sliced off the vampire's forearm. Dropping the gladius, he grabbed the vampire's stump and pulled its torso toward the gap. The vampire tried to get its other clawed hand out to protect itself, but had picked too small of a space to wedge itself into. Its left-handedness only exacerbated its problems as Luke slowly slid his rudis through its armpit and into its heart.

Luke let go of its stump, then kicked it off his rudis before retrieving his gladius. Delilah had worked her way around Luke and kept an eye on the dark alleys, nooks, and dead ends they still hadn't cleared. Luke, startled by a shadow moving across the light, looked up to see Pablo once again stalking across the rooftops. Luke caught Delilah's eye as her gaze drifted to the roofs. Delilah nodded, then moved forward, popping her head around the corner before pulling it back. She gave Luke the "OK" signal, and he darted around the corner. She followed him.

Once they cleared the corner, doors sprung open, and vampires poured out from every hiding place, quickly surrounding Luke and Delilah. Luke didn't wait for them to make the first move and charged the nearest fanger. He shoved a pipe out of his way as it swung toward his head, delivering a stab to the face, and withdrew his sword into a backward slash that bisected another vamp's arm. He followed through with a stab from this rudis. Delilah was doing her best to keep her back to Luke's as she hacked at anything that moved within the range of her machete.

Pablo, having finally made his way to the last mini house, dropped into the back of the alley and worked his way through the vampires surrounding his friends as the vampires between him and Luke were pressed into each other trying to find room to fight. Delilah switched from defense to offense and tried to keep up with the butchery of her companions. As she positioned herself to swing toward her next target, Luke shoved her out of the way, knocking her back into the building. Luke had shouldered her out of the way and was slicing bits off the vampire Delilah had gone after.

Delilah huffed, blocked by a hulking werewolf and Luke. A car horn sounded in the distance, blasting three long honks. The vampires not currently fighting desperately against the marauding slayers ran, jumped, and climbed out of the village. Luke and Pablo put their last vampires down.

Luke, his back still to Delilah, looked around for more vampires to pursue. Delilah thwacked Luke across the back of his thighs with the flat of the machete blade. He yelped, jumped, and turned around. He squatted a bit and squirmed, unable to rub the back of his thighs with his hands full of swords.

"What the hell was that for?!" Luke asked.

Delilah pointed her machete at his chest and shoved him back against the building. She closed the distance, going almost nose to nose with Luke.

"Do. Not. Fuck. With. My. Kills. Ever. Again. Understand?"

"Uh, I, um, I, uh..." Luke stammered.

"I don't want to hear anything out of your mouth except 'understood,'" she ground out between clenched teeth. To emphasize the point, she cocked her arm back, showing Luke the flat of her blade.

"Understood."

Delilah lowered her arm, wiped her blade clean on the shirt of a dead vampire, and shoved it back in its sheath.

Luke turned around and tried to look at the back of his legs. "Is there vamp blood on my pants where you hit me?"

Delilah gave him a quick look-see. "You've got blood splatter everywhere. Not sure I added much. Get to staking, sword boy. We need to get out of here."

She pulled out a fresh stake and worked her way through the bodies that weren't showing signs of having been given their final dispatch. Luke, sheathing his gladius, did the same with his rudis. Pablo, still in his bipedal wolf form, guarded them in case any vampires decided on an encore performance. The silence of their work was only broken by the squelching sounds of decaying vampires and stakes going into torsos. Luke startled as a rattling sound came from inside his hoodie. He fished out the pouch from under his armor and pulled out his cell phone. He stared at the screen, blood rising in his face, his jaw clenching and unclenching, the muscles of his jaw quivering.

"Luke, what is it?" Delilah asked, looking concerned.

Luke thrust the phone at her. She looked at the message. *They took Max. They broke into his home and took Max. Please help! - Pam*

"What number is this? It's not coming up as their camp phone..." Delilah said. "It might be another trap."

Luke didn't answer. He was stomping back and forth, his body shaking with rage. He spied a loose head belonging to a body they hadn't staked yet laying on the ground, reared back with his foot, and kicked it as hard as he could, letting out a scream that was half rage-filled roar and half frustration. It splatted into the metal wall of a shipping container living unit like a rotten melon.

DELILAH DROVE through north Portland toward Hazelnut Grove. Luke, still too angry to talk and, apparently, to drive, had tossed her his keys as they approached the car. Pablo had reassumed his human body and was shimmying into some clothes in the back-seat. Luke fumed, staring out the passenger window. She pulled into their usual parking spot and put the car in park. They poured out of the Volvo and jogged up the bike path. Just before they reached the camp, Pablo put his hand on Luke's shoulder, only to have it shaken off.

"Hey, Luke. I understand. You're angry. But you can't walk in there looking like you're about to demolish the place. Their trusted leader is gone. They're scared. You need to pull it together. OK? Also, if it's a trap, you'll need your calm."

Luke took several deep, slow breaths and forced his muscles to relax. He nodded curtly at Pablo and put on a calmer face. Even if he didn't really feel that much calmer, he could fake it. He was used to wearing façades.

Someone must have seen them approach because Pam and Jim were walking briskly toward them. They waited at the edge of the glow cast by the streetlight. The camp, despite the extremely late hour—it was closer to sunrise than midnight—was a hive of activity. Not sensing any vampires, Luke calmed more. Once they got closer, he could see that Pam had been crying. Her eyes were puffy and red. Jim looked solemn and scared.

"What happened?" Luke asked without preamble.

Jim spoke up first. "Someone woke us up. Said there were suspicious strangers at Max's. By the time we got there, it was too late. He was gone." He paused, looked down, then made eye contact with Luke again. "You better see this."

Jim walked toward Max's place. Pam fell in behind him with the rest of them. As they walked through camp, people gave them frightened and wary glances as they looked up from packing. Jim stopped about ten feet from Max's door. It swung slightly in the early morning breeze.

"Is this how you found it? Door open?" Delilah asked.

Jim nodded. "Yeah. I peeked inside but made sure nobody disturbed anything."

Luke walked forward, bending at the waist, and looking over the ground for clues. Finally, he got to Max's door. Nothing looked disturbed. Everything was still neatly in its place. The only sign of anything out of place was the bed. Luke stepped inside and turned around slowly. That's when he noticed it. The cell phone he'd given to Max was nailed to the wall next to the door, a spike driven through the top of the screen. Underneath it was a folded piece of paper.

Luke pulled it free of the nail, ripping the corner of the fold. He opened it and read,

The night belongs to us. All who dare go out into it belong to us. Portland is ours, and you're next. Leave while you can or we'll come for you next, you two-bit Buffy wannabe.

The bottom was signed with a happy face with dripping fangs added to the line smile. He walked out of Max's house and handed the note to Jim. Pam read over his shoulder. She gasped, covering her mouth, partially hiding the horrified look on her face. Jim handed it to Pablo, who held it so Delilah could read it as well. Everyone deflated. They all stared at the ground, helpless to help their friend. Luke looked around and watched as tents were disassembled.

"What's going on here?" Luke asked.

Jim startled out of his daze. "People are running away. It's not safe here. It's not safe anywhere..." he said the last to himself.

"Don't go north. We just came from the Portsmouth Women's Village. They emptied it," Delilah supplied.

"Yeah. Southeast, I guess," Luke said, recalling his map with all his meticulously plotted vampire kills and attacks. "Deep southeast, further south than Johnson Creek. I don't know if it'll be any safer after this, but it's all I got."

"Wha...what about Max?" Pam finally chimed in.

"I'll do what I can to find him, him and anyone else I can." Luke squeezed the bridge of his nose. "I'll figure something out."

EIGHTEEN

AFTER TWO BATTLES and Max's kidnapping, Luke succumbed to emotional and physical exhaustion and slept past noon the next day while Delilah crashed in his guest room. The sound of knocking on his bedroom door finally dragged him out of the tunnel of nightmares he'd been trapped in off and on all night. The door opened a crack, and Delilah's hand entered the room with a mug of coffee. Alfred pushed his way through the slim gap and hopped onto the bed.

"Sorry about that. He's being insistent. Anyway, brought you a cup of coffee. There's a breakfast burrito out here for you, too."

"Thanks." Alfred butted up against Luke's hand, demanding his morning head scratches. Once Luke obliged, the giant orange tabby burst into his "two pack a day" purr. "Alright, buddy. I'll get up. But I'm pretty sure Delilah fed you already."

Luke peeled himself out of the sheets that had wound around his body in the night's thrashing. Throwing on his robe and grabbing the coffee mug, he joined Delilah at the kitchen table. He peeled the wrapper back and dug into his chorizo breakfast burrito. He exhaled happily.

"I love a greasy, spicy chorizo burrito. It can't solve all the world's problems, but while you're eating one, everything looks alright. Thank you, Delilah."

"No problem. I figured you could use one after last night. There's a message on the group text from Pablo."

Luke took the phone out of his robe's pocket and opened the message.

Yo, what's the news on the GPS tracker? Also, you owe me a replacement pair of button up sweatpants.

"Crap, I forgot about the GPS tracker," Luke said.

Delilah chuckled. "Yeah, I can understand why. Last night was...full."

Luke refilled their coffees and gestured for Delilah to follow him into his office. He sat down at the desk and turned on his laptop, then opened the program he'd installed that coupled with the GPS trackers he'd purchased. He keyed in the ID of the one they'd used last night and waited for the program to track it down. After a few moments, a set of coordinates popped up. He put them into Google Maps and watched a section of map pop up on his screen.

"Hmmm, looks like just east of Pendleton." He clicked the directions button. "About four hours with traffic." Looking up at Delilah, he asked, "Got any plans for today?"

"Not really."

"Up for a road trip?"

Delilah shrugged. "Sure. Pablo coming?"

"No. He has to work. I'll text him where we're going."

"Yeah. No good going out to the middle of nowhere and not letting anyone know."

Luke nodded. "True. Let me jump through the shower, then we can hit the road."

Thirty minutes later, coffee transferred to travel mugs, they headed to the freeway. Delilah tied her phone into the car's blue tooth stereo and played a '90s hip hop mix. Neither of them felt in the mood to talk. Luke focused on the road while Delilah looked out the window, watching the scenery change from city to the trees and rock walls of the Columbia Gorge. Luke turned on the wipers as the steady fall drizzle misted his windows.

"Damn, it's so beautiful here. Everything's so green. Water falls just shooting out of the rock," Delilah said.

"Have you not seen the Gorge before? Did you take some other route than I-84 to get to Portland?

"I came through the gorge, but it was dark, and I was just worried about getting my tired ass to my friend's house."

"Unfortunately, I slept too late and we're on a tight schedule. I want to get there before it gets too late, not that we'd be able to stop at Multnomah Falls, anyway. Some other day."

They passed the pull-off to Multnomah Falls and kept chugging along in Luke's Volvo. Thirty minutes later, Hood River disappeared in their rear-view mirror and with it, the aggressively verdant nature of the west side of the Cascade Mountains. The trees became sparser and grass dominated the hills rising alongside the road. The autumn rains had turned them from yellow to a rich green, easing the transition into the drier side of Oregon. Past The Dalles, even the trees disappeared as the rocky hills changed to scrub brush and grass. The towns they passed through became fewer and smaller as they drove through the Gorge.

Once they began the ascent out of the Gorge, the Columbia River began its northerly turn as I-84 took a more southerly direction.

"We've got to be getting close to Pendleton. It's been a while since I've been out this way, but we should be close," Luke said.

Delilah pulled up the maps app on her phone and checked. "Yeah, about fifteen minutes."

"Grab my laptop. It should be set up to tie into my cell phone for Wi-Fi. Pull up the GPS program. I want to make sure they haven't started moving." The sun was getting close to the horizon, but not quite ready to send up the riot of pinks, purples, and oranges of a spectacular sunset.

"Yup. Still at the same coordinates." She put the numbers into her phone. "OK, about thirty minutes until we're there."

After Pendleton, they began climbing again. Pines, spaced sparsely, broke up the grass.

"Rest area, two miles ahead. I think that's it," Delilah said.

"OK."

"Deadman Pass, one mile ahead. Really? Deadman Pass?" Delilah asked.

"It would appear the vampires have a sense of humor," Luke replied, his tone flat. Luke didn't feel amused after weeks of killing vampires but getting nowhere in their mission to protect Portland.

They pulled off at Exit 228 and found their way to the rest area.

"It's pretty empty. Pull up next to the restrooms. I need a brief detour before we figure out what's going on," Delilah said.

"That's not a bad idea. It'll look more natural and help relieve the pressure on my bladder."

Luke parked close to the restrooms and turned off the car. After Luke came back out, he walked around the building getting his bearings. It was still getting darker as the sunset. A few sporadic lamp posts scattered a bit of light around the parking lot. The trees around the edges of the parking lot obscured his view, but he thought he saw a box van parked in the very back corner of the lot opposite of where they'd parked.

"You see anything?" Delilah asked as she walked up behind Luke.

Luke pointed toward the back corner of the lot. "That's the only other vehicle parked here, and it matches Pablo's description."

"Do you sense any vampires?"

Luke concentrated. "No. It feels clear.

He turned and walked back to the car. He checked his laptop one last time to ensure the GPS unit was still pinging from this location. It was. They got back in and slowly drove toward the van they suspected had ripped out of a Portland parking lot last night dragging their friend. They drove past the van but saw no sign of anyone around. Luke pulled into a parking spot far enough away to not be suspiciously close to the other lone vehicle in the back of the lot. He slung on a baldric and snapped his gladius to it as Delilah strapped on her machete. Luke grabbed a set of bolt cutters and shut the rear hatch. They looked around one more time to see if anyone new had pulled into the parking lot.

Luke and Delilah casually strolled to the van, walked around it, and peeked in the cab. No one. Next, they peeked under the van to see if anything suspicious was going on there. When he was reasonably confident it looked normal, they proceeded to the roll-up door of the box van.

"OK, let's do it," Luke said.

He looked around the lot one last time, then reached down and clipped the padlock, locking the door to the truck's frame. The cut lock fell off and clunked to the ground. Luke set the bolt cutters down, slid his sword out of its scabbard, and checked to see if Delilah was ready. She nodded and pulled out her machete. Luke grabbed the latch, flipped it quickly, and yanked open the roll door. He pulled back, sword leveled and at the ready.

The box was completely empty except for the GPS unit sitting in the middle of the floor. Luke stuck his head in and looked around the box's corners and ceiling for any traps or cameras or any other sign of anything out of the ordinary. He shrugged at Delilah and climbed in. The GPS unit had been centered on the floor. They'd drawn a series of cartoonish hands surrounding the GPS, all flipping the bird. Luke shook his head in annoyance. He took a picture with his phone and sent it to Delilah so she could see, while she kept watch outside for anyone approaching.

"Wow. They're really taunting you."

Luke picked up the GPS and looked it over. Seeing nothing amiss, he put it in his pocket.

"Are you sure that's a good idea?" Delilah asked. "Taking it home. What if they took the number and can hack it?"

"That's a good point." He pulled his sleeve over his hand and pulled the GPS out, wiping away any fingerprints. Tossing it back onto the bed of the truck, he stomped it to pieces with the heel of his boot.

"I guess that solves that," Delilah said. "Did we just drive all the way out here for nothing?"

Luke shrugged. "I guess, but it was a nice drive, and you got to see some scenery."

Delilah nodded. "We should head back."

"Sure. I'll buy you dinner when we get back." Luke hopped out of the truck and headed back to his car.

Delilah opened her door and grabbed some empty bottles and trash and headed to the nearby garbage can. After so many nights in the Volvo, driving around Portland hunting vamps, the debris of drinks and snacks had built up. Luke threw his gladius in the back. With the back hatch open, a breeze blew a piece of trash out of the back and onto the ground. Luke bent over to pick up the empty wrapper. A gunshot ripped the silence, sending glass raining down on Luke as it shattered the rear window of his Volvo.

He hit the ground. Reaching up, he ran his hand over some rough cloth on the way to his gladius. When he pulled the sword out, the Kevlar vest he'd bought for Delilah tumbled out.

"Luke! Behind you!" Delilah yelled.

He scrambled around the Volvo as gunshot sprayed pavement at him from where he'd just been laying. As he ran to the front of the car, he saw Delilah crouching behind the garbage can.

"Get behind a tree!" Luke yelled.

Hunching behind the engine, he pulled the Kevlar vest over his head and cinched it. It felt awkward with all the cloth from his hoodie and T-shirt bunched under it. Foot falls slapped on the pavement. Yanking the gladius from its sheath, he tossed the scabbard aside and ran out from his cover, bellowing to draw their attention. The first person who saw him skidded to a halt. His eyes widened as Luke adjusted his course to intercept him.

Another shot rang out, whizzing by Luke's head. Raising a gun in his trembling hands, the man screamed as Luke hacked through the man's arm just above the wrist. The gun tumbled to the pavement with a clack. As the man hunched over, cradling his bleeding stump, Luke swapped the gladius to his left hand and bent over and picked up the gun, keeping the man between him and the other shooter.

He looked around, trying to locate the shooter. They stood about a hundred and fifty yards back in the grove of pine trees straight behind the man he hid behind. Dashing out, Luke made for the box van to draw their fire away from Delilah, shooting across his body occasionally to force them to duck. Once they dove into the dirt,

Luke barreled around the van, stopping at the front tire so he had the entire engine block between him and the shooter.

Without Luke shooting, he could see signs of life from the other man with the gun. He scrambled along, trying to keep hidden behind the skinny, younger pine trees as they worked their way toward Luke. Setting his gladius on the ground, he rested his arms across the hood of the box van, gripping the pistol with two hands, and took aim. As soon as the shooter broke from their last hiding spot, Luke pulled the trigger, dropping the shooter.

Cautiously, he stepped around the van and walked toward the fence. Without the pops of gunfire, the breeze sounded through the trees carrying the moans of the man missing his hand accompanied by the groans of the second shooter. Luke popped the magazine out to check how many shots he had left — two in the magazine, one in the pipe. He hopped the fence and crouched behind trees, dodging from trunk to trunk, following the pained whimpers. When he saw movement, he dodged behind a tree.

The thrall he'd shot writhed on the ground, groaning and holding both hands over his chest. The closer Luke got, the more gurgly and wet the moans and gasps of air sounded. The shiny metallic silver of the gun contrasting with the natural greens and browns drew Luke's eyes to the semiautomatic pistol. Luke picked up the gun, stashing it in his pocket. Luke had shot him in the chest and his lungs were filling with blood, his eyes fading.

"Hurry! He's killed Benjy and Chip," came a harsh whisper that had grown too loud.

Whoever it was wasn't being careful enough as they moved through the underbrush, breaking twigs and rustling against the dry vegetation.

"It's almost dark. Tell the masters if they want him, he's here."

Luke heard a beep and some cursing. When a branch snapped close by, he raised the pistol and took aim. Another thrall stepped into the small clearing and tentatively raised a gun.

"Drop it, or I'll put one in your chest," Luke said.

The thrall warred with indecision, eyes flicking between the gun in Luke's hands and his face. Luke raised the gun slightly. That was enough for the thrall, who decided to drop the gun.

"Step back and keep backing up until I say stop." Luke stood up and walked to where the thrall had dropped the gun and scooped it up, adding it to his collection. Splitting his attention between the thrall backing away and the ground around him, Luke backed up until he was next to the now dead body of the thrall he'd shot.

"Luke?" Delilah called. "You back there?"

"Stay by the car. I'll be out shortly," Luke replied.

The dying rays of the sun glinted off a small black object on the ground near the body, catching Luke's attention. Something had fallen from the vamp's pocket. Squatting down, Luke took one hand off the gun and picked up a plastic box with a button on it.

"Hey, asshole," Luke called. "What's this?" He held up the box with the button.

The thrall didn't say anything, so Luke stood up and pulled the hammer back on his gun.

"It's a detonator!" the thrall said.

"Why didn't you use it when we were in the van?" Luke asked.

"He wanted your stuff." The thrall nodded toward the body at Luke's feet.

"That worked out well for him. Keep backing away." Luke retreated as well, carefully checking where he was.

When he could no longer see the thrall, he turned and ran out of the little grove, hopping over the fence. He made straight for the car.

Luke scanned around. "Delilah, where's lefty?"

She pointed toward the fence a ways away from the box van. The thrall sat against a fence post, cradling his stump.

"Thrall, you should probably move away from that van." Luke tossed his gladius into the back of his Volvo and dumped all three guns in the plastic tub. "Let's go, Delilah."

He set the detonator on the console and got in. Luke backed up and took off. As they reached the turn that would take them out of the rest area, Luke picked up the detonator and pushed the button. Watching in the rear-view mirror, the van blew off the ground, flames shooting out along the ground. Within a second, the flames reached the gas in its tank and ignited, completing the destruction of the box van. Luke lost the view as they drove under the freeway and turned onto the on-ramp. When they merged, Luke saw the flames licking the sky as they drove away.

"We better get the hell out of here in case someone comes to inspect the fireball that just launched into the sky," Delilah said.

Now that they were safely away from the rest area, Luke grew angrier and annoyed that they'd drove all the way out there just to be shot at by thralls. They'd learned nothing new and nearly been killed —one more fucking dead end in an endless line of failures. All the recriminations that'd been rolling around in the back of his head leapt forward, front and center, blaming him loudly for all the failures of the last few months. If he didn't interrupt this thought cycle, he'd spiral down into full despondency.

Luke shook his head and sighed. "Delilah, I think we could use some road music."

Delilah smiled and nodded at Luke. Her thumbs were busy typing something into her phone. She grinned and looked over at Luke.

"Here you go, Bandit." A banjo and some strings introduced Jerry Reed's lyrics.

"'West Bound and Down?' OK. Although, this isn't much of a Trans-Am..." The silly song choice stopped Luke's growing bad mood as he bobbed his head to the plucky banjo sounds. "Good choice. Thanks."

"AND YOU JUST LEFT THEM ALIVE?" asked Pablo, taking a break from the Howling Moon lunch crowd to get a first-hand account of the previous night's wild goose chase.

"I don't kill thralls if I can avoid it. They might have a chance and turn away from their masters. They didn't cause too much mischief, except killing my car's rear window." Luke raised his pint toward Delilah and nodded in appreciation for all the good work she'd done on their trip.

"We got lucky. That's for sure," she replied.

Pablo folded his arms across his chest. "I'm all for excitement and getting some kicks, but I'm glad I had to work last night. Shoveling spent grain sounds a lot more enjoyable than getting shot at and almost blown up. Where does this leave us?"

"Back at virtually square one, except light several tanks of gas." Luke's tone was biting and annoyed as his jaw clenched and flexed when he wasn't speaking as his mood teetered back and forth between depression and frustration and the warmth being with his friends caused to blossom in his chest.

The furrow in Luke's brow and tightness in his cheeks, coupled with his waspish humor, told his friends louder than words he was frustrated with the setbacks of the last couple of days. Luke collected himself and took a drink of his beer.

"Tonight, let's make a rotation around the camps. We can see if anyone else is missing and if we can find a vampire or two. I'll keep scouring the news to look for anything unusual that might point us in the right direction. Really, though, we need a break. I thought we might get one with our previous attempts, but not so much."

"What can we do to help?" Delilah asked.

Pablo nodded along. "Maybe we can split up and hit multiple spots more quickly?"

"No. As much as I'd like to do that, the groups have been too big. I wouldn't want any of us running into a swarm of vampires without backup. I'm not sure I want to have to recover from another epic beat down." Luke sighed. "Damn it. It never should've gotten this far."

"There's nothing we can do about the past at this point, dude," Pablo replied. "Maybe the pack can help…"

Luke perked up at the suggestion. Having a bunch of werewolves would certainly go a long way to helping him sniff out the vampire nests infesting Portland.

"That would be a boon, for sure."

Pablo smiled. "I'll talk to Holly and see if we can enlist the pack. When we find a vampire, we'll just need to remember to save the clothes afterward."

"Do vampire bodies…corpses…goo smell the same as live vampires?" Delilah asked.

Thinking about it for a few moments, Pablo nodded. "Yeah, pretty similar. Close enough anyway that we should be able to sweep some neighborhoods and sniff them out."

"What kind of range does your nose have?" asked Luke.

"Quite a bit if the wind is right, but I've never done any clinical trials, especially not with vampire remains. We can do some science when we find a vampire."

"It's worth checking out, that's for sure," Luke replied. "When can you talk to Holly?"

"When she gets back in town. She's at a conference."

"A werewolf conference?" Delilah asked, grinned cheekily.

"No. Herbalife."

It was the deadpan delivery that got them. Luke's eyebrows shot up, and Delilah, who had been taking a drink, exhaled, spraying a mist of beer out of her glass.

"Seriously?" Luke asked, while Delilah worked to keep from choking on her beer.

"Nah, I'm messing with you. It's a national conference for public defenders. I can't remember the exact name."

"Holly's a public defender? I didn't know that," Luke said. "Well, I guess I've only had the one interaction with her. She was more interested in asking me questions, so we never got to the usual getting to know you chitchat. I guess that explains her cross-examination skills."

Pablo nodded. "Yeah, she was definitely trotting out 'Professional' Holly. Good thing she's got Sam. Holly can be a little too serious at time, and you've met Sam. So you know what I'm talking about."

"Is Sam Holly's husband?" asked Delilah, who'd finally recovered from her spit take.

"Holly's wife. Samantha, but she prefers Sam. Although, I've heard Holly call her 'Sayumi' a few times when she thinks no one is in earshot. Most of us don't use our birth names on our current documents."

"Yeah. 'Luke Irontree' is the closest I've gotten in a while to my original name."

"Most of the time, I forget you're a couple of old farts, but conversations like this…" Delilah shook her head. "Well, I guess if I need some new papers, I know who to talk to."

"We're a couple of spring chickens!" Pablo protested.

Luke chuckled. "Well, spring chicken, you're driving tonight since you haven't had anything to drink and my Volvo is down a window. If you two are ready, we can continue this conversation on the road."

FOR TWO WEEKS, they circled the city, visiting every camp and popular gathering place with nary a trace of a vampire. It was as if they'd all simultaneously packed up and left Portland. Each night, Delilah, Luke, and Pablo got more frustrated with their lack of progress. The normally copacetic crew began to snipe at each other for no reason. It didn't help that Holly had denied Luke's request to enlist the pack. He knew his friend had done his best to argue their case, but it hadn't been enough.

"She doesn't care if I hang out with you and chase vampires all over the city. It's my time, as long as it doesn't interfere with my pack duties, but she thinks if the pack joins in, it could endanger the pack, its secrecy, and put us squarely in the cross hairs of the vampires. I tried, but she wasn't having it, dude."

Luke understood. The fact that she let Pablo come out with him spoke both of her trust in Pablo and in the fact she wasn't the type of packleader that believed in controlling every aspect of pack life. Luke didn't want to press it too far for fear of losing Pablo's aid and their newly blossoming friendship. Pablo kept coming out with Luke and Delilah when he had nights off, and most of the time he arranged his work schedule so he was free.

The news of strange disappearances and deaths had stopped entirely. No more empty sets of cut up clothes covered in a mysterious dark goo were found. The city was cautiously optimistic that maybe they were coming through this dark fall and hoped for a quiet Thanksgiving. Luke and his crew hoped for any sign of their quarry.

They sat in Pablo's truck, parked along a dark, deserted street in the west hills. They'd started expanding their searches, but to no avail. The silence filling the truck's cab was the result of a terse near-argument they'd had about what to do next. Luke took a deep breath and exhaled slowly.

"You know what? Fuck it. Let's pack it in tonight. Let's also take tomorrow night off. We're starting to wear on each other's nerves. We're not getting anywhere right now, and we could use a night to ourselves."

Pablo and Delilah nodded heartily in response as Pablo fired up the truck and pulled out onto the street that would take them back to North Portland. Luke stared out the window, mind drifting to a time when his life was simpler and his enemies easier to understand.

LUCIUS IIII

THE SCOUTS LUCIUS sent out returned and filled him in on the disposition of the enemy force surrounding the reserve century. The Dacians, according to the scouts, were having trouble finishing off the century. The legionnaires had gone into full defensive mode, presenting shield walls to all sides.

"They're boxed up here," the scout said, drawing a square in the dirt. "They've been mauled pretty good, but they're holding out. I couldn't get a good count through the Dacians and shields. There's probably about a hundred or more Dacians. They have a small force of archers stationed here and here. Looks like mixed force of bows and those Greek bows on a stick, what are they called?"

"Gastraphetes?" Lucius supplied. He wondered if that's how the Dacians had taken out his officers. The gastraphetes had a long range and a flatter flight arc. In the hands of a skilled user, it made for a powerful ranged attack.

"I didn't see any horsemen, and we were thorough in our area sweep."

"Very good. Quirinus, take your horses around and sweep through their archers here," Lucius pointed at one group of enemy archers. "Hannibal, you take your archers and station them along the tree line. When Quirinus hits the first group of archers, you fire on the second group." He drew a line between where his cavalry and archers were. "We'll line up here, three deep, and present maximum frontage. Cassius, take the right side of the second line. Petrocles, you take the left side of the third line."

"Lucius, you might need this." Cassius tossed Lucius something.

He caught it and opened his hands to see the centurion's whistle.

"I figured it might come in handy. He wasn't going to need it anymore. I wiped off the blood."

"Thanks," Lucius said wryly. "Tell your lines to listen for the usual signals so we can keep the lines fresh. Any questions?"

Nobody responded. Lucius pulled out a leather thong from his pouch and strung the whistle around his neck.

"Alright, let's keep silent until the cavalry makes contact. That's our signal to advance."

They nodded and moved to carry out their orders. The cavalry looped back through the woods to set up in a small spur of trees that put them closer to the first group of enemy archers. Lucius organized his three lines while his archers set up on the right. Lucius put the centurion's whistle to his lips and did his best to make it sound like a bird call.

The cavalry got the signal and burst out of the woods, congealing into a loose battle line. The word was passed among the archers to nock and ready. Lucius raised his pilum and pointed forward. The legionnaires stepped out of the woods in a walk. Out of the corner of his eyes, he saw his archers raise their bows as the cavalry neared impact. Some of the Dacian archers had noticed their impending peril but could do little as the cavalry sheared through the lightly armored archers, their bows useless against the weight of the horses and the steel of their riders. The thrum of bows releasing their arrows sounded to Lucius's right, and the other group of archers began falling as the Roman arrows found their marks.

Lucius blew the command to start their attack. He broke into a trot, a raucous battle cry rising from his men as they sped toward the Dacians. Lucius's men were eager to relieve their comrades and rout the enemy. When he judged they were close enough, he launched his pilum. A few of his men's throws, fearing they'd overthrow and hit their own men, came up far too short. Seeing his own pilum drive into the back of a Dacian warrior encouraged him and told him he had his distance. He launched the heavy pilum into the air before pulling the gladius from its sheath on his right hip. His pilum launched, he broke into a run.

Seeing the oncoming legionnaires, the other century renewed their efforts and began shoving the Dacians back. When Lucius's front line smashed into the rear of the Dacians, the two groups of Romans turned the Dacians into mincemeat. They were herded into the shields and short swords of the Romans and couldn't find any escape through the bodies of their countrymen trying to flee the wrath of the legionnaires.

Lucius raised the whistle to his lips and signaled a line shift. Each man in his line tucked to the right and let the legionnaire behind him take his place at the front line, and soon, the fresher line of Romans let the Dacians have it. Lucius, holding the centurion's spot in the front of the line, stepped back for a moment to catch his breath while surveying the situation.

His cavalry had finished the archers and were slashing into the rear of the Dacians, effectively capping Lucius's left flank. His archers had worked their way up out of the tree line and were picking off targets of opportunity. His men were nearly finished with the Dacians in front of them. He blew his whistle again to signal a line shift. The third line stepped forward as the second line worked its way to the back. As the last of the Dacians fell before the combined line of legionnaires, the other century collapsed its box formation and surged against the Dacians on the opposite side.

Lucius signaled a right wheel and got his men swinging to the end of the line so they could curl up the right flank. As they swung around the corner and smashed into the side of the remaining Dacians, he watched his lines wrap around the back of the Dacian formation. With the Dacians outflanked, their defeat was a fait accompli. The Dacians who'd been giving no quarter asked for none, falling to the last man.

As the last Dacian fell, the two centuries collected their breath and shared joy in their mutual survival—backs were patted, hugs exchanged, and tired cheers raised. Lucius was looking around, hoping to spot an officer, when he saw a centurion leaning between two of his legionnaires, limping toward them and avoiding putting any weight on a blood-covered leg. He walked up to Sego, who was still holding their Centurial Signum.

"Legionnaire, where's your centurio?"

"Dead, sir."

"Optio?"

"Unconscious when we left him, sir."

"Who's in charge here?"

"I guess I am, Centurio," Lucius answered. "Decanus Lucius Silvanius, sir." Lucius gave him a crisp salute.

"You've done a good job here today, son."

"Thank you, Centurio."

"Any word from the rest of the cohort?"

Lucius turned and saw Cassius had worked his way over to listen in on the conversation. "Cassius, can you get that cavalryman? Quirinus is his name." He turned to address the centurion. "Yes, sir. A force of Dacians attacked us and wiped out my centuria's officers. After we fought them off, Alaris Quirinus found us back at the camp and filled us in on your situation and the main force. That's how we knew where to find you."

Cassius returned with Quirinus, who filled the centurion in on the last known positions of their vexillation.

"Thank you, Alaris Quirinus. Gather a few men and see if you can get close enough to get some updated intelligence on the situation."

"Yes, Centurio," Quirinus replied as he saluted and turned to carry out his mission.

"So, the only one left was a leader of a contubernium, Decanus?"

"Well, Centurio, it was either fight or die. Everyone kept listening to my orders, so I kept issuing them. When Alaris Quirinus showed up, my comrades said I was in charge…"

"And so here you are, leading an underpowered centuria. What are you? Eighteen?"

"Almost twenty, Centurio."

The centurio shook his head. "Well, your men keep following you and following you well. Check on your men, see to your injured, and get them ready to march out as soon as the scouts get back." He yelled back over his shoulder, "Tesserarius, what's the butcher's bill?"

A broad man with a hook bill nose trotted up to the injured centurion. "Not good, Centurio. I think we can effectively put forty, maybe forty-five men in the field. We're sorting out the wounded from the dead."

Lucius walked off and out of earshot to carry out his orders. The boost the centurion's compliments gave him was nearly enough to buoy his tired limbs. He walked over to Sego and Cassius. "Any injured? Dead?"

"No, we made it through pretty clean. A scratch here, a stubbed toe there. One of the alaris took a fall from his horse. I think he'll be fine, but he's seeing double right now," replied Cassius.

"Alright, pass the word. Get some water and get some rest. As soon as the centurio gives the word, we're marching out again to see if we can relieve the cohort." Lucius walked over and informed his auxilia cavalry and archers to rest and get ready for the final push before stopping to rest himself.

Sometime later, Cassius kicked the bottom of Lucius's caligae to wake him up. "Up, Lucius. The centurio is looking for you. The scouts are back."

Lucius reached up and took Cassius's offered hand and stood up with his friend's help. "Thanks, Cass."

He marched over to the centurion to get his orders. He expected to be folded into the other century and was surprised to hear that he'd be leading his century while the tesserarius would lead the other century, owing to the centurion's injury. The centurion had confiscated the horse of the injured alaris so he could give the final orders when they reached the rest of the cohort.

Lucius got his legionnaires, cavalry, and archers in their marching line. They'd been scrounging the ground for Dacian arrows and pila that weren't too badly bent. While they'd waited, they'd replaced the wooden pins that joined wooden shaft and iron shank and were designed to snap on impact to prevent it being picked up and thrown back. The handful of troops left behind to tend the wounded would also gather up the damaged pila to be repaired for future use.

The cavalry and archers swept the path clean of any Dacian scouts watching the rear while the two partial centuries marched as quietly as they could. They'd hoped to repeat the surprise Lucius had manufactured and hit the enemy solidly in the rear. When they got within eyeshot, they'd expected to see the Dacian's leadership and elites separated from their main force, directing their warriors. However, when they finally found the Dacians' standard, it was engaged in trying to rally its troops and break the box of shields. While the Dacians were fierce and dangerous warriors, they couldn't match the professionalism and intense conditioning a legionnaire was subjected to. The Dacians must have hoped their elite warriors could crack the tough nut of the Roman shield box. Cornered, and with nowhere to flee, the Romans fought desperately.

Lucius consulted with the centurion and the tesserarius as their legionnaires fanned out into their battle line. They'd decided their initial plan would still work. The cavalry was split and stationed on the wings while the archers formed a thin line in front of the Legionnaires. The Centurion raised his hand, gaining the attention of the men, and dropped it, giving the signal to begin.

The archers opened fire, aiming short and adjusting their range to avoid overshooting into their comrades. The center of the line of legionnaires started forward in an open formation that allowed them plenty of space to move through the archers without interfering with their work. When the last legionnaires on the left and right started their movement forward, the two partial centuries formed a shallow "V" with the tip pointing at the center of the Dacians' backs. As the first arrows landed in the back ranks, a few Dacians noticed the oncoming legionnaires and tried to get the attention of their commanders through the din of weapon on shield and cries of anger and pain.

The legionnaires picked up their pace and let loose their pila as they got within range before breaking into what they hoped would be the last charge of the day. As tired as Lucius was, he knew the rest of the cohort who'd been fighting most of the day had to be exhausted. Once pila began dropping out of the sky, a ragged cheer rose from the cohort. They found another reserve of energy and renewed their efforts to break the Dacians who'd surrounded them.

The point of the "V" slammed into the Dacians as they turned some of their forces to ready for the oncoming Romans. It didn't help. The leading edge of the Roman formation sliced through the Dacian lines, crowding them until the fight resembled farmers harvesting a crop of corpses. As the Romans met their countrymen, each wing of the "V" broke apart and swept along the line, one century to the right and one to the left. The cavalry, who'd followed on the wings but a bit back, flared out and began picking off any Dacians who made a break for it.

With one side of the box cleared of opposition, the cohort focused on breaking the remaining lines of Dacians. What had looked like a hard fight but inevitable victory for the Dacians turned into a bad loss as anyone not engaged dropped shield and weapons and made a run for it. Those who couldn't disentangle and run away either surrendered or died.

After they'd mopped up the remaining Dacians and disarmed their prisoners, the Romans set up a defensive perimeter and began sorting through the wounded and the dead. The remaining officers were meeting in the center. Counting the wounded centurion from the reserve century, there were three centurions and two optios left standing. When the day started, there'd been seven centurions and seven optios.

"We were starting to wonder where you were, Adalbern. Glad you could make it to the fight," one of the centurions said.

"We got held up a bit." Adalbern pulled off his helmet, revealing the mousy blond hair and facial features typical of a German. "If it wasn't for Decanus Silvanius here, neither of us would be here to have this conversation."

Lucius stepped forward and gave the lead centurion a crisp salute.

"Decanus?" the first centurion asked before addressing Lucius. "Where's your centurio, Decanus?"

"Dead, Centurio."

"Can you elaborate?"

"Yes, Centurio. The Dacians hit us quick, taking out the centurio, optio, signifer, and cornicen from the tree line. The optio is the only who survived."

"Where is he?"

"Unconscious, Sir. The arrow hit his helm and knocked him out. When we left, he was still alive."

"And you led your centuria?"

"Yes, sir. We finished off the attackers, then Alaris Quirinus alerted us to the situation here. We marched out and relieved Centurio Adalbern's centuria, then headed here."

"Well done, Silvanius. Looks like someone under Antoninus knows what they're doing, although I bet that's more Optio Brabo's doing."

"Where's the Tribune, Tullius?" asked Adalbern.

"The little shit earned himself a glorious funeral when his bones make it back to Roma." Tullius turned and spat on the ground, emphasizing his disgust.

"A lot of good legionnaires paid for that funeral with their blood. Although, everyone getting promotions because of the officers he got killed might not think too unkindly of the dearly departed tribune and his glorious ambitions," Adalbern replied, glancing at Lucius.

NINETEEN

LUKE'S CELL phone startled him from a dream of his youth. At this point in his life, those kinds of dreams were rare. He tried to hold on to them all the more fiercely, but it wasn't to be on a rare night he'd taken the night off for an early bedtime. The ringing stopped when his voicemail engaged, but quickly started again. Sighing, he groggily answered.

"Heh…heh…" A yawn interrupted his greeting. "Hello?"

"Luke, it's Pablo. We've got an emergency. Get down to the house, ASAP."

"OK, OK. You'd better have—"

"Coffee? Yeah, we got plenty," Pablo said, interrupting Luke's sleepy and slurred request. "Get down here."

"Your house?"

"No, the pack has a house not far from the brewery. I'll text you the address."

Usually Pablo wasn't that terse. Something big must be going down. Luke swapped his pajama pants for jeans, slung his swords across his back, zipped up a baggy hoodie, and walked out the door, jumping into his Volvo in case it was needed. The pack house was only a few blocks away from his, just on the other side of Pablo's brewery. One of the younger pack members, one Luke hadn't met yet, was sitting inconspicuously on the deck, acting as a guard.

"Hey, Luke. The door's open; head on down."

Luke nodded at him and headed in. Pablo must have given a description of Luke to the guard. Pablo greeted him in the kitchen with a cup of fresh coffee, then headed toward the basement stairs. Luke followed him down the stairs into the pack's secret labyrinth. The room was set up like an exam room at a doctor's office, complete with the patient table. The room smelled like soldiers about to enter a battle—somber, angry, and frightened. The scent and the palpable tension immediately did the work of a whole pot of coffee and put him on immediate alert.

"You've got a hospital room in your basement?" Luke asked.

"Yeah. The doc runs clinic days here to save the pack members from using the human hospitals for basic needs."

"Smart. What's going on?" Luke asked.

"A young wolf in pretty rough shape showed up at our door tonight," replied Pablo. "She claimed she was being held captive by vampires. That they'd been feeding from her. And here's the big part, that she wasn't the only one. There are lots of people locked up. That's all we've gotten out of her so far. We didn't want to press too hard until the doctor looked her over."

Luke turned his attention toward the girl. She appeared to be very nervous, eyes darting between all the werewolves. Her clothes were filthy, soaking, and tattered. Someone had given her a brutal haircut, leaving a short, jagged mess.

Luke's brows furrowed. "For a werewolf, she seems to be frightened of all the wolves around her. I take it she's not from your pack?"

"No. And she doesn't appear to be from any of the other local packs," Pablo replied. Seeing Luke's confusion, added, "Holly and the other local packleaders share a database of pack members. It's one of the programs she's set up to ensure the local packs get along well."

As the caffeine flowed through his veins, he felt a pit settle in his stomach at the thought of the rough treatment the poor child had undergone at the hands of the vampires. The door cracked open, and Holly popped in with a curvy blonde woman of average height he'd never seen before.

"OK, everyone out! The doctor's here, and she would like some privacy." Holly turned her attention to the girl. "This is Dr. Rabinowitz, one of our pack physicians. She's going to do an exam and make sure you're alright. Would you like one of us to stay in the room with you?"

She squinted and looked around the room, settling on Luke. "The human. The human stays. No wolves. Just the doctor and the human."

Holly turned to Luke with a quizzical look on her face. "Do you mind, Luke?"

Luke shrugged. "No, I don't mind. She doesn't seem to trust werewolves."

The wolves filed out of room, Pablo nodding at Luke as he passed.

"Hi, I'm Dr. Rabinowitz, although you can call me Maggie if you'd like. Can you tell me your name?"

"Gwen, Gwendolyn."

"I brought this for you." Dr. Rabinowitz gave Gwen a reassuring smile and handed Gwen a hospital robe. She had a slight Polish accent to her English. "Would you please put this on? You can change behind the screen."

Gwen nodded and went behind the screen to change.

"That's better. This is probably warmer than those wet rags, anyway. When we're done, you can take a shower, and we'll find you some clean clothes to change into."

"Hey, Doc, let me know when, and I'll turn around to give you two a bit of extra privacy," Luke said.

Maggie nodded in response, then began the examination. Luke zoned out for the initial portion of the exam, retreating into his caffeine-deprived brain until a new line of questioning pulled him back into the room.

"When did you first start identifying as a girl?"

"I don't know. I remember my dad getting really mad at me for wanting to wear a dress. I think I was five or six at the time. The second time I mentioned it, I got a spanking..." Her voice had a slightly dead and clinical tone to it, as if she were recounting something she'd seen through a window.

"Did you come out to your mom?"

"Yeah. She tried to talk to my dad, but he hit her and said no son of his was going to be a queer. She told me to never talk about it again, for both our sakes."

"When did you run away?"

"A couple years ago."

"And you've not been home since?"

Gwen shook her head no.

"Has anyone from your pack tried looking for you?"

"I don't know, I don't care, I'm not going back. If you make me, I'll run away before they can find me again." Her voice was becoming more agitated.

Luke, his curiosity drawing him into the conversation, turned slightly so he could see.

"Don't worry. I'll speak with Holly. She's a good packleader. She'll come up with something." Maggie's face was lined with sadness, care, and a few well-hidden hints of anger. "I think we're done here. We can talk more later. I'll show you up to the bathroom so you can get cleaned up. Luke, would you mind grabbing Holly? I'll meet you both back here in a moment."

Maggie directed the robed kid out of the room. As they passed, Luke gave Gwen a small, friendly smile. Gwen returned a pleading look.

Holly was outside the door when Maggie opened it and stepped in. They stood in silence until Maggie returned a minute or two later, shutting the door behind her. She let out a big sigh. "That's one traumatized kid."

"I don't know what happened to her, but she's terrified of werewolves," Luke commented. "How did she end up here? At a werewolf property?"

"I'm guessing when she had her first transformation, her wolf instinct kicked in and she went looking for the closest pack and found us," Maggie replied. "I'm glad she did find us, though."

"I don't know how many packs you've interacted with over the years, but a lot are not friendly to 'the other.' That's in large part why this pack exists; to give a home to those who would be ostracized, or worse, from their own packs. Some of the better packleaders keep a more open culture. Some of the more mediocre will reassign people to our pack where they'll be welcome and not 'disrupt' their own packs. The other kind, well, they'll snuff out those they view as aberrations; 'cull the pack of weakness' some of them call it. She wouldn't give us any details about where she's from," Holly said, anger evident on her face.

"She wouldn't tell us anything either, so I don't know if it was a bad pack situation or a bad family situation. Even if it was only the latter, the pack didn't do a good job ensuring the safety of all its members. It sounds like her father physically abused her and her mother, specifically about her gender identity," Maggie replied.

Holly's brows furrowed. "What should we do, Maggie?"

"Right now? Make sure she gets healthy. Get her some regular food. We should also look into getting her some puberty blockers if she wants them. I think living rough has staved off puberty thus far. She'd normally be in the middle of it by now. If we feed her and provide a safe place for her, her body will make up for lost time. Blockers will buy us, and more importantly, her, some time. I am concerned about how we're going to take care of her, though. I'm not sure we'll be able to place her with a wolf family, not with her apparent fear of her own kind."

Holly nodded in response. "OK. That gives me some things to think about. She's probably about done showering by now. I'm having food prepped for her. We'll have her brought to the conference room. She can eat while we ask her some questions about the location she described. Hopefully, she'll have calmed down a bit and can give us some clearer answers." Holly grabbed the doorknob but gave Luke an appraising look as she opened the door and headed to the house's meeting room.

THE GIRL HADN'T MADE an appearance yet, so everyone fixed snack plates for themselves and grabbed more coffee. The executive group of the pack was assembled, or at least that's what Luke assumed they were. The kid was too skittish to be in front of the entire pack, plus they didn't need to be here to hear her tale or make a decision. Dr. Maggie Rabinowitz, Sam, Pablo, Holly, and one other individual, a tall, skinny Black man Luke didn't know, were chatting in one corner as Luke took a seat and grazed through his snack plate.

Holly nodded to Luke. "Luke, you know everyone here, except Jamaal. They help me run the pack and were the first responders to my call to meeting. We'll keep the gathering small for now."

Luke nodded at Holly.

The door cracked open, and the girl peeked her head in.

"It's OK. Come on in and close the door behind you, please," Maggie said to her with a warm and comforting smile.

Gwen walked in and closed the door but not enough for it to latch. She'd only entered the room far enough to close the door.

Maggie stood up and gestured toward Holly and Sam. "Gwen, this is Holly. She's the packleader. Samantha is her wife."

Sam gave her a friendly wave and smile.

"That's Pablo, the pack second. This is Jamaal. They're all members of the pack council. The human sitting at the table is Luke, a friend of Pablo's."

Luke nodded at Gwen.

Maggie pointed Gwen toward the food spread out on the counter. "Please, fix yourself some food. But as a medical professional, I'd advise starting light. You've got to be starving after your first transformation, but try not to overdo it. You've been living rough for a while and your stomach might rebel on you."

Gwen walked to the line of food and picked out some rolls and slices of deli meat, as well as a banana, before sitting down in a chair next to Luke.

After Gwen finished eating, Holly directed everyone to silence and said, "Please, Gwen, tell us about the vampires and the jail."

Gwen nodded. "Um, where do you want me to start?"

"Wherever you think you need to start," Holly replied.

Gwen sat for a bit, appearing to think about it. "I've been staying at the camp down on Interstate and Greeley for a while. A few months ago, people started disappearing. I mean, people come and go, but they always take their stuff. At first, it was a few of the rougher people who liked to avoid most of the camp but still stayed nearby. Nobody thought anything of it. Some of the other campers were happy to see them go. Even if they didn't cause too many problems, they scared some people. Others just thought they'd been picked up by the cops."

"Did you see any police?" Holly asked.

"Sometimes, I guess. I always hid when they showed up. I didn't want them taking me in."

Holly nodded. "How many people disappeared?"

"I don't know. It was hard to tell who just left or was picked up by the cops or had...been taken. Max tried to keep an eye on everyone. But it's a big camp and a lot of people just want to be left alone."

"Who's Max?" Holly asked.

Luke chimed in, "I know Max. He kind of runs the camp along with a couple other people. He keeps an eye on everyone. Tries to get people services when he can—"

"I know you!" Gwen interrupted. "You bring stuff to Max sometimes, for the camp."

Luke nodded at her. "I don't remember seeing you."

"I kept out of sight. I thought you were a cop or a social worker."

"Nope."

"Gwen, when were you taken?" Holly asked.

Gwen pulled in on herself. "A couple weeks ago. It was late. I'd heard something near my tent. I snuck out to get Max. That's when I saw some creepers sneak up to his place. He's got one of those mini-houses. The creepers knocked on his door, and when Max opened it, he started talking, then stopped and got all weird. He kind of looked like he'd been hypnotized. Then, two of the creepers carried him away. I was about to yell for help when someone covered my mouth. I woke up in a room with bars everywhere. That's all I remember."

"What happened after you woke up?" asked Holly.

"I... I don't want to talk about it," Gwen replied, further withdrawing into herself.

Maggie settled a hand on Holly to prevent her from delving further in this direction.

"Gwen, do you mind if I ask you a few questions about things like the number of vampires you saw, patrols, security features, things you observed about your surroundings?" Luke gently asked.

She nodded.

"OK, thank you."

Gwen lined out as much information as she could, trying to remember the details Luke was coaxing out of her.

"How did you escape?" Holly asked.

"They came to take me to...they came to get me. I started to panic and then... I changed, shifted..." There was a long pause. "The next thing I remember is running in the dark. I was soaked. I'd picked up the scent of werewolves and came here. I don't know how." Everything was delivered in a detached monotone. "When I got done with the shower, I found these keys in my pocket." She tossed a set of specialty keys on the table.

Everyone's eyes fell on the keys with a mix of responses from disbelief, good fortune, and avarice like someone had just opened the buried treasure a bunch of pirates had dug up.

"Can you tell us where the jail is?" Holly asked, still staring at the keys.

"I don't know. I don't remember how long I ran."

"I might have an idea," Luke commented to Holly. "Gwen, did everything look new and unused, or was it an old jail?"

"Um, new, I guess. I don't remember the outside, but everything seemed new. It was dusty..."

"Wapato," Luke and Pablo said at the same time.

Holly nodded, but Maggie, Sam, and Jamaal looked confused.

Luke deferred to Pablo. "It's in St. Johns, by Bybee Lake. It was this massive jail they passed a bond to build a few years ago, except it never went into use. Wasted millions of dollars. The city tried to rent it out to the Feds or the State, but they didn't bite either. It's been sitting there empty, wasting more money since. Sounds like they found someone to lease it to."

"I'm not sure I'm happy about the new neighbors. The pack has always kept this part of town safe. I'd like to know who knows what and how much down at city hall..." Holly mused.

"That's something we can investigate later," Pablo interjected. "We need to figure out what to do now. This is the first serious break we've had on the bloodsuckers' operation. We can get in there and bust it up and possibly cripple their numbers."

"Yeah, but we have no idea how many vampires are inside. Or what else is waiting inside," Luke countered. "Gwen, how many vampires do you remember seeing?"

"I don't know...maybe fifteen or twenty. My cell didn't have a very clear view."

"Were there other people?" Luke asked.

Gwen nodded.

Holly looked troubled. "How many?"

"Um, lots. I could see about thirty in the cells near me. I heard more though."

Luke's eyebrows shot up. "That changes things. We need to get in and free whoever the vamps are holding before they move them off site or just kill them out of convenience."

"Won't that many bodies point back to the names on the lease?" Sam asked.

"Yeah, but it won't be anyone real or traceable. They'll close shop, suck as many dry as they can, kill the rest, and leave. By the time the city wonders why the rent checks stopped landing in the mailbox, there'll be nothing but a gruesome and smelly mess and leads that go nowhere. Vampires have been operating in the dark for too long to get caught making these kinds of mistakes. They've got their game down. Holly, I'm going to need some information about the pack. I know you protect that closely, but I need to know what kind of resources we have to work with."

Holly didn't respond for a while. "I'll have to discuss this with the council. I'm not sure involving us any further in your war with the vampires is the best idea. Pablo going along with you on hunts is one thing. This opens us to a new level of peril." She sighed, looked down, then back up at Luke. "Do me a favor, please. Take Gwen upstairs and show her one of the guest rooms. The stairs are just outside the door there, and the guest rooms are on the left. Any of them are fine. She looks exhausted and should get some sleep. There are enough council members here to put the motion forward."

Luke nodded and refilled his coffee mug before gesturing for Gwen to follow. "Let's give them some privacy. Grab any snacks you might want and a bottle of water or two."

She did as suggested, then headed out of the room. Luke pulled the door shut behind him and headed to the stairs.

Luke gestured toward the stairs. "This way, little one."

They headed upstairs and down the hall until Luke stopped in front of one of the doors and peeked in.

"This one will work. Bed's all made up. It locks from the inside as well, if that works for you. If it helps, I think the pack here is pretty nice. Although I haven't met most of them, Pablo is my friend and Holly and Sam are very thoughtful and kind."

Gwen nodded before walking into the room and shutting the door. As Luke walked away, he heard the lock click. Taking a seat at the bottom of the stairs, Luke waited for the pack's verdict.

Finally, Pablo popped out, "We're ready for you."

Luke sat at the table on the opposite end from everyone else.

Holly sat up straight and fixed her gaze on Luke. "Luke, we're not sure if we should involve the pack in this business. As it stands, we're split. What you're asking is big. Throughout our history, werewolves have sought to remain hidden, blend in. We hide in plain sight, join the human populace. We avoid getting involved with vampires. We protect our pack and maintain our community. You're asking us to put all of that at risk."

"Whether you join or not, it's risked already. You think I'm about to drop you in boiling water, like the proverbial frog. But the vampires have been slowly turning up the temperature of the pot you're in without you noticing, and now it's about to boil over. I've seen this a lot over the centuries. Witnessed it many times before.

There's a rhythm to it." Luke leaned forward, narrowing his eyes as his gaze intensified.

"First, it's one or two vampires. They feed a little here, a little there. They stay unnoticed. Then, if they decide the environment is ripe, they breed. Instead of a meal, they look for a steadier and more willing source. Violent crime goes up. Strange deaths. Missing people. Darkness." He paused, sighed, and let go of the filter blocking the urgency of his plea.

As he looked around the table, the sure looks had become uncertain and worried. Holly almost looked scared.

"This is your home. Your city. Someone is preying on it. Taking its most vulnerable and using them to further imperil the place you call home. They've taken at least one werewolf that we know of. And yes, she's not from your pack, but she needs someone to advocate for her. Someone to step in for her. I will. I can give you no more reason to do it other than it's the right thing to do, and you have the power to do it if you choose to take up that mantle." He exhaled sharply.

"I know fighting vampires is my lot in life; I'll go in alone if need be. But I'd much rather have strong allies at my side."

Holly took a deep breath and let it out in a long, controlled sigh. She looked at her pack mates, who each nodded slightly, then turned to Luke.

"You're right. We can't shirk our duty to our community any longer. What can we do to help?"

"We need your fighters, and anyone else who is willing to help. We'll also need transportation. There could be a lot of people in that jail, and we won't be able to fit them all in cars. Doc, we'll need medical supplies and probably food. Barring food, we should get liquids. Sports drinks, Pedialyte, or even coconut water will work. If they're being used as juice boxes by vampires, they'll be short on blood and dehydrated."

"Those are all doable. I'll call in the pack. You'll have your fighters, but we'll need more than just muscle. We have a couple buses we use for pack trips. Maggie, I'll leave you in charge of prepping medical and food supplies. Check the pack database for anyone with past medical training. Jamaal, see if you can find any blueprints or detailed information on Wapato."

Luke nodded at Holly. "Thank you. I want to head up that way before dawn to see what the security situation is on the outside, patrols, guards, and the like. I'd like to take Pablo. He's familiar with the scent of vampires at this point; his nose will be useful. Also, if you can spare someone, I'd like to have a driver to keep the car running if we need to get out in a hurry."

"I'll take care of that, Holly," Sam piped up. "Maybe I can keep you two out of trouble." She winked at Luke.

"Yes, but who'll keep you out of trouble?" Holly asked.

"Sam, Pablo, you're with me. We need to stop by my house on the way."

They followed him out of the pack's Kenton house and climbed into the Volvo wagon with Luke.

"Pablo, could you please text Delilah and let her know to check in as soon as she's up?"

Pablo nodded. "No problem. She'd thump you something good if you left her out of this."

TWENTY

PABLO, Sam, and Luke sat in silence as the old Volvo chugged around industrial St. Johns. Luke pulled into the empty parking lot of a giant warehouse. Fortunately, the weekend early morning left the lot empty and an ideal place to stash the car while they proceeded on foot.

Luke popped around back of the Volvo and opened the hatch, revealing the plastic tub he used to stash his gear. He put on his armor, strapped on his back scabbards, and finished by pulling on the giant oversized hoodie he used to hide it all.

Next, he grabbed a duffel bag he'd picked up from his garage. He pulled out three sets of FRS two-way radios and handed one each to Sam and Pablo.

"OK, they're already tuned to the same channel. Pop the earbud in and give it a test. Just push the button on the earbud cord to talk."

"Sweet! I call dibs on 'Bandit!'" Sam called. Seeing the confusion on Luke's and Pablo's faces, she added, "What? We're not going to pick cool CB handles? Spoilsports."

"Anyway, Sam, keep the engine running in case we have to come out hot."

He slid the tub back in and closed the hatch door of the Volvo.

"You're pretty slick at getting all the stuff on by yourself," Sam commented.

"Yeah, I've done it a time or two. Usually not anyone around to help me. Stay safe, Sam. Keep an eye out for trouble and let us know if there's something we need to know."

The men set off at a casual walk, passing various other warehouses and warehouse retail fronts.

"Hey, Luke. Need a harp?" Pablo asked as he pointed to a harp shop.

"They are one of the more versatile and mobile of instruments…" Luke quipped.

They set up behind a hedge that surrounded the parking lot and found a section with a gap at the bottom that would allow them to see through the trunks of the tall camellia bushes. Wapato Jail had cost tens of millions from a voter approved bond yet had never housed a single person until recently apparently.

The recent escape of Gwendolyn had solved the mystery of who was using the jail, but left open the question of how and what Portland's government knew about the less than savory operation they'd leased the huge facility to.

Two guards appeared out of the dark, walking a patrol around the jail. "Humans or bloodsuckers?" asked Pablo.

"Pasty, gaunt, trendy threads. I'm going to say vamp. That and my fanger senses are tingling. What's your nose say?"

Pablo grinned. "Like they haven't taken a bath in a while and are lacking that sexy 'I don't care' musk with a hint of corpse. Vampire."

They watched the undead guards do their patrols. About thirty minutes before sunrise—the first rays of pre-dawn light peeking over the horizon—they were relieved by a set of what were very clearly human guards. Luke and Pablo peeked out from under the bushes as the sun ascended behind them, illuminating the front of Wapato Jail. The pair of security guards strolled around in their rumpled uniforms.

"Human or bloodsuckers?" asked Pablo.

"Definitely humans. Vampires are a bit more graceful," Luke

observed as one of the guards tripped over one of the giant stone spheres decorating the outside of the jail.

Pablo chuckled at the guard's unintended pratfall. "Also, you know, the sun…"

They laid there silently, barely moving as they continued to watch the human patrol. Luke occasionally took some photographs with his cell phone.

"Breaker 1-9, Bandit calling. Looking for Old Man and the Pooch, you got your ears on?" Sam's voice crackled over the radio, imitating a trucker.

"Yeah. Everything OK there?" Luke replied.

"10-4, good buddy. Just saw a smokey bear and wanted to give you a heads up."

"Thanks. I think we're done here. We'll be back shortly."

"10-4. Put the pedal to the metal. The Bandit needs to stop at a choke and puke for a 10-100. Also, the Bandit needs some go-go juice."

"Well, I guess we better get back to the car. Sam needs some go-go juice," Luke said, his delivery deadpan.

"Go-go juice?" Pablo looked confused.

"Coffee, I think she means."

Pablo chuckled. They broke into a light jog on the way back to the car. Instead of taking his armor off, Luke piled into the back seat clumsily, letting Pablo have shotgun.

"These cars weren't meant for people in armor. I barely fit through the back door. Sam, I think that new coffee shop on Lombard by the Taco Bell opens early, even on weekends. We can get you a cup of go-go juice. I could use a cup myself."

"Good, hopefully they have a restroom too!" Sam said.

"For the 10-100?" Luke asked.

"10-4, good buddy."

Pablo groaned and shook his head.

TWENTY-ONE

PABLO LOOKED DOWN at his cell phone, responding to the vibrating buzz of a notification.

"Delilah's out front. I'll let her in." He stood up from the table they'd met at earlier that morning, too early, when Gwen told Luke and the pack about the escape her first werewolf shift had facilitated. A moment later, he returned with Delilah. Pablo cleared his throat to get the attention of the room. "Hey, everyone. This is Delilah. She's been helping us clear up Portland's freelance phlebotomist problem."

Everyone except Sam and Maggie gave Pablo a confused look; Sam was hiding a snicker behind her hand, pretending to cover her mouth and yawn. Maggie rolled her eyes at Pablo's antics, although she grinned a bit.

"You know…vampires. They draw blood…" Pablo waggled his eyebrows.

Holly shook her head and rubbed her temples.

"Anywho… Delilah, the lady with the tattoos is Holly. She's the packleader. The woman with the ponytail is Sam, Holly's wife. The blond woman is Maggie, one of the pack doctors. And the fellow with the locs pouring over the map is Jamaal."

The werewolves greeted Delilah with a mix of nods, smiles, and waves.

Luke filled in Delilah on last night's events, including what they'd learned about Gwen and the initial recon of Wapato Jail. Luke moved over to the map of North Portland they had spread out on the table.

"OK. I think I have a working idea for a plan, if you don't mind?" He looked at Holly, who nodded her consent to continue. "Pablo and I will go in first. We'll take out the guards outside. How many fighters can you bring?"

"Including Pablo, Sam, and me, we've got about eighteen that I can get a hold of now," Holly said.

"When do you think they'll be ready?" Luke asked.

"We're looking early afternoon by the time we get all the people and resources gathered."

Luke's eyes rolled up a bit as he mulled over the numbers.

"It's going to be tight. I'd like to get in before sunset, but better to be properly prepared than rush in. OK, we'll split it this way. Give me a dozen fighters for the jail. That'll leave four to guard the buses and act as a reserve if we need reinforcements. Holly, you'll be on the outside in charge of the evac team." He looked back at the map, then pointed to a spot. "Jubitz Truck Stop. Take the buses and the rest of the evac team and park there until you get the all-clear. It'll be less conspicuous for a couple buses and some extra cars to hang out there. Plus, you can just roll straight down Marine Drive to the pull-off to the jail." He ran his finger along the map to demonstrate.

"Pablo and I will take Sam with us. She'll coordinate communications. The FRS radios I have will work well enough around the jail, but she'll need to stay in touch with you via cell," Luke continued.

Everybody nodded along.

"Sweet! Cool CB handles for everyone!" Sam clapped her hands excitedly.

Holly smiled at Sam. "Jamaal, you'll stay here; you'll be in charge of the pack until I'm back in town."

Jamaal nodded. "Understood."

"What about me?" Delilah asked.

"You'll be going into the jail with me, Pablo, and the were-wolves." Luke turned to Pablo. "Pablo, can you organize our advance team? I'll need four teams. I'll lead two and you and Delilah will lead the other two."

"HEY, BOYS!" Sam called to the two human guards. "Can you help me with my car? It won't start. You look like a couple fellas who know your way around a car." She gave them her most winsome smile and struck a pose that highlighted her curvier assets. The two schlubs looked at each other and came to some sort of silent agreement.

"Sure, ma'am! We'd love to." They abandoned their post and sauntered toward Sam.

"I'm parked over in the Harp store parking lot. I was supposed to meet someone for an appointment at three to look at some harps, but I've been waiting for over an hour, and it's almost dark. They must have bailed. Then, when I went to turn my car on, it wouldn't start. I'm so clueless about things like cars." She added an extra bit of ditz to her routine. She led them to Luke's old Volvo, which was parked behind the hedge, obscuring the view from the prison.

"Ma'am, would you mind popping the hood?" Sam opened the driver's door and pulled the hood release lever. One of the guards slipped his hand under the hood, pulled the latch, and opened the hood. That was the signal, and Luke and Pablo stood up from their hiding place behind the car.

"What the f…"

Sam grabbed one of the guards and slammed his head into the top of the radiator. When his head bounced back up, she slammed a fist into his face with a wicked uppercut that dropped him to the pavement. By the time Sam was finished with the first schlubby guard, Pablo and Luke had knocked out the other.

"God, I can't believe they fell for the old 'damsel and car' bit. Haven't these guys ever watched a movie?" Sam asked.

Pablo chuckled. "Well, Sam, they probably weren't thinking with their upstairs head, and you're quite the adorable little bombshell when you want to be."

"Hopefully the movie magic continues, and these uniforms magically fit us, but I won't hold my breath," commented Luke as he began stripping the guard of his uniform. "There are zip ties in the duffel bag in the back seat. We'll stash the guards out of the way. Pablo, when you're done stripping the other one, give me a hand with this one. I'll grab the shoulders, you grab the feet. No need to drag them across the pavement. We've already knocked them out and stripped them; we don't need to give them road rash on their asses."

The three of them quickly had the guards bound and gagged and out of the way. Luke and Pablo stripped down to their undies and socks. Luke didn't have one of those romance novel cover six-pack bodies, but one that was muscular from hard work balanced by just a touch of love handles. Falling into old habits, he'd began bulking up on calories for leaner times that always came on a campaign. A series of old scars ran down the backs of his legs, peeking out from his boxer briefs. Scars of various sizes and shapes also dotted his torso and arms. Pablo, though stockier, was likewise muscled from lifting large sacks of malt at the brewery. Sam whistled at them appreciatively. As she eyed them up and down, her breath caught when she saw the back of Luke's legs.

"What happened to your legs?"

"Those?" Luke stuck out his leg and twisted to look. "Those I got in training. Centurions were fond of the vine rods as a motivational tool. Vine rods were a symbol of their station and one they liked using heavily. Unfortunately, I was often on the edge of the formation. That, coupled with my centurion's dislike of us 'barbarian boys' and my high performance, meant I got a bit more than average in quantity and quality. I did not mourn his loss when a Dacian arrow split his head open."

As anticipated, the uniforms were a bit on the baggy side. Sam helped them out by pulling the sides of both the shirts and pants around and smartly tucking them into the back, using the belts to cinch everything down.

"That'll have to do. Try not to move too vigorously. And keep your back away from anyone you have to talk to. At least the extra material does a good job of hiding Luke's swords."

Luke snagged the two security ball caps off the ground and tossed one to Pablo.

"We'd better get back before they notice their guards aren't on patrol, but if the guards inside are anything like these two, I don't think 'highly qualified' was anywhere near the top of the list for hiring requirements. Everyone got their radio on? Sam, let Holly and the convoy know they can move to the second wait point."

Pablo and Sam nodded at Luke as they checked the FRS radios he'd handed them. They headed toward the jail, leaving Sam with the car. Once they got back to the jail, they resumed the guards' patrol route.

"Hey, Luke. I was thinking. Do you think they have more human guards inside? What I mean is, would they let hired guards have any contact with the humans they've captured? These guys," he said, plucking his uniform, "don't seem like the scary black bag kind of mercs who would be cold-blooded enough for this kind of job."

"You might be right. We'll have to keep an eye on it. It could be that they have an initial layer of hired help to watch during the day, but it's all outward facing. The human guards likely have no idea what's going on deeper in the building. In my experience, vampires are highly secretive. The humans, or whoever their employer is, have no idea who they're contracting with." Luke looked at the descending sun. "We should keep the conversation to a minimum. I think the vampires will come out to relieve us as soon as the sun's down."

They continued the repetitive path around the jail's perimeter for another fifteen minutes before Luke signaled for Pablo to stop.

"OK, I can feel them. Once we turn the corner, we'll be able to see them. I think they're by the main entrance," Luke whispered. He reached back with both hands and pulled out his gladius and his rudis. He flipped the gladius around in a neat maneuver and offered it toward Pablo, hilt first. "This should look enough like one of the batons the guards carried to get us close. Pointy end goes in the vampire. Try to hit the heart. And careful, it's sharp. The anti-vamp enchantments shouldn't be a problem for you though."

Pablo nodded once and asked, "Won't they see the swords?"

"Here. Hold it like this." Luke demonstrated a reverse grip. "Keep the blade tight against your forearm, and that should do it. Your sleeve should protect you from the silver."

Situated, they turned the corner and kept their casual pace. Pretending to spot their relief, Luke gave the vampires standing just away from the overhead lights near the main entrance a casual wave.

"Anything to report?" one of the vampires asked as they got closer.

"Nothing out of the ordinary," Luke replied.

"Hey, you're not the normal guys."

"They couldn't make it tonight."

The vampires tensed and looked at the two guards still walking toward them. It was too late by the time they noticed the swords weren't batons. "What the fu..."

Luke rammed the rudis home into the vampire's heart, starting his final death. Pablo was a bit slower with his sword and the other vampire, a tallish woman, had turned around and was trying to run back to the entrance. Fortunately, she tripped in a gopher hole, allowing Pablo's heightened werewolf speed to catch up to her. He grabbed her left shoulder and shoved the gladius into her back so hard it sank to the hilt. The vampire fell forward, pulling the sword from Pablo's hand.

"Good catch. You only need to stab them a little bit, not impale them up to your elbow."

"I got a little overexcited; I'm not a sword boy like you." Pablo bent over to pull the sword out but couldn't get it to budge. "It's not coming out."

"Give it a twist. It doesn't have a blood channel, so the flesh can form a bit of a vacuum. Or give it a few seconds for the vamp to start its decay."

Pablo gave it a hard twist and yanked it free.

"Wipe it clean before the vamp goes totally gooey on us, please," Luke added.

The men bent over to clean Luke's blades, then rifled through the clothes and pulled two more sets of keys, making a grand total of five they'd taken from the guards, including Gwen's set. Luke stood up and keyed the radio button. After Luke resheathed the rudis, Pablo returned Luke's gladius to him.

"We appear to have a plethora of keys," Pablo said.

"Yeah. We'll spread them out and leave a set with Sam. Speaking of which…" Luke engaged the mic on his radio. "Hey, Bandit, bring the Trans-Am over."

Sam swung around with Luke's Volvo, then backed it up to Luke and Pablo, who were standing just out of the light. Luke pulled the trunk hatch open and slid out his gear tub. Pablo pulled a ladder and a can of spray paint from the back of the car. Setting the ladder up under the security camera, he climbed up and sprayed the clear plastic dome with black spray paint.

"Hopefully they won't rush out blind. You better get your business suit on in a hurry, just in case," Pablo instructed, taking down the ladder.

Luke shucked his purloined guard uniform and redressed in a pair of skinny jeans and a tight black T-shirt. He pulled on his steel-toed boots and followed them with a set of elaborately engraved steel greaves. Next, he pulled out a scarf, wrapped it around his neck, then pulled out the lorica segmentata armor and settled it around his shoulders. Before he tied up the armor, he slid a manica, an armor sleeve made of segmented plates, up his right arm and fastened it to the inside of the lorica, which he followed by lacing up the armor and cinching it closed. He clipped on his nylon tactical bandolier, attached the rudis to the back, hilt pointing left, and clipped the gladius's scabbard to the left at the bottom just above his hip.

"Sam, please signal Holly to get the evac squad moving," Luke said.

As Luke finished draping a black cloak around his armor, a couple of passenger vans backed up to the entrance and disgorged Delilah and a bunch of men and women in sweatpants. Pablo walked over and got everyone's attention.

"Hi, everyone. For those who don't know," he looked around the

229

crowd, "which is most of you, this is Luke. He's a human and all-around general vampire slaying badass. The Black lady with the cute mini 'fro is Delilah, also human, also a vampire slaying badass. Over behind us are a couple of vampire corpses returning to a more liquid state. Once everyone gets changed, go over and give them a good sniff. You'll want to keep that scent in mind. If it smells strongly like that, kill it. Luke, got anything to add?"

Luke nodded. "The vampires will also be easy to tell because they'll sport huge fangs and their fingernails will convert to claws. Watch out for those. They can disable just as well as the fangs. Don't let them swipe at your throats or you will cease to have throats. You can render them inert by ripping their heads off or stabbing them through the heart with a wooden stake. If you do rip the head off, make sure it can't roll back to the neck or someone else can put it back into place. It can reattach and reactivate the vampire. They are fast and strong. The older they are, the faster and stronger they are, so don't get caught off guard or it will be the last thing you do. Pablo?"

"OK, Holly has given you your assignments. Alpha team and Bravo team, you're with Luke. Follow his instructions as if they came directly from Holly or me. Charlie and Delta Teams, you're with me and Delilah. She'll be handling communication with Luke and his team. Don't let any of the human hostages out of their cells until we've cleared the facility. Luke?" Luke shook his head; he had nothing more to add. "OK, team. Put on your fighting faces. It's time to rumble."

"Yay, team! Go Team! Rah, rah, ree; kick 'em in the knee!" Sam cheered them on.

The sound of a door opening behind them caused everyone to turn around. A head popped out the door, eyes going wide at the sight of a bunch of burly werewolves. Luke thought he mouthed the word "fuck" before disappearing back into the jail.

"That's their scout figuring out what happened to that camera. Let's go before they can get too organized," Luke ordered.

All the wolves, except for Sam and the other two divers, stripped off their sweatpants and tossed them back into their vans before beginning their shifts. A few moments later, Luke was surrounded by a dozen werewolves in bipedal hybrid form. The drivers of each of the vans had opened the back doors and pulled out boxes full of stakes attached to bandolier-style belts. They handed two to each of the wolves. Pablo strung on a pair as well. By the time they were done, they looked like a nightmare version of a Chewbacca cosplay convention.

Luke looked at Pablo, who nodded in reply. "Let's do it. Everyone behind us."

Luke and Pablo walked to the front doors, inserted their pilfered keys into the locks, and opened the doors. Two wolves followed up by dropping large rocks to prop them open. Luke drew his gladius and darted forward to the next set of doors.

TWENTY-TWO

THE KEYS LUKE and Pablo had lifted made short work of the doors that separated the various sections of the jail. As suspected, the few guards they initially met were human security guards who hadn't been relieved for the day yet. They were quickly disarmed and zip tied out of the way. When they found the main security office, they shut down the video surveillance system once they collected the usable information.

"Why haven't they attacked us yet?" Pablo asked.

"I don't know. Maybe they got sloppy, and we caught them off guard. It won't last for long, though. They've had enough time to set up some surprises for us deeper in," Luke said, scratching his chin thoughtfully. "Be careful, buddy."

"You too," Pablo replied.

As they proceeded into the heart of the jail, they came to the split in the hallway they were expecting that led to the two separate wings of the jail. With their plan in effect, Delilah, Pablo, and their teams split off to the right while Luke and the Alpha and Bravo teams went to the left. Luke held up his closed fist, directing his team to stop.

"There are a couple vamps coming up. Stay clear of my blades and don't let them get past you. Nothing gets through. Don't get separated. Stay close to each other."

The wolves nodded in response. Luke took the opportunity to pull the rudis from its scabbard. With a rudis in his left hand and gladius in his right, Luke halted as he heard the approaching footsteps and snatches of conversation. He readied himself, a coiled viper about to strike the unaware mouse.

"That last one last night didn't taste very good. I'm tired of dining on the homeless dregs of Portland."

"Sure, the flavor is crap, but these meals don't fight. The free-range meals have gotten a lot more dangerous."

"Sauce, man, savor the danger."

"Dude, pay attention. They've got to be here somewhere." He sniffed. "Fuck, they're—"

His words were cut off as a rudis plunged into his heart. His buddy stood agog, staring at the wooden blade sticking out of his dissolving friend's chest. He only caught a brief spinning flash of black and silver as a gladius separated his head from his neck. The soft sound of paw pads and claws giving a quiet golf clap rewarded Luke's lethal moves. Luke bowed with a flourish and pulled his rudis free from vampydee and quickly stabbed it into the headless vampydum chest cavity to ensure he wouldn't rise to give more one-star yelp reviews of Portland's houseless population.

They worked their way up the hallway, clearing each room as they passed. Luke sent in a team of wolves here or there, sharing the fight and probably in the wolves' eyes, the fun. Nothing undead remained ambulatory. While Bravo Team cleaned out a larger cadre of vampires, Luke watched the hall with Alpha Team.

"Spartacus calling Foxy Lady, status check." Sam had insisted everyone else get cool call names, partially because it amused her and partially to keep some semblance of privacy, and had settled on "Foxy Lady" for Delilah.

"Light to medium resistance. About to enter Block 1. Out."

"Same here, entering 3. Over and out." Luke closed the radio's button.

Once they walked out into the main hall where he might be overheard, Luke switched back to hand signals with the team. Alpha team formed up with Luke while Bravo took off to the left side. Luke carefully inserted his key into the lock and pulled the door open slowly to keep it from making any kind of noise, then signaled, *"Go."*

Bravo team went in first and broke right along the wall; Alpha followed and stayed along the wall that ran toward the back from the door. The wolves might as well have been ghosts for all the noise they made. Luke gently closed the door and caught up to Alpha Team. No amount of carefulness could keep the metal stairs from rumbling, but they still progressed as quietly as they could after finding nothing on the first level. The second and third floors proved similarly empty.

Luke walked back down the hall so he could check in with Pablo and Delilah quietly. "Spartacus to Foxy Lady. Block 3 clear, proceeding to Block 2. Out."

"Roger. Block 1 clear, no resistance. Proceeding to Block 2. Out," Delilah replied.

Luke's teams met back up at the next locked, barred door. Luke pointed to his nose and then dangled two fingers from his top teeth like vampire fangs, pointing down the hall.

They piled in as soon as Luke unlocked the barred gate. Luke closed the gate, but just before it clicked shut, he heard feet hitting concrete hard and the jingling of metal. He spun around just in time to see a vampire sling a chain around the bars of the door and barred frame and click a large padlock shut. The vampire stuck his hand between the bars, gave everyone the bird, then pulled his hand back through before Luke could spin around and lop it off.

"Bravo, you're on rearguard. Stay close but don't cluster up. The exit is blocked." Luke worked his way forward. "This is Spartacus. General notice, we've encountered some shenanigans. All parties step up your vigilance."

"Roger, busy pistol whipping some guys who said shenanigans too many times, out," Delilah replied.

A pained yelp from the rear brought Luke's attention back to the chained gate. The back of his platoon pushed forward. The smell of smoke and gasoline wafted down the hall. Once Luke got to the back of his formation, he saw several wolves patting out the sparks in each other's singed fur. He whipped his cloak off and used it to help smother the last of the sparks. Several of the wolves had nasty looking burns.

A short yip, just loud enough for him to hear it, drew him back to the front. Somewhere ahead, a door slammed shut as the clarion calls of battle yells rang out. Luke stepped out in front, giving himself room to work, and signaled his wolves to stay back. The first vamp sprang through the dim light with lungs bellowing and an arm cocked back with a machete ready to spring down on Luke with all the speed and power a vampire could muster. Luke slapped the machete away then sidestepped before raking the sharp steel & silver edge of the rudis across the vamps back. The bellicose bellow turned to a pained shriek as silver burned and kept the wound from closing. The fanger staggered forward, his momentum carrying him into the waiting claws of the now enraged werewolves.

Behind him, he heard a gory mix of juicy meat splattering and bones shattering as the werewolves took their revenge. Parrying the next vampire's attack, Luke delivered a quick stab in the face, and as the vampire recoiled and covered her face, dropping the machete she was swinging, Luke finished her with a precision heart shot. The next vampire caught Luke with his gladius stuck in the ribs of his previous foe. He shoved the dead vamp out of his way and managed to get a nearly powerless stab in the stomach, but the weight and speed of the onrushing vampire carried the blade deeper. Luke let the vamp's body close with his as he spun, shoving the vamp into the eager wolves.

The ferocity and speed with which Luke had broken their charge caused the trailing vampires to slow their approach. A whistle caught Luke's attention as a thrown stake whipped by his ear and thudded to a halt in the lead vampire's chest, eliciting a gasp before she collapsed in on herself. The wolves had had enough. They broke ranks and charged the remaining vampires, tearing into them with snarling teeth and shredding claws. The vampires dissolved into chunks and pieces. Luke used the distraction to recover his gladius.

Pained yelping drew Luke's attention back to the fracas. Another group of vampires had sallied forth from a side door behind the werewolves. One was down on the ground holding its hamstring; another had a fire axe stuck in its shoulder blade. Trying to regain control of the engagement, Luke let out a primal yell and charged at top speed into the back of the vampires and laid about with swords, both steel and wooden.

The vampires, thinking they'd potentially routed the invaders, soon realized that their compatriots were no longer whole and fighting at their backs but gooifying into very stylish piles of sludge. Luke dispatched the last, checked in the closet they'd sprung out of to make sure it was cleared, then barreled down the hall. Another group of vampires had opened the gate leading in from the other cell block when Luke's speed and fury caught them completely by surprise. The remaining wolves collected themselves and charged after Luke, ensuring he wouldn't be overwhelmed.

The vampire's advance began to melt, in some cases literally, before the methodical and brutal charge, while the werewolves who had finally reengaged were picking up the pieces. Finally, Luke burst through the door, beheading the vamp trying to get the gate closed again.

Chaos boiled throughout Cell Block 2. Pablo's team had made it through on their side before Luke and his squad. Fights raged on multiple levels. The outnumbered werewolves were doing their best to handle multiple targets, but in some cases had been separated from their packmates. Luke couldn't see Pablo but hoped his friend wasn't lying hurt and unseen somewhere. Delilah was sticking close to one of her squads and was laying about with stakes and a machete. Luke shut the door after the wolves made it through, then sprinted off to the first engagement he could reach.

Luke's swords blurred through the air, lopping off arms when heads weren't reachable. If he had to duck, he took out knees, quads, or hamstrings. If he couldn't kill, he maimed or distracted, allowing the werewolves space to recover and finish the vampires. With each werewolf freed, the tide shifted slowly away from the fanged and toward the furry. On the other side of the cell block, some wolves had managed to group back up and were rallying to their over-whelmed friends.

Rushing toward a wolf about to be taken down by two vampires, Luke saw the wolf go down with a piteous yelp. Before they could press their advantage and kill the wolf, Luke roared at them as he sprinted to the wolf's aid. One of the vamps, seeing the angry sword-wielding man barreling down on them, broke and ran for it. A leg shot out from between the bars of the nearest cell, sending the vampire flying forward and landing on its face with a grunt and a crunch of bones and splat of blood. The other one backpedaled into the bars of the cell behind her. An arm reached out and wrapped around the throat of the vampire, their fist white knuckling the bar to keep the vampire and its superior strength locked in place just long enough for Luke to dispatch the vampire with a quick stab to the heart. The fanger with the freshly smashed face was simultane-ously struggling to get back up and run, making for another quick kill for Luke.

Breathing heavily, Luke looked around the room. The last few vampires were going down. That's when the noise slammed into Luke. In the heat of battle, terrified human screams mingled with the pained whines of injured werewolves.

"Hey! Hey, Luke!" Luke turned to see Max frantically trying to get his attention. It had been Max's arm that'd assisted Luke a moment before.

"Max, I didn't see you there. I was a bit distracted. Are you OK?"

"I'm...I'm not sure. I've been gnawed on by these...these..." he said, gesticulating clumsily at the vampire goo next to his cell.

"Vampires?"

"Fuckin' vampires!" He looked a bit wild about the eyes. "And now, there's giant damned dogs here to replace them."

Max wobbled back to the bed, sitting down with his head in his hands. A shaky laugh occasionally punctuated his mumbling and cursing.

"Max. It's all right. I can understand. This is a hugely big pile of fucked up, but you're OK now. I'm here. The werewolves won't harm you. You're safe inside your cell. I won't open it until it's safe. Understand?"

Max perked his head up, making eye contact with Luke and then nodded. Luke turned in time to see a naked Pablo limping toward him.

"That was a bit touch and go there for a minute, man."

"Yeah, I was worried we weren't going to make it out of that hall. We left a wolf or two back there. The injuries didn't look fatal. Do you think we're ready for the evac team to come in with some medics? We need to get these wolves cared for and moved so they don't inadvertently lash out at the civilians."

Pablo grimaced a bit before responding, "Yeah. I think we're good. We'll be sure to have them bring in some extra escorts, though. I'm not sure if the vamps who locked us in the hallways are still lurking about out there. Shit, I hope they have some fire extinguishers."

"You, too?"

Pablo nodded.

"Yeah, that was a good move on their part. Fortunately, no one took anything worse than some singed fur and a few burns that'll heal fast on a werewolf. Can you get a few more wolves to shift over to human? The civilians are all looking a bit wild-eyed right now. First vampires and now werewolves…"

Delilah walked over to join them. "According to Sam, the evac buses are on site."

"Shit, let them know there may be some loose vampires heading their way," Luke said.

"I did. They're prepared if any pop out the front door. I'll lead them back. Pablo, mind lending me two of your fuzzboys as an escort?"

Pablo nodded in reply and signaled two of his packmates who were still in wolf form. "You two are with Delilah. Keep her out of trouble."

Luke nodded. "Yeah, we'll want to keep a few of the in-control wolves in their fur tuxedos in case we get more uninvited guests. I don't want any mistakes."

Pablo concentrated and sent out the order. Soon, about half of the werewolves began their shift back to human, causing a rise in the distress and associated noise among the civilians trapped in their cells.

Luke pushed the talk button on his radio. "This is Spartacus. The civilians are secured. Foxy Lady will be coming out to escort in the second wave. Medics needed but send in with heavy escort. There may be a few fangers unaccounted for. Over."

"Copy, Spartacus. Hot Momma and the Evac Team are coming in. Over," Sam replied. Hot Momma was the name she'd come up with for Holly.

"Bring some bolt cutters and fire extinguishers. Over and out." Luke let go of the radio's toggle and walked back to Max's cell. "Well, Max. This is quite the pickle you've gotten yourself into."

Max appeared to be calming down, or at least was at the point where the shock was simulating the same. He stood up and walked over to the bars. "Yeah. This was not how I wanted this winter to go."

"We're about ready to start opening the cells. We've got buses waiting outside to take everyone to a safe place where we can treat people's injuries. How many of the people here are from the camp?"

"I'm not sure, but quite a few. There are others I don't know, but everyone looks like they arrived in rough shape and most haven't improved under these conditions. What's up with all the naked people?"

"The werewolves didn't bring a change of clothes. I'll be right back. I need to check on a couple of things." Luke saw Pablo heading back toward him. "I'm going to start opening the cells and getting things organized. There's a couple of injured wolves down the hall we came down."

"Yeah, I sent a team to bring them out. Everyone is ready on our end."

"I'm going to release Max first so he can help me keep things calm with the civilians." Luke walked down to the panel with the manual gate releases and found the one that corresponded with Max's cell. Even with the open door, Max stayed in his cell.

"You sure it's OK, Luke? I don't want to get bit."

A passing werewolf chuffed at the comment and kept walking.

"You're safe. They're friends, and they're here to help. Everyone's under control."

Max's head peaked out cautiously, followed by the rest of his body. "Wh…what do you need me to do?"

"I want you to start looking for people you know and who can help you out, the calmer ones. Let them out first. Then start assessing who is injured and can't wait. We have medics coming in who can take care of them. The people who are ready to go need to be organized so we can get out of here as quickly as possible. We've cleared the two blocks on both sides of this one. Is there anywhere else we need to look before we get out of here?"

Max licked his lips nervously. A look mixed between panic and revulsion filled his eyes. "The infirmary," he answered, pointing to a door in the middle of the block opposite of them.

Luke nodded, then walked briskly over to the door. He pulled out the keys and tried several before picking the right one. As soon as he opened the door, he was nearly blasted off his feet by the charnel house stench of blood, shit, and decay. He turned his head and coughed back a gag before pulling in his resolve and heading into the hallway.

TWENTY-THREE

LUKE PEEKED in the first door. It was a supply closet filled with industrial cleaning supplies. The second room, however, proved to be far more interesting. Beds filled with human bodies strapped down with leather cuffs and thick leather waist bands lined the room; every mouth was gagged. Luke slowly pushed down on the doorknob lever, cracking the door an inch before he peeked in. Finally, he opened the door enough to slide inside. Save for the bodies in the beds, the room was empty. He walked to the closest bed and checked for a pulse, one body after another, but found none. Body after body, dead.

Two thirds of the way down, he placed his fingers on the neck of a woman, feeling her pulse. She struggled against her bonds, screaming into her gag. Her eyes shot open and looked about wildly, unfocused. Luke lurched backwards, tripped over the bed, and tumbled over the corpse he'd just checked before crashing to the ground in an unceremonious heap. He leapt to his feet, making sure he hadn't attracted further unwanted attention. Luke walked around the bed making soothing noises, trying to calm the woman.

"It's OK. No one is going to hurt you. I'm going to free you."

He repeated the words over and over until they finally seemed to sink in, and she calmed. Her eyes, still full of terror and near panic, finally focused on him. Her breathing was labored but steady. He sheathed his gladius and set the rudis down on the bed next to the woman's.

"I'm going to get that gag out of your mouth, OK?"

She nodded as best as she could with her head strapped to the bed. Luke reached toward her head to unstrap her head, all the while speaking soothing words. With the strap undone, he tried to pull the gag out from her mouth but couldn't. It was too tight.

"OK, I'm going to have to try to untie this. Can you turn your head for me, please?" She complied, but Luke couldn't get the knot to budge. "Shit, this thing is tight. I'm going to have to cut it. I need you to lay absolutely still, all right?"

She swallowed and nodded. Luke pulled out the poniard from its sheath on the inside of his left forearm. He worked a finger along her cheek under the gag. "Sorry, it's scary looking, but it's the thinnest blade I have, and I don't have anything with a single edge. Hold still."

Luke carefully slid the thin tip with the flat along his finger until he had enough blade under the gag to give it a gentle sawing motion. Once the fibers frayed and split, the cutting became easier until the last bit gave way. He resheathed his dagger, then gently removed the gag from her mouth. Initially, she opened and closed her jaw, working it around to loosen it up after it being savagely bisected by the coarse material of the gag.

After a few moments, she spoke, "Please. Please, get me out of here. I don't want to get eaten, please..." Luke loosened the buckles on all the straps, freeing her.

"Take your time getting up; work some blood back into your arms and legs. I'm going to check to see if anyone else is alive." Luke continued his procession but found no life. The woman was the lone survivor in the horrid chamber of death.

A scream ripped Luke's attention away from his musings. He found the source; the woman he'd freed was plastered against the wall sliding toward Luke, her attention fixed on a bed. Luke followed her stare and saw one of the bodies he'd checked thrashing wildly against its restraints. Luke ran to the trapped victim to free it. As he got closer, he noticed the movements were wrong. A clenched fist uncurled, revealing rapidly growing claws. The beds didn't contain the dead; they birthed the undead.

Luke yanked his gladius and rudis from their scabbards as he approached the writhing vampire reanimating in its bed. Razor sharp fangs descended from a mouth clenched in a feral snarl. The vampire's predatory gaze landed on Luke as he scrambled around the foot of the bed. The vamp's eyes conveyed one thought: lunch. It redoubled its efforts to break free of its restraints, shaking the bed and raising a racket as springs and metal stressed and groaned. Luke slammed the gladius through the baby vamp's ribs into its heart, forcing a violent screech filled with fury and pain from its throat before it began dissolving into the sheets and mattress.

"Get out of here. If you go right, it'll take you back to the main cell block. My friends are waiting there. Hurry, go!"

She shook her head violently, her face a mask of terror.

"Please, don't make me go. There might be more of those things out there."

Luke made a snap decision, and replied, "Fine, just stay behind me and away from the beds."

He put his gladius back in its scabbard, keeping the rudis out and ready. He jogged down to the end of the line of beds, slid the rudis into the chest of the next undead body twitching with unlife. Taking advantage of the restraints, he performed the ritual that transferred the vampire's vitality to him by placing his forehead on the pommel of his rudis as he spoke the ancient incantation that activated the rudis's true power. The silver engraving and edge glowed, starting at his forehead and then down to the chest of the staked and back up until it disappeared from the pommel into Luke.

Newly juiced up, he jogged to the next bed and systematically staked corpse after corpse whether they were starting to reanimate or not, figuring a stab wouldn't matter to a corpse and that it was better to be safe than sorry. Unfortunately, he couldn't move fast enough to get all the beds in a timely manner. The last several shook like a scene from a horror movie, bouncing off the floor. Luke sped up as the sound of metal bars groaning past their tolerance was accented by welds snapping. Several of the new vampires were using their newly found strength to rip themselves free of their restraints. Luke freed his gladius from its sheath, hoped the woman stayed close enough to protect but far enough away not to entangle his movements, and prepped for battle.

"Get in the corner and stay back. I need room to work."

He caught a flash out of the corner of his eye as the woman darted into the corner, squishing herself back as if she were trying to dissolve into it to reduce her profile. Knowing she was as safe as she was going to get in this charnel house, he set about disassembling the vampires before they could get entirely free. Triaging the ones who were further along in their progress, Luke stabbed, sliced, and hacked any bit of flesh he could, parting heads from bodies, arms from torsos, and if the opportunity presented itself, a kill shot to the heart. As the numbers thinned, Luke began cleaning up the remaining unstaked.

"That was a close..." Luke's sentence was cut off as a powerful blow struck him in the back, tumbling him to the ground, his weapons flying free of his hands. Air whooshed out of is his lungs and stars exploded in his eyes as his head hit the concrete floor. He tried pushing himself up, but his hands slid in the liquid goo that had been vampires only minutes before. Whatever had tackled him was scrabbling up his back but also tangling themselves in his cloak.

He couldn't get any purchase on the slick floor with a writhing mass on his back, and his swords were just out of reach. Collecting enough awareness, he felt something slide up along his left side. A hand was trying to claw its way through the scarf he wore to pad his neck against his armor. He punched out, hitting a face with his left fist, a weak connection, but solid enough to force the body that'd crawled on top of him to recoil and shift to his right side. He slammed his manica covered elbow into its face and heard the crunch of nose cartilage snapping. The body went momentarily limp, allowing him the time to roll it off him. He snatched up his gladius and spun to meet his attacker.

The woman he'd rescued shook her head, trying to clear the daze;

the black ichor that was vampire blood flowed thickly from her nose and over her needle-sharp fangs. Luke sighed as he lopped off her head. Picking up his rudis, he sent her on her way with a stake through the heart and a quick draining to patch him up some. Hope and optimism and her seeming life had fooled him into turning his back on her. He'd wanted to save at least one person from this hell room.

TWENTY-FOUR

LUKE SHOOK off the last of the daze from hitting his head and gave the room a quick sweep to ensure he'd gotten them all. Then he walked out of the room. The door across the hall led to another room identical to the one Luke just cleared, though unlike the last room, there were no bodies strapped to metal beds. The next room was clearly the source of the all-pervading stench that permeated Luke's senses.

He thought he'd become used to the stench, but when he opened the door, it bowled him over. He thrust the door shut and fell back, gagging and coughing. Shredded bodies filled the room. Arms ripped from torsos. Heads smashed with skulls being held together with strips of scalp. Chest cavities exposed with jagged ribs sticking out, some broken in half or ripped apart by a ravening animal. Nothing was whole or intact; nothing was alive.

Luke knew what he'd find in the next rooms. The evidence was too overwhelming, but he'd been denying the clues that'd been laid out before him. He walked to the end of the hall and looked inside the small, reinforced security window. The door had been further strengthened with huge steel crossbars fixed into brackets like a castle's gate or door. It was designed to withstand huge amounts of force, force that a newly born vampire could generate before it came into its control.

Several new vampires stalked about the room like predators in a too small cage. Bodies hung from the ceiling on thick chains, bodies that no longer resembled the humans they'd once been, bodies that would soon be taken down and go with the other waste meat down the hall. Even though there was no blood to draw from the cadavers, some of the vampires still gnawed on a leg here, an arm there just for the satisfaction of the rending motion. Luke saw the look in one's eyes; it chilled him to the bone. Hate and hunger and rage, all traces of humanity erased. The corners of Luke's vision blackened and narrowed as he slid down the wall, his knees losing the will to keep him upright. He breathed rapidly and shallowly, his head held in his hands.

"It's starting again..." he mumbled to himself over and over again.

Luke didn't know how long he'd been there before he heard a voice rise out of the deep water of his horror trapped brain.

"Luke... Are you back here? Luke! Fuck, it stinks back here. Luke! Oh, there you are." Pablo jogged up and knelt beside him. "Are you OK, buddy? I hadn't seen you in a while and got worried. Your friend Max said you came in here to check for more survivors. Did you find any?"

Luke shook his head slowly, still looking between his knees at the floor. WHAM! Pablo jumped back, falling on his butt as something repeatedly hit the door they'd been sitting by, each time a little harder.

"They heard us..." Luke whispered.

Pablo stood up and walked slowly to the door, trying to keep out of the line of sight of the window. He peered into the room. WHAM! Pablo flinched away and stared back at the ravenous face trying to claw its way through the door and window.

"What in God's name?"

"There's no god in there..."

"Luke, what is this? What's going on?"

"It's a nursery." Luke coughed.

"A what?"

"A vampire nursery." Luke's voice was losing the detached, spacey quality the more he talked as he pulled himself back to the surface. "They drain their victims, feeding on them in the process, then they feed them vampire blood. That's what they were doing back there." He vaguely gestured toward the other room down the hall. He continued, "They stash the newly made vampires in this room until they learn control."

"What?"

"Newly made vampires only know insatiable hunger, not just to feed, but to rip life apart. This jail is a vampire breeding center."

"It's a gate to hell," Pablo muttered. Luke nodded his agreement.

"Help me up?" Luke extended his hand so Pablo could give him a hand up.

"What are we going to do? Can we go in and kill them?"

"Probably not. They're at full strength and have zero control. I finished a handful of newly awakened ones back there, but they were still weak, for a vampire that is. I'm not sure I could handle this lot even with your help."

His brow wrinkled. Pablo looked scared. "We can't leave them, though, can we?"

"No…we can't."

Luke looked around the hallway, hoping for inspiration as the slamming against the door resumed. When his eyes raked over the fire suppression station, he got an idea. He jogged over and opened the door. Inside was a spooled fire hose and a fireman's axe. He yanked the axe off its hooks and ran back to Pablo.

"The first door in this hallway, the one closest to the exit, is a supply closet. I think I saw rubbing alcohol in it. Get every bottle and bring it back here. Bring some gauze, too. I'm going to see if I can get this window out of the door. They won't be able to come out through that."

"Good luck, dude. That's security glass. That's some tough shit."

"I know. I guess we'll see who's stronger?" Luke picked up the axe, and Pablo turned to run down the hall. "Pablo! Don't look in any of the other rooms. You don't want that in your brain; trust me."

Pablo nodded, then turned and ran down the hall, avoiding the other doors. Luke got in position and began a steady, powerful rhythm, using the pick side of the axe to bash at the center of the small rectangular window. Pablo made several trips to the supply closet, bringing back arm loads of supplies. Luke's progress was slow, so he flipped to the bladed edge and continued bashing away. Finally, the window frame gave way, and the security window flew back into the face of the ravening vampire on the other side of the door.

Pablo was busy taking the caps off everything he'd brought. When he finished, he stuffed lengths of gauze into the opening of several metal cans. Luke grabbed a large plastic jug of alcohol and squeezed it into the opening the window had left, soaking the vampire reaching through. He pulled out a lighter from his pocket and sparked it up. As he moved his hand toward the opening, careful to avoid falling within range of the vampire's clawed hands, the alcohol vapors and droplets the searching arm was flinging about lit up and ignited the vampire. Screeching an unholy shriek, the vampire flailed away from the door and disappeared back into the room. Another quickly took its place.

Luke repeated the process until the vampires stopped grasping out the window. While they were relentless, they weren't entirely mindless. They could see what was happening to their roommates. He peeked into the window and saw several more standing back, occasionally dodging the lit vamps flailing about wildly.

"They're not coming close enough to spray. I don't think throwing will work, either."

"I'm workin' on something…" Pablo replied. "Save me one bottle of alcohol, but throw the rest in. Try to spread them around so the alcohol spills out and covers as much area as possible."

Luke did as instructed, occasionally hitting one of the watching vampires if he could. He turned to grab another bottle, realizing he was down to the last one, and picked it up but didn't throw it.

"OK, done!" Pablo had made a dozen long wicks out of the gauze that each ran into a metal tin of cleaner, plugging them. The rest of the gauze he'd tied into a long rope with one end still rolled up. "This industrial cleaner shit is mega-flammable. It'll make a big bada boom! Let's slide it through the opening. It doesn't matter if they land on the bottom or not. The gauze will keep them reasonably plugged."

Luke set down the alcohol and alternated back and forth with Pablo dropping the improvised bombs into the vampire nursery. When they had dropped the last one in, Pablo picked up the rope of gauze from the ground.

"Pour some of that alcohol on this… Careful, man! Don't spill it on me!"

"Sorry, it kind of gushed there for a second."

"OK, that should do it. Now take the rest and squirt it over the cans." Luke followed the instructions. Pablo took one end of the roll and held on but dropped the rest into the window and let it unspool down into the pool of alcohol. He looked around until he saw the axe. "That'll work. Hand me the axe, please."

Pablo set the axe head down on the floor and propped it against the door. He took the loose end of gauze and tied it around the handle to anchor it. Next, he bent over and squished the gauze pile around on the floor so that it had soaked up as much alcohol as possible, and it was spread as evenly as he could make it. He took one end of the soaked pile of gauze rope and tied it to the end of the first roll of gauze wound around the axe handle, then began walking his alcohol-soaked rope down the hallway.

"Let's blow this popsicle stand," Pablo said.

"Let's just hope they don't rip that gauze to pieces…"

Pablo grinned wickedly. "Don't worry. As much alcohol as is on it, it's already dripped all over and down the inside of the door. That'll keep the fire moving."

Luke followed him down the hall. The vampires, seeing nothing outside the window, again surged forward, ripping at the window space, hoping to widen it enough to escape and feed. Luke and Pablo opened the door back into the cell block. Delilah was waiting for them.

"Hey, boys! We've got all the injured civilians out and most of the others. You two ready to go?"

"Luke, prop that door open," Pablo instructed while still stretching out his gauze rope.

Luke and Delilah watched him work as he whistled a jaunty tune.

Someone Luke didn't know popped their head through the cell block's exit door and yelled to them. "Yo, Pablo! The last of them just left the first cell block. We're all clear here, so get your asses moving! Holly wants to go, NOW!"

"We're on it. We'll be hustling along shortly. We just need to light the birthday candle," Pablo called back.

The guy in the doorway gave Pablo a strange look before disappearing back the way he came. Luke offered Pablo his lighter.

"No thanks, man! My hands are covered in alcohol. I think I'll step back a bit and let you light it up."

Luke turned to Delilah. "Delilah, would you like the honors?"

"What am I doing?" she asked.

"Just light the end of the gauze…and then…" Pablo finished by pantomiming a massive explosion.

Delilah grinned back at him.

"Get ready to run. I'm not sure how much of a bang this is going to make, but let's not take any chances," Luke said.

Delilah bent over and lit up the end of the alcohol-soaked gauze and watched the flame take hold, then shoot down the length.

"RUN!"

They took off running toward the exit. Luke spared a last glance to see the flame disappear into the doorway to make its run down the hallway. Delilah dropped behind a bit, unable to match a werewolf and vamp-juiced slayer in speed or endurance. Luke slowed to match her.

Big bada boom was right. The flame finally reached the tins and lit them up, letting off a series of "whumps" as they exploded. The three kept running as fire alarms went off, but no sprinkler system kicked in to accompany it.

"Where are the sprinklers?" Pablo yelled.

"No, idea. They must have disabled them," Luke replied.

They sprinted through Block 1 and then out into the hallways that led to the exit, coming to a gasping halt outside.

"Fuck! The guards! We can't leave them tied up in there," Luke yelled.

Luke turned around to head back in when Sam caught him by the shoulder.

"Luke, we already took care of it. We cut the zip ties from their legs and sent them away. It'll take them a while to raise any alarm. We're almost ready to go."

Sam walked off to get into an SUV with Holly and some other werewolves. The last of the civilians were getting on their buses. Luke jogged over to his car and pulled out his plastic storage tub. As quickly as he could, he pulled off his cloak, tossing it in the back of the wagon, followed by the swords and the lorica segmentata. He left on everything else—the greaves, left wrist brace, and sheathed poniard. Finished, he slid the tub into the back before closing the car's back hatch door.

"Hey, Luke. I'll ride with you. Also, you've got an extra passenger," Delilah said as she pointed at the small figure inside his car sitting in the backseat trying to look inconspicuous.

Luke sighed and turned to get into the front seat.

"Go easy on her. She didn't want to stay with the werewolves. They terrify her. She snuck out and hid in the back of one of the buses. When I came out to get the second wave, I found her and sent her to your car so she'd be safe enough and in a human's car. If you want, you can chat with her, and I'll drive."

Luke smiled and nodded and climbed into the passenger side.

"Hello, Gwen. It's fine that you're here, but we're still not all the way out of this. You know what was in there," Luke gestured toward the jail. "If we run into anything on our way out of here, I need you to listen to me and follow instructions, OK? You're still a bit under-sized and a lot under trained to be jumping into any fights. Your best strategy is to listen to one of us."

Gwen nodded, then stared out the window as Delilah climbed in. One of the buses sounded its horn, signaling it was time to roll. The trucks and SUVs belonging to the pack moved out first, followed by the two buses. Delilah joined the line of vehicles that brought up the end of the caravan as they wound their way through the industrial north side of the St. Johns neighborhood on their way to the St. Johns Bridge. Luke stared out the passenger window into the darkness, his mind drifting to the past.

LUCIUS V

THE LEGIONS of Rome assembled outside the ruins of Sarmizegetusa Regia. The capital had been set on fire and burned by the Dacians as the Romans were about to break through their walls. The Dacian king, Decebalus, fled before he could be captured and committed suicide, slicing his own throat with his falx. He refused to be paraded through the streets of Rome. As Imperator Traianus prepared to leave Dacia and return to Rome for his Triumph, he performed one last duty to the legionnaires who'd brought him victory and the accolades that went along with it—awarding honors to those who'd earned them.

"Last, but not least, the XXX Ulpia, named after our victorious Imperator! Henceforth, you shall bear the name XXX Ulpia Victrix in honor of the victory you helped to achieve!" the emperor's herald cried out.

The men of the XXX Ulpia Victrix sent up a hearty yell in response, knowing their deeds would become the basis for the lore and history of the legion, and even after they were gone, their legend would outlive them. The herald, standing next to the seated Imperator, waited for the men to quiet down before continuing on to the individual honors. Names were called and promotions and honors given as they worked through the legionnaires.

"Tesserarius Lucius Silvanius of I Centuria, VI Cohort!" the herald cried.

Lucius marched, ensuring his steps and turns were of the highest quality, to the platform where the Imperator sat. He issued his crispest salute before standing perfectly still, back straight.

"Tesserarius Silvanius, for exemplary service to your centuria and legio, you are awarded this silver phalera." The primus pilus of his legion walked forward and placed the silver disc bearing the image of the imperator on the left side of the harness Lucius wore, over his heart and opposite of the bronze phalera he'd been awarded the previous spring for his actions in saving his vexillation.

"Next," the herald continued, "for your actions organizing a half centuria and coming to the relief of the X Cohort of the XXX Ulpia Legio and saving the lives of over 350 of your comrades, you are awarded the Corona Civica."

There were a few moments of stunned silence before the men of the legion broke into loud cheers. The Corona Civica was rarely awarded and required direct testimony from the person whose life had been saved fighting off Rome's enemies. One or more of his comrades must have attested to his actions, earning him the highest honor a common legionnaire could earn. The primus pilus stepped back out. This time he carried a chaplet made of oak leaves and branches with acorns clustered about it.

"Kneel, Tesserarius Silvanius," the legion's highest-ranking centurion commanded.

Lucius knelt before the centurion as the older man placed the chaplet on his head.

"This is an honor few men earn, even fewer of your age. Congratulations," added the primus pilus — the highest-ranking centurion of a legion. "You may rise now."

Once Lucius was standing again, the imperator rose from his chair and approached Lucius.

"Centurio Brabo tells me the men call you 'Ferrata'?"

"Yes, Imperator."

"Based on your deeds and service, it's well earned." The imperator reached out and attached a gold phalera to the center of the harness just above Lucius's sternum. It bore the eagle of Rome's legions on it. "Centurio Brabo has requested you as his optio. You've been given one of Rome's highest honors and a promotion to optio into the I Cohort. You've done well for yourself for one so young. I look forward to hearing what you'll accomplish next. The legions need more men with your iron will."

The imperator returned to his chair and nodded at the primus pilus of the XXX Ulpia Victrix. The centurion returned the nod, then addressed Lucius.

"Report to Centurio Brabo for details of your new position. Well done, Optio Lucius Silvanius Ferrata."

The herald called out to the legions, "Optio Lucius Silvanius Ferrata."

Lucius walked over to Centurion Brabo to the sound of the cheering legions. He stopped before Brabo, back ramrod straight, and saluted the centurion. "Thank you, Centurio."

"You've earned it, lad. When we're done here, get your gear and report to the primus pilus for your tent assignment."

"YOU JUST GOT PROMOTED to Tesserarius, Cassius. I think it's a bad idea to use your position to sneak out of camp in the hope some Dacian girl will lead you to a hidden treasure cache," came the voice of Sego from the shadows behind their tent.

Lucius slowed down and silently edged forward.

"Always playing it safe, Sego. If it weren't for the fact that you stand at the front of the line with nothing but the Centurial Signum in your hands, I'd think you were a coward."

"Fuck you, Cassius. I'm not one of your new little cronies, always begging for your favor. You can't goad me by calling me a coward. I like my place. I've earned it. I don't need to chase after imaginary riches, hoping to rise above my station. Have fun with your Dacian but leave me out of your schemes."

"Fine. Go spend the night with that Aegyptii, Amosis. I've seen you eyeing each other since he transferred into the centuria."

"I think I will. He's much better company than you, Cassius. I won't rat you out, but neither will I cover for you."

Lucius heard hob-nailed caligae marching away from the tent. Cassius muttered, "Coward" as Sego walked away for an assignation with Amosis.

Lucius was still standing there when Cassius emerged from behind the tent. Spying the newly minted Optio, Cassius stopped, his eyes opening wide and his mouth forming an "o" of surprise.

"Cassius…"

"Eavesdropping is a bad habit for an *optio*," Cassius replied, rendering "optio" into a sneer.

Lucius ignored the comment and the tone. "Planning some unauthorized nighttime reconnaissance?"

"It's none of your business. Why don't you go play with your oak leaves and kiss Brabo's ass some more."

"Hades below, Cassius. Is that any way to talk to your friends?"

"Friends? Aren't we all just out for ourselves, *optio*?" Again, "optio" dripped with disdain.

"Cassius, whatever you're planning, don't do it. Your new centurio is not someone to mess with. He's not like Brabo. Apparently his old centuria calls him 'Centurio One More.' Whenever he breaks one of his vine rods, he doesn't stop, he just yells for another one. If you get caught, this won't go well for you."

"I'll take it under advisement, *optio*." Cassius walked toward Lucius, slamming his shoulder into Lucius's side as he walked past.

"Cassius!"

Cassius kept walking.

"Tesserarius!"

Cassius, hearing his rank and the tone of command, turned around, made a rude gesture, then saluted. Although technically correct, it couldn't have been delivered with more venom. He turned around and walked into the darkness.

Lucius sighed, sad that the friendship he'd forged with Cassius seemed so fragile and easy for the other man to throw away over jealousy. It was a good thing Lucius was being transferred to another century. Perhaps distance would heal the gaping wound in their friendship. He ducked and entered the tent he'd shared with his contubernium. Somehow, all eight of them had come through the last two years of fighting alive and intact, physically at least. It only seemed to be the friendships they thought they'd made that were becoming the casualties. Lucius gathered up his meager belongings and headed toward the area given to the I Cohort, where he'd be the optio for the V Centuria.

Lucius's fortunes had launched him ahead of the other new optios into the prestigious I Cohort, which only had five centuries, but each was double strength. He'd be second in command of his 150-man cohort and outrank most other optios in the legion, save for the optios I-IIII of I Cohort. He tried not to let Cassius's bad attitude dampen the pride he felt in accomplishing so much by his twenty-first year. He wished he could share news of his success with his father.

Once he got his new assignment, he found the tent he'd share with the optio of the IIII Cohort. The optio of the I Cohort was the only optio to get his own tent. The tent flap was propped open, letting the brisk spring air into the tent. An older man, probably in his early thirties, was sitting at a camp desk shuffling through some paperwork.

"Optio Demetrios?" asked Lucius by way of getting the man's attention.

"Yes." The older man turned, his eyes brightening upon seeing Lucius. "You must be the new wonder kid Brabo brought with him. He dropped off your rank crest and feathers earlier before heading to a meeting. I set them on your bed."

Demetrios turned back to his paperwork and let Lucius settle in. He stowed his gear and affixed the blue crest, which matched the legion's emblem colors and ran front to back, to his helmet, then added the two white feathers, which attached just above each ear and stood straight up.

"It's quite the feeling the first time you get to wear your rank on your helmet. Makes you a good mark in battle, but it'll make you visible to ours too. Although, looks like I'll be losing the pool."

"Pool?" Lucius asked.

"Yeah, me and some of the optios bet on how long it'd take you to make it out of your contubernium and into a crest." He stopped to think. "Shit, Brabo is probably closest. But he'll have a tough time collecting since he's the one who promoted you." Seeing the look of shock on Lucius's face, Demetrios added, "Don't worry, you've earned the spot. We've been watching you since you pulled the X's bacon out of the fire. Brabo selected you because he trusts you. I've got to turn in these reports. We'll talk more later."

Demetrios gave Lucius a companionable pat on to the shoulder and departed the tent. Lucius sat on the camp chair, staring at his helmet and its new adornments. Finally, he made a decision, strapped on his helmet, grabbed his scutum out of its case, and marched back to his old tent. Everyone stayed clear of the young optio with his purposeful step and determined and angry eyes. When he reached his old tent, he grabbed the flap, pulled it aside, and stuck his head in. He was unprepared for what he interrupted—Sego and another man splayed out and nearly nude.

Lucius pulled his head out as fast as he could, catching his new crest on the tent pole before clearing it to get his head out of the tent. Flipping the tent flap closed, Lucius stood blushing from the top of his head to his scarf covered neck. A legionnaire with dark black skin Lucius didn't know came running up and spoke through the tent wall.

"Shit, sorry, Amosis. He walked by while I was distracted." The legionnaire turned to Lucius. His eyes drifted up, finally seeing the marks of rank. Straightening up, he saluted. "Optio."

Sego and a darkly complected man who must be Amosis popped out of the tent, hastily settling their tunics and fastening belts. They both straightened and saluted, likewise saying, "Optio!"

Sego looked past the helmet and crest. "Lucius? Wow, the crest fits you. Um, about what you saw a moment ago…"

Lucius raised his hand, interrupting his friend. Amosis stood rigidly straight, as if waiting for inspection.

"No, it's OK, Sego. I'm sorry for interrupting. So Cassius wasn't kidding?"

"No, we've known each other for a long time. Cassius knows where my interests lie. Are we going to have a problem here?"

Lucius shook his head. "I doubt you're the first legionnaires to enjoy each other's company. I'm not here to police who you have sex with. I'm going after Cassius before he gets himself demoted...or executed. He hasn't been talking to me lately. Do you know where he's going?"

"I don't know where this mysterious treasure of his is, but I know where the woman is. She's got a tent on the edge of the camp where the followers are. Shit, you probably shouldn't go by yourself. You might need some help getting Cassius to come back. Amo, can you and Bomilcar help?"

Amosis had finally relaxed now that he knew they weren't in trouble. "Of course, Sego. Bomilcar?"

"Why not? Nothing else going on, and this beats losing at dice." Bomilcar shrugged.

"Get geared up and meet here as soon as you can. If you see anyone you completely trust, bring them," Lucius said.

While he was waiting, a couple of his old contubernium mates showed up and decided to pitch in. When Sego's lover and his friend returned, Lucius had six men counting himself. His men fell in behind him as they marched to the gate nearest where the camp followers had set up. Lucius gave the pass code and headed out into the evening.

Striding out in front, Sego waved everyone behind the tent they were about to pass by. The men ducked into the shadows. They soon figured out why Sego had motioned them into hiding.

"You couldn't get anyone to come with you?" a woman asked, her voice raised and irritated. She spoke in a heavily Dacian accented Latin. "Either your friends are cowards or you can't even lead your own piss to a latrine trench."

Cassius reared back and let loose a heavy slap. Lucius expected the woman to crumple. Instead she caught Cassius's hand at the wrist, halting his arm mid swing and squeezing his wrist until Cassius flinched.

"If you try that again, I'll slit your throat and let the dogs have your corpse, Roman." Her words dripped with disdain as she threw his arm down, letting go of his wrist.

Looking around to ensure no one saw his humiliation, Cassius rubbed his wrist. Lucius waved his small squad further into the shadows and ducked the rest of the way behind the tent so not even his head was visible.

"Will you still take me to the hiding spot?" Cassius's voice carried a wheedling note to it.

"Fine, follow me."

Lucius peeked out quickly to see which direction they were headed. Seeing that it was directly away from the camp and away from their hiding spot, he gave them time, periodically checking to ensure he knew where they were going. Cassius seemed entirely focused on what was ahead of him, ignoring what might be creeping up behind him. Feeling confident they could move out without being seen, Lucius waved his men from their hiding space. Instead of the purposeful march they'd used before, they snuck through the shadows, keeping low in case Cassius checked behind him. He didn't; his mind was apparently focused on the woman and the treasure he was already counting in his head.

If they continued in the direction they were going, they'd be in the rugged hills that surrounded the ruins of Sarmizegetusa Regia. It wasn't long before Cassius and the woman disappeared into a copse of trees straddling a rocky formation jutting out of the ground. Lucius signaled they should pick up their pace. They jogged toward the copse until Lucius waved them down into the tall grass. In the darkness ahead, they saw a torch flare to life, illuminating the opening to a cavern. Lucius signaled for his squad to move forward.

They crept into the cave, keeping the light visible in front of them. Eventually, they came upon an occasional lighted torch stuffed into a ring in the wall. They tried to keep to the sandy dirt to muffle the hobnails of their caligae. Lucius raised his fist, halting his squad.

"You promised me gold!" Cassius shouted, sounding as if he were just around the upcoming corner.

"I promised you treasure beyond your imagination. I never specified gold," the woman replied.

The sound of a gladius leaving its scabbard put everyone on high alert, hands reaching down to gladii of their own. Lucius waved them down.

"I've had enough of your promises! Take me to the gold, or I'll shove this fucking sword into your lying guts."

"That won't be necessary, will it? Drop the sword, Roman."

The sound of steel hitting the rock floor caused Lucius to slowly withdraw his gladius from its sheath, making next to no noise. The other five legionnaires followed suit.

"You foolish Roman. Now, the only treasure will be for me. You could have had so much. Please lie down." There were more sounds of metal shuffling against rock. "Very good. Mmmmmmm."

Lucius waved his men forward. They crept up the cave and edged around the corner. Lucius planned to take advantage of his friend's occupation with his playmate. The scene opening before Lucius as he rounded the corner just ahead of his men was not what he'd thought he'd find. He'd expected to find Cassius and the woman enjoying their tryst in the cave. Instead, Lucius found Cassius on his back, a look of ecstasy on his unnaturally pale face. The woman, however, was clamped to his neck, blood dribbling out of the corners of her mouth. Lucius looked down; a pool of blood collected around Cassius's neck and shoulder. The weight of one of his men bumping into his back, not having expected Lucius's stop, jolted him out of his shock.

"Get away from him!" Lucius shouted. He took a couple steps forward.

The woman leapt up. Cassius's blood coated her face, chin, and neck, dripping down two long, needle sharp fangs that descended from her upper jaw. Where her fingernails should have been, she had long, animal-like claws. Lucius would never forget the looks of hunger, lust, and hate in her eyes as she lunged for him.

He barely raised his scutum in time to keep her from ripping out his throat. She shoved him back with the strength of several warriors. He dug in, putting all his strength into keeping his shield between him and the monster thirsting for his life. Lucius swung his gladius below the shield to catch her in the legs and relieve some of the pressure, but she dodged. It wasn't until she tried to climb over the shield to get to Lucius's head that he caught a break. Training and reflexes kicked in as her left arm rose, exposing her ribcage and armpit. The lightning quick stab caught her by surprise as the point of the gladius parted her ribs and sank into her heart. She shrank back as Lucius twisted the blade and withdrew it before lopping off her head.

The deed done, Lucius dropped his shield and sword and slid into the dirt next to his friend, covering the gaping wound in Cassius's neck with both hands.

"Oh, Cassius…"

Lucius's squad stood around the two men as Cassius, now paler than newly bleached linen, gasped for breath, unfocused eyes twitching left and right as Lucius struggled to halt his friend's lifeblood from spilling into the dirt. Tears streamed down Lucius's face.

"Lucius, I hear someone coming from deeper in the cave. Lucius?"

The five men fanned out, blocking the cave with their shields and putting a wall between whatever was approaching them and Lucius and Cassius.

"Halt! Who goes there?" shouted one of the legionnaires.

Cassius's movements became fainter, his breaths shallower, until the blood stopped pumping out of the hole in his neck. Lucius closed his eyes and hung his head over his dead friend. He disappeared into his grief, his tears mingling with the blood of his friend.

"Lucius, we need you. Lucius. Someone's coming."

"Wha…what?"

"Someone's coming from deeper in the cave. We need you."

Lucius pulled himself together. He found a clean patch of dirt and grabbed handfuls of it, trying to get the blood off his hands.

Once he judged them sufficiently free of blood, he picked up his scutum and gladius.

"Sego, you're the best runner here. Get back to the camp and bring help. We'll hold them off as best we can."

Sego hesitated, then nodded, slamming his gladius back in its sheath and setting his scutum against the wall before taking off at a fast run.

"We may have to hold out for a while. Amosis, Bomilcar, step back. We'll hold the gap. When I signal, you'll switch with Julian and Hector. Let's keep as fresh as we can. If things get dicey, we'll fall back."

They set their lines and just in time. A howling horde of Dacians burst out of the back of the cave, one or two outstripping their comrades significantly. They pushed back the initial attack, but things did get dicey, and they were pushed back and forced to abandon Cassius's body. Lucius kept his small squad rotating, never taking a break himself. They just didn't have enough men. His goal was to keep them moving backwards so they wouldn't get run down from behind trying to flee. Lucius, already worried, was getting even more concerned as his men's movements slowed, fearing the next rotation wouldn't be enough, and the Dacians would break their line.

A cooling breeze pushed up against his sweat-covered skin. They must be nearing the entrance. Not only did the breeze bring a bit of relief, it carried with it the sound of feet marching and men shouting in Latin. Relief had come.

"Everyone on the line!"

The men in relief surged forward, bolstering their comrades. Soon, fresh legionnaires pushed through the gaps and pushed back the Dacians, who, seeing the tide was turning, broke off in ones and twos and fled back down the cavern. Lucius and his men worked their way to the back, dripping sweat and gasping to catch their breath.

When the last of the Dacians had fled or been killed, the legionnaires searched for Cassius's body but found only the blood-soaked dirt he'd bled out in. His body had been dragged away along with the creature that had killed him. Lucius's friend was truly gone.

TWENTY-FIVE

A STEADY LINE of brake lights flared red as the convoy of cars, vans, and buses ground to a halt in front of Luke's Volvo a few moments after it had climbed onto the St. Johns Bridge, pulling Luke out of his nostalgia. Delilah slowed behind the bus and put the car in park but left the engine running.

"What the... Delilah, would you keep the engine running in case we need to move out quickly. Gwen, stay with Delilah. I'll be right back." Luke popped the door open as Pablo came jogging back. "What's the hold up, Pablo?"

"Some weird shit, man. That's what's up."

Luke raised a questioning eyebrow.

"Like shit that's up your alley, if you catch my drift. The bridge is blocked off ahead. All I can see is a line of headlights blaring and the silhouette of some dude. He's got one of them big shields, and he's beating on it with a stick or a sword or something. It's eerie as fuck. There's got to be more of them hitting on stuff, because they're raising a big fucking din, all in rhythm."

"All right. Help me with my armor?" Luke asked as he headed to the back to pop the hatch. Pablo grabbed the lorica segmentata and held it open at shoulder height so Luke could shimmy in. Luke stuck his right arm in first, sliding it into the manica armor. Once Luke had the armor settled on his shoulders, he adjusted the manica to ensure proper fit and laced up the front to close the armor around his chest. Pablo pulled out the rudis in its back sheath. Once Luke finished lacing the armor, he raised his right arm so Pablo could settle the tech nylon bandolier-style belt over Luke's shoulders. Luke grabbed his scabbarded gladius and clipped it onto the loop at the bottom of the bandolier on his left hip.

"Cloak?"

"No. I'll go without." Luke reached into the back of his wagon and pulled out a huge rectangular package covered in leather. "Pablo, mind grabbing the bottom of the case?"

Pablo grabbed the bottom edge of the leather on the end opposite of Luke and held it. Grasping each edge with both hands, Luke pulled out a massive curved rectangular shield, the famed scutum of the Roman legionnaire. Painted a glossy black, the dim light reflected off the silver of the central boss and the metal rimmed edge. He handed it to Pablo. "Can you hold this please?"

With his hands free, Luke reached in for another, smaller plastic tub. He opened the lid and pulled out a shiny helmet. The neck guard sloped down at an aggressive angle just below the brass covered ear guards. Along the crown running from ear to ear and from front to back ran two perpendicular brass-covered thin steel bars that reinforced the steel of the main helmet. Two jaunty, stylized eyebrows swept up from the rim of the helm. Luke set the helmet down and pulled out a crest made from long, black horsehair. Luke quickly attached it to the helmet in the transverse position reserved for centurions that aligned the crest from left ear to right. The crest was much longer than the standard crest and swept down and over the neck guard and would reach part way down Luke's back.

Pablo whistled in appreciation. "That's a boss brain bucket, bro."

"It keeps my brain where it's supposed to be." Luke stowed the helmet under his right arm and grabbed the scutum with his left hand. "Let's go see what our shield-bearing mystery date wants."

Together, they walked up the line of cars to the front car where Holly, Sam, Tony, and a couple other werewolves stood eyeing the figure blocking their exit. As they got closer, the steady rhythmic thrum of metal on board caused Luke to straighten up while a small smile tugged the corners of lips ever so slightly up.

"Hello, old friend," Luke whispered.

"Do you know that guy?" Pablo asked.

"No, that sound. It's the sound of sword on shield. It's been a while since my ears have experienced it." They halted as they reached Holly and the rest. "Hey, Holly. What's going on?"

"Nothing new since Pablo went to fetch you. I can make out some flashing red and blues down at the end of the bridge and down along the off and on ramps. They're blocking our way out and probably anyone else's way on."

Luke nodded at her. "I'm guessing that's not their only force. We should set up a line behind us."

"I planned for this. Pablo, run back and grab Archie. He's got some official-looking signs and barricades he can set up to keep any innocents from joining us. Once he's got that set up, tell him to pull ten or twelve wolves to help him watch the back line." Pablo nodded his affirmation and trotted back to carry out her orders. "Sam, you take four wolves and guard the people on the bus…"

"The hell I am! You know I can fight, probably better than most here. I'll have Beckah organize that."

Just before she took off, Luke added, "Can you have Gwen get on the bus? There's a spare sword in the back of my car. You'll see it. Give it to her and tell her to stay on the bus and help guard the people. I don't want her wandering out into the middle of this mess."

Sam nodded and ran back.

Turning back to Holly, Luke continued, "Holly, we're going to need to make sure all the vehicles have a person behind the wheel."

"I don't know what's waiting out there. We're going to need every wolf we have. I should have called one of the other packs for reinforcements," she mumbled the last to herself.

"No helping it now. I guess the humans we rescued will have to pitch in on that end. Get the spryer ones organized and make sure they stay put and don't panic. We'll need to get out of here in a hurry, and I don't want a driverless car blocking our escape."

Holly nodded at Luke and gave orders to one of the wolves Luke didn't know. A moment later, Sam returned, carrying a large Naginata.

"I'm going to stroll out and see what our friend across the way wants. I'll try to delay as long as possible so you can get everything set up. It's obvious he wants to talk, or they'd be on us already."

He set his shield down and leaned it against his side. He tested all the leather thongs, ensuring they were in the right place before settling the helmet on his head and tying the straps under his chin. "Well, here goes…"

"WHO COMES before me dressed in the costume of the Roman legions?"

Luke took a stutter step as the words processed in his head — Latin, classical Latin.

"A centurion of the Roman Legions," Luke responded in Latin.

"They're all dead and dust, just like the empire."

"One Roman remains alive. And unless my ears are playing a cruel trick, one remains undead."

"Lu… Lucius?" came the uncertain reply. "How?"

"I could ask the same thing, Cassius. I saw you die."

"But you didn't see me rise," he said bitterly. "I serve new masters now. Who do you serve?"

"Humanity."

Cassius chuckled as they walked toward each other, meeting near the center of the bridge. He switched to English. "You always had an overinflated sense of yourself. In the grand scheme, we're but bugs to be used or squished when more powerful creatures will it."

"You always were a cynic. Duty, honor, and loyalty were never enough for you, my friend," Luke replied in English.

Cassius laughed in response. "It's been nineteen centuries since we were friends. I'm not sure either of us is entitled to that word anymore." They stared at each other until Cassius broke the silence.

"So you're the one who's been killing our pups, eh? My masters are most vexed with you."

"I'd say I'm sorry for inconveniencing a former friend, but… Yeah, no. Not really feeling it right now. So you've spent the last nineteen-hundred-years spreading the vampire plague?"

"Plague?" Cassius laughed harshly. "We're the solution. We're the ultimate step up on the evolutionary ladder. I'm immortal. What is a human's life compared to that? You've somehow managed to slip off the yoke of death. Why restrict yourself to crawling with the other bugs? Why associate with the howling animals I can smell behind you?"

Luke shook his head at his friend. "Always grand schemes with you… I'm one of those bugs you want to squish. I fight with them and for them. I fight alongside the wolves because they've chosen to stand up in the face of darkness. Some of them are my friends. Surely you can remember what it's like to fight alongside a friend?"

"I haven't forgotten. I haven't forgotten, but where did that get me? Dead and bleeding out, breathing my last gasp at the hands of a vampire. Where did that get the empire? Dead and destroyed at the hands of ravening barbarian hordes. I know what matters now. I know how the world works. You and a handful of slavering dogs can't stand in the face of our might."

Cassius had come far enough forward that the headlights no longer rendered him a silhouette. He was wearing a shiny legionnaire's helmet, much like the one he'd died wearing in the spring of 107 CE. He had a scutum bearing the classic red and gold eagle wings and lightning motif most associated with the Roman legions. Instead of the matching chest armor, he wore a black tactical ballistic vest.

"Nice helmet. An original?" Luke asked.

Cassius chuckled at Luke. "Nah. You can get this shit online. I just got nostalgic when I heard some fool in Roman gear was killing MY FUCKING VAMPIRES!"

Luke shrugged, then grinned at Cassius. "Sorry, not sorry. Killing vamps is my business, and business has been booming, brother."

They'd both halted and were eyeing each other across about fifteen feet.

Cassius got a curious look on his face as he looked down at Luke's legs. "Are you wearing skinny jeans under those greaves?"

Luke spread his arms to open the view and looked down at his jeans. "Yup. They make my ass look glorious." He winked at Cassius.

Cassius sighed. "I don't suppose I can talk you into coming over to my side? You'd do quite well with us."

Luke shook his head.

"Well, I can offer you a clean death. You can fall on your sword, or I can end it for you quickly. A quick stab through your spine just below the skull? For old time's sake?"

"Your mercy is overwhelming," was Luke's deadpan reply.

"Well, I guess that ends the pleasantries portion of the festivities. We should probably get to the meat of the matter or our audience likely to get bored. By the way, love the crest, very in this year. Shall we?" His hand drifted behind his shield and pulled out a falx which had been hanging from his left side, hidden behind his shield. The sleek, wooden handle was a foot and a half long, while the slightly longer blade had a single curved edge that ended in a wicked point. The sight of it sent a shiver down Luke's spine. It had been almost two thousand years since he'd last seen one wielded against him in the hills of Dacia, but the devastatingly effective weapon brought horrible memories of friends and comrades killed and maimed. It was particularly designed to wreak havoc on the armor of a Roman.

"A falx? Really?" Luke asked as he shook his head. He settled his hand on the pommel of his trusty gladius and pulled it free of its scabbard. "I'm glad I wore the manica..."

With that, he charged—shield raised before him but pulled in tight to his body while he held the sword up and ready—arm cocked back. Cassius, with vampire quickness, closed with Luke. At the last moment, Luke launched himself into the air, pivoting to the right around Cassius's shield. Luke punched out with his shield, pushing Cassius's out of the way and used the recoil to twist his body and unleash a brutally quick stab into the back of Cassius's shoulder.

Cassius cursed and staggered forward. Unfortunately for Luke, the tactical vest Cassius was wearing turned the sword and absorbed some of the force, and while the stab had done damage, it hadn't rendered Cassius's left arm useless as intended. Luke landed and crouched behind his shield with his sword hidden behind the scutum, eyes peeking over the rim as he advanced on Cassius, who reset in a defensive position.

"You're pretty nimble for a human," Cassius taunted.

He swung his falx down toward Luke's head. Luke rotated the shield and caught the blade on the long edge and followed through by rotating his shield. He finished the rotation, sliding the falx away and his shield back into position. Luke's shield hand was now in the reverse position with his palm up and the bottom of the shield now at the top. He punched out with his shield, slamming into Cassius's shield and forcing him back, resetting the engagement.

The combatants circled each other, looking for an advantage until Luke lunged to the right, punching out toward Cassius's head. Cassius fell for the feint and met Luke's shield with his own before hissing in pain as Luke whipped the edge of his gladius across Cassius's leg just above the knee. Luke took advantage of Cassius's distraction and rammed his shoulder into Cassius's, knocking him off balance. Cassius staggered back as Luke pivoted on his right foot, spinning around and launching two rapid thrusts into the vampire's lower back. Cassius grunted in pain. Luke finished by pulling in his shield and shoving Cassius in the back. Cassius used the momentum to stagger forward into a run, opening some distance between him and his former friend.

"That fucking hurts!" he said as he spun around to present his shield. "Is there silver in that poker?"

"Something like that..."

"That's not factory spec."

"Depends on what factory you're sourcing from. Do you think our audience is being entertained?" Luke asked.

"I should hope so. Otherwise, I'm taking these hits for nothing. That silver burns! When was the last time anyone saw two Roman legionnaires going head-to-head?"

"Sorry. Should I have given a handicap? I just figured if you'd been around for a couple millennia, you might have learned some new moves."

Cassius rolled his eyes at Luke and raised his hand with the falx in it to his face, using his middle finger to scratch his nose, simultaneously flipping Luke off. Luke clacked his sword against the front of his shield twice and stalked toward Cassius.

"Shall we?"

Cassius grimaced before darting forward, using all his vampiric speed. He delivered a series of shield bashes interlaced with lightning quick hacks and slashes with his falx. Luke parried and blocked but was driven back each time before seizing an opening to take control of the engagement, driving Cassius back on his heel. Man and vampire were breathing heavily, sweat beading on foreheads as their eyes focused with supreme concentration, jaws clenched. Luke's finesse was balanced against the speed and power the vampire used to smash at him.

They were evenly matched until Cassius turned his strength up a notch and drove Luke back. The vampire's powerful blows rained down, getting sloppier and sloppier as Cassius tried to overpower Luke. Just as Luke was about ready to shift the engagement back in his favor, his heel caught in a tiny pothole. As he windmilled his arms, trying to maintain his balance, Cassius slammed the edge of his shield up and into Luke's wrist, sending his gladius flying. Cassius took advantage of Luke's flailing, hooked his shield, and sent it skittering across the pavement. He pushed Luke down to his knees, pulled back, and prepared to deliver the final blow.

TWENTY-SIX

A MIGHTY GRUNT ripped from Cassius's throat as he poured all his vampiric strength behind the swing he delivered toward Luke's head and shoulder. Luke ducked, leaned to the left, and raised his manica covered arm to protect his head. Cassius had fully committed to his swing, leaving no room to change his angles. The curved bill of the falx clanged against the steel of Luke's manica, skittering and screeching over the overlapping plates and shooting down off his elbow. Luke pulled the poniard from his wrist sheath, rotated on his knees, and delivered a pinpoint stab through the tech vest into the vampire's kidney.

Cassius's scream, an inhuman blend of rage, pain, and fear, blasted out of his mouth as his body convulsed, and with super-human strength, he flung both his falx and scutum away from his body as he curled backwards around the knife in his back. Luke rotated around to avoid his falling foe. Cassius landed on his back, driving the poniard further through his kidney until it protruded out his stomach and tented the front of his tech vest. Luke stole a dagger from its sheath on Cassius's belt and crawled on top of Cassius, but Cassius had recovered enough to pull his knees to his chest. As Luke crouched over Cassius, dagger poised over the vampire's heart, Cassius kicked his legs out, launching Luke backwards.

Luke landed on his back with a clatter and slid, armor against pavement sending up a brutal din. Once Luke stopped, he rotated his legs and flipped back on his feet. Cassius, cursing and unsteady, rose to his feet and hobbled to his falx.

"Luke! Catch!" Samantha shouted from behind him.

Luke turned his head to see a katana still in its scabbard flying toward him. He reached up, snagging it out of the air by the scabbard with his left hand. Placing his right hand just below the hilt guard, he pulled the blade out and stashed the scabbard under the bandolier belt. He strode forward a few steps and settled into a ko gasumi stance, his body bladed with his left side facing Cassius. His weight shifted to his back leg, and the blade settled parallel to the ground at eye level with his arms crossing as his right hand held the hilt just below the guard, and the left holding the end of the hilt. Every muscle in his body was taut and ready to spring into action.

The tip of Cassius's falx scraped along the pavement as he stumbled toward Luke. Cassius chuckled and coughed.

"You watch 'Kill Bill' a couple times and think you're a Samurai?" He chuckled again before coughing and hacking up a bit of blood he spat to the side.

He took a deep breath and seemed to gather and prepare himself before summoning a last reserve of vampiric strength, letting out a harsh battle cry and sprinting toward Luke, falx poised and cocked above and behind his head. Luke stood statue still, eagle eyes squinted and taking in everything as his ancient friend charged toward him. Just as Cassius uncoiled his arm, preparing to loose a death blow, Luke's tightly coiled body sprung into motion.

The gleaming steel of the katana arced back, down, and around in deadly a windmill ripping up into Cassius's side above the left hip and continued through his rib cage, exiting just through his right armpit, slicing into his arm slightly. Making choking, gasping sounds, Cassius dropped his falx and fell to his knees before tumbling to the pavement and landing on his face.

Luke flicked his wrist and whipped the oozing vampire sludge off the blade. He shoved his foot under the side of the twitching body on the pavement and flipped him onto his back. Cassius's face twitched as bloody air rasped in his throat. An air bubble of blood formed, expanded, and popped as his eyes moved around in an unfocused, animalistic panic.

"That and soldiering up and down Honshu as a Ronin for fifty or sixty years. But go ahead and crack wise, I'm not the one with a gaping torso," Luke said in near perfect 17th-century Japanese. Cassius gave no indication that he heard or understood Luke as his legs weakly kicked and dragged over the road, and his fists clenched and unclenched. "Also, don't buy shit body armor next time."

Switching back to English, Luke said, "You never could control your strength or swings. I'm sorry it had to end this way, my friend. And you *were* my friend…" Luke's sadness was evident in both his voice and the pitying expression on his face. He reached over his shoulder to grab the rudis, which would permanently end the existence of the vampire that had once been his friend.

"Halt, Centurio!"

Luke's head whipped around to his left and saw a shadow emerging from the flood of headlights coming from the vampire-occupied end of the St. Johns Bridge.

The solidifying shadow continued in Dacian-accented Latin, "Even though this waste of space has so thoroughly failed in his mission, I still have need of him."

Two more shadows split off from behind him to flank him on either side.

Luke left his rudis undrawn and brought the Katana to readiness. "By right of conquest, this cadaver is my plunder. Turn around and walk away."

Despite the bravado of the words, Luke didn't back them with the confidence of his conviction as a note of uncertainty crept into his voice. He was too distracted by the Dacian-accented Latin speaker walking toward him. Two more silhouettes split off from the shadows flanking the voice, forming a wedge stalking toward him. The voice began to solidify into visibility. He wore a cassock. His long, wispy hair blew in the wind. A silvery beard contrasted with the dark fabric of the robe. With five to one odds, Luke reluctantly backed away from Cassius's still twitching body. Despite the damage Luke had done to Cassius, it wasn't enough to kill the vampire, not without a stake to the heart or a fuck ton of gasoline and a match.

"Stand down, Centurio. This is a fight you shan't win with naught but a pack of gutter dogs at your heel."

Luke heard the approach of footsteps behind him. Taking a moment, he peeked over his right and then his left shoulder. Werewolves in bipedal hybrid form, one wielding a naginata sword-bladed spear, sidled up along his right and left sides. He briefly made eye contact with the wolf he recognized as Pablo and nodded in acknowledgment before returning his attention to the blast from the past stalking toward him. One more set of shadows split from the last pair to increase the oncoming wedge to seven predatory figures.

Once the wedge drew up to Cassius's body, the robed beard made a couple gestures, and the darkly dressed vamps to his immediate left and right took Cassius by his feet and armpits, lifted him, and carried him back toward their lines. The vamp in the cassock turned and followed them. One more set of shadows split off from the end of the wedge while the two vampires at the front closed the formation, blocking Cassius, beardo, and the pallbearers. The vampire wedge advanced to meet Luke and his werewolf contubernium, which grew as more quietly padding feet joined him and the first wave of werewolves.

Luke closed his eyes briefly, centered himself, then set his body and sword into a versatile stance designed to handle both offense and defense. He heard growls and rumbles as his lupine allies readied themselves to plunge over the precipice into supernatural-on-supernatural violence.

"Once more into the breach, dear friends, once more…" Luke muttered a few levels above a whisper.

LUKE WASN'T sure who made the first move. The two lines stared at each other for what seemed like an eternity but was probably only a handful of seconds until the tension broke and they surged toward each other, the vampires hissing as they moved with supernatural speed while werewolves growled and sprinted toward their enemies. Claws ripped into each other as a wolf grasped a vampire's head and wrenched it off before chucking it violently at another vampire, knocking it off balance.

Luke took advantage of the cranial ballistic and brought the katana down, removing the vampire's right arm before bringing the blade around for another pass that sent its head tumbling one way as its body fell the other. He punted the head away to ensure it didn't make its way back to the vampire's neck before turning toward another target. The battle raged around him, but no vampire was within easy reach, so he took a moment to survey the scene.

The werewolf with the naginata was engaging two vampires, the big spear making precise slices as she slowly dismembered the over matched vampires with trained, lethal precision. The other wolves seemed to be taking some injuries, but were giving better than they got, at least for now. However, another couple groups of vampires sneaked along the edges of the bridge, hoping to take Luke and the werewolves by surprise.

One of the lead vampires screeched as a crossbow bolt sprouted from its chest. Joining Luke and the wolves, Delilah had grabbed the shiny, new high-tech crossbow Luke had gotten to experiment with and was putting it to good use, breaking up the momentum of the vampires trying to join the fight. While she held the right line, Luke dashed off to the left to engage the other group. Just as he was about to make contact, a large beast in full wolf form flew over his head and landed on the lead vampire, shoving it to the ground before ripping its throat out. Using the distraction provided by the violent wolf attack, Luke swept in and took a head off before following through and catching another vampire at the elbow, lopping off part of its left arm.

A few other wolves joined the swirling chaos to dart in and hamstring vamps then dart away, avoid slashing claws and violent fangs. Luke followed and dismembered the fallen vampires, taking their heads to leave them near dead or their limbs if he couldn't get to their head easily to render them impotent.

A pained yelp pulled Luke's attention to one of the bipedal werewolves who'd been dragged down by a couple vampires. He rushed over to help, lopping off the head of one vamp while raking the katana's blade across the ass of a second vampire, trying to get to the wolf's neck. The sudden deep-cutting swipe caused the vampire to arch its back and present its head for a near perfect executioner's decapitation. The headless body flopped back down on the werewolf, black ichor sluicing out of the neck onto the wolf.

Luke kicked the body off the werewolf and offered a hand to help him up. The wolf accepted and pushed his way up awkwardly. He rose unsteadily with a right leg that looked badly bloodied.

"Get back to the bus with the civilians. Relieve one of the guards and send them up. I'll cover your retreat." The wolf looked like he was about to disagree and head back into combat, but instead nodded once before limping toward the back of the line.

He caught sight of Delilah. She'd abandoned the crossbow and was darting about, hacking at vampires with her sizable machete. She was playing it smart, keeping the bigger and faster werewolves between her and the vampires, darting out when the fangers were distracted to lop off a hand or arm or sweep her blade across legs. Each swipe rendered the vampires less efficient and easier for the werewolves to finish.

Catching a slight movement out of the corner of his eye, Luke spotted an unattended vampire sneaking toward Delilah. She hadn't notice it; her focus was on the main melee. The vampire's attention seemed entirely on Delilah, so Luke jogged toward it, building up speed while trying to keep his footfalls silent. Finally in a full sprint, he ripped his katana through the back of the vampire just as it was raising a blade to plunge into Delilah. Realizing her danger, she spun around and brought her machete through the neck of the would-be assassin, turning it into a gory Pez dispenser. Luke halted his momentum, spun around, and finished the decapitation. As the body fell, he noticed the blade the vampire was about to stab Delilah with was his missing gladius.

"There you are, buddy!" he said as he reached down to pick it up off the pavement. He nodded at Delilah before heading off to see where he was needed.

With a katana in one hand and his gladius in the other, he darted about, assisting the werewolves by lopping off whatever he could get his blades on or, when possible, stabbing the vamps through the hearts with his gladius, sending them to their final rest. The fight appeared to be largely heading in favor of the werewolves when he heard a sound he hadn't heard in ages—the blowing of an oxen horn. Looking toward the line of headlights blocking the west side of the St. Johns Bridge, he waited to see what new trap the vamps were sending their way. Then he heard another horn from far behind their own lines.

Before he could prepare for another onslaught, the vampires began to disengage. Those who were able went into full vampiric fast sprints, fleeing the wrath of the werewolves. Any stragglers were quickly swarmed over and destroyed. Some werewolves appeared to be about to launch a pursuit. Luke put his fingers between his lips and whistled shrilly to get their attention.

"Wolves! HALT! Return to your lines," he bellowed, using his battlefield command voice. One of the wolves punctuated his command with a loud howl. The wolves stopped their advance and backed toward their initial line. Luke joined them. He met up with a heavily breathing Delilah.

"Shit, I need to do some more running or something if it's going to be pitched battles in the streets all the time."

"Yeah, battlefield conditioning is something else entirely," Luke replied, trying to mask the fact that he was winded himself. "Got enough energy to jog back to the line and see what's happening?"

"Yeah. Sure." She took off at a steady jog. He turned around and saw one of the bipedal wolves shifting back to human form. Once he saw it was a woman, he turned his head, allowing the wolf some privacy.

"You can turn around," came Holly's slightly ragged voice. "Wolves are used to casual nudity."

"So are legionnaires, but I always like to defer to the mores of the times."

Luke turned as Holly pulled on the T-shirt she'd been wearing earlier. Her lean muscles rippled under her pale skin.

"You've been fighting vampires for a long time. Are they going to keep attacking?"

"I haven't fought vampires in these numbers in a while. I'm not sure what's going to happen next."

Their questions were quickly answered as the line of headlights and the vehicles attached to them began to back away and drive off.

Luke squinted, watching the lights move. "Well, looks like they've given up for now. Hopefully."

They turned as the sound of someone jogging toward them caught their attention. Delilah, huffing and puffing, halted before them, placing her hands on her knees as she caught her breath.

"I've really got to start jogging more often. Shit." After a few moments, her breathing calmed, and she stood up to face Luke and Holly. "Looks like the vampires back there have withdrawn as well. The wolves are ready though if they come back."

Hearing the news, Luke offered the handle of the katana to Delilah, pulled a cloth out of his pocket, and wiped the gladius clean before resheathing it. He took back the katana, repeating the cleaning, before turning his back to Delilah.

"Can you hand me the scabbard, please?" Delilah pulled the wooden saya out from under Luke's bandolier and handed it to Luke.

"Was anyone hurt badly?" Holly asked.

"A few cuts. There were a couple wolves who were sent back to the bus with more severe injuries. I don't know much about were-wolves, though, so I don't know how bad the injuries really are," Delilah replied.

"If they're still moving or haven't made the final shift, they'll heal." Holly's relief was evident. "We'd better get this caravan moving again before the police show up. Everyone shift back."

As if on cue, the sound of sirens off in the distance deep in St. Johns punctuated the need to hurry. Peering off into the distance, trying to see if he could catch a flash of red and blue lights, he noticed a red glow and thick cloud forming near where Wapato was located. The bomb they'd set off in the vamp nursery had kept burning and had engulfed the jail. The authorities would have something far more pressing to worry about than what they didn't know was happening on the St. Johns Bridge.

"That'll keep them distracted for a while," Luke said, pointing to the growing inferno in the distance.

The wolf with the naginata walked over to Luke and handed him the sword-bladed spear before she began her shift. When she was done, Samantha stood naked before him.

"Mind holding that for a few more moments while I put my clothes on?" She winked at him before turning to walk toward the pile of clothes that belonged to her. When she returned, she said, "You're pretty good with that katana, although your Japanese is a bit rusty. It's also quite archaic."

"Thanks, it's been a long time since I've used my Japanese and even longer since I learned it. You're pretty handy with that naginata." He handed her back the katana first. She slid it under the belt she was using to hold up her jeans. He returned the naginata to her. "Holly, I need to check on the vamp bodies they left behind and ensure they're properly staked. Mind if I borrow Sam to watch my back? Also, I probably should be last in line of the caravan. I can sense the vampires and should be able to see if anyone is following us. I'll want to drift back quite a bit."

"Right, good thinking. Sam, go with Luke. You can help guide him to the farm if you get too far behind."

"I'll collect Gwen and help get everything ready to go," Delilah said. She bent over and picked up Luke's crossbow before walking back to the line of cars.

Sam fell in with Luke as he headed back out to the center of the bridge. Luke reached over his shoulder and pulled out his rudis and began working his way through the various bodies, staking them through the heart and leaving piles of dissolving and disintegrating bodies.

"Why do some turn into goo and others puff out into dust?" Sam asked.

"Freshness. The gooey ones are vampires that have been turned more recently. The dust bunnies are older vamps. I'm surprised there are as many old vamps here as I'm seeing. I must have taken a good chunk of their young ones out recently. Typically, the old ones use the young ones as expendable foot soldiers. They can be replaced easily." He continued his work. After a few more bodies, he looked up at Sam.

"Onna-bugeisha?"

"Yup." Sam smiled at him and nodded.

"I thought so. Your forms are more classic and practiced. More true war forms." Luke walked up to a vampire that had been hamstrung on both legs and was missing an arm. She was trying to crawl back toward her now vacant lines with only one arm. "Not so fast."

Luke placed one knee on her back, halting a half-assed attempt to escape before he shoved the rudis between her ribs and into her heart. He placed his forehead on the pommel and mumbled the formulaic incantation that activated the true power of his rudis. The fine silver filigree glowed, starting at the sword's pommel and running down its body and into the fanger, before it slithered its way up, ending at the small silver nub at the end of the pommel before disappearing into Luke's forehead.

"What's that? Why did you only do that on this vampire?" Sam asked.

"It's a secret," Luke replied as he stood up and walked toward another headless vampire.

"Bullshit." Her eyes widened as a realization dawned on her. "That's how you get your power, isn't it? You're like some kind of, I don't know, vampire vampire…"

Luke looked at her before returning his attention to a partial body in need of a staking. He nodded lightly before saying, "I'd prefer if you'd keep that fact to yourself."

"I can't keep it from Holly, nor would I want to. She's my wife and my packleader."

Luke pulled his rudis out of the dissolving body and faced Samantha.

"Nor would I expect you to. You and Holly seem like a wonderful couple. I wouldn't want to interject one of my secrets between you two. Besides, I expect that Pablo has already informed her. Then again, he might have kept it to himself since it didn't affect the pack. I just ask that you keep it between you and Holly. I think this is the last one. I need to collect my shield so we can get the hell out of here."

Together, they walked over to the site of Luke's duel with his former friend. Once he got there, he took out the cleaning rag, wiped down the rudis and stowed it safely in its back scabbard. He picked up Cassius's falx and handed it to Samantha. "Mind carrying this for me?"

Sam leaned her naginata against her shoulder, freeing up one hand to take the falx. Luke bent over and picked up his shield before walking over to pick up Cassius's.

"What kind of weapon is this, anyway?" Sam rotated the weapon to look at it from various angles.

"It's a falx. The Dacians liked them."

"Those guys you were telling us about at Pablo's house?"

"Yeah. It kind of works like a sickle. The curve allows for maximum force to be applied to a broad area. With a two-handed swing, it could punch armor or helmets. It could rip a shield apart or easily lop off a hand or arm. That's why I'm wearing all this gear," he said, roughly gesturing at himself. "This helmet has reinforced steel crossbars on it. The armor sleeve—it's called a manica—is designed to take the blow of the falx and direct the blade down to the elbow where the plate is thicker."

"Cool!"

They walked back to the caravan. Everyone was in a vehicle, and all the engines were running. Luke chucked both scutums into the back of his Volvo wagon, removed and stowed his helmet, and took off his swords and the bandolier that held them.

"Just throw the falx into the back with the shields. We need to get on the road." He unlaced the leather thong that held his armor closed and turned toward Sam, who was unscrewing the shaft of her Naginata.

"It'll fit in the back better this way," she commented, catching where Luke's gaze had landed. "Need some help with the armor?"

"Sure. It's always awkward to get off." Luke shimmied out of the armor, then took it from her and put it inside its storage tub. He shoved the whole box back into the wagon, then pulled down the hatch door. "Let's go."

Luke walked up front. Delilah was already in the driver's seat, so he climbed into the passenger side, and Sam got in behind Delilah. Gwen was already strapped in the back right seat.

"Gwen, you remember Samantha?"

"Hi, Gwen. You can call me Sam." She offered her hand to the skittish girl sitting next to her.

Gwen gave her a wary look and a tiny wave, avoiding shaking Sam's hand as the caravan finally started moving again.

"Delilah, once we get off the bridge. I need you to fall behind the rest of the caravan. Sam will guide us to our destination. I need to make sure we're not being followed by any toothy tails."

TWENTY-SEVEN

THE CARAVAN MOVED up Highway 30 with Luke, Delilah, Sam, and Gwen bringing up the distant rear. So far, Luke hadn't felt any vampires behind them.

"Hey, Sam, are there multiple ways to get to this farm?" Luke asked.

"Yeah, why?"

"Maybe I'm just being overly cautious, but I don't want any unwelcome visitors. Can you direct Delilah to an alternate route? If there are any vamps behind us, hopefully that'll let the caravan get safely to the farm."

"OK. Do you want to make any unscheduled stops to help throw off the scent?"

"Sure, why not. You'd probably better let Holly know what's up."

"Yeah. She'll worry. Delilah, just stay on Highway 30 for now." Sam fished her cell phone out of her pocket and called Holly to explain what they were doing.

Luke twisted around to his right and saw that Gwen had fallen asleep against the window.

"Sam, I think you can reach my backup cloak—the one not

covered in vampire gore. Would you mind spreading it over the kid?" he asked after Sam finished her call. "What time is it?"

"About four a.m.," Sam replied.

"Let's head to Astoria. The Pig 'N Pancake opens early. I'll buy breakfast, then we can lay out the next part of the trip. You good to keep driving, Delilah?"

Delilah nodded. "Yeah. But you owe me some coffee with those flapjacks. This has been a long night, and it's not over yet."

Luke chuckled in response. "Thanks again for driving. You can have as much coffee as you want and anything else."

Delilah smiled at Luke and nodded before sticking her right hand into her jacket pocket to pull out her phone. She unlocked it with her thumb, then handed it to Luke.

"I need some road tunes. I have an old-school punk radio station on Spotify. I need some upbeat bops."

"Apparently of the blitzkrieg variety?" Luke waggled his eyebrows at Delilah.

Delilah snorted, trying to keep from laughing at Luke's word-play. She rolled her eyes at Luke. "I hate that I laughed at that."

Luke hooked her phone up via Bluetooth and hit play. The Buzzcocks' "Ever Fallen in Love with Someone You Shouldn't've?" filled the quiet with its steady beat and catchy guitar riff. The car settled into silence as classic punk and post-punk songs from the late '70s and early '80s kept everyone's heads bobbing as the old Volvo steadily ate up the miles to Astoria.

ABOUT NOON, the gang, tired and flagging, pulled into the tiny town of Birkenfeld deep in the wooded hills of the Coast Range, the mountains separating Portland and the Willamette Valley from the Oregon coast.

"Take a le..." Sam yawned, cutting off her directions. "Sorry, take a left after The Birk."

"The what?" Luke asked from the driver's seat.

"The Birk! You don't know The Birk? Oh man, it's great. It's a fantastic little roadhouse. Beer, food, music. It's owned by the pack! We'll take you there for burgers. It's on the left as we pull into town. The road leading up to the farm is just after. Once you get on the road, keep going until the gate. I'll key us in, then you drive up to the main house."

The Birk looked like an old storefront attached to a house. The big metal letters across the front proclaimed Birkenfeld Country Store. A smaller sign underneath had the current name, The Birk. Luke pulled off 202 onto a well-maintained gravel road that led back into the woods. They crossed a bridge over the Nehalem River and then pulled up to the gate. Luke moved up so the gate keypad was next to the back left window. Sam rolled the window down, reached out, and keyed in the code. A moment later, the gate swung open, and Luke continued down the gravel road for another few minutes. Finally, they pulled into a clearing with a large house. Behind it, there were several smaller outbuildings of uniform size and build.

"The pack has events up here, so we have a lot of little cabins where people can stay the night. That's one of the reasons Holly wanted to bring everyone up here. Plenty of beds, plus it's way out in the middle of nowhere. We have a couple pack doctors and some nurses too. They've probably been triaging the people from the jail and our wounded," Sam said.

Luke reached over and gently shook Delilah's shoulder. "We're here. You fell asleep after we left Astoria.

Delilah yawned and unbuckled her seatbelt. "Crap, I didn't get to see the coast. I've never seen the Pacific Ocean."

Luke turned to the back seat. "Gwen. It's time to get up. We're here."

Sam reached over and gave her shoulder a little shake. Gwen shot awake and immediately pulled her legs to her chest as she flailed about with her arms, her eyes wide and panicky. Sam scooted away to avoid getting hit by accident.

"It's OK, Gwen. You're with friends. No one here is going to hurt you. It's OK. It's OK…" Luke kept talking in a soothing voice until the startled girl finally calmed her breathing and relaxed somewhat.

"Sorry," she muttered, her face looking at the floor of the Volvo.

Luke smiled gently at her. "We're here now. There's probably a spare bed you can borrow for a nap."

"If you're hungry, I can make you a sandwich," Sam offered.

Gwen just nodded and got out of the car and stretched. Sam and Luke made eye contact. Sam's sad look mirrored the sorrow Luke felt. He sighed and joined everyone else outside as they stretched, trying to get some life back in their limbs after a long night followed by hours in a car. Holly and Pablo came out of the door.

Pablo waved. "Hey, Luke. How you doing, dude? You look beat."

"Thanks, Pablo. You're not the freshest daisy yourself."

"At least I showered," Pablo teased, grinning at Luke.

Luke turned toward Holly as she and Sam embraced.

Breaking the hug, Holly turned toward Luke. "Did anyone follow you?"

"I think we got away clean. I never felt so much as a twitch. Between all the vamps we've killed lately and those on the bridge, they may be running thin on numbers."

"Good, good. We can talk strategy later. There's coffee and tea inside. Also hot showers."

"Dibs!" Sam shouted and ran into the house.

"She does that every time, even though she knows there are multiple showers in the main house. She's headed to the room we use when we're out here. It has a bathroom en suite," Holly muttered, shaking her head. "Gwen, I've had a bed made up for you in the back of the house, so you'll have some quiet. There's a large closet full of clothes for younger people in it. There's bound to be something you'll like and that'll fit. I'll show you where it's at." She gestured for everyone to follow her. "Luke, Delilah, there are showers for each of you and rooms as well."

Luke went to the back of the Volvo and pulled out a couple bags. He handed one to Delilah and followed Holly inside.

"Shoes off, please. You can set them next to the door on the racks. There's plenty of space."

Everyone followed orders and picked a spot on the rack to set their shoes. The entry opened into a large room with dark hardwood floors and plenty of cushy armchairs and sofas with small tables next to them. Holly led them to the back of the room and up a set of stairs with a dark red carpet runner covering its hardwood. She stopped at the end of the hall next to another set of stairs leading up to a third floor.

"Luke, you're on the left. Delilah, you're on the right. Each of your rooms has a small bathroom attached. Gwen, your room is next to Luke's. The door across from it is a bathroom. I'll leave you to it. We'll be assembling down in the kitchen when you're done. There will be snacks ready, too."

LUKE WAS the last to exit his room. Dressed in a tunic in a shade that could only be described as Roman red and a pair of baggy, gray linen trouser-like leggings, Luke padded silently down the hall in a more modern pair of cotton socks. The tunic was caught up at the waist in a belt that was hidden beneath a fold of the tunic that draped over the top. The hem came to mid-thigh.

As he passed through the large sitting room, he saw Gwen sitting in a chair in front of a window. She'd turned the chair to face out so she could stare out into the woods. A cup of tea steamed next to a beat-up paperback and a plate with a partially eaten scone on it. Luke walked over to her, making sure to walk heavily so he didn't startle her. She was dressed in a pair of black jeans and a black T-shirt. Her dark brown hair was short and ragged and in need of a good cut and style to help it grow out evenly.

"Hi, Gwendolyn. You doing OK?"

She nodded but didn't say anything in response.

"Do you need anything before I go talk with the others?"

She shook her head.

"If you need anything, let me know." He offered a kind smile before turning and entering the kitchen.

Pablo had a cup of coffee waiting for him on the table. He picked a fruit scone off the pile and sat down. Holly and Sam sat next to each other, their hands resting in each other's on the table. Delilah was leaning against the counter, dipping a tea bag into a steaming cup. Maggie, the doctor he'd met the other night at the pack's house in town, was sitting next to Sam. Max, Luke's friend from the house-less camp, looked nervous sitting at a table full of werewolves.

"Thanks for joining us. You can get some rest when we're done here if you want. I've kept the gathering small to keep things simple," Holly said.

Luke nodded at Holly. He looked over at his friend Pablo, who was quivering in his chair, trying to hide a smirk behind his hand.

"What the hell are you wearing, dude? Got a date at the Colos-seum later? Debating Cicero at the Forum after? Invading the Greeks before lunch?" Pablo could no longer hold in his snickering.

"Clothing can provide more than mere physical comfort..." Luke replied airily before taking a nibble of his scone while the others smiled at Pablo's antics.

Luke sighed, wrapped his hands around his coffee, and stared at the still, black liquid steaming in the cup. "Last night, I fought a man I saw die over nineteen hundred years ago. I found his body with a woman attached to his neck. I shouted at her. When she raised her head to look at me, her face was smeared with blood. She hissed at me. But it was the fangs I remember most, the huge, gleaming, needle-sharp fangs dripping the blood of a man who had stood next to me in battle for two years and who I'd trained with for two years before that. She flew at me. Fortunately, I had my gladius out. By that stage of the war, my reactions were hair triggered and wire tight. I caught her against my shield and plunged the blade through her heart, twisted it, ripped it out, then beheaded her. It was my first vampire kill. He was my friend... And last night, I took a katana and split him nearly in half."

Pablo stopped laughing and reached over to squeeze Luke's shoulder. "I'm sorry, Luke. I was just ribbing you."

Luke reached up and patted Pablo's hand but kept staring at his coffee. "I know, my friend. I know." Picking up his cup, he blew over his coffee before taking a sip. "They're comforting. They remind me of a time before I knew there was such a thing as vampires and my whole world was a small village near the Hallerbos."

Silence settled over the group as they enjoyed their warm, caffeinated beverages and tasty snacks. Pablo stood and grabbed the carafe of coffee to refill his cup.

"Any refills?" Pablo offered. Several hands raised as he made the rounds.

"Thanks, Pablo," Holly said. "Now that we've had some coffee and a bite to eat, we should probably open this discussion. Max, thanks for joining us. Do you feel comfortable representing the humans liberated from the jail?"

"Yeah, I know most of them, at least by sight. I won't make big decisions regarding their fates, but I can speak on their behalf and look out for their interests." He was getting slightly more comfortable as the normality of sharing space with fictional creatures became his reality. Or maybe he just was numb to it after the tumultuous events of the last eighteen hours. The dose of extreme fatigue and the hardship of his time imprisoned by the vampires didn't hurt, either.

"Luke, what was going on in that jail?" Holly asked. "Pablo wouldn't give me any details."

"Something I've been fearing for a while. It's become a little more extreme than a few vampires wandering into town and making a few more vampires." Luke sighed and took another drink of coffee before making eye contact with Holly. "They were using the jail as a feeding and breeding station."

"Breeding station?" Sam asked. "Is it, like, you know, in the movies?"

Luke let out a bitter chuckle. "No, the movies romanticize it. The premise is similar, but only in its most basic form. A lot of vampire movies are partially propaganda. Vampires want you to think they're sexy and misunderstood. They make the process of creating vampires seem dangerous and erotic with only a reasonable amount of pain."

"Wait, there are vampires in Hollywood?" Delilah asked incredulously.

Luke shrugged. "Vampires seek out fame, power, and fortune. They use glamour and wealth to move in influential circles where they can seduce and use their magic to control those who control the levers of power."

"Wait. It kind of sounds like a cult," Sam said.

"Or fascists," Maggie added.

Luke nodded at Maggie. "Vampires do not reproduce sexually. When they make a new vampire, they suck their vessel almost completely dry. Then they open a vein and let the nearly dead victim drink it. Some do it willingly for the power, but the unwilling can be turned. A vampire's glamour is a strong magic. Vampires don't really believe in consent, just what they can take."

Luke took a drink of coffee. "Once that blood hits the victim's mouth, it creates an insatiable urge to drink deeper. Then, the vampire's blood goes to work and burns out the human blood and, along with it, the person's soul. The process is excruciating."

"Have you seen it?" Holly asked. Everyone was looking on with fascination.

"Yeah, I've seen it a time or two. The shrieks of pain as the victim's humanity is burned away are branded into my mind. Watching a human die that way is not something I'll ever forget. That's what was going on in Wapato. The first room I found in the infirmary section was the transition chamber. There was a giant row of beds filled with bodies strapped to them. All of them filled with vampire blood about to be resurrected into darkness." Luke stood up to grab another pastry before pacing around the kitchen.

"I killed them all. Hours before, they'd been humans. Living beings exposed to terrible pain and terror, but humans. The vampires fed on them, then forced them to drink their death. When they rise, they're at their weakest, for a vampire. They're still incredibly strong, but they've not fed on human blood yet. Their hunger is all-consuming."

"What do you mean?" Sam asked.

"After their first blood, they become truly demonic. They're strong, fast, and hungry, but have no control. They will rip the world apart to drink, then they'll satisfy their lust for carnage by ripping your body to pieces.

"Pablo found me next to the room where they put vampires for their first blooding and the subsequent mayhem of their first days." Luke sat back down and looked Holly in the eyes.

Taking one look at Luke's face, Holly recoiled before recovering and giving him a look of profound empathy.

"They'd lowered humans into the rooms on chains. They feed on fear and terror almost as much as they do blood. When they finished with the bodies, they piled the tattered remains in one of the other rooms in the infirmary. No human should have to suffer that pain and terror. No one should have to have their soul blasted from their body so they can become the foot soldiers of darkness."

"Is…is that why you fight them?" Sam asked, standing behind Holly with her hands on her shoulders, providing comfort and reassurance.

"I can't stop…there's no end…" Luke trailed off as he tried to bring his emotions under control.

"I know I can't say this enough or ever pay you back, but thank you for getting me…us out of there." Tears streamed down Max's face as his hands trembled on the table.

Pablo got up and pulled out a bunch of bucket glasses, then grabbed a nearly full bottle of whiskey from another cabinet and poured two fingers into each glass before handing them out. "It's a bit of a rougher spirit, but I don't think any of us are in the mood for something subtle or genteel." He took a big drink and sighed as the whiskey burned its way down his throat.

Luke held onto his glass and stared into it for a while before taking a sip of his own. It seemed to fortify him some, so he took a larger drink and grimaced as the rough whiskey reminded him who was in charge.

"You're not kidding, but good choice." Luke sighed again and composed himself. "We've dealt them a severe blow tonight. I've—"

"We've…" Pablo and Delilah interrupted simultaneously.

"We've," Luke corrected, nodding at Pablo and Delilah, "put a big crunch on their numbers over the last several weeks between all the vampires we've killed in the streets. Last night, we shut down their feeding operation and eradicated their breeding stock. Next, we killed a bunch more on the bridge. There were a fair few older ones there. Cassius and his masters have got to be hurting on numbers. I think that's why they let us go tonight. We proved too much for them, and they couldn't lose any more bodies. They'll be back, though."

"We can't do much about that right now. We have more immediate matters to figure out. We can't turn all these people back out on the streets just to be swept back up by vampires," Holly said.

Luke nodded at Holly. "I think things will calm down a bit for a while. They have to find another suitable location, but that doesn't mean they won't continue with more modest operations. But you're right, we can't put everyone back out on the street. Vampires can find those they've fed on."

Everyone tensed at hearing this.

"Can they track them out here?" Holly asked tersely.

"No, certainly not this far out. But back on the streets of Portland, they'd be cattle to the slaughter. They're going to want to erase the evidence."

Getting to the logistics, Holly sat up straighter. "What can we do?"

"Can they stay out here for a while? I know this is pack property, but it's the safest option for now. It keeps everyone together where we can protect them. We can provide for their basic needs. I'll give you money, so the burden isn't on the pack. It'll give some time for the link between predator and prey to weaken."

Holly nodded. "Thank you. We can contribute as well. I think that's the best option for now. Max, what do you think?"

"There are some that have family they'll want brought out here, but most have no place else to go and will be happy to have a roof and some food."

"We've gone from being a secret to bringing more people into it," Holly said to herself, shaking her head. "I guess in for a penny, in for a pound." She looked back at everyone else. "The pack has a few LCSWs and other people in social services."

"L-C-S-Ws?" Luke asked.

"Licensed Clinical Social Workers. They can help people get services. Some are more geared toward providing therapy. No doubt that'll be needed in high supply after the horrors you described. You're lucky you made friends with Pablo, Luke. Other packs are definitely not as service oriented to their communities as ours." Sam smiled at Luke.

Luke, a thoughtful expression on his face, came to a conclusion. "I think I can contribute more than money. I own an apartment complex that's nearly finished with a full remodel. Once it's done, we can move them back into town and house everyone there. Your social workers can run it."

"Can you afford that?" Pablo asked. "Don't you need to rent it out?"

Luke chuckled. "No, I'm good. You don't live for as long as I have and not get good at managing wealth. I have properties scattered around the world. I have more than enough to spare a building and some funding. Holly, does this sound like a good plan?"

Holly looked thunderstruck, as did everyone else at the table.

"Yeah, yeah, I think so. Max?" Holly asked.

Max shook his head. "That's too much. We owe you our lives already. We can't hope to pay back even more."

Luke held up his hand to stop Max. "You can't repay that which isn't owed. It's not a handout or a loan. It's a chance for people to get off the streets. Holly, I'm guessing the pack has businesses that need employees. The benefit of having a workforce that knows about your unique circumstances can't be discounted."

"This is going to mean a lot to these people, Luke. Some of them just haven't recovered from the crappy economy. It's hard to get a job if you don't have an address or a shower." Max turned to Holly. "Others, though, are going to need some help from your social workers. There are some who are fighting some personal demons or are mentally ill."

Holly nodded in response. "The pack also has a host of other medical professionals we'll make available. Luke, how long until your apartment building is done?"

Luke shrugged. "I'm not sure. I've been a bit distracted lately. I'll find out as soon as we get back to town."

"Thanks, Luke. Maggie, how is the health of everyone?" Holly asked.

"Most are a bit dehydrated and hungry, as Luke said they'd be. There are a few who are in a rougher condition, although I'm not sure if that's a result of their time at the jail or if they were that way before they went in. There are a couple in worse shape. I'm not sure if they'll make it. We lost one on the way here. I've put in what plasma we have, hoping to get their blood volume up, but we're short on donors. Wolf blood won't work, and we only have two humans here who aren't already short on blood."

"You should probably exclude me from that number as well, Doc. I'm not sure what my blood would do in someone else," Luke said.

Maggie raised an eyebrow questioningly but didn't pursue it further. "And either way, I'm not sure Delilah has enough to spare to help out all who need it. I'll work some connections to see if we can get some more out this way. We may also want to hold a blood drive with the human pack members."

"I can check with the other packs as well," Holly added. "Are the two who won't make it lucid?"

"Lucid enough to consent to the bite?" Maggie asked. "Yes. Although they're in pain from their ailments and neglect, they're still fully in control of their mental faculties."

"What's the bite?" Max asked nervously.

"At times, we've offered a solution to sickness to various people we could help. Lycanthropy, if they survive the transformation, will essentially cure a person of anything. Anything physical, anyway," Maggie replied.

"There are several pack members who survived the AIDS crisis thanks to the gifts given to them via the bite," Holly added. "It's not a decision to be made lightly, or without the ability to consider the drawbacks."

"Everything will be discussed with them?"

Holly nodded in response.

"And if they say no?"

"We'll make them as comfortable as possible and do whatever we can to help them, but we won't force them to do anything they don't want. Not without their consent," Maggie stated.

Max thought about it for a bit, then agreed they could propose the option to those in need of it, but he had more questions. "And you'll take care of them after? You won't turn them out into the world alone?"

"No. They will remain with us while they learn about their new life and all the advantages and disadvantages. If they eventually decide this pack isn't right for them, we'll help them find one that better matches their personality," Holly said.

"And if they don't want to be part of any pack?" Max asked.

"That's unusual, but it does happen…at least for a while. The pack link is more than just a community. It provides stability and reassurance. Once a person is linked to a pack, very few want to let go of that connection. They find the world outside the pack to be a cold, barren existence. Also, the packs provide resources for their members—jobs, health care for human family members, housing if needed. We take care of our own and make sure everyone has the opportunity for a fulfilling life."

"At least the packs run by good packleaders," Sam said, looking fondly at her spouse.

Max nodded. "OK. I'm placing a lot of trust in you. Luke trusts you…"

Luke nodded at Max.

Max smiled weakly. "I don't know why, but a lot of people look to me to keep an eye on them. You've done right by us so far. If you can offer them a new road, I'm on board."

"I think it's fairly obvious why they look to you," Delilah commented.

"Now, the last piece of business for today: Gwendolyn," Holly stated.

"I don't mean any offense, but I don't think she'll agree to live with other werewolves right now," Delilah said.

"I agree," Maggie replied. "She's had a rough experience with her werewolf family and likely, their pack too. We'll have to find other options to help her for now." Maggie gave Luke a less than subtle look, which he missed, but Holly didn't.

"I'd offer to let her stay with me, but I'm still living on a friend's couch until I can find a job and an apartment," Delilah offered.

"You're planning on staying in Portland for a while?" Luke asked.

"Yeah. I still have unfinished business here," she replied cagily.

"Well, we can certainly find you a job with one of the pack businesses. What are you qualified to do?" Holly replied.

"Besides sit in a library and research a master's thesis? I waited tables and bartended all through my undergrad and grad program. Occasionally, I'd spin records and DJ. If you have a restaurant or a bar I could work in, preferably not the late shifts since I have other priorities for that time window."

"Pablo, do you have anything available in the pub?" Sam asked.

Pablo eyed Sam for a moment. "Yeah. I'd planned to add some lunch hours, plus I have a feeling my pack duties will be picking up some under the current circumstances. If you can provide a resume and some references…"

Sam threw a wadded-up cloth napkin at him. It landed on his head and draped over his face.

"I kid! I kid!" Pablo responded, swiping the napkin off his head. "I'd love to have you at the pub. I'm always looking for reliable help I can trust."

"I'm sure we can find a room for you to rent until you can find an apartment," Holly said before turning a very direct gaze on Luke. "As far as Gwen, though…"

"What? Oh, no! I don't know anything about kids. I also don't know anything about trans kids." Luke felt slightly panicked and was sure he looked wild about the eyes.

"In two thousand years, you've never had a family? Kids?" Sam asked incredulously.

"No…" Luke shook his head.

Maggie smiled calmly at Luke. "She already seems to have latched on to you, Luke. Building trust with someone is the first step to finding some stability and security in her life. She needs a place to call home and a person to show her kindness and ensure her wellbeing. For whatever reason, she's chosen you for now. You can provide her with a home where you'll both have access to the resources of the pack. Eventually, we'd like to bring her fully into the pack. There are several trans pack members who can provide guidance. I also know a few therapists who work with trans people and can provide assistance for you and guidance and therapy for her. That's a bit more long range, though. Right now, we just need to get her off the streets into a place where she'll be safe and secure. And most importantly, where we can ensure her medical wellbeing. She just had her first werewolf shift. That's a good sign she's about to launch into puberty."

Luke looked around the table, his breathing a bit uneven. The looks he got back were a mix of hopeful and kind. Seeing the support of the first non-feline friends he'd made in many years steeled his wavering resolve.

"OK... I really don't know anything about kids," Luke repeated. He knew what Maggie was saying was correct. For some reason, in the whirlwind of chaos of the last forty-eight hours, the homeless girl had identified him as someone who would look out for her. "...but I'll try. I've got a guest room she can stay in."

Maggie smiled warmly at Luke, easing a bit of his anxiety.

Holly clapped her hands once. "Good! Maggie, you and Luke should exchange information. I think we're done here for the moment. We have some good rough plans in place. We should plan another meeting to go over the next steps after everyone gets their information together. Maggie, you can get back to your patients now. Luke, Delilah, you can go get some rest. I don't think there's anything else you can do at the moment."

Luke nodded and stood up. He walked out of the kitchen and back over to Gwen to check on her before heading up for some much-needed sleep. The kid was passed out in the chair. He flagged Delilah down and waved her over.

"Poor kiddo, she's got to be completely exhausted," Delilah said.

"Yeah, I'm feeling about the same, and I get regular food and sleep in a nice house." Luke picked up the small end table and carefully moved it out of the way, then scooped up the underfed and undersized kid and carried her through the maze of couches and chairs toward the stairs. Delilah followed him. They stopped in front of Gwen's door.

"Can you open the door, please?"

Delilah slid around Luke and the sleeping Gwen and opened the door before stepping in. She pulled down the covers and moved out of Luke's way as he sidestepped through the door, carefully avoiding bouncing Gwen's head off the door and waking her up. He placed her on the bed with her head on the pillow, then pulled the covers over her. Luke and Delilah quietly left the room and shut the door behind them.

"She's so light. Just skin and bones," Luke said.

"Sounds like she was on the street for a long time. Hopefully you can provide her a bit of stability for now."

Luke nodded. "I've fought vampires for centuries, but the thought of having a child in my house is far more terrifying."

Delilah chuckled. "You'll do fine. Besides, I think Holly and Sam and the rest of the pack are likely to pitch in anything you need."

"Yeah. You did good last night, by the way. You probably kept a lot of wolves from getting hurt worse or even killed. You played it smart. I think you impressed a lot of the pack out there, and most importantly, Holly."

"Thanks! I do appreciate..." she interrupted herself with a massive yawn, "...it. I need to get some beauty sleep. Momma's tired!"

"Sleep well, Delilah."

"You, too, Luke."

EPILOGUE

LUKE AND GWEN were adjusting to life with each other. Luke wasn't used to having another human in his space. Alfred, on the other hand, adored having a new set of hands around to pet him. He spent most of his time with Gwen, getting belly rubs and ear scratches. The orange tabby's presence comforted the pre-teen as she struggled to come to grips with two years of homelessness, followed by a terrifying two weeks held captive by the vampires in their feeding station and nursery.

The first morning, Luke had found her sleeping sitting upright on the floor with her back in the corner, her blankets wrapped tightly around her. He let Alfred wake her up with a combination of kneading and his aggressive purr. From that morning on, the two had been nearly inseparable. He followed her around like a puppy. When she was sitting, usually with her nose buried in a book, Alfred was in her lap or lying next to her.

She'd only left the house a couple times for visits with Dr. Maggie. She'd refused all of Luke's attempts to get her to join him when he went to meet with Pablo. About the only person she didn't actively avoid, besides Luke, was Delilah, who stopped by periodically to check in on Gwen and make sure Luke was handling the change to his lifestyle as well as possible.

Luke finished the last touches on the dish he was making for the holiday dinner at Pablo and Tony's house. He washed his hands and went to let Gwen know he was leaving. He knocked gently on her closed door.

"Hey, Gwen. Mind if I come in?"

"OK."

He cracked the door and popped his head in. Gwen, as was usual, sat in the wingback chair he'd moved into her room. She had an open book in her lap.

"I'm about to head to Pablo's. Everyone would love to see you. The food's going to be amazing. Tony is a great cook."

"I don't want to go. I don't celebrate Christmas."

"Me either, really. I'm technically a pagan. It'll be fun, though. Delilah will be there. I think Sam is coming, too." About the only wolf that had seemed to get through her anti-werewolf barrier had been Sam. Her kind and open nature had even worked on Gwen. "You don't have to talk to anyone if you don't want. I'm sure you can watch TV. The food will be good, and it'll do you some good to get out of the house."

Gwen sighed. "OK. I'll go."

She untangled herself from the fuzzy blanket she'd wrapped around herself. She wore oversized baggy black jeans and a hoodie that matched the jeans in both color and sizing. She grabbed a knit beanie off the dresser and pulled it over her messy hair. The aggressive and poorly done hack job the vampires had given her was looking even worse now that it was growing out in uneven patches. The beanie had become her armor, protecting her head from the stares her hair got from the indignities done to it.

"Great! Let me grab my jacket and the salad and we can go."

"MIND KNOCKING on the door for me, please?" Luke asked. He raised his hands, which were holding a large glass bowl with tinfoil covering the top.

Gwen knocked tentatively. A few moments later, Pablo opened the door.

"Luke, Gwen! Come in, come in! Happy Holidays, Gwen. Happy...Saturnalia, Luke! That's the right holiday, correct?" Pablo came in for a hug as Luke juggled the bowl to one side and propped it against his side so he could awkwardly return his friend's hug.

"I think it ended a couple days ago, but I appreciate the sentiment. Thanks for inviting us, Pablo."

"Of course! I'm glad you could make it. Let's take that to kitchen." He directed a beaming and friendly smile to Gwen. "Welcome to our home, Gwen. Can I take your hoodie and your hat?"

She shook her head vigorously.

"OK, no worries." He turned around and beckoned for them to follow.

In the kitchen, Tony was in the same position as when Luke first met him, working away at the food. Pablo took the bowl and set it on the counter with the other bowls and containers. Pablo turned to Tony, wrapped his arms around his waist, clasping them in front of Tony's stomach. He gave his husband a squeeze and a kiss to his cheek.

"We have guests, love." Pablo said, letting go of Tony and walking over to the kegerator in the corner. "You don't get a choice this time. I saved a keg of my holiday ale just for today!"

"Merry Christmas, Luke." Tony set the towel down and gave Luke a cordial hug before turning to Gwen, who was standing off to the side of Luke and just behind him, trying to avoid any hugs. He offered her a warm smile in lieu of a hug. "And you must be Gwendolyn. I'm Tony. Merry Christmas, and welcome to our home. We have juice, soda, sparkling water, or still water if you'd like. Just let Pablo know, and he'll get you whatever. Honey, when you're done with their beverages, take them out to the living room. I'm sure Gwendolyn would like to inspect the holiday cookies and candies."

"Can…can I have a sparkling water, please?" Gwen asked. Her voice was nearly inaudible.

"Sure thing! What flavor would you like? We have grapefruit, orange, cherry, and…" Pablo opened the fridge and pulled out a drawer filled with cans. "And some lime."

"Cherry, please."

"Cherry, it is for the young lady. Can't stand them myself, but Tony loves them."

"That's because I have better taste than you," Tony quipped.

Pablo rolled his eyes in mock annoyance. "I know. You chose me, didn't you? Let's leave the food artiste to his masterpieces."

He led them to a side table in the living room covered in cookies and fancy homemade candies, each labeled with a place card hand-written in a stylish calligraphy. Gwen's eyes lit up at all the variety and bounty of treats she'd probably not seen in years, or maybe ever.

"May I have a peanut butter ball, please?"

"Grab a plate and pile it high! It's everything a growing wolf needs," Pablo said.

Her eyes darkened slightly at the mention of wolves, but she followed his invitation and went over the offerings, selecting the ones that matched whatever criteria she had for sweets. The sound of knocking forced Pablo to set down the plate he was assembling.

"Delilah! Welcome! Happy Holidays!"

"Hey, Pablo. This is my friend Clarvetta."

"Hi-ee!" said an unfamiliar voice.

Luke wandered over to greet Delilah. When he turned the corner, Pablo was taking a covered pan from Delilah, who was standing next to a short, brunette woman with pale pink skin.

"I'll put this in the kitchen. When you're ready, Tony can help you finish it up."

"Hey, Luke, Merry Christmas!" Delilah gave him a hug. "This is Clarvetta. She's been kind enough to let me couch surf until I get a place."

"Hi-ee! Nice to meet you." She offered her hand to shake, which Luke did.

"Hi, nice to meet you, Clarvetta."

"Is that Gwen?" Delilah asked as a beanie covered head peeked around the cover. "I'm going to go say hello."

"I'll take Clarvetta to the kitchen and get her a drink." Pablo gestured toward Clarvetta with his head. "Follow me to beveragetopia!"

Luke followed Delilah as she made her way toward Gwen. He stopped at the snacks table and popped another peanut butter ball in his mouth.

Seeing Delilah, Gwen's face brightened. "Hi, Delilah."

"Hey, Gwen, I'm glad you made it out! Can I give you a hug?"

Surprising Luke, Gwen nodded shyly. She hugged Delilah tentatively, and then a bit more fiercely.

"Merry Christmas, kiddo. I have a little present for you." They broke the hug. "I'd like to take you out for some girl time! We'll go visit my hair stylist friend Ananya. She's got a couple cool ideas for haircuts that'll work with what you have. Then we'll go get lunch and hit a shop or two. See about getting you some more clothes. My treat! Does that sound fun?"

"Mmmhmmm," Gwen said "Um, thank you."

"Do you mind if I join in? I know a great place that makes some amazing milkshakes!" chimed in Sam, who'd just entered with Holly while Delilah was presenting her offer to Gwen.

"What do you say, Gwen? Can Sam join us?" Delilah asked.

"Uh huh. OK," said Gwen, the first genuine smile anyone had seen cracked her face.

Delilah and Sam exchanged numbers and a tentative date or two that might work.

"Hey, Pablo!" Sam yelled. "What's it take for a lady to get a glass of wine around here?"

"You know where the kitchen is!" called Pablo's voice. "I'm setting up Clarvetta with a glass right now."

Delilah and Sam strolled into the kitchen.

"Dee, you didn't tell me Luke was so foine!"

Luke blushed all the way to his hair.

"Ananya did a nice job on the hair and the beard, but great idea putting him in skinny jeans! That butt!" Clarvetta continued.

Luke walked to the other side of the room hoping he wouldn't hear any more and continued to blush furiously. Gwen giggled at his discomfort. Eventually, everyone but Tony joined Luke in the living room with their drinks. The conversation was light and friendly and kept to strictly non-paranormal topics, avoiding any mention of vampires or werewolves or other strange things, since Clarvetta was firmly not in the know about Delilah's extracurricular activities.

Throughout, Tony regularly refreshed the appetizer table. Gwen had found "We Bare Bears" on Netflix and was binging her way through several episodes. It had been a long time since Luke had celebrated any sort of holiday, let alone with friends, and for the first time in ages, he felt a bit less hopeless. It felt nice to have friends. Where he used to avoid people, he found himself reaching out to them to hang out. It was a change, but one he felt good about.

"Well, shoot. I think I'm fortified enough to head to my parents' house. I'd better call a Lyft," Clarvetta said. "Thanks for having me, Pablo. It was so nice to meet everyone!" She gathered up her things and bundled up. "I'll see you later, Dee."

After Clarvetta left, the conversation shifted to recent events.

"I'd like to find out who at city hall knows anything," Holly said. "Once the holidays are over, I'll ask my contacts."

"Do you think you'll be able to find any paperwork? It'll probably lead to a dead end, but you never know, we might be able to squeak some information out of it," Luke said.

"I'm not sure. Typically, they don't let defense attorneys rummage around in the file cabinets. I have a few friends in various departments that might be able to get us a look, though."

"We should probably think about inserting a few pack members into some city jobs," Pablo said.

Holly nodded, looking thoughtful. "That's not a bad idea. We'll have to keep an eye open for jobs and match them with pack members. I'm sure we can get a few hired."

"Do you really think they'll be back?" Sam asked. "After we destroyed their entire operation and killed a ton of their vampires, won't they just go away?"

"We've thwarted them for now, but they'll want vengeance. We hurt them. We took out some older vamps, but mostly just easily replaceable foot soldiers. They'll be back," Luke said.

The prospect of another round left everyone a bit less cheerful and slightly deflated. Gwen had scooted closer to the TV and had turned up the volume a couple more notches, keeping her back to the group and staying focused on her show.

"Well, on that note, I'll go get everyone another round of holiday cheer," Pablo said.

The conversation returned to lighter topics until Tony called everyone to the table for dinner. They sat around the ornately set table and passed dishes around family-style, filling their plates. Before they could dig in, Pablo raised his glass.

"I'd like to thank y'all for joining us today! Holly and Sam, this pack has given me a home when I needed it most. For that, I'll be eternally grateful. To our new friends, Luke, Delilah, and Gwendolyn, I hope this is the first of many gatherings for years to come. Last, Anthony, each year with you is better than the last. I don't know where I'd be without you!" He turned his attention to the whole table. "To each of you, cheers and good health and joyous holidays!"

Everyone raised their glasses, even Gwen, who drank cherry sparkling water from the wine glass Tony had given her. "Cheers!"

"Now, please. Enjoy this marvelous feast Tony has prepared for us and all the dishes everyone brought to share."

They all followed Pablo's advice and dug in. The feast featured a perfectly roasted turkey, as well as a rack of lamb. The crowd enjoyed Luke's farro salad and liked that they got to experience a bit of Luke's Roman heritage, even if it was only the farro that counted. Delilah's mac and cheese was a big hit, with everyone going back for seconds and even thirds for a few people. Gwendolyn found it particularly delectable.

"This is amazing," Gwen mumbled around a mouthful of food.

Luke was so surprised by her statement—she'd barely talked at all since they arrived—that he let her table manner faux pas slide.

"The mac and cheese is exceptional, Delilah. I'd love the recipe," Tony said.

"It's my granny's recipe. I'll write it down for you, but only on the condition you don't add any weird shit to it like celery or raisins."

Tony chuckled. "I promise I'll respect the recipe. Everyone ready for some—"

Phones went off, setting off a cacophony of vibrations and ring tones. Luke was the only one besides Gwen—who didn't own a phone—who didn't reach for his phone to check what was going on. When he sat there quietly, everyone looked over at him.

"What? Everyone who would be texting me is at this table."

"We need to turn on the news," Holly said.

Chairs pushed back from the table as they got up and filed into the living room. Pablo grabbed the remote and turned on one of the local news stations. The chyron scrolling across the bottom of the screen read:

Breaking News: Mayor Tom Jorgens has been abducted.

"…was sitting down for dinner with his family when armed perpetrators broke into the mayor's residence and abducted the mayor and his girlfriend. There is no word as to the identity of the perpetrators and no explanations or demands have been received. Portland police and FBI agents are on the scene." The newscaster put a finger to her ear and looked distracted for a moment. "We are getting word that City Hall is about to make a statement. We'll go live to Melanie Yakamoto who's standing by at City Hall. Melanie?"

"Thanks, Stacey. We've just been informed that Casper Clay, a spokesman and security consultant for City Commissioner and Police Commissioner Fred Bealer, will be coming out shortly. Ah, here he is now, being escorted by several Portland police officers."

The camera cut to an empty podium with a man approaching it from out of the dark. A tall man with sandy blond hair and a navy-blue suit stepped into the spotlight behind the podium. Luke's eyes went wide, and his jaw dropped. He instantly recognized the man he'd fought on the St. Johns Bridge three weeks ago.

"Cassius…" he whispered. He wasn't the only one to recognize the commissioner's spokesperson and security consultant.

"Him!" Delilah hissed.

Luke turned to Delilah and saw tears streaking down her cheeks.

Sam, who had been standing next to her, took her hand and squeezed it comfortingly. Everyone else turned to face Luke and Delilah.

"Who is he, Delilah?" Sam asked.

Delilah didn't answer, her eyes fixed on screen.

Luke narrowed his eyes as he watched his young friend. "You all saw him three weeks ago on the St. Johns Bridge. We fought until I used Sam's sword to split him from hip to shoulder."

"Apparently, he's recovered," Pablo said.

"Apparently." Seeing Tony's confusion, Luke added, "Cassius was my friend when we were in the legions, before he was turned into a vampire."

Everyone turned back to the TV just in time to hear Caspar, aka Cassius, tell the reporters that he'd not be taking any questions.

"Well, looks like we may have a lead on how the jail got leased," Holly said as Cassius turned away from the cameras and walked back into city hall.

Delilah finally spoke. "He murdered my father…"

To be continued in Dark Fangs Raging…

Keep reading for a brief excerpt.

LEAVE A REVIEW

Reviews are the lifeblood of every indie author. Even a simple star rating means the world to us. If you enjoyed this book, please leave an honest review at Goodreads, BookBub, or your preferred online book retailer.

Would you like to join other readers who enjoyed this book? Join my Facebook Reader Group!

facebook.com/groups/CThomasLafolletteReaderGroup

Thank you!

C. Thomas Lafollette

LUKE IRONTREE WILL RETURN IN

DARK FANGS RAGING

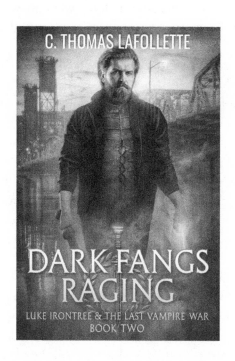

DARK FANGS RISING: BOOK TWO

Chapter One

LUKE REACHED up from the backseat of Pablo's pickup and patted Delilah on the shoulder. "It's time."

"Remind me why Pablo can't drop us at the front door?" Delilah folded her arms across her chest, looking mildly disgruntled.

Pablo shook his head. "I'm not particularly interested in having my pickup and its license plate recorded by any nosy bouncers or security cameras. We're trying to keep this anti-vamp operation of ours under wraps. They don't need to know Clark Kent is really Pablo Sandoval."

"He's right," Luke agreed.

"Yeah, but it's raining, and I don't want to walk through it," Delilah replied, her tone laden with annoyance and just a hint of a pout.

"It's just a good Oregon drizzle. You'll dry off before you get your drink," Luke replied.

"I better not have to wait that long for a drink," Delilah mumbled.

Delilah and Luke popped out of their respective passenger side doors and strode down the block and around the corner leading to the hottest new club in town—Red Velvet Room. They set a pace and bold stride that would have looked cool and dangerous in slow motion. A gust of wind caught the corner of Delilah's dark red leather three-quarter trench coat and flipped the bottom portion out.

Their cool quickly ended as they queued up with the rest of people waiting to get into the club. Eschewing his normal plain black hoodie, Luke's hooded jacket was stylish and simple. He coupled it with expensive shoes and designer jeans, hoping the combo would ensure Luke's entrance—that and a $100 bill he planned to palm to the beefy guy at the door. Delilah, with a few more months of growth on her teeny weenie afro, wore her trench and tall soled, heavy boots and looked like a stylish hero in a 1970s Blaxploitation film. Luke ran his fingers through his slightly curly hair, his hand coming back damp but smelling nicely of product.

"Don't mess with your hair. You need to look good to get in. The damp is good on the curls, though." Delilah inspected his hair to ensure everything, waves cresting like whitecaps in a rough sea, remained in order. "OK, you didn't mess anything up."

"Thanks." Luke smirked at her.

"And you're sure everything is set up?" Delilah asked.

Luke nodded. "Yes. We're good. You ready with the soundtrack?"

"Yeah, although I don't see why you asked. They have a DJ, don't they?"

"They do, but you've got better taste…most likely. Besides, when the action goes down, I'm guessing the DJ is going to be MIA when it comes to spinning." He added the "most likely" to goad her a bit. Delilah always insisted that her taste was impeccable, and certainly better than Pablo's and Luke's.

When they got to the front, the musclebound guy gave their IDs a once over then collected their door fee—and Luke's gratuity—and sent them inside. They made for the empty table near the DJ booth which was situated under one of the speakers dangling from the ceiling, allowing the sound to project over their spot without being louder than they wanted.

"I'll get the drinks," Delilah said, casting a glance toward the bar. "He's serving the women first."

"Good idea. I don't want to give him an opportunity to give me too much of a look over if Cassius has nosed around my description. I'll take a pilsner." Luke tucked into the booth so he could watch the room.

The bartender gave off strong vampire vibes that pinged Luke's vampy senses and made his fingers itch to pull the gladius that wasn't currently on his person. Returning a few minutes later with a couple beers, Delilah set them down and slid into the other side of the booth. The bartender's gaze had flicked to Delilah a couple times as he'd watched her cross the floor. Luke hoped he was admiring the tall Black woman's curves and not eying them suspiciously.

Delilah, ostensibly watching the dancing, surveyed the area, getting a feel for the space and obstacles. Luke had shown her pictures he'd taken when the club was empty, but seeing 2D images was different from being in the room. She'd said she wanted to familiarize herself with the layout and fix any danger points in her mind, especially with the dark setting and the flashing lights of a club full of dancers.

"Where's the other exit?" she asked. "In case we get cut off from the main one?"

"Past the bathrooms. It leads out to the delivery entrance. The door's locked right now, but I'll unlock it before we get ready to kick off the party."

"You still have the keys?" Delilah asked, brows furrowed.

"I paid a lot of money to play janitor so I could get in when they were closed. How do you think I got those pictures?" Luke forced his glance away from the bartender. He couldn't help it. His mind wanted him to focus on the only vampire threat in the room.

"Luke. Quit staring at the bartender," Delilah hissed when his gaze swung back toward the bar. "You're going to draw attention."

"Sorry. He's the only vamp here, and being in his presence is like nails on a chalkboard." He shifted in the booth so he could focus on something else.

Delilah rewarded Luke with a smile. "Any chance your old pal Cassius will show up?"

Luke shrugged. "I don't know. He's not really the reason we're here."

Delilah sighed and slumped into the booth. "I know, it's just…"

"I understand. We both owe him a lot of pain, and when the time's right, we'll deliver it without hesitation."

"It's just… I'm tired of waiting." Delilah drew back the curtain in her eyes she hid the pain behind.

Luke empathized with her. "I know. I really do. I'll do everything in my power to help you take him out, but tonight's not the night. We're just not ready yet."

Delilah clenched her jaw and nodded curtly. She'd agreed with this assessment before, but it clearly galled her. Luke wasn't sure how Delilah's father had been involved with vampires. She'd refused to share any details other than she'd walked in on Cassius committing the deed. When she'd attacked him, he'd ripped out a bunch of her locs, necessitating the big chop and the short afro she now sported. Luke hoped Cassius didn't show up tonight, afraid Delilah would forget their mission and jeopardize their lives.

He still had trust issues, even though he considered both Delilah and Pablo to be friends. He'd lived and hunted by himself for decades before they forced their way into his life. Though he was glad to have their help, he had a lot of his own issues to work through. Forcing his eyes off the bartender again, he got up and went to the bathroom. When he returned, he shifted the conversation to non-business topics while they waited until it was Luke's turn to chastise Delilah.

"You're going to put a crick in your neck periscoping around like that. Also, you're drawing attention." Luke indicated the bar with his eyes. He wasn't sure if the vamp bartender was eyeing her because he was attracted to her, or if she'd genuinely caught his attention with her nervous surveillance of the club.

Delilah took in a deep breath and let it out slowly, forcibly relaxing her shoulders. Slumping in her seat, she tried to put on a more casual pose. "Sorry."

"No worries. There's no guarantee he'll be here tonight. Owners don't always show up, and he's not the reason for tonight's visit. And if he does, it'll probably be under heavy escort. When we go after him, I want to control the engagement so it ends in our favor."

He gave Delilah an understanding smile. "I know it's hard but be patient. He's not going anywhere. He's too entrenched in his and his masters' plans. They've put a lot of work into this city. Somehow, the vampires are involved with the disappearance of the mayor. Why else would he be working for the city commissioner? He'll go down, and we'll be the ones to do it. I promise."

He tried to pour all his confidence and affection for Delilah into his gaze. She met his eyes, then nodded, relaxing visibly. She settled into her seat and began bobbing her head along to the rhythm of the DJ's song selection and beats.

"I'm surprised you actually approve of the DJ."

Delilah shrugged. "He's not bad."

"Better than you?" Luke raised an eyebrow and the corner of his mouth in a smirk.

Delilah rolled her eyes at him. "As if. Another round?"

Luke checked his phone to see what time it was. "Yeah, we should be good for another." Delilah started getting up when Luke halted her. "Never mind, I see a server coming around."

He paid for their drinks with cash, then waited until she was gone before resuming their conversation.

"When do you want to start this party?" Delilah asked.

"When there are enough guests of honor to make it worth our while. They probably won't be out until late."

"Why are we here so early then?"

Luke shrugged. "I wanted to make sure we got in. Plus I wanted to ensure we controlled the timing from start to finish. We choose when we engage, not just where. We're here to make a statement to the vampires. We need to make some noise. The bigger the crowd at the club, the more effect this mission will have."

"Are you sure this is a good idea? Just the two of us?" Delilah looked nervous as she leaned across the table.

He swept his eyes around them quickly to ensure no one was close enough to overhear. "That's all we'll need for this. We're not here to clear it out, just to make it harder for Cassius and his ilk to hunt. He needs to know he can't hide from me, even if it's in plain sight. We make a mess for him, then clear out. This place gets a bad reputation, and the fangers have to figure out a new way to get easy prey. It's what I've been doing by myself, so two people is more than enough."

Delilah nodded, though it seemed less than enthusiastic. Over the couple of hours they'd been hanging out, the club had filled up with rich twenty and thirty-somethings from the Pearl District eager to be seen and the crowd from the 'burbs eager to say they got into the

Red Velvet Room. It was a potent cocktail of affluence and gullibility.

As the floor filled, the lights dimmed, replaced with red mood lighting that matched the bar's name. When the affluent and expendable reached a critical mass, more vampires joined them, targeting the former for longer term parasitism and exploiting the latter for a quick snack. Luke, his body vibrating with the tension of being so near too many vampires, was ready to move.

"OK, it's about time. You have the play list ready?"

"Yeah." She pulled out an old MP3 player they'd picked up in a thrift shop. Jamaal, the North Portland Pack's head of tech, had formatted it to ensure it wasn't traceable. "I put the songs you requested in with the rest of the play list. There's some old school stuff in that list. You've got interesting taste. Where'd that come from?"

"I had cable in the '80s and '90s and watched a lot of MTV, especially 'Yo, MTV Raps.' The internet didn't really exist at the time, so I went to a lot of matinées. Pop culture kept me distracted, especially Black pop culture—Friday, Boyz n the Hood, House Party, stuff like that. I didn't really have any friends to speak of, and I was sliding into isolation more and more. Exploring this new entertainment kept me going outside the door to do more than just look for vampires." He shrugged, giving a clinical assessment of his more recent past. "Plus I had to do what I could to blend in when I went hunting where the youth of the day gathered. Had to look the part."

Delilah raised an eyebrow skeptically. "Did it actually work? Did you blend in? I mean..." She held up her hand and gestured toward him.

Luke shook his head, chuckling. "Yes and no. I didn't really blend in well with the kids. I looked like someone's dad or a narc."

Delilah let loose a loud laugh before tamping it down to avoid attracting attention.

"But at least I was on the scene when a fanger showed up."

Delilah looked delighted at the thought of Luke trying to blend in as an '80s hip-hop enthusiast. "Please tell me you have photos of you in an old school Adidas tracksuit?"

Luke winked at her. "Maybe sometime I'll show them to you, if you're nice to me."

Delilah rolled her eyes and stuck her tongue out at him.

"It's time to put on my dancing shoes." Luke shifted to get out of the booth.

"Dancing shoes?"

"Yeah. I'm going to dance."

Delilah snorted but tried to wipe the smirk off her face when she saw Luke's serious face. "You're going to dance? You? Pardon me, but you don't seem the type."

"You'll see..." He gave her a knowing smile.

"This ought to be good."

He headed to the back of the club toward the restroom. He slid behind a large potted plant and watched for an opportune moment before darting into the back hallway that led to the supply closet and the office. He fished a set of keys out of his pocket, opened the supply closet, stepped in among the brooms and mops, and shut the door behind him. Flipping a mop bucket over, he stood on it, moved the panel from the false ceiling out of the way, and pulled out the large duffel bag he'd planted when he was undercover as the janitor.

His next stop was the manager's office. He grabbed the gladius and unsheathed it in case someone was in the office watching the cameras. A different key unlocked that door. The office was empty. Either he was lucky, they were overconfident, or they just used the camera to corroborate anything they needed later, relying on security on the floor and at the door to maintain order. Stepping in, he pulled the door shut behind him and locked the door.

He flipped on the security monitor—a nature documentary played from the media device he'd spliced in. He chuckled as the screen panned across a central American jungle. When the vampires checked the security footage, all they'd find on their recording was a nice show about vampire bats. He hoped they watched it all the way through. He'd added an homage video of the Beastie Boys "Sabotage," although he doubted the fangers would find it as funny as Luke did.

He stripped off his shoes, jacket, and the button down under it and folded them into a neat pile. Opening the duffel, he pulled out his armor padding and drew it on over his undershirt. Next, he wrapped a thin black scarf around his neck to prevent his armor chafing and help cover the shine of steel.

He slipped into the armor and cinched the leather thong tight. He'd already set up the tactical bandoleer in place before they'd packed the armor. All he had to do was sheath the sword and the wooden rudis.

Both sword blades were partially visible in the semi-open scabbards Luke used to ensure quick draws over the shoulder didn't catch. The one set for his right hand was made of a steel alloy with some silver in it and was covered in crisp engravings, the visible side displaying a rising sun with flickering flames lashing out and down the blade. Its handle was made from dark wood at the pommel and an oval-shaped guard with a bone hilt. The other weapon—the rudis—was a wooden sword shaped like a gladius. The dark brown and intermixed golden tones of Persian ironwood glowed in the dim light of the office, and the silver inlay shimmered when it moved, catching bits of light. A steel-silver alloy rim formed the cutting edge, making it just as deadly, if slightly more fragile looking, as the steel gladius in the other scabbard.

Shaking out the wrinkles in the button-down shirt specially tailored to fit over his armor and swords, he slipped it on and added the custom hooded sport coat, arranging the hood to cover the pommels of the swords. He looked bulky; the armor gave him the physique of a linebacker.

He pulled out the last thing in the duffel, a backpack, and put his pile of clothes in along with the duffel bag after he'd collapsed it down. He didn't want to leave any evidence, plus he liked the clothes he'd added to his wardrobe with Delilah's help. He checked his appearance in the floor-length mirror to ensure he'd pass muster on the dance floor, then looked at the clock hanging above the mirror.

It was time. He closed his eyes briefly and took a deep, calming breath. Just a few more minutes until the waiting would end and he could get to the action. Exhaling slowly, he opened his eyes, grabbed the backpack, and headed back to the dance floor.

Get Dark Fangs Raging Now!
Available April 19, 2022

NEWSLETTER

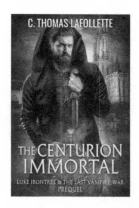

The Centurion Immortal is a Luke Irontree prequel novella and is exclusive to the Dispatches from C. Thomas Lafollette newsletter. Please sign up for your free copy and you'll also receive a twice-monthly newsletter with news, book updates, recipes, drinks tips, and other fun stuff. Your email will never be given out, rented, or sold.

CThomasLafollette.com/newsletter/

GLOSSARY

Auxilia - Units of cavalry, ranged, and infantry fighters who assisted legions and filled specialized roles. Roman citizenship was not required. Citizenship could be earned by completing a 25-year term of service in the auxilia.

Centuria - A unit of 80 legionnaires plus servants led by a centurio

Centurio - The basic equivalent of a modern captain. He commanded his 80 men in combat and coordinated with the other centurio and higher officers.

Cohort - A unit of six centuria, 480 men at full strength

Contubernium - A tent unit of eight men who slept in the same small tent. The basic platoon unit that fought and worked together.

Decanus - The leader of a contubernium. A corporal.

Falx - One of the prime weapons of the Dacians. It had a long, curved blade with the inside edge sharpened that ended in a pointy tip. The handle was typically slightly longer than the blade. Combined, they were about three feet long. When wielded with two hands, it could easily slice through limbs, punch through armor, or tear apart a shield.

Gladius - The short sword used by the legions. It had a sharp, stabbing point that formed the main attack but was balanced and could slash just as well. Romans were trained to stab vital areas or slash at exposed flesh.

Legio - A legion, composed of ten cohorts. A legion usually had several auxilia units assigned to them.

Miles - The term for a Legionnaire

Optio - Chosen by the centurio to assist his leadership and to take over if the centurio wasn't available to lead the unit for whatever reason. The modern equivalent of a lieutenant.

Pilum - The specialized throwing javelin of the Roman legions. The shanks, made of softer iron than the tip, were joined to the shaft with a wooden pin. After the battle, pila (plural of pilum) would be collected, their shanks straightened and pins replaced. Each legionnaire carried two into battle—a light one that flew longer for the first throw and a heavier one for the shorter, second throw.

Scutum - The classic Roman shield. It was held by a bar in the center that ran parallel to the top and bottom. It could be used defensively and offensively.

Tesserarius - The legionnaire in charge of assigning guard duty for his centuria. The equivalent of a sergeant.

Tiro - A recruit (tirones is the plural)

Vexillation - A vexillation was a group split off from its legion and given a special task or mission. Vexillatio in Latin.

ACKNOWLEDGMENTS

I'd like to thank all the people who made this book possible.

Suzanne, your editorial eye has made this book and series infinitely better. Your belief in my vision for these characters has made this a kick ass team effort.

Ravven, your covers are amazing and really capture the essence of Luke and his world.

Amy, you're my alpha reader and my line editor. These books wouldn't be possible without you.

Doochie, you've been my earliest reader and a great hype man as well as a wonderful friend.

To my critique group, you've only gotten to see the first few chapters late in the process, but you've had a truly positive impact on making the opening chapters so much better. I look forward to sharing the rest of this series with you as we go.

All the beta readers, your words and opinions have helped make this book what it is.

ABOUT THE AUTHOR

C. Thomas Lafollette is a writer of Urban Fantasy and Historical Fantasy and is the author of the forthcoming Luke Irontree novels. He earned a degree in Ancient History with a specialization in Classics at The College of Idaho. He's read poetry on stage with Yevgeny Yevtushenko* and dined with the Belgian Prime Minister**. C. Thomas has lived in Portland, Oregon for over Twenty years. He lives with his wife, fellow author Amy Cissell, his stepdaughter, and his three jerkface cats. He and Amy also run their own freelance editing business - Cissell Ink

*Yevtushenko was friends with a professor at C. Thomas's college. He was studying Russian at the time and Yevtushenko decided he wanted the Russian students to read with him on stage at his performance.

**This was purely coincidental. C. Thomas's host took him to dinner at a restaurant in Mons, which was Elio De Rupo's favorite spot. He'd had a pie thrown at him earlier that day and was having dinner with some friends. C. Thomas is still not sure what kind of pie it was though.

twitter.com/CTLafollette

facebook.com/CThomasLafollette

tiktok.com/@cthomaslafollette

instagram.com/CThomasLafollette

bookbub.com/authors/c-thomas-lafollette

amazon.com/C-Thomas-Lafollette/e/B09JMTR7W7

goodreads.com/cthomaslafollette

ALSO BY C. THOMAS LAFOLLETTE

Luke Irontree & The Last Vampire War

Book 0 - The Centurion Immortal

Book 1 - Dark Fangs Rising - March 22, 2022

Book 2 - Dark Fangs Raging - April 19, 2022

Book 3 - Dark Fangs Descending* - May 17, 2022

Book 4 - Blood Empire Reborn* - July 12, 2022

Book 5 - Blood Empire Avenged* - August 9, 2022

Book 6 - Blood Empire Burning* - September 6, 2022

Book 7 - Blood Empire Collapsing* - October 4, 2022

Book 8 - Ancient Sword Falling* - November 29, 2022

Book 9 - Ancient Sword Unyielding* - December 27, 2022

Book 10 - Ancient Sword Shattering* - February 7, 2023

The Luke Irontree Historical Adventures

Rise of the Centurio Immortalis - April 5, 2022

Fall of the Centurio Immortalis* - May 31, 2022

The Moonlight Centurion* - November 1, 2022

The Highway Centurion* - January 24, 2023

*Forthcoming

Made in United States
North Haven, CT
19 November 2023

44277510R00211